I0678855

Find Your Way

JAY JACUZZI

Copyright © 2011 Jay Jacuzzi

All rights reserved.

The characters portrayed in this book are fictitious.
Any similarity to real persons, living or dead, is coincidental
and not intended by the author.

No part of this book may be reproduced, or stored in a retrieval system,
or transmitted in any form or by any means, electronic, mechanical,
photocopying, recording, or otherwise, without express written
permission of the author.

Published by Jay Jacuzzi
ISBN-13: 978-0615556079
ISBN: 0615556078

LCCN: TXu001582277 / 2008-07-30

For Richard & Dalton

*I thank my lucky stars every day
that my way led to you*

ACKNOWLEDGMENTS

Among the many ideas important to *Find Your Way,* one that stands out for me involves the intersections of lives and how we are moved, motivated and even redirected in both subtle and obvious ways because of these random occurrences. Reality certainly inspires fiction, my own course having been touched by many special people.

Thank you Steve Schaeffer for the endless support, encouragement and friendship. You are as generous as you are talented, and your insight, both personal and professional, is valued and respected (and keeps me from losing my marbles).

Thank you Todd Harris for believing in my writing for as long as I can remember and for all of your efforts with *Find Your Way.* You are a great friend.

To Buzz Kaplan, an amazing mentor and friend, thank you for many years of advice, support and laughs.

My sincerest gratitude to Kenita Ashley for reading my manuscript and providing so much enthusiasm throughout this process.

Thank you Davonne Lewis for proofreading and cheerleading.

And Robert Ivanschitz, for your kind, motivating words over the years.

Thank you Dad and DeeAnn for your love and support.

And always to my guys, Richard and Dalton. Thank you for a great life.

CONTENTS

CHAPTER 1
OCCUPATIONAL HAZARDS

Sophia Connors viewed life like chapters, compartmentalizing most things into segments that either continued on or ended with certain separation and definite punctuation. Occupational hazard, she supposed, something of which her life was filled plenty. From chapter to chapter and project to project she went, literally and figuratively, occasionally by choice, but usually by evolution. "That's life," she'd say with a certain level of disconnect when one thing ended or something new began. To the naked ear, this casual-toned remark might present itself as a statement, but a better-trained, more observant one would catch a hint of a vocal upturn indicating she might have meant it as a question.

Once upon a time, Sophia had been what she lightheartedly considered obsessed with fairytales and fables, a conclusion with which others around her undoubtedly would have agreed. As an adult, she came to realize this attraction contributed to her magnetic pull to what she called "the R & W"—the "R" stood for reading, the "W" for writing—her compatriots during school days and beyond. There was something about those grand stories, their extreme characters and the fantastic conclusions

1

that hooked her at an early age. While she supposed she was no different from most kids in that these stories were both entertainment as well as a foundation for understanding the world, she knew she took these stories more seriously, often taking major precautions to protect these special objects of her affection. Time and time again she proved cautious in ways others were not, even at the earliest age.

Sophia's parents regularly brought up tales of her as a child, mostly to embarrass her in front of friends, describing how she never left her books alone at school for fear others would take them. If she went to the bathroom, then so did they, a regular occurrence that caused teachers and students alike to wonder what this unusual girl could be thinking.

Ben and Diane Connors would also tell others that she founded what she called the Connors library. What they went on to explain was that Sophia's compulsive and protective nature drove her to go so far as to institute a library-like checkout system for her siblings whenever they wished to borrow her prized possessions, hence the name given to formally identify Sophia's institutional-like procedures. Long before she could completely understand the relationship between cause and effect, she knew that extreme circumstances demanded extreme actions. That was how seriously Sophia enjoyed her stories, and as explained by Ben and Diane, her selection of a career was as obvious and clear as writing on the wall.

Sophia did indeed love the written word for she found there was magic in the construction of a sentence made up of random or deliberate words. Her love, like most, began with the fairytales and their happy endings, but it was the fables that received preferential regard for they told tales of purpose greater than pushing characters through a series of challenges only to ultimately and predictably realize satisfaction and glory. Fairytales were beautiful and validating, but fables had real teeth and weren't afraid to bite. They lived on because of their grip and because they stood for something larger than themselves, and that was something that commanded her attention and admiration. She respected their sense of morality and judgment.

As she got older, she questioned this preference and wondered if it made her cynical, if her attraction towards stories darker and more twisted meant she was equally dark and twisted. Regardless, she believed happy endings were possible, but she identified more with fables and needed to believe that there were lessons to be learned in every story, including her own. She and those around her saw this childhood obsession grow up and mature into her ambition to be a novelist, a dream she continued to pursue. She wanted to write stories with meaning and purpose.

The day started with the alarm screaming hatefully—no different than any other workday—an unwanted necessity that extracted Sophia from a comfortable but anticipatory slumber. Like recent days, there would be no run today before going into the office. Demanding deadlines had resulted in long hours, and the compromise the past few weeks, maybe even for the remainder of the month, was exercise. More work required getting as much rest as possible whenever possible, a decision she easily justified with the additional consideration the temperature had been consistently hovering around thirty degrees outside. January was flexing her winter muscle and Sophia was none too thrilled about it.

After showering, she hovered over her coffee cup, toweling her hair and wondering if it had snowed the night before like the botoxed newsman said it would. She didn't consider him a reputable source though. How could she trust someone whose face didn't move, whose real expression she could not see, regardless of whether he was announcing clear skies or a tornado? "No emotion, no devotion," she always said.

She also found it criminal someone should make so much money for making such general predictions. "It's going to be cold tomorrow," he'd say, which would result in her inability to stop herself from talking back to the television.

"Of course, it's cold. It's January in New York, you idiot."

She gave a quick glance out the window onto 79th Street and saw a subtle blanket of white she assumed had probably already frozen over. She knew she would have to be careful walking today until the heat of the city's inner core had a chance to melt it all away.

While refilling her cup, her cell phone began ringing. She located the phone on the counter and saw Kate's name flashing on the screen.

"Morning," Sophia said. "This is an unusual time for you to call."

Kate laughed, gravel still in her voice, the sounds of the city behind her. "What? I'm not allowed to call you this early?" Her tone wore its usual sassy defiance. "When did we establish that rule?"

Kate sounded noticeably stirred up, especially considering she rarely spoke to anyone before ten o'clock. Kate was Sophia's closest friend at the agency as well as in the city and Sophia knew very well that she went out of her way to never schedule meetings or participate in any kind of interaction before she had had a few hours to settle into the day.

"You can call me whenever you want," Sophia responded, a smile in her voice. "You just never do. That is, unless you've been arrested. Everything alright?"

"Funny girl, I've never been arrested. Well…never that I've admitted to you anyway," Kate teased before getting to her point. "Griffin wants the team in as soon as possible."

Sophia was excited by this news. "Do you think we're finally going to hear today?"

"Sounds like it. I got a call from the Headmistress," Kate explained, using the nickname Sophia had given to their boss' mean-spirited secretary several years ago. "I told her I'd call you myself, even though I know you'd love nothing more than talk to the Sea Witch this early in the morning."

"Thanks for the protection. I appreciate that," Sophia said. "Did she explain the urgency or give you any info?"

"She wouldn't budge, only it does sound like he's got news about the Turnbow pitch. My guess is they selected us as their agency. Why else would they need us immediately? And I'll bet money we've got deadlines for projects that were due last week. Isn't that always the case?"

"That'd be great," Sophia told her and then clarified, "Winning the account, that is. Not the insane deadlines part."

Sophia sipped at the lip of the hot cup, remembering the hours they'd spent the past several weeks creating layouts for what had to be one of the worst possible account prospects ever. Turnbow was a consumer products manufacturer, and while the account would be a huge win for the team, one of the brands they were pitching to represent from their family of business was Mom T's Hemorrhoid Cream. Needless to say, this brought endless jokes from Sophia and Kate's advertising team, becoming as Sophia called it, "the butt" of all their adolescent attention for the past month. Their jest, however, made their senior account supervisor, Russell Griffin, extremely nervous and uneasy, which in all reality was not very difficult to do. An intense, overly self-conscious man they all suspected had not had sex with his equally frigid wife in heaven knows how long, he squirmed when anything was stated that might insult or upset an existing or potential client. Sophia considered Russell a seasoned account man—the term she defined as meaning irreversibly tainted—for he lived to please the hand that fed. He was without a doubt loyal, but that loyalty was always directed upwards to his superiors, and rarely in support of the needs of his team.

The fact that Sophia disliked Russell as much as she did was not typical for her nature. The truth was she was not particularly rebellious, that she was quite agreeable in most circumstances, more so than many of the other copywriters she had worked with in her years of advertising. But she felt that equally important to loyalty was morale. She came to know how significant this was at the agency, as well as how a little enjoyment went a long way in an environment like advertising, which typically was like hanging out in a den of snakes.

Of the two of them, Kate was the one more prone to making biting comments, saying things like, "Russell should take his ventriloquist act on the road. He's so good at throwing his voice when his lips are firmly stuck to the client's ass."

While funny, Sophia reminded her that a comment like that was particularly unsettling when made in reference to the

Turnbow clients because when it came to the account they were pitching, butts were already such sensitive subjects.

"I'm leaving in a minute," Sophia told her before hanging up to finish getting ready.

When Sophia arrived at RGB's midtown offices thirty minutes later, Tricia, the head receptionist, directed her to join the rest of the team in Conference Room Rothko. RGB (named after the primary colors red, green and blue from the additive color model) had been founded by Trevor Duncan, a former hippie and art student who insisted on naming everything in the building after something from the art world. Conference rooms were named after artists including Van Gogh, Picasso and Renoir. Floors had different color palette themes and were referred to as such. Hallways and bathrooms acted as galleries for imitations of the original masterpieces. Sophia liked the concept but felt it was taken somewhat overboard. It was all a little too cool for school, especially since Trevor regularly demonstrated that his love for commerce outweighed his love for good art. She also suspected his actions were driven by what he thought other people would think was creative, that he himself had left his ability to recognize style and trend back in the '70s. But with the silent criticism, she also gave him credit for establishing and growing a successful and reputable agency. Trevor was smart enough to surround himself with intelligent and talented people who supplemented, even overshadowed, his shortcomings. She knew that recognizing when one needed the strengths of others was a talent unto itself.

Sophia entered Rothko and saw Trevor and Russell standing in front of the room talking to one another, neither making eye contact with her. In his usual fashion, Russell leaned uncomfortably to the side and Sophia told herself he looked like he needed a tube of Mom T's famous product. When she turned to find Kate, she discovered her friend pointing at the seat saved for her and began moving in its direction.

"Good morning," Sophia whispered to Kate, who was holding her cell to her head, wiggling the fingers in her free hand and mouthing, "Hi."

Sophia pulled off several layers of clothing and made herself more comfortable. Trevor and Russell remained intense in their conversation so she took out her own phone to check her email. As she did so, she noticed their art director, Bill, walk through the door. She was relieved she wasn't the last to arrive.

As she pulled up her email, Sophia saw one from Kevin. Happy to see it, she opened it and read:

Hey, doll. Hope you had a nice night last night. We leave Chicago in a couple hours. Last night's dinner meeting was amazing. There's A LOT to tell you. Big stuff! Calls for big celebration tonight. I got us into Le Bon tonight at 8. See you there. XO Kev

Le Bon, she considered. The news must be really big! They probably made him partner, finally, after all of the promises. *Wouldn't that be great?*

Sophia had had a feeling lately that something was up with him, not that he had said anything specifically to confirm her suspicions. But his step, and his attitude, had seemed more aggressive, maybe even more proud? Making partner meant more money, but she knew it also meant much more to him. And hadn't he always said that once he made enough money, when he had established himself and felt he'd really achieved his own independence that he would be ready for them to talk about bigger things, the next steps? She re-read the email and felt the warmth of his X and O. In the three years they had been together, he had always been sweet like that, never afraid to show affection. It was one of the many things she loved about him.

Sophia looked up and glanced over at Russell. There definitely seemed to be something up with him this morning, and she noticed his eyes twitching awkwardly the way they did when he was unhappy. Maybe Kate was wrong? This wasn't the appearance of a man who had just won a major account. Sophia turned to Kate as she closed her phone, "I'm not so sure you got your facts right," she began to say.

But before Kate could respond, Russell interrupted. "Now that we're all here," he said, eyes emoting a nervous flutter, "I have some news."

Russell, notorious for unnecessarily stretching things on and prolonging the inevitable, be they good or bad, hesitated. Sophia looked to Kate for feedback and saw she was getting irritated, as expressed by the direction of her eyebrows. Russell recovered after a deep breath and began. "Believe it or not, despite what we know to be fantastic efforts by the team, the news I have is unfortunate."

The mood in the room dropped noticeably as if someone had just dimmed the lights.

"We did *not* get the Turnbow account," Russell continued, more direct this time. "All of you did an impressive job and really came to the plate with your best efforts, but unfortunately, they have decided to go another direction."

There was a collective sigh. Sophia felt a rush of disappointment and knew her twelve teammates were experiencing the same letdown.

"As you know, Turnbow's parent company, Lewis Industries, is one of our largest accounts and the one all of you work on," he said, indicating there was more to announce.

Kate turned to Sophia for answers as her eyebrows did a one-eighty. Both women shrugged their shoulders in unison before looking back at Russell. Where could he possibly be going with all of this? And why was Trevor in the room anyway? He never came to team meetings unless something *really* major was happening.

"As it was explained to me," he continued, "Lewis Industries was so blown away by the creative presented to their subsidiary during the pitch process that they have hired them to handle their own account."

Something major *was* happening but it took a few seconds for this statement to register and sink in.

Kate responded first, in true Kate form, from the hip and for the jugular, and with irritated eyebrows back to assist her. "That's bullcrap. They can't do that!"

She, like everyone else in the room, was scrambling to make sense of the news, and she did so in a manner that showed how different her account management approach was from Russell's. But even she was concerned where he would take the conversation next.

"But they can," Russell replied, his face taking on a pinched appearance, one that was worse than Sophia had ever seen. "While we've managed the Lewis business for years, we haven't been under a contract with them for almost twelve months. We tried to get them to commit but they skirted the issue. Now we know why—they've been interviewing agencies. They can take their business anywhere they want, and unfortunately, there's nothing we can do about it."

"What does that mean?" Sophia asked. "Will we be reassigned to other accounts?" She hated the idea of not working on the same account as Kate but things could be worse.

And they were.

"No," Trevor said, finally stepping forward. He was looking at Sophia but she got the impression he was actually looking through her, or at least trying to.

Sophia then realized other people had entered the conference room through the doors behind them. One of the men was someone Sophia remembered meeting at an RGB holiday party a couple years before. His name was Bob, or maybe Jim, and he worked in human resources. She recalled for certain though that he had stale breath and was not very interesting. She had been surprised he worked in human resources because there was nothing very human about him. Bob or Jim moved along the conference room table to where Trevor was and handed him a stack of papers. Trevor must have seen the comprehension in Sophia's eyes because he immediately ripped off the metaphorical bandage and got to the point. "We thank you for the service you have provided this agency over the years. Unfortunately, we no longer have positions for you. Each one of you will receive a minimum of four weeks pay as well as reimbursement for unused vacation time. Additional severance pay is dependent on your length of employment with RGB. On behalf of the organization, I wish you all the best. With that, I will hand it over to Vic Stevens from H.R."

Oblivious to the fact she misremembered Vic's name, Sophia became engulfed by a weird and warped slow motion tunnel vision, like a scene from a bad movie where everything is shot with a fuzzy, psychedelic filter, and with distorted sound. What happened next, as best as Sophia would be able to remember later because of this unconscious, blinded haze, were only snippets.

Trevor and Russell disappeared. The boring H.R. guy handed the team sealed envelopes and pink slips, only they weren't pink. She would remember wondering, *How long did you know this was going to happen?* It was a question she would begin asking herself regularly. Each employee was then paired off with a security person, which erupted a fire in Sophia. "What kind of corporate mischief do you think I'm capable of?" she demanded of the man assigned to supervise her.

"I'm just doing my job, ma'am," he told her.

But Sophia had shifted her focus on Kate, who was being escorted through a door on the opposite side of the room. Her friend made a finger phone with her hand by her ear and told her to call her later.

After Kate disappeared, Sophia thought she heard her yell, "Bullshit!"

Sophia would remember feeling like they were in a slaughterhouse, that each of them was being ushered into their own stall to be butchered. She would remember scattered moments of taking pictures of Kevin and her family off her desk and walls and placing her small collection of sweaters and shoes into the cardboard box they provided her. *Such hospitality,* she would remember thinking, venom and disbelief seeping through her skin. And there was a sense of humiliation, knowing that others she had seen almost every day for years were watching, feeling pity for her, as well as fear about their own survival.

Before Sophia knew it, she was swept out onto the street, standing in the middle of the busy sidewalk outside the doors to a building she had entered more times than she could count, wondering if the people passing by could read her dumbfounded astonishment and understand the abandonment she felt. In perfect poetic harmony, snow began falling from the sky and landed on the box in her arms, which not only carried her possessions but seemingly her career as well.

She stood there bewildered for some time thinking about how she believed in fables. What would the moral of her own story be if someone asked her at that very moment? What would she tell Oprah or Ellen or Barbara if they asked her to describe her life's theme or motto? It was a ridiculous fantasy, she knew, but who didn't want the privilege of sitting on an infamous couch and have the opportunity to jump up and down like a crazy person and talk about career, love and life?

"That's a hard one, Oprah," she might say, being a little coy because she wanted to sound thoughtful and like she didn't already have an answer. But she *did* have an answer and it came to her right there on the street.

"I guess if I had to sum it up with one simple statement," Sophia would say, "I guess I would say, 'you just never know.'"

Yes, Sophia told herself, turning away from the building she had spent a huge chunk of her life the past five years, keenly aware of the imbalance suffered between work and personal lives. *You just never know…when one chapter is going to end.*

CHAPTER 2
THAT OLD SINKING FEELING

It was like being on the worst of all possible dates. There Sophia was, back in her apartment and alone with the box, wondering how she was going to get herself out of this mess. She stared at the object from across the room, deliberately sitting in the middle of her loveseat, trying to fill up as much empty space as possible to reduce her sense of isolation and abandonment.

Her head was beyond overwhelmed, the surface still thawing out from too much time spent out in the brutal winter day while the inside felt steamrolled by this unexpected turn of events. As fortune would have it, however, and as the one positive she could claim for the day, the awkwardness only lasted a few minutes because her cell sounded off and broke the uncomfortable tension. She was grateful for the interruption, regardless of who was calling, even if it was a telemarketer. She was that much more thankful when she saw it was Kate.

"You survived the bloodbath?" Sophia asked. "Can you tell me what just happened?"

"I know! How messed up was that?" Kate said.

Sophia could tell she was now laughing. Even in the face of such a morning, Kate could always manage to remain upbeat and unfazed.

But Sophia did not share the same resilience. "I'm still processing it," Sophia announced. "Frankly speaking, you sound a lot better about this than I feel."

Kate interrupted, "Will you hold that thought? Don't go visiting Pity City without me. Meet me at MaryAnne's in thirty?"

Sophia looked at her watch. "It's a little early for a margarita, don't you think?"

"Watch your mouth," Kate said with another laugh. "It's *never* too early. Besides, after what just happened, I think we have cause."

Sophia couldn't deny she was relieved to have an excuse to leave her apartment, knowing full well she would have plenty of time there soon enough. She was certainly concerned, if not more than a little freaked out, by the sudden reality of being unemployed. The truth was she didn't have a lot of money in her savings account and the severance check she just received would only go so far. But she knew she wasn't alone in this. Kate was in the same boat. They would support each other and figure this out together. And Kevin would surely make things better as well, softening the blow from this surprising twist in life's course. Besides, he had good news to share with her and that had to count for something. So she grabbed her bag and keys, layered up again and left her little corner of Manhattan.

Sophia took her time as she walked towards the restaurant several blocks away, stepping slowly across winter's icy blanket, but becoming conscious of all the people everywhere going about their lives. Who were all of these people? And what were their lives like to afford them the morning hours when so many others were chained to their offices? Were they unemployed as well or did they just live different schedules?

Unemployed. It was a term that would take some getting used to. Being off in the middle of the day to meet a repairman at the apartment or while on vacation had always been a surreal experience for Sophia. These were hours she had been conditioned to feel owned by someone else. She had become a vampire of sorts living for the night. But that had all changed unexpectedly. Those who had controlled those hours had given them back and not for generous reasons. She had been released from duty. Kicked off the team. Thrown in the recycling bin as if they were saying, "You're good for someone, just not for us anymore."

As she made the trek, she tried to reach Kevin but only got his voicemail and realized he might be in a meeting or in the air. "Welcome home," she said. "I got your message. It sounds like you've got some news. So do I...just probably not as exciting. I'll see you tonight at eight."

She decided she would reserve her news for later that evening, maybe even tomorrow, depending on how things went tonight. He had seemed excited in his email and the last thing she wanted to do was rain on his parade. If he had been promoted, this was huge news he had worked towards for so many years. While hers was significant, she didn't mind prolonging its inevitable announcement, especially if it meant not putting a damper on his celebration. There would be plenty of time later for him to console her.

When she arrived at MaryAnne's, Kate met her with an enthusiastic wave from a corner table. She was using an unnecessary amount of energy to get Sophia's attention, especially considering the place was mostly empty at this early hour. Two margaritas and a basket of chips also greeted Sophia. As Kate would say, "It's a party and everyone's welcome."

After Kate completed the greeting with a hug, her unpredictability reached an all-new zany high. "We're going to Paris," she said, licking the salt along the rim of the glass, her eyes glowing from the idea.

Sophia wondered how many drinks Kate had already had. "Excuse me?" Sophia responded, surprised for the second time that day.

"We...are...go...ing...to...Par...is," she repeated, effectively extending the words for dramatic effect. Her grin was huge and she was clearly impressed with herself.

"We…are…look…ing…for…jobs," Sophia responded, shaking her head at her friend who seemed to have lost her mind.

"I *think* better in Paris," Kate stated.

"And I think better when I know I can *pay* my rent," Sophia told her. "Besides, you've never been to Paris."

"Now is the perfect time to go. When else are we going to have eight weeks off to go travel like this?"

Kate was fearless. Sophia had always known this but never knew how solid, or maybe the better term was pliable, her backbone really was until this moment. Pushed into a corner, Kate still came out swinging.

"I'm serious. Let's go!" she continued.

But Sophia just shook her head, mostly in disbelief, and partially as an instinctual answer to Kate's invitation.

"Come on! Come with me," Kate said, leaning forward, grinning like the Cheshire Cat. "Screw New York City. Let's go see France! I've got plenty of miles for both of us, so the airfare is taken care of. Let's get out of here and go enjoy our freedom."

"You've lost your mind, Kate. We're not free. We're unemployed. And in about two months, I'll be on the street because I can't pay my bills."

Kate giggled. "Well, it'll be spring by then and the weather won't be bad, so we can sleep in the park."

"Yes, Kate," Sophia said sarcastically, now gulping her margarita. "That sounds like a great, well-thought-out plan."

"Well, I'm going to Paris, my dear," Kate told her. "And I want you to come with me."

They sat across the table from each other in a deep stare until suddenly there was nothing but silence between them. That was when Sophia realized Kate was pulling one of her sales strategies on her. "Throw your demands out there," she had once told Sophia, "and then shut up until they respond and give you what you want! I mean it. Don't say a word. Shut up and let *them* do the talking. They are more likely to dig their own graves and give you what you want than deal with the misery of confrontation."

Kate was a master of confrontation, completely unafraid of war or turmoil. If she thought it was appropriate or necessary, she wouldn't think twice about causing a scene or going on the offensive. This morning, for instance, if she had thought a fit would have changed the results, she would have started doing some major pitching. Sophia realized she should have anticipated Kate would throw responsibility into the wind.

But Sophia was less bold. She was quick-witted but overly self-aware in most situations. She often thought twice before speaking, usually because as a writer she had the opportunity to edit her choice of words before committing to them. Even then, she might overanalyze the words she had decided to put out there, questioning or regretting her choices.

Sophia had displayed plenty of courage in her life but unemployment was something she had only dealt with one other time and it had been when she was much younger, when living at home seemed an option that minimized the situation's crash and burn effect, and when far less seemed at risk. New York was an expensive place to stay afloat, and it demanded a lot. Losing it as home was a difficult proposition.

Kate must have realized she was not making progress because she rolled her eyes and gave in a little. "You have until tomorrow morning to tell me you want to join me for this once-in-a-lifetime opportunity. I'm thinking about leaving Friday. You can come back any time you want but I think I'm going for six weeks. I'll have all the details worked out later today."

"You've lost your mind," Sophia told her.

"I know," she said. "I wish you'd lose yours, too!"

Le Bon was grand and spectacular, a virtual cathedral of visual splendor, just as Sophia had expected it would be. Deliberate splashes of cranberry paired with swipes of harvest and pumpkin were layered around the room atop lighted panels framed with teak and metal. These tall walls were capped with an illuminated glass mosaic ceiling complementing and completing the design. All of it was stunning, Sophia thought, looking around for Kevin. She did not see him at the entrance so she walked past the host and into the adjoining room where she found him sitting at the bar, his back to the door.

As she made her way to him through the crowd, it dawned on her that this would need to be the last supper—her last meal out now that she was unemployed, at least for now. She was back on a very limited budget which meant lunches and dinners out like the ones of today would temporarily need to be privileges she would have to do without and would definitely miss.

Kevin turned around when she reached him as if he sensed her presence behind him. He greeted her with a wide smile and a "hey." He looked handsome as ever in his navy pinstriped Hugo Boss suit, the blues of his shirt and tie making his aqua eyes pop. It made her chest fill with warmth and suddenly everything seemed right in the world again.

"Hello," she said, leaning in to kiss him on the cheek. He smelled clean and inviting like soap. "Been here long?"

"Not long," he said, returning the kiss, moving his lips alongside her cheek until it landed just right. "Long enough to order you a glass of wine. They said our table will be ready in a couple of minutes. Here…"

Sophia sat down in the open chair next to his and took the glass he was offering. He lifted his own and tilted it in her direction for a silent toast. She followed his lead and then sipped to whatever they were celebrating. Clearly something had happened on his trip. He was glowing. His eyes gave away his excitement.

"Good news?" she asked, ready to hear what he had to share.

"Mmhmm," he replied, nodding in agreement.

"Really? Did they promote you to partner?"

Kevin nodded again and looked directly into her eyes, a little more humbly this time. "Yep, sure did."

"Wow!" she announced, instantly glad she had reserved her drama for later. This was too important and exciting to overshadow with something that would be just as much of a problem tomorrow as it was tonight. It could wait. It *should* wait because she felt good news should come before bad. "That is so fantastic!"

Despite an apparent attempt to control his excitement, Kevin gave in to his emotions. "Yeah, it is."

After a moment's pause, he said, "I'm really glad you're so happy for me."

"Of course. This is big news! When's the promotion effective?" she asked before taking another sip of her wine. She was thrilled for Kevin, proud as much *for* him as she was *of* him, and joyful that all of his hard work was really paying off. She knew how invested he was in his work and what he wanted to achieve in his career.

"Immediately," he responded. "I'll start taking over my new duties right away."

"That is really great, Kev. This *is* cause for celebration!"

Kevin reached the bottom of his glass with his next sip. Then out of nowhere, his joy was suddenly interrupted by something, a thought that had come to the forefront of his mind. Sophia saw this, and as he looked back at her, he seemed to recognize she was aware something had just happened.

"What is it?" she asked. "Are you worried about how much work it'll be? Remember you've earned this. You've busted your butt for years. You may be one of the firm's youngest partners but you deserve this."

Kevin looked into his empty glass and then back at Sophia. "It isn't that," he said.

"What is it then? What's wrong?"

He paused again and then said, "I thought about waiting until later to bring this up but there's no time like the present. Right?"

"What do you mean? Bring what up?"

"They want me in Chicago. They want me to move there."

It took a few seconds for this information to sink in. Kevin would be moving to Chicago. *Oh, my God,* Sophia thought. *Could today deliver any more change?*

"And?" she asked, knowing how unnecessary her question was even before it left her lips. "You're going to do it, aren't you? I assume you are, right? This is too big to pass up."

Kevin nodded, presenting a look of relief that was mixed with something else Sophia couldn't put her finger on. "It means so much to have your support," he told her. "You need to know that."

The glow in his face had vanished. As soon as Sophia realized this, her mind did its best to analyze the situation and do some fast thinking. So what if Kevin had to move to Chicago? She was no longer tied to New York the way she had once been. Sure there were all those thoughts she had earlier in the day about not wanting to leave it and, of course, she really loved New York but she really loved Kevin, too. Wasn't Kevin more important to her? And with the day's events, she was now free from the responsibilities that would have perhaps complicated her thoughts previously. Maybe their timing was working out just fine. Maybe it was a sign, even though she didn't believe in such things. But then again, perhaps she had been wrong all these years. Maybe life was littered with evidence of directions, such as "go this way" or "turn back and run, fool!"

"Don't worry about me," she said as casually as she could, smiling to bring him release from the concern she could read on his face. "We can make this work. We can do the long-distance thing for a while. And if you love it, if we love it, then I'll move there, too."

Kevin smiled. "You're so sweet, Sophia. I don't deserve you."

Sophia pushed back at his statement. "Of course you do."

Kevin got nervous again and Sophia knew there was more, that what she said didn't bring him the relief she thought it would. "And you know how much I love you, right?"

"Of course," Sophia said, realizing the time had come for her to follow Kate's sales advice. *Shut up and let him do the talking.* Where exactly was he going with all of this lead-up?

After another noticeable silence, he finally spoke again. "I love you, Sophia. I love you a lot. But I think I need to go to Chicago alone."

There was more silence. Not because Sophia was waiting for more of his response but because she was waiting for her own.

"What did you say?" she finally asked, not sure she heard him correctly.

"I've thought a lot about this. And I think I need to go to Chicago by myself, without any commitments in New York. I think it'll be better for both of us."

"*Both* of us?" Sophia asked, stunned. *Did he say this would be better for both of us? Have I become an obligation? And how long has he known about this?*

That old sinking feeling—the one with the surreal tunnel vision she had experienced earlier in the day—returned to her and she fought it off as best as she could.

"Are you breaking up with me?" Sophia asked for clarity, beyond surprised the words were coming out of her mouth. Never in a million years would she have expected this to happen. Not tonight. Not Kevin. Not ever.

Kevin squirmed and pulled himself back into his seat, the excitement in the conversation completely dissipated. His eyes avoided Sophia's at all cost while his actions and silence answered her question.

Sophia's world had shifted on its axis once more and it had all been too much for one day, so she stood up.

"Please," he said. "Don't leave. Let's talk about this. This is not how I wanted it to go."

The tears welled inside Sophia's burning face but she swallowed, forcing them down. He had pulled the world out from under her and she did not want to give him more than she already had.

"Talk about what?" she asked. "What's there to say? You seem to have made your decision and apparently you did it quite easily without me."

Kevin stood, looking around in hopes of not making a scene, pleading, "Please stay, Sophia. Stay for me. I want us to celebrate together. You are the most important person in my life. And this is the most important thing to ever happen to me. It means so much to me to share this with you."

Sophia began to pull her coat back on. Having been

dumped twice in one day, she wanted to do her best impression of Norma Ray meets Kate, to stand on the bar and yell, not "union" but "bullshit!"

"Please, Sophia…"

She yanked the strap of her purse over her shoulder. "If you only knew the kind of day *I* had. This just tops it off perfectly. And you can rest assured knowing you have certainly 'shared' this with me. Thanks for that," she said, the hurt escaping despite her best efforts. "This is an experience that has solidified our relationship forever."

"But…please don't go," he said, making one more attempt.

"And just so you know," she told him, now staring deep into his eyes, unable to help herself, *"you* were the most important thing to ever happen to *me."*

Sophia then walked out, retracing her steps through the bar and toward the front door until she found only minimal comfort from the winter night. As the brutal wind slapped her face, the emotion she had been fighting with the past few minutes gained ground and the tears finally broke through. Suddenly desperate to make sense of this nightmare of a day but at a complete loss of what to think and do, she unconsciously threw her hand in the air to hail a cab. It was an act that in her mind felt like a drowning woman involuntarily flailing for help. Her own thoughts denied her until a cab pulled up, when from nowhere and without explanation came something to fill the void. What she heard was the old Gomer Pyle catchphrase, "Surprise, surprise, surprise!" Only television's Gomer had been charming and there was nothing heart-warming about any of this. And she was certainly not in Mayberry.

CHAPTER 3
LISTS

1) Me. Oncoming traffic. Pushed.
2) Gum (me, again). Shoe. Step.
3) The ball (me, again). Any sport. Swing, kick, throw.

Lists were a way of life for Sophia. For as long as she could remember, she had put her thoughts to paper, usually in the form of short, numerically organized lists designed to help her create a sense of order, albeit knowingly a false one. It was a technique she had relied on for years, perhaps at times even abused, not only for her writing and the characters she was creating, but to protect her from the calamity of life in general. Her girlfriends kept diaries, her writing friends kept journals, and she kept lists inspired by specific topics, themes or character situations. Sometimes they provided writing practice or an outlet for her stream of consciousness. Today they were her survival.

4) Ground. Open. Swallowed.
5) Rug. Pulled. Humiliated.
6) World. Implodes or explodes. Either will do.

There once was a time when Sophia's lists floated around on little pieces of paper, receipts, yellow stickies, gum wrappers and the such, eventually to be stored in a wooden keepsake box she acquired from her mother at some unremembered time, or taped in a notebook—the kind kids buy every August before school is back in session—and of which she once had a large supply. Sophia believed taping was better and easier than rewriting, and while less attractive, she found it a more reasonable solution, organizing her random thoughts into a personal mental scrapbook.

Mostly driven by impulse, there was no concrete strategy to the practice. If the mood struck her, *if* she could find something to write on—hence the long list of options—*and* she happened to have access to a writing instrument, the notes were drafted and her mind found temporary freedom from an idea as well as from the fear that some important sliver of a thought might fade away.

She knew, however, there was inconsistency in her methods and madness—that while she was trying to make order in the world she was in fact creating disorder in her purse, gym bag, work bag, etc. But she chose as her top priority the exploration and cementing of these thoughts and ideas since the potential benefit was more significant to her big picture goals. Secondary was the physical organization of the vessels themselves.

As fortune would have it though, the practice changed for the better in the early days of the new millennium as Sophia was catapulted like so many others into another era. When the technology boom made one of its seemingly loudest and largest explosions, she was introduced to new tools she quickly adopted in support of her habits and hobbies—writing fell into her habit category because she considered hobbies as projects involving play while habits were ones you simply can't help yourself from doing.

It was then, during the boom, that Sophia experienced her first real love affair. Boys before Kevin had come and gone with little notice, but her love affair with her BlackBerry had changed her life forever. Suddenly gone was her dependence on finding scratch paper at the most inopportune times—which was usually the case—when her creative mind was flushing ideas she frantically fought not to lose because she knew that if she didn't trap them by writing them down then they would be sent back into the right brain abyss and lost to her forever. Creativity was fleeting after all and required the use of any means necessary to weigh it down and prevent it from leaving as fast as it had arrived.

Her BlackBerry was indeed heaven-sent, the device's mini keyboard and notepad capabilities delivering independence and efficiency as well as a happy divorce from her own clunky handwriting. It was always nearby and her words always found room on this most convenient of resources. Plus, it offered the added benefit of allowing her to email these notes to her computer, thus making it easy to convert them into her much larger, greater electronic master list also known as the bible. While the bible was not always as organized as she'd wanted, it was a centralized source for her free-flowing and often miscellaneous thoughts. Scanning for ideas using the search function and a few key words to find the location of her notes was far easier than flipping through gum wrappers and trying to interpret her personal hieroglyphics. Technology was a miracle as far as she was concerned.

> 7) *Salmon fighting their way upstream. Brown bear waiting.*
>   *What's the point, salmon?*
> 8) *Soda pop left on metal. Eaten away. Good gone bad.*

The lists Sophia created today though only found life in her shattered mind. Awake for more than an hour, she remained congealed with her sheets, staring at the ceiling, unable and unwilling to move. Her cell had rung multiple times since last night but she could not and would not answer it. She remained hung over with despair, denied by any self-worth she once possessed.

Two days had passed since her world had collapsed and no matter how hard she tried, there was really no making sense of the events. One minute she had a job, the next she did not. And one minute she had a serious boyfriend she practically lived with, and then she did not. Creativity, she thought, was not the only thing in her life that was fleeting.

The day after everything hit the fan had been bad. The night after—last night—had been worse. Day two so far felt practically indescribable, and yet, because she didn't know what else to do, she tried.

She had waited until the morning after her dinner with Kevin to call Kate and give her the news. Stunned and shocked, she had needed the time to let it all sink in, to prepare herself because she knew Kate would jump on the opportunity to promote her idea of the trip to Paris—one that had initially not seemed a very practical idea but took on a whole new attraction considering the latest development. How could she refuse such an offer, an opportunity to escape her troubles, even if only temporarily?

Truth be told, she had thought about leaving RGB time and time again. There had been countless moments when her climb towards career success seemed so steep she was certain she would slip and fall, not because she wasn't qualified, but because of the type of person that world demanded she be. The bottom line was that it was a sales environment, even in the writing department, and she was not a salesperson. She was a writer. And while she had confidence in her abilities, most of the time, the pressures and demands of life as a copywriter regularly forced her to wonder if it was all worth it. She questioned if her love for the written word could sustain such subjective blows in the competitive ring of advertising, where her work more often than not met the scrutiny of others who all thought they knew better. RGB promoted teamwork, but most of the players, including the clients, were in the game for themselves and thought they were the only ones on the field. Sophia had stopped counting years ago the number of times she had heard from Kate or her other account managers that a client thought a certain idea or slogan they themselves had come up with was clever and that the agency's campaign should be created around it, when in fact, the idea was actually quite horrible and would appeal to no one other than that specific client representative.

There were times when she felt she had lost herself in this world, when she felt she was so off-track from her real goals that she might never get back. She had wondered on more than one occasion if she had sold herself short, if the allure of a steady paycheck and the presumed job security had guided her off-course. As it turned out, she was realizing her assumptions were probably correct.

Losing her job was one thing. It left her in a bind that more than anything was uncomfortable and unsettling. She had spent five years with the agency, a timeframe comparable to a high school or college degree, and having earned her diploma, she was kicked off the campus. However, she told herself, at the end of the day, it was just a job.

But what she had had with Kevin was real, or so *she* had thought. At what point had Kevin realized he had moved on, or even sensed that she had become disposable, something tradable? Had she reacted too quickly at dinner? Could she have said something that would have changed his mind? Although it was unlike him, perhaps he had been testing her to see if she really wanted to be with him?

She began a new list. Beaten down by her thoughts, simple and concise words were all she could muster now to describe what she felt. There would be no more metaphors or analogies. That ability had gone back to sleep.

1) Confusion
2) Disbelief
3) Bewilderment

Bitter taste filled her mouth as her mind followed this direction of thought. Who wanted to be in a relationship with someone who had to be begged to stay? Not her. Not with anyone, Kevin included, for that matter.

What continued to press on her was her desire to know how long he had known, not just about this job, but that he also didn't want her to go with him. How long had he been aware she was a compromise he was willing to make, that she was literally the tit for that tat?

And how long, she demanded to the emptiness of her room, her blood returning to a boil as she continued to stare at her ceiling, had he held this relationship with less significance than her? Hadn't he always seemed so content? Hadn't he always told her that he was?

Sure there were times when they didn't connect as fluidly as she thought they should. And, of course, their schedules and the pressures of their lives made them occasionally feel like they were keeping each other company more than creating romance. But wasn't that a relationship, to nurture and care for one another, to eventually grow old together, and to be there until the very end? When had he stopped thinking of her in those terms? Or, despite his spoken words to her on countless occasions over the years, and as she considered it now for the first time as an option, had he ever really thought that way to begin with?

4) Desperation
5) Abandonment
6) Devastation

As she reviewed the timeframe and logistics of it all, she grew even more lost. He clearly had known about all of this, that he would so easily give her up for his new life in Chicago, when he was inside her Saturday night, when he whispered in her ear that he loved her.

And what about the pancakes he had made for her the following morning, their last breakfast in bed, the naked caresses afterwards? If she was soon to be a memory, was the stack of flapjacks all just a pile of guilt, a distraction, a last hoorah, or worse, a passage of time? Was he only postponing the inevitable until his promotion and plans were confirmed?

Her mind sunk to darker places as more unimaginable thoughts came to her, taking her over. What else did she not know? *Is there someone else?*

All of these questions haunted Sophia, begging for answers she wasn't sure she really wanted but couldn't help herself from thinking about anyway. She despised the sense of deception overtaking her, the doubt that it's possible to really ever know someone. *Can you truly ever know another person?*

It was a terrible thing to have started planning a future with someone, to have let him in to become part of your life, just to have it all stop instantly one day. She wondered if she could have been any more stupid, blind and vulnerable.

7) *Butchered*
8) *Broken*
9) *Crushed*

She was certain that sometimes it was best not to know. During her first year of college, she found herself living with a skyscraper of a girl named Debbie who was built like a giraffe and drank like a fish. For a while, they were perfect roommates, sharing space and friends. But soon enough, their relationship became taxing and confusing, and Sophia started noticing Debbie drinking too much, too regularly, and acting out in unusual, passive-aggressive ways towards her. She at first attributed Debbie's complicated, dramatic flair to her love of opera and Maria Callas. But after more than a few uncomfortable scenes, Sophia made the mistake of reading Debbie's diary, an object that Debbie herself practically dangled in front of her face. Sophia forever regretted giving into the temptation. She was also sorry to see the terrible things that were written about her by this young woman she thought she knew and who clearly wanted things from their relationship she could not give her. Debbie's frustration and unhappiness had developed into cruelty. Sophia fortunately found an escape exit out of that living situation within a couple of months.

But that situation was different and Kevin was no stranger. They had shared the past three holiday seasons together. They had shared their bodies and their secrets, most of them anyway, so Sophia thought. They had been vulnerable to each other. Or had they been? As doubt took over, she began to question all of her beliefs about their relationship. Could it be, she wondered, that Chicago was Kevin's escape exit from her?

Sophia had decided to wait to call her parents and tell them all that was happening, afraid she knew what they would say, that they would again make a case for her to return for good to San Francisco. She wasn't sure she had the backbone to resist their advice, and even though they would be upset with her for not sharing this significant news with them immediately, she chose the path of least resistance. *No news is good news?* She admitted to herself that the only "good news" this "no news" was good for was that she had one less battle to fight, until, of course, she picked up the phone to make that call.

Sophia had always had a strong ability to protect herself, regularly demonstrating a decisive streak and proving she felt it important she make her own way in the world. Her mother had always considered Sophia somewhat of an anomaly when it came to their family, the loner in many ways her siblings and parents were not. Her older brother, Twain, was an athlete and a leader. Extremely popular in school and sports, Sophia called him Colonel Popular, The Chosen One (nicknames for the people and things around her was pretty much a way of life for Sophia). Twain was proud of this title and not at all shy about sharing it with others to perpetuate its use. He relished the praise he received from his social activities—and there was plenty of it—including girls lining up to date him and calling at all hours for longer than Sophia could remember them not.

She called their younger sister, Austen, Mama's Girl, The Protected One. Austen was a girlie girl who from day one dreamed of living in the Barbie mansion married to Ken and making Barbie Corvette-loads of babies and boxed lunches. Her main aspiration was and always had been to love and be loved. She was maternal, nurturing and dependent—all qualities Sophia had fibers of but were not exactly her dominant traits.

Sophia herself was neither chosen nor protected, nor did she want to be. She relied upon her creativity, and until Kevin, her independence, and she liked it that way most of the time. Amongst the Connors clan, with her sharper edges instead of rounded corners, Sophia had developed a reputation for being the square block to the family round hole, making choices her folks would probably never make, not to spite them or because they would disapprove of her decisions, but because Sophia ultimately did what Sophia felt she needed to do. She had made plenty of mistakes along the way but at least she knew they were her mistakes and no one else's.

Sophia and her parents were no strangers to uncomfortable discussions and the awkward silences triggered by the disconnect between their separate desires. When she graduated from college in California and told her parents she was moving to New York to be a writer, her mother's face dropped like a broken soufflé. In her usual fashion, Diane Connors had turned to Sophia's father for assistance, defaulting to him because, as in so many other instances, she did not know how to handle the situation or her daughter. "Who is this child and where did she come from?" was usually the message her face communicated.

Ben Connors had stared forward at Sophia to allow the news to sink in. Then in *his* usual fashion, he tilted his head as if he were asked a question for which he didn't have the answer— the expression he gave when anyone in his family said or did something he didn't fully understand. It was a response Sophia always felt was his way of either buying time to collect his thoughts or in hopes the other would cave before he had a chance to respond, a strategy perhaps related to Kate's.

"Are you going to do anything about this, Ben?" her mother demanded.

"Mom, please don't be upset. Be supportive," Sophia said, trying to be as casual as possible and coach her mother into a positive outlook. "Every writer should live in New York at some point in their life."

Sophia's father, a lover of the written word himself, shrugged and looked back at his wife. "She's right, Diane. She's got a point."

Diane was not pleased with this reaction. "Oh, what do

either of you two know about it?" she said, now irritated with them both.

Then she directed her attention back to Sophia, "I do not understand this fascination you have with New York. You've had it since you were eight years old. Well, let me tell you…there is nothing in New York we don't have here in San Francisco, that's for sure."

Ben said nothing, knowing there was no argument that could be made to change Sophia's mind. His daughter was grown now and ready to fly from the nest. There was nothing left for them to do but let her go.

"I cannot believe either of you," Diane told them with complete disgust.

She stood up and walked towards the door. But before she got there, something in her shifted and she stopped. She then slowly turned around and walked back to Sophia, her tone tamed by the time she returned to her daughter's side. "You know I support you in *everything* you want to do. Don't pull that crap that I don't support you. You're not in the sixth grade anymore. I just don't understand why you need to live on the other side of the country to write. There are plenty of writers in California. And forgive me for being selfish but I'd like to be able to see my daughter more often than on Christmas."

That was when Sophia knew she had received her mother's blessing and that this was as good as it was going to get. She also knew she was about to start crying. So to distract herself from letting that happen she jumped up and hugged her mom tight, whispering in her ear, "Thank you!"

Diane and Ben Connors were and always had been a tag team, passing the baton from one to the other, two halves of a single whole, not quite as effective without the other. They had been that way as long as Sophia could remember, something she sometimes found annoying but usually sweet and always enviable. Salt and pepper. Laurel and Hardy. Yin and yang. They made a complete and complementing set.

But today, back in New York, it was best to not call them yet. They would perhaps be a little angry with her for holding back this important information, maybe even hurt, but in review they would remember Sophia needed to do things in her own time and way.

When her phone rang again, she answered it, because this time it was not Kevin. It was Kate.

"Are you gonna make it?" Kate asked.

"I'm coming. I'm leaving now," Sophia told her and hung up.

CHAPTER 4
IT'S TIME

Leaving her apartment after the better part of two days, the vitality and energy of the city gave Sophia a much-needed shot in the arm. New York was a land of distraction. Out roaming its belly, her problems were not lost but were diluted for a few minutes among the masses. The city, consumed by a never-ending sense of disinterest, offered a shield of anonymity. It was a relief that no one knew her as far as the eye could see, that no one would stop her to ask how she was, or where Kevin was and how he was doing. There would be no awkward and forced conversation about work or life, both volatile topics the wildly disharmonious chaos of the city made Sophia feel comfortable in forgetting for the moment, as if it was acceptable and even expected to believe that she just did not matter. Some might find this transition into something microscopic and insignificant discouraging, and think it would add to Sophia's sullen mood, but this was not the case. Sophia believed that New York City was a place where anything could happen. Today, at this moment, she wanted to believe that she would disappear.

Sophia entered the subway station, passing through the

turnstile and climbing the stairs just as a downtown train approached. The arriving train was the local she wanted. While the local was a longer train ride than the express option, it would not require her to switch trains along the way in order to get to her final destination. As it pulled in, cold air was pushed through her hair and down the neck of her coat. Winter was an unfriendly guest she wished would go away already despite knowing hers was a request far too premature to begin making. She regrettably shared the same wish about a lot of things in her life at the moment.

As she stepped onto the train, she looked around, examining the availability of seats and the quality of the crowd. In Sophia's electronic collection of observations and stories, she had compiled lists over the years of subway details from travels between destinations. The subway was the true New York Petri dish, a melting pot test environment to watch what would happen when you introduced any variety of elements in a closed but not-so-controlled setting. While not the purest example of the scientific method, it certainly produced interesting results.

Like most New Yorkers, she felt she had probably almost seen it all, both bad and good, and much of it took place on public transportation, and the rest in other public spaces. As the train ran the track, bumping and grinding its way downtown, her mind wandered to some of the unappealing and surprising situations: the angry yells of those pissed off about more than just the fact that someone took the seat they wanted; the mad push and sensation one receives feeling like a cow in a herd; the impatience of parents showing hostility towards their children; the loud, self-centered students on their way to and from school; the smell of a self-soiled individual passed out after a long, hard night of self-abuse; the vomit; the people rudely sitting spread eagled and deliberately taking more than one seat; the litter bugs (she wondered if people still used that term); the addicts frozen in drug-induced, slow-motion suspension; excited tourists with cameras and maps acting like they could not believe their eyes; the fights; the fear that something really awful might happen again one day in New York.

Sophia was all for giving credit where credit was due, and the fact was that she had collected plenty of wonderful stories from her under-city travels, too: happy children interacting with their happy parents; adults on their way to or from a ballgame; young lovers discovering one another; thumb fights; the son proudly taking a phone photo of his dad; the mom who walked jokingly outside the train window to keep up with the car as it moved out of the station to make her children—still on the train—laugh; the man who stood at the doors until they closed, kissing his hand and waving it towards his partner inside the train; the tourists with cameras and maps acting like they could not believe their eyes (Sophia felt this item belonged in both the good and bad lists); the subtle, friendly gestures, such as people holding the door for one another or telling someone their bag was unzipped and contents were falling out, which reminded her there were plenty of New Yorkers who really did look out for others.

When Sophia arrived at Kate's building, she walked past the doorman who recognized her and waved her on as if he was expecting her.

"Big day!" he said, flashing a mouth full of bright white teeth.

"Sure is, George," she said, certain he knew all about the trip.

"Will you make sure I get a postcard?" he called out, leaning over the front of his station.

"You got it," Sophia replied before the elevator doors closed.

At Kate's apartment, she rang the bell three times before her friend finally opened the door.

"Sorry," Kate said, unusually flustered. "I'm sure I've forgotten something. I just know I have."

"Don't forget to send George a postcard. He's awfully excited about this trip."

Kate laughed. "Naw, he just wants to sleep with me. Sometimes I think he loooves me."

Kate stalled immediately after the second sentence,

regretting having made the joke. Love, even in the playful context of her doorman's flirtatious lust, was not a topic to make light of given Sophia's current state. Sophia saw this reaction on Kate's face but dismissed it with a response. "Please," she told her friend as she sat down on the sofa, "I'm not *that* fragile."

That was a lie, of course, and they both knew it, but it did make Kate feel better as she was about to embark on this adventure. The last thing Sophia wanted was for Kate to feel the burden of her heartbreak.

"You know it's not too late to change your mind," Kate said, continuing to run around her apartment, frantic in her attempt to finish packing. It was a sight Sophia found somewhat comical and cartoonish.

"Yes, I seem to recall you've told me that about fifteen times in the past twenty-four hours. Don't get me wrong, I really do appreciate it, but it's not likely to happen. And stop feeling guilty you're going and I'm not. I'm at peace with it, so you should be, too."

Kate ran into the bathroom, made a ruckus that included sounds of shattering glass, and then came out with her hands full of bottles and tubes of products she poured into her suitcase. "There! All done," she said, finally stopping, putting her hands on her hips as if showing her bag she was the boss.

Kate studied Sophia's face and then just came out with it: "You look like shit."

"Thanks. That's so sweet of you to say."

"Sorry. I'm just making an observation."

"Well, I thought it only fair that we both have bags. Of course, yours are for traveling."

Kate looked Sophia dead in the eyes with an expression so compassionate, so unlike Kate's usual fly-by-the-seat-of-her-pants attitude, that it made her nervous. "For the sixteenth time, it's not too late to change your mind. We can get you a ticket. If it's too late to get you on the same flight, I could push back mine so we can travel together. Or…"

Sophia interrupted her with a smile and the internationally symbolic hand, "Stop. Please. I need to stay here and dig myself out of this mess."

Without a doubt, this had been one of the most difficult decisions Sophia had ever had to make because her impulse was to do what Kate was doing—to say "screw it" to reason and responsibility, and to break with her past with a good, long trip to France. While it was something the doctor had ordered, it was also something didn't have coverage for.

She saw calculations taking place in Kate's face, so she added, "And don't you dare think about staying. I don't need you taking care of me. I'm a big girl, you know, and I can manage for a couple weeks without you. Although, of course, it won't be easy and you'll be missed terribly."

She threw that last part in there to stroke Kate's ego, even though it certainly didn't need it.

Kate wasn't entirely sure she was being told the truth, but she, like Ben and Diane Connors, knew she could not make Sophia change her mind.

"I'm sure I'll kick myself forever for not going but I know this is for the best right now. When the hell did I get so responsible?"

"Will you promise me one thing?" Kate begged, now sitting down next to Sophia. She grabbed at her hands and wrapped them with hers. "Will you please promise me you'll shoot a flare if you need me? Please. And know you're not alone. You'll never be alone. Not now. Not ever."

Sophia began to cry, which was the last thing she wanted to happen right now. She had wanted to come over to her apartment and give her friend a proper New York sendoff while showing her how strong and brave she was. But right now, with her strongest friend getting soft on her, she just couldn't muster it.

"Yes," she promised, tears streaming down like a leaky faucet. "I will."

Kate hugged her for a minute until Sophia pushed out of the embrace. "You need to get going if you want to avoid traffic to the airport."

Kate stood up and put on her coat. "You better email me while I'm gone."

Sophia wiped away her waterworks. "All the time."

"And you better call your parents. The longer you wait to tell them, the worse they'll be."

Sophia said nothing in return, both because she knew Kate meant well *and* because she was right. When it came to the Connors family, Kate was biased. They were her surrogate family. Her own parents' relationship had imploded three weeks before she left for college and, like broken bones that mended but did so with residual effects and imperfections, things were never quite the same for her and her siblings. Ben and Diane did their best to fill the need in Kate, whom they considered a Connors.

Sophia stood up and grabbed one of Kate's suitcases, laughing because her friend had packed so much it seemed she had a new outfit for each of the twenty-eight days she was going to be gone. Sophia quipped, "I'll help you with your bags if you help me with mine."

Sophia waved as Kate's cab pulled away going east on 8th Street. Once it had blended into traffic and vanished from sight, she began working her way through the crowded sidewalk back to the subway station. Her chest ached as if she had just said goodbye to the last recognizable piece of a life that was no longer. She knew the thought was melodramatic but she couldn't help herself. These past few days had rubbed her nose in the reality that life was so temporary and that someone or something could be a part of your life for the longest time only to one day disappear. She had issues with that finality.

Despite the noise and activity around her, loss absorbed her again as it dawned on her that Kevin would soon become a stranger. This man who had at one time been her present as well as her future would inevitably fade away into the past. He would no longer be the one person who knew practically everything about her, the one with whom she shared her fears and aspirations. Neglect and experience would eventually make them unrecognizable to one another.

It also saddened her when she realized her dreams were now hers and hers alone. Kevin had pressed many times to read the half-written draft of her novel but she would never let him, even though he seemed to understand its crude, incomplete state and promised to be generous with his praise. Sophia wondered now if it was a good thing she hadn't shared that part of herself with him. Would it have made a difference if he had seen that other side, the deepest part of her?

She had wanted him to be the first to read her novel when it was finished, to discuss her thoughts and intentions behind it all, to give him the opportunity to ask what he would be inclined to ask. But now he would not be beside her when that day came.

But when will I be ready?

This was something she had wondered for so long, knowing she really only had herself to blame. What was she waiting for? While Kevin had somehow been constructing a future without her right under her very nose, she had managed to stall, to take steps in the wrong direction, like a real life version of Chutes & Ladders. Kevin climbed to the triumphant finish line while Sophia seemed to be sliding back to the beginning.

It will happen. I will finish.

By that time, she considered, he wouldn't even be in her life. If one day she was lucky enough to get published, and if he cared at all, perhaps he would buy a copy of her book and read it. But by then he would probably no longer *know* her. Would he see things in her writing and still think he knew who she was and what she was all about? Would it make him miss her and long for her the way he once had? Or would time disintegrate everything, like the soda pop eating away the metal that she had added to her mental list earlier in the day? Would there be any recollection of the intimacy they once shared? Or would it all be stripped away? She wondered what it was all for, why anyone even bothered if all things eventually and unavoidably came to an end and faded away.

At that moment, when Sophia felt totally destroyed and perhaps at her worst, something remarkable occurred: she vividly experienced a mental flash of her grandmother's face and of something she used to say.

Nonna had been one tough cookie, so much so that the family jokingly called her "Little Mussolini" because of her dominating, dictator-like tendencies. A strict woman insistent on having her way, Sophia had many clear memories of her running the family and her world with iron-fist discipline. She was blindingly adamant in everything she did, from the way she demanded her children hear and follow her every instruction, to the subtle details that spoke so loudly to what she was all about, including how she stuffed her tiny but fat feet into shoes that no longer fit because she refused to accept they no longer did—a horrible sight which scared all of the grandkids because of the way the folds of her feet poured off the sides. She was willful and focused, and a force with which to be reckoned.

One of Sophia's more amusing memories was the time the whole family watched *American Graffiti* together. As she recalled, there was a drag racing scene when a guy flashed his naked butt through a car window. Without missing a beat, Nonna pointed at Sophia and the other kids, then spoke to Ben and Diane, "Are you going to let them watch this?"

But what was made the moment so funny was how she then pointed at Sophia's parents in the same way she did their children and yelled at her own husband, "Are you going to let *them* watch this?"

Sophia's grandmother was famous for delivering hardcore advice, most of the time to innocent bystanders who hadn't even asked for it. Nonna lived by two main rules. First was her often-used personal statement, a catchphrase of sorts, that always generated surprise since it came from the old, tough-as-nails, four-foot-five woman. "Shit or get off the pot!" she would say, meaning it with all of the implied severity. In other words, get to it or get out *now*.

Nonna's second rule of life, which never really explained

her unabashedly coarse attitude towards everyone and everything, was communicated in the saying, "It could always be worse."

Isn't that the truth, Sophia thought. She herself had used the expression a zillion times, but there was something about that moment while in the depths of her overwhelming personal challenges and the search for a fragment of reason that its meaning really struck her.

This made Sophia recall her brother, Twain. As kids they had had their share of ugly battles, fighting for perceived territory or other difficult-to-remember things that at the time had inspired catastrophic sibling struggles. Austen, having been born so many years after them and posing no immediate threat to either, somehow earned their sympathy and support and missed most of this abuse. With each other, however, Sophia and Twain fought regularly and with intensity, and one such fight in particular stood out with clarity and detail. There was his older brother arrogance, his dismissive disregard and refusal to hear her requests. There was her pride and strong will. There was his village built from Legos. There was screaming and then pushing, and before she knew it was over, like Godzilla's tour of Tokyo, she had kicked and demolished every structure and vehicle he had spent weeks constructing, stepping through walls and formations with her bare feet. As scratches and cuts replaced her fury, tears replaced his blind bullishness and he crumbled to his knees. Across from each other they stood, exhausted and defeated from battle.

But a few minutes of silence later, Sophia witnessed something she would come to recognize as typically characteristic of Twain. Incapable or unwilling to hold onto anything for too long, Twain's emotion left him as fast as it came. He stood, shrugged his shoulders and said while surveying the destruction, "Oh, well. It's time to fix it."

Twain's rubber band resilience was unlike her. Just like that, he had experienced his anger and sorrow and was able to move on, as if he had gotten it off his chest and was no longer controlled by it. She wanted that for herself today and, therefore, declared she would do what she could to make that happen. *It could always be worse.*

Hypnotized by the city's underground tunnels passing by the subway window at an increasing speed, Sophia told herself she would allow herself to mourn what would not be, to get it off her chest as best she could, even though she felt torn wide open while the brutal wind of sadness blew frost through her insides, burning her terribly and permanently. She felt lonelier today than perhaps ever before. The events of the past several days had completely derailed her, stampeding her real world the way she once did to her brother's imaginary one. Sophia would surrender to her pain—today, tomorrow, as long as it took—with blind hope that it might ultimately make it go away. Maybe, just maybe, she told herself, she would one day mean it when she shrugged her shoulders and said, "It's time."

CHAPTER 5
P-DAY

The concept of magnetism—the forces that brought people and things together as well as drove them apart—had always fascinated Sophia, and her recent personal circumstances certainly did nothing to discourage this.

For as long as she could remember, she had been drawn to New York. There was no better way to describe or explain the sensation that pulled her to the city. And without really even knowing much more than what was introduced to her by books, movies, television and a few short vacations, she dove in and moved to Manhattan with the little money she had scraped together from graduation and the job she had worked her senior year at The Giordano Public Relations Group. Other than a couple boxes of clothes, she brought with her a scheduled interview with a temp agency, which proved to be her most useful possession of all.

Sophia loved the city from the minute she arrived, but soon learned from new friends that her experience was somewhat unique, that many others found their first months in New York, even years, to be filled with culture shock and transition, as if they were very little fish dropped into a mammoth lake learning to swim for the first time. Sophia realized the city had tremendous power over people, that it played games with their heads and, if ill-prepared, it would chew them up and spit them out. This harsh awakening shed light that went beyond the scope of New York, for they were all transplants, the children of small cities and little towns, discovering the world was a very large and complicated place. To survive, and survive well, in Manhattan would require fast walking, smart talking, and a good deal of money. For many, their conditioning or nature had not equipped them properly, and they found themselves scrambling to make sense of it all.

Sophia had never experienced homesickness, not because she didn't miss her family, but because she had always been a forward-thinking person. She insisted there had to be something profound in her future and that it wasn't going to arrive without her going farther than a few miles from where she grew up. She also didn't romanticize the past as if her high school days had been the pinnacle of her life, years by which to compare all others. They were good ones, that was for certain, but she left it at that. And while some of her new friends longed for days and places past, she found her first months and years in New York both challenging and thrilling, and in spite of everything that occurred, her senses tingled in ways she had always suspected possible but never truly felt firsthand. There were those who struggled to find their equilibrium, as well as others who planned their inevitable departures, but Sophia had her sea legs the moment she stepped foot onto the island of Manhattan. She had felt at home—a feeling she had held onto until recent days. Today, however, she wasn't quite sure of anything.

When she did arrive in New York, her parents, on the other hand—her mother especially—had needed time to transition. Initially, they thought she was crazy. But once she was settled and working, and a little time allowed them to get used to everything, they began warming up to the idea. Sophia suspected the new support had a lot to do with the responses they were getting from family and friends.

"I saw Jodi Meyers at the grocery store last week," her

mother once told her in those early days. "She was so excited to hear you moved to New York. She said you always were such an adventurous girl."

Sophia was grateful to learn someone other than herself was doing some public relations work on her behalf to win them over.

Then, when the towers fell, they quickly changed their minds, returning to the idea it would be best if their daughter lived in California.

Sophia's first job in the city had been at the Lincoln Personnel Agency, a bandage of a job that ended up providing much more stability than she originally expected. Her arrival happened to coincide with the burst of the dot com bubble, and as many of the infantile companies failed to deliver on paper promises and bad business plans, venture capital money dried up and took a trickle-down toll on the New York job market. Companies still needing help but afraid to hire permanent staff made use of Lincoln's services, liberating themselves from the burden of long-term commitments or employee benefits. This worked out in Sophia's favor and she found herself consistently busy working a variety of office jobs all over the city, proving her worth to the agency and managing to scrape by financially.

For an extensive list of reasons, working for Lincoln was not a great job. But in addition to a paycheck, it allowed Sophia a privilege she knew anyone could appreciate—the views of New York—for everywhere she went, whether uptown or downtown, high or low, she got the chance to see Manhattan from hundreds of different angles and perspectives, and all within the first few months of living there. She called the sights "the nooks and crannies" of the city, a term her advertising-abused mind had picked up countless years before thanks to the Thomas' English Muffins folks. Years later, in an interview at RGB, she actually claimed that this adoption of advertising language was a clear sign she was destined to write advertising copy. She knew the minute the statement stumbled off her lips that it was contrived, but she also knew she needed more money than what she was making at Lincoln and that she needed healthcare benefits, too.

Sophia had come to New York to see things and that was what she was doing. If there ever was a place for her to discover more about the world, and herself, this was it.

But there were some experiences she wished she could erase, that no one, not even a writer, should experience.

Sophia had been working at Kopp & Kaminski two weeks under her first long-term assignment when she heard the loud grumblings from the conference room. The room, which had been filled with new hires brought in from local New York, Connecticut and New Jersey offices for orientation and training, had been stirred up by something far more commanding than K&K's employee manual. The ruckus was too great for Sophia and her co-workers to ignore, causing a congregation to assemble together in the room. As each new person entered the room, their eyes followed those of the crowd out the large panoramic window in search of downtown. All the way from K&K's 16th floor offices on 28th Street and 7th Avenue, they could see the smoke coming out of one of the World Trade Center towers. Surprised and confused, they stood there and watched, questioning and discussing, as many did that morning, what could have started a fire in the building. But the collective concern in the room gave way to something far worse when moments later they saw the second plane hit the other tower.

When it happened, Sophia and her colleagues could not believe their eyes, that together each of them had seen the large metallic object, which seemed from the distance to be a small commuter plane, fly through the morning's perfect blue sky down the Hudson River into the building. The room erupted in audible disbelief and panic, and they knew something unimaginable was taking place.

Sophia ran to her desk and dialed her parents. It was only shortly after five o'clock in California but she knew from having grown up with earthquakes that the phone lines would soon be busy and that dialing out would be nearly impossible.

Her father picked up after two rings. "Uh, hello?" he said, sounding asleep.

"Dad, it's me, Sophia. I'm fine," she replied, prepping him.

"But I wanted you to know that something is happening here in New York."

There was a thoughtful pause and an attempt to gather his focus through his state of slumber. "What? What do you mean?" he asked, awakening quickly.

Sophia wasn't sure what to tell him because at that point she still didn't know much. She didn't want to worry him either, and while wondering if she should sugarcoat her words, they ended up slipping out without time or thought to edit them. "We're not sure, but the World Trade Center towers are on fire. We saw something in the sky from our offices. We think a small plane hit one of the towers after the other tower was already on fire."

"Oh, my God!" her dad cried.

Sophia could hear her mother stir in the background. "What is it? What is it, Ben?"

"Tell her I'm fine," Sophia insisted. "I'm nowhere near downtown. I wanted to call you to tell you I'm ok, whatever's happening."

"Sophia's fine, Diane," Ben told his wife. "Turn on the television."

"Dad, I should go and see what more I can find out. I'll call you later, ok? I love you guys."

"We love you, too, baby! Be careful," her father said, before they both hung up.

She felt herself get choked up. The fear, the not knowing what was happening, the desire to be with her family—it had all created a knot in her stomach that began to climb into her throat.

When Sophia returned to the conference room, everyone was deeply agitated and noticeably worse off than before, mesmerized and shaken by what was happening across the city. She looked back out the window and saw that the smoke from the towers had grown far more alarming, that the second tower seemed just as devastated as the first. It wasn't long before the unthinkable occurred and the entire room broke into uncontrollable, inconsolable sobs.

K&K's managing director announced moments later what was happening, that he had seen on the television in his office what had and continued to occur only a few dozen blocks away, and that everyone had the option of staying in the offices or going home. Sophia, opting to get as far from downtown as possible, returned to her desk, swapping out her work heels for the pair of sneakers she was grateful to have in her gym bag, and left the building as fast as she could. While leaving the building brought her relief, what she experienced outside the building that day would be burned forever into her memory.

In every direction as far as she could see—across the street to Madison Square Garden and Penn Station, down the street towards Chelsea, up the street towards Macy's—people had poured into the streets, stunned looks of horror reflected in their faces. *Zombies,* Sophia thought, *that's what we look like.* Never before had she seen so many people fill the streets, and yet their collective effort managed to produce a silence so horrifically deafening. The whole city seemed to be out around her, only there was so little noise. And where was the traffic? There were no cars driving down 7th Avenue. The city had been altered.

She worked her way uptown, first darting across 34th Street to get as far away from the shadow of the Empire State Building as possible. Whatever was happening, she wanted to avoid the largest buildings and landmarks in case the last of the terrible things had not yet occurred. Determined to get to 9th Avenue and be closer to the Hudson, she then followed a path north to the Upper West Side.

Along the way, she stopped to get money from an ATM and pulled out as much cash as she could. Then, closer to home, she stocked up on bottled water and canned food at the corner bodega, the line of others proving they shared the same survival instincts. After the cashier rang up the man in front of Sophia, the customer announced he was four dollars short, and in his desperate state of confusion, he stood there perplexed and unable to figure out how to resolve his problem. He was in shock. Sophia tapped him gently on the shoulder to get his attention and then pushed a five-dollar bill across the counter.

The man turned around and attempted a smile, his mouth thanking her while his shell-shocked stare pleaded for answers. "What the hell is happening to our home?" commanded his expression. To this day, Sophia wasn't sure if she donated the money to be humanitarian or because she so badly wanted to be home.

Sophia then returned to her apartment, relieved by the false security of her own environment, knowing she was probably no safer there than she had been ten, twenty, thirty minutes earlier. But in her own space, she could tell herself she was out of harm's way, without the faces of others to remind her she could not be certain of anything. She avoided the mirror for days, unable to bear the terror she knew was there waiting for her, her expression probably looking no different than the man in the bodega.

Sophia rose before eight in the morning, the earliest she had awoken since "D-Day," or "Dump Day," as she was now calling it. After all, she figured, a historic occasion such as being dumped twice in one day by both your employer and your boyfriend certainly demanded the respect of its own unique title.

It didn't take her long to learn to appreciate the daytime hours and to fear the evening ones. Her first instinct had been to sleep in as long as she wanted or needed, and stay up as late as she felt inclined, figuring that if she was going to be out of a routine, she might as well enjoy a flexible schedule—a privilege she hadn't been in possession of for many years. What she hadn't expected was what happened when the sun went down: what seemed fine in the daylight suddenly became something entirely different in the darkness, when the only light on the city street outside her window came from the solitary lamp two doors down, and when the winter sky, consumed by the weight of its own desires for better days gone by, offered no condolences because it had none to give. The evening hours, which came far too early this time of year, brought with them cold and overwhelming thoughts, and Sophia began developing a sense of dread that reminded her of a college friend she once knew who had suffered all his life from night terrors, a disturbing sleep disorder far worse than nightmares. His condition caused him to awaken, on several occasions, in their dormitory's courtyard screaming bloody murder at two o'clock in the morning. She, of course, acknowledged that her situation was different, that she could put herself to bed and know she would be able to stay there until hope arrived with the morning light, but her anxiety regarding the evening hours felt, as best as she could tell, the same. When Sophia realized a couple days into her new routine that night was not to be trusted, she committed herself to busy days of work and early nights to bed. Structure and sleep, she discovered, slowed the pace, at least a little, of her world spinning out of control.

She had assigned a special title to today as well—"P-Day," or "Parents' Day"—deciding it was time to tell her parents about the events of the past week, to get past this one major hurdle in the way of returning her life to a semblance of normalcy.

After spending a couple of hours sending resumes and emails to contacts in the advertising field as well as other industries, Sophia picked up the phone to make the call, knowing her parents would be awake by then.

"Hello?" Diane Connors said when she picked up the phone, acting like she didn't know who was calling, even though the whole family knew how obsessed she was with her caller ID.

"Hi, Mom. It's me."

"Sophia, dear!" she returned, still pretending to be surprised. "Did your sister call you? You heard the good news then?"

Good news? This was a call for bad news. Sophia had no idea what her mother was talking about, and just as she was about to say so, call waiting—another Connors family favorite—clicked and commanded her attention. Glancing down, she saw it was Austen calling her on the other line.

"Mom? It's Austen. Can you hold on a minute?"

"Sure, dear."

Sophia jumped over to her sister. "Hey, I'm on the other line with Mom."

"She didn't tell you, did she?" Austen asked with a tone of disgust.

"No. Tell me what?"

"You swear she didn't? You know how she is. I will be sooooo angry if she did."

"I swear, Austen. *I* just called *her*," Sophia insisted, wondering how she had managed to land in the middle of something. "What is it? What's going on?"

Austen sighed with relief just before she screamed, "I'm engaged! Robert and I are getting married! Can you believe it?"

What did you say?

If Sophia's life came with a sound effects machine, something which she had thought most of her life would be extremely useful, this would be a moment when it would be going off, making some old car horn's "ah-ooh-ga, ah-ooh-ga" cry, or a cartoon's "wah-wah-wah" sound, like when the Road Runner once again foils Wile E. Coyote's plans. Sophia felt her torso tighten immediately, not because she wasn't happy for her sister, but because the universe seemed to think this needed to happen during perhaps the worst week of her life.

Her tongue tied, her head did its best to calculate the news and construct a response. Her baby sister, who was so much younger than her, was getting married, ahead of her, and was announcing the news now. All she could get out was, "Wow!"

But it only took a second or two before she felt herself stepping outside of her own body, beyond her own issues, and into the joy she knew her sister was experiencing and had every right to celebrate. So she followed up her feeble initial response with "This is fantastic news!" This time, as she spoke, she realized she whole-heartedly meant her words, too. It was just taking her head and tongue a little time to catch up.

"Mom didn't steal my thunder, did she? I told her I wanted to tell you myself. Please tell me the truth."

"No, she didn't. I really had just called her when you buzzed in. Your timing is perfect because she didn't have a chance to tell me anything."

Austen took a deep breath and, like a talking doll with its

wind-me-up string pulled, she released in a single, uninterrupted comment, "He proposed last night...we were by the Bay and he got on one knee...it was just so romantic...I am so lucky...he is just the sweetest, most perfect guy...God, I love him so much!"

Wow!

"That's so wonderful, Austen! I'm really thrilled for you two," Sophia said, her private initial shock melting away and her truly happy feelings for her sister breaking through. How could she be anything but thrilled for her sister?

"Thank you! Thank you! Thank you! I'm so happy! I can't believe how lucky I am."

Remembering their mother on the other line, Sophia told Austen, "Let me tell Mom I'll call her back."

"Oh, yeah! I forgot. No, talk to her and call me when you're off. Okay? I want to make a few calls. Call me when you're done, alright?"

"You got it!" Sophia said and clicked back to her mother.

Seconds later, Sophia was sharing the excitement with her mother, "Wow! That's great news."

As she spoke the words, she knew she really felt their meaning. Robert was kind and thoughtful, and he made Austen very happy. He was good *to* her and good *for* her. And Sophia had known, like they all had, that it was really only a matter of time before this happened.

"Your dad and I think so, too. We just love Robert and we know how great they are together."

Good for her.

Sophia let it all soak in, happy to have *that* news to distract her from her own. But it only took a moment for it to begin slipping away as her mind became aware of where this conversation was going. How long before her mom brought up...

"And once you and Kevin decide to take the plunge, too," Diane Connors said, "then *all* my babies will be married, and you'll be ready to start making babies of your own!"

Too late, Sophia realized. Like a fish fresh out of the water, that mom of hers was a slippery one.

"Yeah, Mom, about that…"

"Oh, I am so pleased each of my children have such wonderful…"

"Mom, please," Sophia said, trying to stop her mother before the pile of salt she was adding to her wounds became too much to take.

"I know! I'll stop pushing. I just can't help myself sometimes. And with this news…well, it makes me so pleased."

Sophia moved the phone to her other ear. She had unconsciously begun pressing the handset into her ear and it had started to hurt. Maybe, she decided, she should hold off on telling her parents her news until another day, letting her sister and Robert have their important and well-deserved moment. Yes, she decided right then and there, rubbing the sting from her ear with her free hand, that was what she would do. P-Day could happen another day.

"What is it?" her mother asked. "What's wrong, Sophia?"

Uh-oh. Stop the bleeding. Get out before it's too late.

But Sophia's grave mistake was her hesitation, something her mom noticed immediately, and her usual approach in such situations was relentlessness.

"Honey, what's going on? What's wrong?"

Again, despite her mind telling her to run, Sophia froze. Her brain just wasn't up to its usual fast-thinking, "get-me-out-of-this" conditioning. She had lost herself in confusion, tripping and stumbling as she tried to think of something clever in a non-clever moment, and it only served to secure her demise. Before she knew it, Diane Connors could be heard distancing her mouth away from the phone, yelling into some far-off land in the background, hollering for her husband, "Ben, on the phone, now! Something's wrong with Sophia!"

"Mom, really!" Sophia finally mustered, a lie about to follow.

"Everything's fine!" she added, scrambling to bring a sense of security to her mother as well as herself. Today was Austen's day. She would not lose sight of that fact, using that detail to find strength in defending herself from her parents. Her problems could cry on their shoulders another day.

"BEEEEEENNNNN!" Diane Connors screamed, much louder this time, confirming there may be no way out for Sophia. "PHONE! NOW!"

Sophia heard her father pick up the other phone, then drop it, then pick it up again and shift it around until it was nestled into the nook between his shoulder and head. If Sophia had had that sound effects machine she fantasized about so many times, about now it would be playing cheesy horror film music, the type of ditty playing when the stupid teenager making her escape from the killer stumbles over something and ends up dying because of it.

"What's all this yelling about, ladies?" he said. "What am I missing?"

"I don't know," Diane told him. "That's what I'm trying to figure out."

"Really guys, I'm fine. Maybe we could talk about all of this another day. Let's celebrate Austen's good news right now."

"'All of this?' What does *that* mean?" Diane responded, and Sophia suddenly envisioned her mother as they spoke packing her luggage to come rescue her.

Sophia knew she was doomed. Her mother could not resist pulling an exposed thread to find out where it would lead and what would unravel.

"Oh, crap," her father said, knowing too she was onto something.

"So I'm right," her mother added, the Sherlock Holmes of the West Coast. "I knew it! There *is* something wrong."

"Mom, please!" Sophia said, trying to negotiate the situation.

"What is it, baby?" her father pleaded with a crack in his voice. "Please tell us what's wrong."

The charade was over. There was no going back with these two.

"I got fired," she blurted out. "And Kevin dumped me. On the same day."

The conversation from there on out became parental ping-pong—a session of doting that at the same time managed to comfort *and* embarrass her.

"Oh, honey!" pinged her mother. "This is terrible! Are you alright?"

"I'm fine," Sophia insisted, lumping a scoop of fat lie on top of her messed-up-life sundae. "It's really not that big of a deal."

"Not a big deal? It sure is!" ponged her father. "Do you need money? How are you holding up?"

"No, really. Thanks, but I'm fine."

"Oh, Sophia! I am so sorry. And so disappointed for you. Why don't you come home?" pinged her mother again, demonstrating her predictable inability to resist the urge to try and lasso her daughter home.

"I'm fine, guys. I really am. Please don't worry about me. I'll admit, it's not a great time, but I've been through worse," she declared, even if she knew that really wasn't the case, placing the balderdash cherry atop her fat lie.

"I am so sorry, sweetie!" ponged her father, staying in the game, trying his best to keep pace with his wife. "Can we do anything to help?"

"I called you because I wanted you to know what's going on. Not to worry. Just to know."

Sophia knew that if she let them dig at the topic too much she would break down. Considering Austen's announcement, the only tears she felt were appropriate today were those of joy for her sister. "I promise I'll call you if I need anything. Let's all focus on Austen's great news. This is *her* day."

After a few more attempts at helping his daughter, Ben left Sophia with an open-ended offer for assistance and then broke from the conversation. A couple of minutes and an exchange of several details later, Diane "let her daughter go," as she always put it when she had run out of things to say. Sophia hung up feeling confident she had successfully dissuaded her mother from jumping on the next plane to New York.

Relieved the deed was done, yet still reeling from the news, Sophia hadn't enjoyed more than twenty seconds of peace before her cell rang again, her brother's name flashing this time.

Are you kidding me?

She would have bet money their parents had gotten to him. That was the twisted Connors universe: what one Connors knew, all others found out within minutes. She answered the phone, "Yes?"

"Do you want me to kick his ass?" Twain asked.

"Was it Mom or Dad?" she inquired with deliberate sarcasm.

"You mean who called me? Both. They're concerned."

Sophia managed a laugh, imagining her parents each double-fisting phones. She could see it in her mind, her mother yelling across the house, once again making dial-demands of their father. "You...Twain! Me...Austen!"

Better yet, she pictured her mom hollering the instant she hung up with Sophia, barking with the exact same singular and precise commands she used during their conversation and as long as she could remember, "BEN! PHONE! TWAIN! NOW!"

"I hope you told them not to tell Austen," Sophia told her brother. "Not today anyway. She deserves the chance to celebrate without concern for anyone else."

"I told them to hold off, but you know them. They can't help themselves."

"Yeah, I know," she told her brother, aware this was an uphill battle best not pursued. Their parents were consistent in their ways and rarely fell susceptible to pressure or pleading. Sophia had made her request but knew their parents would ultimately do what they wanted. After all, a Connors never fell far from the family tree.

"How *are* you doing?" Twain asked, getting the conversation back on course.

"I've been better," she said, feeling her throat begin to tighten again. There were things she would tell Twain that she wouldn't tell her parents, not over the telephone and three thousand miles away anyway. "I'm not gonna lie. I'm a little lost."

"It'll get better. I promise."

"Oh, how do you know?" she joked. "You've never been fired *or* dumped!"

It was the truth. Twain's relationships with his wife, Judy, and his job had both lasted over ten years.

"That's what they say in the movies," he offered back.

She laughed. Leave it to Twain to know how to melt the ice. "We'd know about that, wouldn't we? All those years Mom and Dad brainwashed us by forcing us to watch movies and read books?"

"No, really," he said, interrupting her digression. "Do I need to worry about you?"

"I'll be fine," she insisted. "But right now I feel like I've been beaten with the shit stick."

"It'll be fine, sis. Just give it some time and try not to take it all too seriously. You know what I mean? You need money?"

"No, I'm good. I have a little to keep me from working the streets any time too soon. Key word, of course, is 'little.' And I signed up for unemployment yesterday. That was quite an experience, I can tell you."

"My sister the street walker. Now that would be a sight."

Sophia laughed. "Yeah, as if I haven't had enough rejection lately. I'd be the sorriest, poorest hooker there ever was."

"Oh, please. I have several friends who'd pay to have sex with you."

"You're disgusting," she said, laughing. She and Twain had always shared a unique banter.

"I'm sorry about all of this," Twain said in an unusually gentle tone. There was love in the pause that followed, an allowance of concern through words unspoken. "You know you can call us…me, any time. For anything. Okay?"

"I know," Sophia replied. "I appreciate that."

"Here," he said. "Hold on a second. Someone wants to say, 'Hi.'"

Sophia heard the phone being passed. On came a little voice, young and curious. "He-wo?" said Twain's three-year-old, Pete, still unable to form certain letters.

"It's Aunt Sophia," she heard her brother say in the background.

"Hey, Pete! It's Aunt Sophia," she repeated.

"Hi, Aunt Soapia." Pete returned.

"How's my little monkey?"

Pete laughed at the description.

"How are you?" she asked again.

"Pine."

"What are you gonna do today?" she asked.

"Pay," he told her, meaning, "play."

"You gonna watch some TV, too?" she added in her regular journalistic style, knowing Pete had not yet become much of a phone conversationalist.

"Yes," was his only answer.

"You gonna watch cartoons?"

"Yes."

"I love you!" she told him.

"I wub you," he repeated, and then hung up the phone.

Sophia heard the final click of the phone and then nothing after that. Laughing with surprise, she realized Pete probably associated that statement with the end of a conversation. *Love equals the end. Just like a man.*

But Sophia didn't really mean the harsh thought, not much anyway. She knew there was a small part of her that did—not towards Pete or her brother or their dad certainly—but towards other men, or maybe just life. This emotional shot allowed her to give face and blame for how she was feeling, even if it wasn't entirely justified or properly directed. Wasn't she entitled, just a little right now, to let off some steam this way as long as it only remained something she felt temporarily?

"Bitter, party of one," Kate always joked about herself when something didn't go her way. Sophia liked the expression and repeated it when it suited her own circumstances. They both knew, however, it wasn't a characteristic either wore very well for long.

Besides, Sophia acknowledged as she thought about the men in her family, she would do her part to make sure Pete grew up to be a thoughtful, considerate man just like his father, and just like theirs.

Sophia felt relieved she had completed what she had set out to do. There she was on the eve of yet another birthday—a topic she was completely avoiding at the moment—and she still felt the pull of her parents' approval. While it wasn't something that overwhelmed her, it did matter. What they thought still impacted her, and she knew how lucky she was that, despite the occasional disagreements, they were always in the stands rooting for her. Theirs was the ultimate seal of approval, which she doubted would ever go away.

As for today, she would focus on her sister's happy news and soak in the priceless love of her small nephew who was able to enjoy the simplest of pleasures. *How lucky he is.*

CHAPTER 6
THERE IT WAS

It took Sophia twenty minutes to convince her former co-worker, Sandy Smith, that the idea was feasible. It took another twenty minutes to get her to execute the plan.

"Oh, I don't know if I can do that," was Sandy's first reaction.

"Please, Sandy! No one will ever know. They don't do background checks. Heck, I'd be surprised if they even look at IDs."

"You have to promise not to say anything. I could get into a lot of trouble if anyone finds out about this," Sandy told Sophia with the severity of someone discussing secret service work.

"I promise you I won't say a word," Sophia assured her. "Besides, it's not as if we're breaking the law here."

"Of course not, but the company will be really angry if I refer a professional for this vodka focus group."

"Sandy, I'd hardly consider myself a professional drinker," joked Sophia.

"You know what I mean. The focus group company doesn't want professional ad or marketing people."

"I'm unemployed. How professional is that?"

"They want to make sure the people used have nothing to do with the industry so they can get some valuable consumer data for their clients. Your marketing and advertising insight affects your opinions. They know that. I work with these folks a lot. They will be really ticked if…"

"I promise, Sandy! Don't think another thought about it. Honestly, I'll never say a word. And I could really use the money."

"Uh-huh" was all Sandy said in response. She didn't seem convinced this was a good idea, but Sophia thought her persistence was beginning to wear her down.

"Today I'm just Plain Jane off the street," she added.

"Uh-huh. The pay *is* really good."

"I think I'll be…" Sophia continued, thinking up her alias for today's focus group, "an executive secretary for a banker. Yes, that'll be my new identity."

"Whatever, Sophia. Just don't start spewing ad lingo. Don't get 'overachiever' on me and they won't know the difference. They pay cash. Did I tell you that?"

"Yep, you sure did. That's great news."

"Ok, good. Well, good luck today."

"Thanks again," Sophia told Sandy. "I really appreciate the referral. I owe you one."

Sandy's contact at In Focus, a company that provided research support for hire for agencies and corporations testing products and services, many of which were still in development, was a woman named Mabel, who called soon after Sophia hung up with Sandy. As Sandy had explained, the focus group they discussed was for another agency, not RGB, so there was little chance Sophia would run into former co-workers.

"Is this Sophia?" bellowed the deepest smoker's voice Sophia had heard in some time. It came wrapped in a thick Long Island accent.

"Yes."

"This is Mabel, Sandy's friend at In Focus. I understand

you've got some time to be in on a focus group for us."

"I do," Sophia told her, resisting the temptation to tell her she had all the time in the world.

Mabel asked a slew of questions trying to understand Sophia's "profile." They discussed a variety of topics that did nothing for Sophia's fragile state of mind, such as marital status, age and occupation.

"Are you a drinker, dear?"

"Sure," Sophia said, hoping she was passing the test.

"You like vodka, don't cha?" Mabel stated, giving Sophia the impression she was now being guided more than questioned.

"Oh, yes. Of course."

"That's good, dear," Mabel said, sounding disconnected as if she had been asking questions like these for as long as she had been smoking. "Like I told Sandy to tell you, I got an opening for a group this afternoon. This other gal cancelled on me. Oh, how I hate when they do that to me last minute."

"Yes, Sandy told me all about it. Where do I need to go and when?" Sophia asked. "And don't worry about me, Mabel. I'll never cancel on you."

"Thank you. I tell you, I could die when they do that to me. Messes up everything."

"And feel free to call me for other groups, too," Sophia said, throwing into the conversation, "My schedule is…uh, flexible."

"I'll do that," Mabel said. "You know I'm really not supposed to assign people to groups more than once every six months, but between you and me, we'll see what we can do."

"That's wonderful, Mabel. Thank you so much!"

"Dear, you are so sweet. No wonder my girl Sandy is looking out for you."

The appointment was in a corporate office building on Fifth Avenue and 40th Street, a building built in the '60s with a dated wannabe contemporary look that stood out now just as it had during its day, and not in a good way.

Eleven flights up in a lobby more appealing than the rest of the building, Sophia signed in for the three o'clock session just as Mabel had told her to and then sat patiently waiting with others until they were called into their meeting room. As she waited, she re-read the email she received from Kate earlier on her phone, one of several she had gotten since her friend arrived in Paris.

Hello again from Paris!

All is fabulous here. Très magnifique! You sure you don't want to join me? (That would be my fortieth time asking that, right?) It's not too late!!! I cannot believe I've only been here a week and a half. I'm being a good girl and am not spending a ton of money on clothes, although you know I'd love to! I'm following the suitcase rule. If it won't fit in the bags I have, then I can't buy it. (But I could always buy a new bag, too. Right?) Hee hee.

Glad to hear you're sending out resumes. May I play devil's advocate? (You know I'm going to regardless of how you answer that question because I'm only looking out for you.) Do you really want to go back into advertising? Maybe you should stay strong and hold out for the right opportunity? You need to be writing. I know you said beggars can't be choosers but you're not a beggar! You're a great writer and it's time you write something more substantial than ad copy. It was a good job for you for a little while but now it's time you do what you were born to do. Just think about it…

I've been hanging out with a fun group of Parisians I met a couple days ago. Some fun folks you would totally love, if you change your mind… (I know, I know…I don't stop. I don't think I know how.)

More later! I love ya!
Kate

In Sophia's emails back to her friend, she went out of her way to appear fine, to present herself as standing solidly on her own two feet. The last thing she wanted to do was rain on Kate's Parisian parade. Kate deserved to have the time of her life and not worry about her friend back home.

Kate certainly had a point. Why go back into a business she had thought about leaving so many times? It wasn't too late to shift gears, to take the train off the track and put her career on a different course. There were plenty of things she could do with her skills to pay the bills until she was writing full-time. For the past five years, advertising had drained the life out of her, demanding a schedule that didn't allow her to work on anything else. How long had it been since she had touched her novel? She couldn't remember and that scared the hell out of her.

There it was, Sophia realized. There was the confrontation she had dreaded but knew was unavoidable, that at some point she was going to have to make a decision to somehow create or adopt a lifestyle that supported her writing ambitions. For some time, she had thought the opportunity would present itself naturally, but she now realized it was not going to happen that way. She would have to make the time as well as the decisions and compromises that provided her the time and energy to write. There were more occasions than she cared to remember when she had every intention of going home after work and picking up her story where she had left off. But as things unraveled at work, so did they in her personal life. Late nights on the clock at work meant little or no time at home, and certainly no creative juice left over for the minimal spare time remaining.

Sophia's thoughts evaporated when someone came out from behind a door and said, "Everyone in the three o'clock group? Please follow me into conference room F, please."

At the end of a long hallway lined with different rooms tagged with letters, the group reached and entered their opened room.

"Please help yourself to a drink and snack, and then find a seat," the host told them.

Sophia examined the assortment of desserts and candies in every corner of the room, probably intended to give the interviewed subjects a sugar kick to keep their energy levels high.

Sophia knew the tricks of the trade, not that she, the banker's executive secretary for the day, would ever say anything. She had attended conferences where the rooms were set up in similar ways with the same deliberate strategies. Grabbing a water, she walked to the end of the table and sat down.

Moments later, Sophia did a quick head count and discovered there were now fourteen people in the room finding their seats at the long, oval-shaped table. Three additional people who looked like they worked for In Focus hovered about, waiting for the room to settle. Sophia also noticed the wide, mirrored observation window and wondered how many people were on the other side of the glass, hoping there was no one in there she might know.

One of the standing employees began to speak. "Thank you for joining us today," she said. "As I think you've all been told, we're here to get your thoughts about some vodka products, including packaging and taste. We encourage you to voice your opinions and to tell us exactly what you think about what we share with you."

As the speaker said all of this, a mouth-smacking sound distracted Sophia's attention. She turned her head to discover the repulsive sound was coming from the woman next to her as she devoured a plate full of goodies she had collected on her way into the room. Sophia turned away from her and then realized others were chomping away with the same disturbing intensity as if they hadn't eaten in weeks. Catching eye contact with her, the guy across the table smiled and winked at Sophia without missing a second of chewing time. With all of the crazy feeding going on, the hour-long session began on a questionable note and only continued to spiral downwards from there.

Once the procedures for the focus group were explained, the leaders directed a discussion about a new pomegranate vodka product their client, a major spirits company, was introducing later in the year. The In Focus staff attempted to guide the conversation with subtle, leading inquiries. First, they reviewed bottle and box packaging designs, and the comments heard from the participants included a variety of useless suggestions that traveled beyond the borders of subjectivity. Several members of the group pretended to understand design and marketing, using terminology that made no sense either in or out of the current context, while others pointed out details that were irrelevant to the mind of anyone who might actually purchase this product or, for that matter, any other. Sophia was both amused by them and embarrassed for them at the same time. And she was definitely sorry for the employees on duty that day. If this was what all focus groups were like, then where was the value?

Then they reviewed multiple drafts of print campaigns, which only triggered more of the same banter, as well as an unnecessary and significantly heated debate between four hyper-aggressive, "I think I'm cool," A-type personalities. Sophia had seen this competitive behavior before, but with a better-educated and better-dressed crowd holding a firmer grasp on the English language *and* their emotions. She began to feel a little afraid, and she started to feel sorry for herself as well.

Finally, once the unexpected and inappropriate boiling conversation mellowed to a simmer, the participants tasted four versions of the yet-to-be-finalized product. Sophia found two of the concoctions—the best description for the vodka—to taste just as one would expect from a factory or laboratory: artificial, contrived and unappealing. The other two options were interesting but still somewhat off-target.

But by this point, and before she could share her ideas, the introduction of alcohol to this sugar-frenzied crowd was proving to be a terrible idea, and the inmates went from scaring the guards to taking over the asylum in no time flat. Like a pack of ravenous hyenas that just escaped from their cages, the aggressive ones became more fired up, jumping at each other, making wild accusations about brain sizes, mothers and wives, and suggesting stepping outside to settle matters. The passive ones cowered in their corners and tried to hide. If it weren't for the boardroom environment and poor packaging designs, Sophia thought she might have taken a wrong step at the corner of Fifth Avenue and 40th and landed in the middle of some cable nature special. She just shook her head, certain that very little good was coming from this gathering to drive the future of this new product, and was reminded that being on a jury of her peers didn't always give her the greatest confidence for the future of the planet.

In addition to the one hundred and twenty-five dollars in cash, Sophia left the room with clarity. Kate was right about this advertising world, that she had thought about quitting the business a thousand times but rationalized why she shouldn't or couldn't do it. She had been blinded by the security of a paycheck and controlled by her fear. Right now, she was freefalling, and there was no doubt about it that it scared the hell out of her, but the idea, she knew, of returning to that life and staying there for the next thirty years was far worse. She had to believe there was something hopeful in the distance, a glimmer of a promise in that realm of uncertainty that something unknown might be better for her in the long run than something known, that there was the potential for greater reward in breaking from the pack. While she felt she just might drown in the process, she wasn't going down without a fight.

CHAPTER 7
FULL CIRCLE

Much to Sophia's relief, the cold spell finally broke, allowing the temperature to climb into the forties for the first time in over a month. She had kept a steady eye on it, regularly cross-referencing what she read on the Internet with the thermometer she had mounted outside of her window when she first moved into her apartment several years ago. Weather watching was a hobby to her, especially this time of year when cabin fever became increasingly trying. Her grandmother had relished the pastime and had played a large role in the semi-compulsive behavior living on in Sophia.

Nonna, she realized, would have loved The Weather Channel, a twenty-four hours a day smorgasbord of weather patterns and warnings. She would have loved it so much so, Sophia considered as she laced up her running shoes, that QVC and The Home Shopping Network might have witnessed major declines in sales.

Nonna rarely left her home those last few years, the result of failing health as well as declining social interest. A spitfire to begin with, her crass tendencies became more pronounced as the years went by, solidifying her status as "one tough broad," as she liked to call herself after Sophia introduced her to the term. But towards the end, she remained glued to her chair in front of the television, refusing to sleep in her bed after her husband died a few years earlier, and having discovered the subtle comfort of talking, even yelling, at her TV. Such practices, she had explained to Sophia once, worked well for her, having spent nearly a lifetime dealing with feelings that hurt far easier and faster than hers ever had, and never quite understanding the reasons why. "Why so sensitive?" she'd bark with contempt whenever she saw tears. This electronic relationship was also devoid, to her relief, of the Italian Catholic guilt that eventually reared its ugly head, even for her, when her old world manner failed to translate in this modern one.

It wasn't until Nonna passed away that the family really understood the depths of her relationship with the television shopping organizations. First was the discovery of piles and piles of purchased goods, each wrapped delicately in tissues and stored carefully in her husband's clothes dresser. As they went through the unfortunate task of sorting through her possessions, Ben unearthed hundreds of little trinkets stashed away for some unknown future purpose, perhaps, as he told the family, to be given as gifts for future birthdays and holidays.

Then came the condolence card. It arrived at Ben and Diane's home, forwarded like the rest of Nonna's mail in case there was some incomplete something to which needed tending. Somehow, one of the salespeople Nonna had spoken to regularly got wind of her passing and thought to send the family a condolence card. It was addressed to "The Family of Mrs. Isabel Gallo," and offered kind words about Nonna and how the employees considered her a part of their QVC family. Diane responded by contacting the name on the return address to tell her how much she appreciated the thoughtful gesture and that the kind effort left an impression on the whole family.

During the discussion, one that allowed Diane more time with her mother even though she had been buried weeks before, the woman shared tales of how Isabel would call to make comments about the sets or guests on the show, how she would share her thoughts about how lovely the hosts might look one day or the next, how she did her darnedest to get to speak as a caller on television as many times in a week as possible. "I think it was like a sport to her," the representative, Pamela, giggled.

"It's fairly common," the woman told Diane. "You know, for older people to call in. But your mother was special. We always welcomed her calls because we just loved her so much."

The idea of Nonna being lonely in her final years had always nagged at Sophia and she knew it had the same effect on her mother, despite the fact she was constantly surrounded by "intruders," as she called them—basically any welcome or unwelcome guests stopping by to play cards or visit.

"What do I want to visit with people for?" she would clamor. "What do I have to talk about? I've been talking for eighty years. I'm tired of talking."

Sophia loved that her grandmother had a secret life. No matter how basic the details of this confidential side, they gave her hints of complexity no one else knew anything about.

As for Nonna's love for Sophia's grandfather, Sophia was happy she had those memories to bring her comfort. To feel that way about someone she shared fifty years of her life with was enviable and beautiful.

Winter's temporary reprieve provided the opportunity Sophia needed to attempt her first outdoor run since the New Year and everything else that had happened since D-Day. Bundled up, she left the apartment, ready for the release that inevitably came from exercise and that she so desperately needed. It would also provide her a chance meeting with George Grant.

Even in winter, stripped of color and prosperity, Central Park was one of her favorite places. Her first instinct was to follow her usual course, crossing 77th from her apartment to the entrance of the park, making her way uptown following the path around the lake and The Great Lawn, then traveling downtown by running parallel with Fifth Avenue as much as possible. She would inevitably move toward the center of the park so she could cut through The Mall, a spot among many that never failed to charm her in this complex and wonderful oasis. Then, continuing down Fifth until she reached the lowest stretch of the trail along 59th, she would take Central Park West—another favorite stretch of the city—back north to her starting place. Today, however, she decided to embrace her current mindset of shaking up habitual behavior by running counter-clockwise. Somehow it just seemed the appropriate thing to do.

The cold felt shocking at first, scratching harshly at whatever bare skin she left exposed, but she knew it was only temporary. Running was therapeutic, allowing Sophia the rare chance in this crazy city to really clear her head. Stripping away everything like nothing else could, it enabled her to see things in a fresh, new way and recharge her battery.

She reached the park in no time and began her journey in reverse. It was odd, to say the least, to force herself to do something that did not come naturally, because for as long as she had lived in New York, she had always taken the same course—a path she had forged once that seemed to fit so well that she adopted it for what she thought would be life. But life had thrown her some curveballs, so why shouldn't she toss a few back in its direction?

When it came down to it, Sophia was really a creature of habit, although she would never admit such predictability to her family. They pictured her, or so she thought (acknowledging to herself how impossible it was to truly know how one may be perceived by others), as the free spirit of the family, the most impulsive one of the bunch who was so regularly full of surprises, especially in her teens and twenties, that the only way she caught them off-guard was through the specifics of her random actions, not through the actions themselves. There were road trips and last minute getaways to far off places, many of them to locations her parents themselves had never seen or knew very little about. There were countless other decisions as well that triggered that "what-are-you-thinking?" Connors response.

While over the years, the decisions she had made may have been somewhat rash and a little controversial to her liberal but by-the-book family, one category in which she never applied that same decision-making process was in the way of love. Her casualties in that regard were often the result of slow infiltration. She was rarely one, unlike many of her friends, to just dive in. For her, the walls lowered slowly. Regrettably though, she would admit, a few undeserving but persistent individuals had managed to get through while she wasn't paying close enough attention. As her shoes bit into the ground step after step and her mind ran its own course, she knew that having a love life was one area she was not and would not be ready to think about going clockwise or counter-clockwise any time soon.

The run in the wrong direction felt right. It also felt similar to making her left hand do things for which she had always depended on her right: it was familiar but not quite an experience of which she felt complete ownership.

After a few minutes, she reached the corner of the park near Columbus Circle. Her mind felt clean, like toxins had been draining the past twenty blocks, and her limbs tingled with renewal and invigoration. Her iPod drove her physically and mentally, providing motivation when and where her body would not. She praised music and the iPod regularly, certain that they were two of the world's greatest inventions. Sophia felt confident she wouldn't be running, much less living, if she hadn't had either of them to keep her going.

59th Street passed beside Sophia in the distance as she continued her trek. Horse-drawn carriages and tourists with cameras journeyed in the vicinity but now she hardly noticed them. She was ready to assign herself a topic to concentrate on: a scene, a conversation, a character. It was what she did, or had done once upon a time, when she was actively and regularly writing. Since then, however, the runs had become just about hearing the music, but not *really* listening. There was a difference, she knew, between being casually entertained by song and finding inspiration as if the music was her own personal score. Music had once helped drive her characters from one place in their lives to another, motivating Sophia to write their emotions and explorations. She had since stalled, unconsciously abandoning her characters in the unwritten abyss of her glassy computer screen. There was no denying it. *But why?*

Sophia didn't remember exactly when the writing stopped. She had told herself for some time it was a temporary state, that it would remedy itself eventually. It didn't just happen one day, but it *did* happen, and when she thought about it in depth, she felt broken down like an inoperable car on the side of the literary highway. *But why?*

She reasoned there were many issues. There was the fact she had spent so much time working on her first novel all at once, filling every free moment it seemed with writing. She had been proud of the long strides accomplished during those days, but it caused her to take a much-needed break to heal the burnout and, somehow, she was never able to get the train back on the tracks.

There was also the job. Work had stolen her voice and replaced it with one of a corporate spokesperson or commercial actor. The language of her writing had become promotional and influential, not in a human, life-affirming way like the topics of her personal interests, but in a business, assembly-line way. She had become a business robot, a cog in the wheel, and while for some it wasn't a bad way to make a living, for her it was a good way to make a dying. Lost was her motivation to write, slipping slowly from her grasp. She knew this now, two weeks away from the demands of RGB. Perspective might not help pay the rent, but it certainly helped give focus to her priorities.

The other realization that came to Sophia as she made her way north up the eastside was that blame wasn't productive for anyone, especially herself. It was only good for helping her figure out what not to do again—what mistakes not to repeat. She admitted she loved the idea of being able to blame her lack of writing on her career but no one made her make those choices. *She* chose to spend long days at RGB to advance her career. *She* chose to spend her free time on other things. Life was one big process of elimination and she couldn't always know what she wanted until she knew what she didn't want.

As the park continued to pass her by, she also conceded to herself that she would love, perhaps more than anything, to blame Kevin. *Kevin. But why?*

There was that name. It sounded odd now, foreign and awkward. Funny, she considered, how you could learn the distaste of a name with time, not that the thought of him affected her much at the moment thanks to the endorphins shielding her vulnerabilities. Her relationship with Kevin had taken much of her time over the past three years, but was it fair, or more importantly, accurate, to claim that it prevented her from writing?

Sophia pondered if that was what happiness did: blinded and misled its victims, steered them off course like some Greek tragedy in which the ship that was just about to reach its home or loved ones or treasures, crashes upon the rocks. Kevin was an independent type, but no different than Sophia. They had juggled their careers and free time fluidly and effortlessly. He was not too intense with his affections, nor too reserved. The overall balance of all of these qualities had attracted her to him and made her believe in their future.

Our. We. Us. Words describing a pair. They were words she could no longer use, that she would have to add to a list of others that she no longer had any right to speak, not about him anyway.

Perhaps, she considered, it was that balance between them that served as one of the reasons the relationship came to its disappointing end. Was there not enough need, enough "I'll-die-without-you" or "who-was-that-on-the-other-line?" jealousy to keep it compelling or interesting? Weren't the women in those TV movies her mother got her hooked on always so hungry for drama between themselves and their men? But Sophia, even at her lowest point, scoffed at that idea and then at herself for even considering it a possibility. If she had even suspected Kevin had been disloyal to her, she would have had her shoe so far up his rear that he wouldn't have been able to sit down ever again. She had trusted him always and never had, until now, any reason to do otherwise. But she did find it oddly interesting, however, that the things one could love about someone could turn into some of their worst qualities in the end.

Yes, she knew, she would love to blame anyone and everyone, anything and everything, but that just wouldn't fly, and she could not pretend or make herself believe otherwise. If she had to blame or be angry, if necessary, for letting anything bad happen, she had only herself. And she also knew that the positive part about owning that responsibility was that it meant she could take it back, take control, and reverse what needed reversing.

When was the last time? It bothered Sophia that she could not remember the last time she had worked on her novel. A year? Two years? More? Frankly, she thought, she didn't want to know because it no longer mattered, because there was nothing she could do to go back in time. But she did wonder, now that she was unemployed, could she still call herself a writer? *Writers write.* Did her lists count?

She shook off the negative thoughts. What now mattered was the present, the future, and what she did with that time. *Shit or get off the pot.* Nonna was right.

Should she pick up where she left off with her existing draft? The story seemed distant but familiar, like a friend she had not seen in years. She had once been so passionate about it, but maybe starting anew was just what the times were demanding. And, of course, she could always go back to it one day. Perhaps beginning a new story, from scratch, would be best. She had plenty of ideas and notes to weave into a new story, and the creative process of coming up with the intricate details of a new novel could be just the thing needed to get her excited about writing again.

As the positive chemicals rushing through her body began to command her to conquer the world, Sophia told herself that she would *make* the time to write, and that time to start was *now,* that all of this happening in her life she would consider, for lack of a better description, a sign. While she didn't necessarily believe in such magical thinking as "signs" or "destiny," she was fascinated by the concepts and included them in her writing.

People, including her, loved the idea their lives were designed with purpose.

There was no more time to waste. She was determined to get herself back on track, moving in the right direction. She reminded herself that running and writing were similar: get out of the habit and it was hard to get back in. But once in the rhythm, the attraction and experience were like nothing else.

What would she want to write about this time? What kind of statement would she want to leave the world with once she was gone? She thought about her love for her grandmother, as well as the undying love Nonna had for her grandfather. She thought about her own disappointment with love. There was something there. This would be her topic to focus on for the day. Like her mother, Sophia saw a loose thread, a creative one, waiting to be pulled to see where it would take her. So she pulled and pulled. It was how the process went. While it was not always easy, it was for her today. It was, as the saying went, "a walk in the park."

The thread produced George Grant, clear in her mind as anyone she had ever known, a strong and powerful man limited by life's circumstances. Once a young man with the love of a good woman, the years of his life met with terrific disappointment. Before her untimely death, the two had a daughter and a son. George's oldest child, the daughter, would run away while Dirk was still a boy. She had to get away but no one ever knew why. The son grew up bitter and hungry for more than he was been born into, more than George's declining spirit or skills could ever provide. The years passed them both but not without turmoil and hardship, and the roles both were designed to play unfurled to an explosive ending. Sophia continued pulling at the thread until she realized she had completely opened the creative floodgates.

So she stopped running just after passing the lake and removed her BlackBerry from the zipped pocket in her jacket. Doing her best to keep up as the words flowed out of her, she created a new list, this one the story draft for what would be her new novel.

George Grant, broken man, the embodiment of disappointment and heartbreak

Farm land, contradictions of emptiness and prosperity, goodness of the earth and badness of mankind

Greed, corporate greed, personal greed

Lifetimes, years, span of generations

Multiple perspectives, each chapter jumps from one character to the other

Sophia typed as she walked, digging at these thoughts to find what else she could uncover and how she could link them all together. She wanted to write something about love, a story about sacrifice and compromise on behalf of that love. She remembered her father reading *Sir Gawain and the Green Knight* to her and how he explained its fantastic tale of humility and morality, as well as how Gawain's fate was driven by his commitment to honor, loyalty and truth. It had left an impact on her forever. It would be her inspiration and she would weave it into her own variation of a fable.

Someone forced to make a difficult decision, the right decision despite all or who are sacrificed or compromised. She will be called Anna.

Before Sophia knew it, she had come full circle, completing a lap around the park and heading towards home, her head and BlackBerry brewing with ideas. By the time she reached her apartment, she had lost count of the number of times she had stopped to add additional notes, unable to type and walk at the same time. She felt stimulated and grateful for choosing her imperfect loop going "the wrong way" because for the first time in some time she felt that she just might be headed in the right direction.

CHAPTER 8
PROLOGUE

Sophia wrote until midnight, not noticing the bewitching hours had been upon her as long as they had been or that the sadness hadn't come knocking. George Grant had led Sophia to his son, Dirk Grant, and then to Anna McCormack. Dirk and Anna would have a child, a boy, and he would need protection from Dirk and from the greater evil alliance of which Dirk would become a part. With several ideas drafted about where to go with the story and how to get there, Sophia wrote her prologue, a scene slightly disconnected from the narrative of the rest of the book and intended to read as a dream foreshadowing her modern day epic. She wrote it to seem like a scene from the final sequence of the fourteenth-century story, *Sir Gawain and the Green Knight,* in which Gawain goes to fulfill his part of a deal made in honor of his king, Arthur, and to face his fate—to meet up with the Green Knight who will have his chance to kill Gawain. That tale, which to her seemed more like a fable than the poem it was labeled to be, would play a critical role in her story. *Sir Gawain and the Green Knight* had moved her, almost haunted her, with its dark, romantic beauty and intricate story. She decided she wanted to intertwine it with her own characters' lives to give the story an additional level of symbolism and depth.

PROLOGUE

It was a sign or, more specifically, a warning, arriving in a dream formed of things both foreign and familiar to her. But by the time Anna McCormack would remember it and realize its significance, it would be too late, destiny already set in motion and her role in a struggle about which she should know nothing already played.

Her first moment of clarity in the dream came as she realized she was lost, not in any land she had ever known before but somehow in a forest, deep inside a fortress of nature and fear, unaware of how or why she was there. Terror, viscous and hostile, pumped through her veins, making her certain she would double over at any moment, welling her eyes with fractured memories that floated past in the tears running down her face. She tried to pull her focus together, desperate to gain control of her body and mind, but it was so difficult, too difficult—a dream from which she could not awaken.

Peering into the small pool of water at her feet, she caught the reflection of the dark sky hovering above a woman she did not recognize. Only the vulnerability marked in the eyes looking back seemed familiar, but that fragility floated away on tiny waves as a frozen wind blew through it, the chilling breeze telling nothing of the secrets it carried from behind her or of what lay ahead. The unknown face staring back became as distorted as her memories, running away from her, spreading out in every direction.

She was outside of her own world and could not be sure she knew the woman she had seen looking back. Yet something in a deep corner of her mind, a sliver of a memory barely standing out like a hint of a piece of paper stuffed long ago into a book, told her all of this belonged to her—this place, this sense of abandonment, this isolation—and that there would be no escaping. She became aware of the cold chill climbing the back of her neck and her chest responded with a cry of sadness and fear.

She looked up, searching for answers in the cracks between the streaks of light and dark covering the forest, wondering how she had come to be there…and why? Shadows taunted her with all they knew and all she was not allowed to know. No matter how hard she concentrated, nothing permitted her to unlock in her mind how she had come to this place. The one thing she did know was that she was in the danger. But how would she escape? What path would lead her away?

Her instincts, like an animal being hunted, told her to continue moving. There would be no answers, no safety, standing in one place, so she forced her feet to start in motion as if they were machinery separate from her. And as she did so, she caught a glance from outside of herself, a moment on a fragmented timeline hinting that this was merely a slice of something larger, a snapshot from a life trapped like a scene in a snow globe for someone else to observe. It was then she felt the presence of another and the contents of this snow globe world were shaken up, sending her into motion.

Snap. The crack of broken twigs from up ahead.

As she looked up, she caught a shadow moving behind a tree. Light into dark, dark into light. Her eyes were playing tricks but somehow she knew she needed what was out there, that she had to run to it, not away from it. That was where her escape would be. Without thought, her feet pulled her toward the fleeing enigma. Was it human or animal? Would she even know the difference in this world?

Mud filled her shoes as she stepped deeper into the shadows, icy water and slush moving aggressively between flesh and fabric. The sting between her toes was terrible, but only for a moment until she became aware of the burning on her arms. Looking down, she discovered rips on her skin, crimson red bleeding through newly opened folds inflicted by thickets of wild bushes telling her she didn't belong there. But she continued to run.

Slice. Slice. And the scratches continued as well.

What was she pursuing? She did not know, only that something greater than herself consumed her, drove her into the heat of a sprint. Somewhere in the recesses of her mind a light illuminated, a thought presented itself. And she heard a voice. Danger, it told her.

She recalled a memory, but could not be sure it was her own. There was hunting, and much of it. She saw a deer, chased from the safety of high ground, cut down and killed. And on a separate occasion, a huge boar, ferocious and old, driven from his own herd. Then the brutal skinning of a fox as ravenous dogs watched on, hungry and angry to devour its flesh on a day when the world hung with frost, this ill-fated creature not cunning enough to avoid its own murder. Was Anna the hunter or the hunted? Was she to endure the same fate?

Her breath became heavier as she chased after the shadow. Was this what she really wanted? Did she have a choice in the matter? She continued to run until she was no longer sure she was following anything. It was then she realized she had come to the top of a little hill where a cave suddenly appeared. Perhaps, she considered, what she was following had run in there. She thought about turning around but as the idea crystallized, she heard that sound again.

Snap.

Whatever she was following was nearby. Then she remembered something else, that there was much at risk.

She walked toward the cave through a thickening mist, resisting its long arms as they stretched around her, wondering if this was all just a trap. But she forced her way forward anyway and found the mist swallowing her as it formed an ever-bending wall. It disguised any reasonable evidence that she was not merely walking in circles, that she might inadvertently walk off a cliff or into a ravine. It mocked her search while protecting any clue of where she should next direct herself, rescuing time from any sense of beginning or end. It taunted her with each step, ridiculing her efforts.

Click. Another sound. And with it came so much fear, as well as another piece of knowledge. She must find the chapel. It was her fate.

But what was the chapel? And why must she find it? She could only be certain that there was no other choice. This was what she must do.

Light suddenly shined from over her shoulder, throwing a glow up the wall of fog before her. It caught tiny bits of precipitation, producing mirrored reflections like ornaments. She stopped and looked closer, amazed that within the orb-shaped molecules were dew images staring back, projecting moments from what she assumed had once been her life before all of this had happened, before she had been thrust into a world no one could have ever imagined. Tension stung her temples and pressure attacked her chest. She thought to look at her hands and discovered the markings on her palms and finger tips disappearing, erasing. Her identity was vanishing.

Fear made her impatient and words came to her from nowhere. Why did she know these words? Had she read them before somewhere? "If you want me, come to me quickly. Now or never, be done with it."

The mist surrounding her fell to the ground like a curtain disconnected all at once from its hooks. She stood back at the mouth of the cave, which wasn't a cave at all but a chapel, and it dawned on her that every moment of her life had led her to this one. She remembered why she was there.

"You came. You can be trusted."

He stood before her, draped in shadow at the mouth of the chapel. His face was recognizable without being seen.

"You kept your word. Now give me the rest."

She knew what he wanted and followed his direction. Lowering her head to the ground and fulfilling her promise, she saw the ax in his hand, the light catching its bold polish. As he raised the ax toward the sky, it produced a brilliant and blinding glare, and a lifetime of memories splashed before her. She knew it would only be moments until they flew away, like her, into the darkness, and that world would be lost to her completely. A tear escaped from the corner of her eye and she asked a question for which she already knew the answer, "Does this have to be?"

He remained silent, waiting for her to stop moving.

"Deliver my fate," she demanded of him, "and deliver it quickly."

Her final thought presented itself in slow motion: "What will it be like afterwards?"

As the ax struck, her life splintered, spilling like puzzle pieces from a box. One decision for Anna had changed everything. There would be no afterwards.

Sleep came slowly to Sophia that night, her head spinning from the thrill of new ideas. She declared she would channel her sadness through Anna, using the character to express her desperate need for reason. Dirk and George, on the other hand, would be her muses through which she'd exercise her frustration and anger. She would play all of them like pawns on a paper landscape to flesh out her ideas on love and loss, greed and ambition, faith and science.

As she laid in bed staring into nothing, she became aware that this was *her* prologue, too, that its symbolic nature—a beginning inspired by the past and drawn toward a destined future—made a statement just as much about her as it did Anna. Sophia had discovered a source of strength and optimism, something that could hold her up and keep her standing on her own feet. She would learn the next day just how good it was to have begun laying down such a foundation, and just how much she needed it, when she braved her first conversation with Kevin since D-Day.

CHAPTER 9
THE BIG FISH BOWL THEORY

Meeting Kevin three years ago had happened by accident—a happy accident, Sophia once believed. Random were the ways people often found each other in New York City, which was less like a big apple and more like a big fish bowl, its inhabitants swimming around from location to location, occasionally discovering new things and bumping into new people along the way. Big on hypotheses and generalizations, this was one of Sophia's favorite theories, which gave credit to a city so vast and complex that one couldn't be sure what was awaiting them around the bend.

It was Halloween weekend and Kevin, who had been scheduled to leave the city for work, was dealt a change of plans due to an air traffic controllers strike grounding all planes and preventing him from getting to Chicago. After the breakup broke, Sophia reflected upon these details—particularly the Chicago specific—and considered with focused hindsight how life just might have provided her all of the evidence she needed right then and there to learn how the relationship would eventually play out. She could not deny that this insight tortured her a bit, making her suspect it was over before it even began.

Thanks to the lone home economics course she took in grade school, Sophia was outfitted in a costume she made herself: a green dress with a single shoulder strap—to match her single status—and a leafy exterior. Her plans that night involved a costume party with friends, Kate included. In those days, Sophia had been more social, certainly more so than she was now. Meeting people had always easy for her, even in a city like New York where walls could be high and personalities guarded. In spite of this, she had met quite a few people in the city that she liked if for no other reason than she thought they were interesting. There was no shortage of great stories and, even better, big ambitions—the fruits of those trees in endless production in this city—and both were always sources of inspiration that fueled Sophia's writing.

But over time she came to realize and accept that she was irreversibly socially monogamous, not so much by choice but by nature. As the last few years began to show signs of picking up the pace—something her mother had warned her about—she felt *she* was slowing down and becoming more content with the idea that less was more. Where some wanted hordes of friends, she needed only a few. She had begun to embrace her contentment with quality, not quantity.

She also became aware of her generation's flight pattern, that she belonged to an age bracket for a transient bunch. They came in droves to the city for what turned out to be only a short stay before either moving out to the suburbs to start families or going back home, wherever that might be. Not everyone found the city to be a permanent residence, which stirred a certain sense of loss in Sophia because it meant that what they shared had an expiration date, that they were merely ships passing in their New York nights, so to speak, friends for a moment until the next destination or chapter of their lives summoned. In a city so filled with history, it was surprisingly made up of millions of moving parts that came and went. While certain that she and the city would continue to function without those parts she came to know and care for, Sophia knew she would feel a void, a loss, an abandonment—even if it wasn't personal and although she knew she was perhaps being selfish and irrational. In many ways, the experience was similar to her love for Nonna and Kevin: it was difficult to let go of something she became aware of existed, something that once made her feel connected to the world, that reminded her of the possibilities of life. It was hard to imagine the magician's hat without the rabbit once she knew the rabbit had been pulled out of it.

Additionally, her social status contended with the reality of stamina, a relevant consideration. While she had established several good friendships since arriving in New York, her schedules with work and Kevin became increasingly demanding, and those relationships, with Kate being a clear exception, slipped without intention into a backseat position. There were, as her father would say, just so many hours in a day.

But isn't that life?

She had considered that question so many times, reminded more than she cared to admit of the temporary nature of the human experience, the deception of time, the fragility of body. It was *all* just for rent. A loan. No one owned *anything* forever.

Memory was both a generous and baffling thing to Sophia. It had a way of softening experiences, erasing some altogether and putting others on pedestals. Of that night, at the party, she could remember some pretty specific details, some of them unusual and abstract, while others had completely abandoned her forever, including elements she thought she would, or should, remember but couldn't, even though she hadn't had more than a couple sips of a single drink.

For instance, Sophia remembered she spent a good amount of time in the corner of her friend's dining room, and that he was one of the few acquaintances in her extended circle who had such a large apartment that actually had a formal dining room, considering the guy had *only* three roommates. How she could remember *that* fact she was not sure, but she *did* know the host was dressed like Dracula and had just left their conversation, even though she couldn't remember who he was or what he looked like, other than his costume and fangs dripping with blood.

She could recall the mahogany-stained wood paneling on three sides of the room and the tall window on the fourth wall about five feet from where she stood. While she would not be able to say who she was talking to, or what they were discussing at the time, she remembered she was drinking a vodka with tonic, her first cup, newly filled, with a twist of lime floating on top, and her friend, whoever she was, was drinking some blood red orange drink that may or may not have been punch served at the party.

And she recalled, with vivid focus, the first time she saw Kevin. He had just walked through the door wearing green medical scrubs, looking engaged in conversation with someone, another person she could not remember. He wore gray Nike sneakers and a surgical mask that was hanging loosely under his neck, just below a necklace made of twine. Just as quickly as he had entered the room and as fast as she had seen him, he made eye contact with her, and there was a shift in the room and, so it felt, in the universe. Their eyes locked and Kevin sent over a smile that could have melted Antarctica, Sophia thought, the kind that showed in his eyes as much as it did his mouth. It made her chest grow warm and slushy. His was the calm, satisfied expression of someone who knew how lucky he was at that moment, who said with his whole being, "There you are. I've been looking for you." Sophia's stomach dropped like the bottom was falling out from under her, like she was on the Six Flags amusement park ride that once thrilled her, the one like an open elevator car that drops straight down ten stories.

She remembered that Kevin, who was with a guy she didn't know or had ever seen before, stepped towards her through the crowded room and away from his friend, whoever he was, while still in mid-sentence.

"Hello," was Kevin's first word upon reaching Sophia, simple and direct, unremarkable on paper but noteworthy in context to Sophia, greeting her with that same big smile that had never left his face.

Sophia laughed only because her nerves made her do so. It was an involuntary reaction to help her sober up from the intoxication of the moment, to help her collect her thoughts and assess what it meant that they were both drawn to each other so powerfully from the moment they saw one another. Her nervous tendencies had always caused her to jest at unusual times, although at that moment she felt far more excitement than fear. "I think your friend was still talking to you."

"Oh, really?" Kevin said but didn't bother to look back.

"Yes," she continued, adding another laugh. "I'm pretty sure. Must not have been very interesting, whatever he was telling you."

Kevin clearly wasn't interested in talking about his friend. "I'm Kevin," he blurted out with excited haste like a nervous schoolboy asking her to the junior high dance. But there was also something so natural about it, like he had been waiting for some time to say those words, not to anyone but to *her*. She noticed that, as he said them, his smile somehow managed to widen even further, which only made her stomach bubble more. This guy— with the eyes that looked deep inside her and the smile that went on for days—had a name, and it was Kevin.

Remembering she had been talking to someone also, Sophia pointed at her friend, whoever it was, and said, "This is *whoever.*"

"Nice to meet you, *whoever,*" Kevin replied but never took his eyes off Sophia. "And *you?* What's *your* name?"

"Sophia," she told him, certain she was blushing, feeling her face flush from his attention focused on her.

"That's a beautiful name."

Sophia was at a loss for words, which was quite something for a woman whose world was built around them. Also unusual was the fact that her walls did not attempt to shield her. She was completely accessible to him.

It would be incorrect to describe Kevin that night as "smooth," for if he had been Sophia would not have been interested, and the unbelievable physical attraction they both felt would have stopped when he crossed the room and opened his mouth. In all reality, she was attracted as much to the flaws of an individual as their perfections because the combination was what gave them character. Sophia thought "impulsive" was a better description. He was not calculating and his deliberate demeanor and presence felt natural and sincere, like he knew that what was waiting behind door number three was for him, like he had just found something he'd spent a long time looking for. Without words, without having to explain herself, she felt the same way. The attraction was immediate and then validated, for their connection and all that followed fit like a link in a chain.

The conversation went around and around in those first moments together, but having never been in this position before, she found herself unsure of what to say next. Somehow, it didn't quite seem to matter.

Kevin was close to her now, his stare constant. Flinching involuntarily, she forced a response, "Thank you."

"For what?" he asked, forgetting why he was being thanked.

"For the compliment," she told him. "About my name."

"Oh, yeah," Kevin said, blinking and breaking from the stare, now embarrassed, concerned he made a fool of himself.

He looked her up and down. She became nervous he was checking her out just to check her out, but that didn't seem to be the kind of guy he was. Then she was relieved to remember she was wearing a costume.

"Let me guess," he told her, giving it a second before asking, "She-Hulk?"

She laughed at him again. It was an amusing guess considering her all-green attire. "No, but I can see where you'd get that idea."

"Really? I was sure that was it!"

"You want a second chance?"

"Yes, please."

"Ok, then. Go for it."

He thought about it more and scratched at his chin. "Well, you can't be a Smurf because they're blue. And Barney is purple and doesn't wear a dress. Betty Rubble?"

"Really? Betty Rubble? That's your next best guess? The last time I saw Betty's dress, I don't think it had leaves on it. Want another guess?"

He shook his head. "No, I don't know. You got me," he said, humbled by his inability to answer correctly. "Am I total idiot?"

"Are you joking? What planet did you grow up on? I'm the Jolly Green Giant!" she told him.

Kevin slapped his forehead and laughed a cute "a-ha" of a laugh, showing he felt stupid for not identifying the icon. "Of course! I *am* an idiot! I should have gotten that." Kevin was now the one blushing, and it brought them both at ease and closer together.

"The Jolly Green Giant is pretty well-known! But I think I can let it slide."

The party went on without them, not that either of them noticed. Sophia did not remember what happened to the friend she was with, or how and when she left them alone to talk, only that the conversation flowed smoothly as if they had known each other for the longest time. She did remember the many laughs, the sharing, the curiosity, the desire to know more. It was the beginning of them not being able to get enough of each other, like reading a book neither wanted to put down or finish.

"You're beautiful," he told her later in the evening.

"Well, then," she replied, deflecting the compliment. "Aren't I glad I didn't paint my face green tonight?"

"You'd still be beautiful," he told her.

"So would you," she told him back.

Facing her, searching for her soul through her eyes, he slipped his hand into hers, as if it had been made to do just that, a perfect fit.

"I sure do hope those strikers get what's coming to them," he told Sophia. While at the time she had no idea he was talking about the reason he had been unable to fly to Chicago that day, she agreed completely with him. He seemed right on so many levels, so certainly he had to be right about that, too.

"You answered!" Kevin said. "Wow! I'm a little surprised. I've tried you I don't know how many times but you never pick up."

Sophia didn't want to admit she already knew this but was

determined not to lie about it either, knowing it would make no difference to the situation. Besides, she was certain Kevin knew it as well. Three years as a couple, practically living together the entire time, there were few secrets left…or so, until recently, she had once thought.

"Why are you calling, Kevin?" she asked, the simple math in her head telling her he'd be leaving for Chicago soon.

The minute the words came out she was aware they sounded harsh, probably even mean. Part of her wanted that, to lash out and wound him like he did her. But there was another part that didn't, that wanted to guarantee she wasn't the one to cause irreparable damage to the relationship, that maybe even left room for a reversal of his decision. It had been a struggle to take the high road when the flood of disappointment and contempt was unavoidable. Her solution instead had been to cut him off as a way to save herself, which may have provided some preservation on the surface but hadn't yet done much for the internal bleeding.

The breakup with Kevin had unearthed well-hidden emotions, many she was not aware she had or had managed to forget, not just for their relationship but for others as well. Many of the memories involved her grandmother, which had started around D-Day and continued on with full force to this day.

Nonna had never had these kinds of problems in her day, or if she had, Sophia knew nothing about them. What would Nonna have done if a man called—not with a telephone, of course, but in person—and she didn't want to see him? Had Nonna ever been scorned? What would *her* line of defense have been?

Sophia remembered two important details Nonna shared about those early days of her love life—not that that was what her generation had called it, especially in the small Italian village she spent her childhood in. First, that younger Nonna lived with her father who apparently was the inventor of tough love. Secondly, gentlemen calling back them meant a whole other experience, a process Sophia's grandmother apparently had thoroughly enjoyed. Nonna's take on the story, which Sophia's mother claimed should always be filtered through reservation and skepticism, was that she was quite the heartbreaker in her day. The topic, which Sophia found entirely too bizarre to discuss, was thrust upon her before she had met Kevin. At only twenty-three, Sophia was threatened by Nonna with the "old maid" label, and Sophia imagined the woman sewing the giant letters O and M on all of her clothes.

"I had many suitors, you know," she had told Sophia. "The boys used to chase me all over town. And I let them, I did."

"You were a tease," Sophia told her.

"I had to see which one really wanted me the most. Besides, it's not teasing to let them think what they will. You can't control what's in a man's mind, now can you?"

The way Nonna said it made Sophia think that just perhaps her grandmother *could* control the minds of men, at least back in the day.

"You love with your head too much, sweetness," Nonna told her. "Love doesn't think. It *does*. It makes you generous in ways you never knew were possible before. It makes you give of yourself without thought of what you get in return. It's wanting more for another than you want for yourself."

"I don't think it's ever going to happen," Sophia confessed.

"It will, my little old maid," she said with a wink. "And when it does, you will know it. It's unmistakable."

Missing Kevin reminded Sophia of how much she missed her grandmother and how much she wished she was still alive today. It reminded her of the tremendous regret she carried with her that she didn't say all of the things she should have said before it was too late. It made her wonder what she could have done differently with Kevin as well.

"That's not very nice," Kevin replied, countering Sophia's inquisition over the telephone. "Especially considering I called to wish you a happy birthday."

It was her birthday! Her writing frenzy had actually erased it from her mind. Insecurity then made her question if he was calling out of obligation or because it was something he wanted to do. And what about next year? Would he call then? Would he one day stop calling altogether?

"Oh, thanks," she said, feeling conflicted, and mostly uneasy just to be talking to him.

"Do you have any big plans?"

"Just to do some work. Look for a job," she told him. Her answers were direct and short, which was the best she could muster.

"I heard. I'm sorry. Kate told me all about it, when she called to rip me a new one."

"I told her not to do that. I wanted her to stay out of it."

"She told me that, too."

This Kevin sounded like the same Kevin she knew and loved so much, but this one had somehow moved on without her, too. How could he continue his life without her when she wasn't sure if she could make it another day without him? How could he sound so calm and collected when she was broken into a thousand pieces?

Stay focused, she told herself. *Stay strong.*

"I have a box of your stuff here for you to pick up," she told him, feeling herself place a protective layer around herself, brick by brick, in slow-but-methodical motion.

"I have one for you as well. How about I bring yours over and pick up mine? Can I see you?"

"I don't think that's a good idea," she told him. "When can you come by? I'll make sure I'm not here."

There was a pause before he replied. "How about later today? If that's no good…"

"No, that's fine. I'm going to run out for a few hours, maybe soon. Does that work?"

"Sure," he said. There was disappointment in his voice which confused Sophia because she wasn't sure what it meant. She wanted it to mean he realized he had made the biggest mistake of his life and couldn't live without her, but then she received confirmation that wasn't the case.

"I'm leaving in a few days," he said.

"I wish you a lot of luck," she told him, trying to seem in control of her emotions even though she knew better.

"I want you to be happy for me."

There were those words again, self-centered and devoid of emotional responsibility. With that, a button was pushed and Sophia's sadness turned into anger. "Really? Do you think that's realistic at this point in time? Well, I want *you* to be sad for *me*. Try that on for size and see how selfish your request is."

She could now hear her heartbeat, thunderous and angry, a rush of blood flowing through her body. She thought she heard him gulp.

"All I'm saying, or trying to say, is...what I mean is that I want us to one day be able to be friends. I never want to lose you in my life. But I feel that right now is the time for me to go out on my own and do some things I need to do."

"I'm sorry I was holding you back, Kevin."

"Don't say that, Sophia. You know I never felt that way."

"Kevin, at this point, I don't know anything for certain. Not anymore. You come out of left field to tell me that you're leaving town without me, and you want me to help you celebrate? I'm sorry but I can't do that. Maybe I'm weak for telling you all of this, and maybe you can't deal with it, but guess what? I am pissed off, *and* hurt, *and* heartbroken, *and* it isn't anyone's fault other than *yours*. And the minute you can really appreciate and respect what *I'm* going through, then maybe we can talk about celebrating this 'good news' of yours."

Kevin was silent. He clearly hadn't expected an outburst from Sophia, who was normally so calm and rational.

"You're right," he finally told her. "I'm sorry. For a lot of things. And it wasn't exactly what I meant to say, or how. You're the one who is good with words."

Sophia's emotions turned on her and she could feel her eyes start to well. She knew the timer was counting down, that it was only a matter of time before the tears came.

"I wish you well, Kevin. I really do. I hope you find what you're looking for, and that life is fulfilling and rewarding. I have to go now. I'll be gone in a few minutes, probably for the rest of the afternoon. Please come by before five."

With that, she hung up.

Memory was a strange thing indeed. There were the things Sophia wanted to always remember and hoped she would never forget, and there were the things she wanted to forget but couldn't if her life depended on it. Easy to remember yet hard to forget would be many of the moments and details collected over the past three years with Kevin. The way he fit in with everyone, that everyone liked him. The sweet smell and softness of his hair. The warmth of his body next to hers. His weight on top of her. The way he snorted when he laughed too hard. His predictable responses in certain situations. His unpredictable ones in others. His dry sense of humor. The list of losses went on and on.

The city would continue to remind her of what was missing as well, whispering of experiences and happier times, forcing her to remember, and making it impossible to forget.

Kevin would be spared all of that. Chicago offered a clean slate that he was lucky to have, not that the whispers were even calling him to begin with.

CHAPTER 10
A STAR IS BORN AGAIN

After hanging up with Kevin, Sophia immediately declared she would flee. She would respond to an instinct that had proven valuable and worthy of being passed down from generations and generations of animals, her species included. Yes, she would flee, scoot, run off, abscond, fly the coop, high-tail it out of there to some far away place, far from the dangers of her life on this island of Manhattan. She could join Kate in Paris! Or she could take the next flight out anywhere. She could go visit the Grand Canyon—she had always wanted to see that. And Sedona, Arizona. And Santa Fe. Or she could cross the Atlantic and go to London for a couple of days before taking the train to Paris. There were so many options. Maybe Kate was right, that what she really needed to clear her head from all this crap was an adventure.

Yes, she would leave the Kevin drama and the job hunt behind. She would kick off the first day of *another* year in style, a spoiling that under normal circumstances she never would allow herself, but one she certainly deserved. She would prove she could do anything she wanted and that *she* was the one in control of her life. She would go into her desk drawer and grab her passport and the emergency credit card she had in case an occasion demanding access to extra cash suddenly arose (the same card that remained hidden away because Sophia knew herself too well, that she would have justified its use if it had been within arm's length).

Then she thought of her unrealized character, Anna McCormack, sitting on the edge of that imaginary creative abyss, and her story of purpose that had yet to be written. If Sophia stepped away from her writing now, how would she get back on track, especially if she forced her own hand by making bad financial decisions she would certainly have to account for upon returning? Wouldn't the added pressure only make matters worse in the long run?

Sophia verbalized her disgust with herself for having no backbone. "Chicken shit," she said aloud, grabbed her bag and coat, and left the apartment.

The farthest she would escape that day was to Union Square to see a movie, a film that of course took place in New York. "You can run but you cannot hide," she would tell herself.

Going to the movies on a weekday when kids were in school and adults were at work was a treat Sophia had taken advantage of several times since becoming unemployed, and it was something she rewarded herself with every few days as a way to encourage long stretches of productivity, a carrot she dangled in front of herself to keep moving. When the days she pre-determined for mid-day movies arrived, Sophia found herself anticipating the basic pleasures of the experience. Everything was as easy as it could possibly be on those days, from buying the tickets to selecting any seat she wanted. It was usually like having her own private screening room, and *if* anyone was actually in the theater with her, she hardly ever noticed and would just pretend she was there alone. Sophia had grown up with movies and had loved them all her life, which was part of the reason why what happened that day was so remarkable.

Sophia arrived at the theater, sailing through the process of purchasing her ticket and ascending the escalator to the second floor where she was told her movie was playing. The entire place was abandoned with the exception of a handful of employees tending to their stations. Approaching the empty concessions stand, she ordered her popcorn and rolled her eyes at the injustice that snacks cost as much as the movie ticket itself.

As she approached her theater, an attendant was just pulling closed the doors, telling her, "It'll be just a few minutes. We need to clean it."

Sophia acknowledged his comment with a nod but wondered how dirty the theater could possibly be if only a few people had seen the first showing of the day. The wait was fine with her. It was a worthy compromise since she had escaped her apartment and a possible meeting with Kevin. Chewing a few kernels of popcorn, she took a seat on a bench and looked at the new and old movie posters illuminated behind glass frames on the wall across from her. She thought she was alone until a voice let her know she wasn't.

"Have you seen that?" the voice asked, deep and sultry with a hint of Europe.

Sophia turned her head to see an older woman, dressed nicely, wearing large round sunglasses that covered about fifty percent of her face. People and their sunglasses perplexed Sophia. Why was this woman wearing them inside? She bet she was also the kind to wear them at night, too.

"Which one?" Sophia asked politely, not knowing the movie the woman was referring to because she couldn't see her eyes.

Working Girl," the woman answered, her lips moving slowly to pronounce each syllable with deliberate affectation.

Sophia looked back at the poster. "Yes," she stated, turning back to the woman. "I hope they don't decide to remake it like they've done with so many other great movies. I'm a firm believer that the classics shouldn't be remade."

"Classics?" the woman said with a laugh. "You have just dated both of us, I am afraid."

Sophia smiled. "I'm sorry. I didn't mean anything…"

The woman held out her left hand to stop her in mid-sentence, and Sophia spotted the huge, hard-not-to-notice gem boldly set in a band of platinum and white gold. It was more than a ring; it was a statement and it said, "I don't need a man to buy me jewelry."

"There is no need to apologize," the woman told her, the "o" in "no" stretching on for days in an accent Sophia could not identify. "And I completely agree. I *do not* understand why they must remake everything."

"Why do they feel the need to re-do what was pretty perfect to begin with?" Sophia replied. "Are there no new stories out there? I'm a writer and I can tell you I have plenty of them, just not enough time to sit down and write them."

The woman must have liked what she heard because she pulled off her glasses, leaning forward to whisper to Sophia. This time, as the woman spoke, Sophia noticed she avoided using contractions. "I could not agree with you more. Did you know that I was offered the Sigourney Weaver role?"

Sophia looked into the woman's face. It took a few moments, but she knew who this woman was. "Oh, my gosh! You're Natasha McGavin!"

What she wanted to say was, "I thought you were dead!" Hadn't she read somewhere that she died?

The woman smiled as if expecting the reaction and nodded with feigned modesty. "Yes. Yes, I am."

"You were offered that role? Why didn't you take it?"

"Did you ever see *A House Like Ours?*" Natasha asked.

"Of course!" Sophia replied, unable to control her excitement about discussing this infamous movie role with the actress herself. Natasha had portrayed Beverly Class, the well-known, real-life actress who was the poster girl for mean and abusive. Practically *everyone* knew the movie and her role. "It was wicked, and what a juicy character! You were so wonderfully nasty!"

"Oh, thank you," Natasha said, soaking up the praise. "Well, I was so typecast after that. Everyone only saw me as Beverly, so much so that I was afraid of playing another bitch and getting stuck like that again."

Sophia was giggling inside. She was sitting next to Natasha McGavin talking about famous movie roles. And she just said "bitch."

"It's a movie that'll never be forgotten. That's not exactly a bad thing, you know?"

"Yes, I know. You are sweet for saying so."

"It's the truth. My God, what a film! You have had quite the career."

Natasha seemed impressed. "You hardly seem old enough to know my career. But I did do many movies before that and was never typecast."

"Oh, I *know* your career. My parents are big movie fans. We went all the time, and rented them all the time, too. I remember seeing *The Dreyfus Affair* with my mom on television. One of our local channels always showed afternoon movies. I think I've seen it maybe three or four times. We'd always make a big bowl of popcorn and she would, as she called it, 'educate' me. My dad—he's an English professor—he focused on teaching us kids all about literature. And our mom, she made sure we knew all the film classics."

"'Classics?' There is that word again," Natasha said. "I supposed that is what *I* am now."

"I'm sorry," Sophia responded, feeling bad for potentially offending Natasha, as well as for rambling on the way she was. "I didn't mean that in a negative way. I think it's an incredible accomplishment. Isn't that what any artist wants? To leave behind a piece of work or a career that outlives them?"

"It is a double-edged sword, dear. In one way, I know I leave something for the world to remember me by. That is comforting, I will admit. But on the other hand, the downside is that people place me in time. You get frozen in their minds, and people can be very unforgiving when you age. They expect you to stay the way you were, and looked, five, fifteen, fifty years before. It is impossible to satisfy their expectations. And if you are a woman, and have had children, well, then you can forget what your body used to look like."

"Do you *have* to satisfy their expectations?" Sophia inquired, still spinning because she was talking shop with an acting legend.

"I am an actor. What do you think?"

Sophia remained silent but nodded. She could not possibly know the pressures this woman, or any other public figure, dealt with. She was glad writers were rarely found interesting enough to come out from behind the desk. They did, after all, make a living that had little to do with appearance, with the exception of book tours, of course. As far as Sophia was concerned, writing was the best of all worlds because all the acting, directing, set planning and cinematography was done by one person who was spared budget battles, weather problems, and so on. And that better world typically was uninterested if her butt got big, her breasts started to sag, and she no longer looked so good in a bathing suit—not that Sophia was about to confess any of this to Natasha.

"Do you have children?" Sophia asked.

"Is that your way of asking me how my body came to look like it does?" Natasha asked with a smile to indicate she was kidding around with the younger woman.

Sophia, liking this woman's quirkiness, laughed back, "No, of course not."

"No. I have no children. In my day, it would ruin your career. Plus, women did not have children out of marriage. They also did not run around like these girls do today. If they did, they were a lot more discreet about it. Besides, I am not the motherly type."

"I'm Sophia, by the way," she said, introducing herself, realizing she had not given her name in return.

Natasha extended her hand in a ladylike way, the type of motion seen rarely today. "Nice to meet you."

"You, too. I was actually named after an actress," Sophia added. "My brother, Twain, was named after Mark Twain, and my sister, Austen, was named after Jane Austen. My mother insisted on naming me after Sophia Loren—not a writer—which is a little amusing considering I'm the writer of the three of us."

"She is a lovely woman," Natasha said.

"Sophia? You know her?"

"We met briefly."

Sophia did not want to ask too many questions for fear of looking star-struck, which she rarely was, but definitely felt today. "How did you get into acting?"

"You *are* a writer, are you not, you inquisitive young thing?"

"Comes with the territory, I suppose," Sophia told her.

Natasha donned a serious expression, and then said in her best affected voice yet, as if she was unveiling the world's most important invention, "I was discovered."

Natasha allowed a moment to let that statement sink in before following it up with, "I do not think people are discovered anymore, are they?"

"I don't know," Sophia said, unable to remember a recent story like the ones she had heard on the old movie channels about Hollywood's so-called "glory days," when a waitress in a diner or a gas station attendant could be plucked from obscurity to become the next Jean Harlow or James Dean.

"I miss the good old days," she confessed. "You are probably too young to remember this, but you used to be able to smoke anywhere you wanted."

That made them "good old days?" Sophia thought, but instead said, "Really?"

"Oh, sure. Even in the late '80s I could sit here in the lobby and smoke a cigarette. Not that I *do* smoke, mind you."

Sophia gathered that this last remark was said deliberately so Sophia would not think Natasha was a smoker, not that Sophia would have cared either way. She wondered if Natasha was trying to appear current and chic, hoping to seem she was keeping up with the times. Did she not think Sophia could smell the smoke emanating off of her jacket?

"You said you are a writer," Natasha stated, as if to change the subject. "I had wondered what you were doing here during the middle of the day. I usually have the place all to myself."

"Actually, I'm unemployed. My day job was just eliminated," Sophia told her, unsure why she felt so free to share her troubles. "I was a copywriter. We lost the account and the agency cut staff. So I'm looking for another job and am working on my first novel as fast as I can."

"Are you any good?" Natasha asked.

Sophia wasn't quite sure what to say to that question. Most of the time she had confidence in her abilities, even though it came and went occasionally, and the past few weeks had force-fed her a combination of both rejections and affirmations. She also didn't want to sound like she was bragging, and she certainly didn't have any proof other than years of copywriting, short stories, an incomplete novel, and one in the works as they spoke. But she did think she had promise. "I think so."

"I always thought being a writer was a romantic trade," Natasha told her.

"I don't know about that," Sophia said. "Poverty, rejection, constant creative angst…not so romantic, if you ask me."

Natasha laughed. "I know about creative angst. Maybe you can help me write my autobiography."

Sophia looked closely to see if she was joking. "Are you serious?"

"I am," she said. "I would love that. It is something I have wanted to do for some time. And this 'classic' is not exactly getting any younger."

Sophia knew she had a "wow" expression on her face but let Natasha continue her thought process. "I would write it myself but writing is not my talent."

Sophia considered this sudden and amazing opportunity. Then she remembered Kate's advice to hold out for something that supported her own writing goals.

"Would we be able to work on it as a part-time job? Say a few days a week, like three or four? So that I could use the rest of the time to work on my novel?'

"I see no problem in that," Natasha said. "That seems acceptable to me."

The usher opened the theater doors, looked at them and said, "It's all yours, ladies."

Sophia was suddenly grateful the usher had used their theater to take his break. "I would love that, Natasha."

Natasha opened her bag and looked for something. Pulling

out a pen and paper, she wrote down an address. "This is my home. How about if you come by on Friday? Say around nine, and we can get started. I will let you speak with my lawyer about pay and all of those important details I am sure you will want to discuss."

"Wow, this is fantastic, Natasha. You won't regret it," she told the actor. "It will be the best autobiography ever. Everyone will want a copy!"

"Wonderful," Natasha said, getting up and putting her sunglasses back on. "Well, enjoy the movie. I will let you enjoy it in private."

Sophia stood up to shake Natasha's hand once last time, more as a "I-really-appreciate-this-opportunity-you're-giving-me" gesture than for reasons of etiquette or manners. "See you Friday!"

Certain Natasha wanted the privacy more than she did, Sophia found a seat far away, as well in front of the actor, so she wouldn't feel she was being watched from behind. But Sophia was the one having a difficult time concentrating on the movie, her head excitedly reeling faster than the movie, thinking up the many ways they could tell Natasha's story. From the few things she knew about Natasha and the details they had just discussed, she was certain she could turn her life into a great book.

When it was over, she stayed through the credits to give Natasha the opportunity to leave without her, not wanting to crowd the star newly back from the dead, the star who had been born again. Natasha McGavin, she considered, as the long list of production talent rolled up the screen, was certainly full of surprises—a first impression it would take only a little time for Sophia to realize was more correct than she knew.

CHAPTER 11
STUCK LIKE PASTA

Before going home to the certain confrontation that Kevin had come and gone in her apartment, and life, Sophia extended her stay downtown, allowing herself to savor the best news she had received in weeks.

The first thing she did, as she followed the cement path around Union Square Park, was phone her parents, who had called to wish her a happy birthday while she was watching the film.

"I thought she died!" her mother said.

"Me, too," added her dad, on the phone in another room.

"So did I," Sophia confessed, still feeling weird about that detail. "Why is that?"

Her mother fielded this question. "I remember a story about it a couple years ago. I *guess* it turned out to be a rumor. But you know the media…they never come back and tell you something they reported was wrong."

Sophia wasn't sure she entirely agreed with this statement but decided not to debate the issue. Before the younger Connors could say anything further, her mother demanded, "What's she like?"

"She's interesting," Sophia replied. "I don't know exactly, I just met her, but she seems to have a lot of interesting stories to tell. I'm mean, look at that list of movies she's been in."

"How come she hasn't been in anything lately? What with cable and everything, she should be working," Ben added.

"My dad, the agent," Sophia laughed, and her mother joined in.

Sophia managed to keep the conversation short, aware she benefited from juicy news. The more interesting the news, the faster her parents "let her go" to conduct their Connors telephone marathon, mass dialing all family and friends to share the conversation. And she knew this one would go far and wide.

"Good luck at home," Diane told her before they hung up, having been told about Sophia's conversation with Kevin. "Just keep thinking about all the good things in your life."

"Yes, baby," Ben added. "Call us if you need to talk."

As Sophia watched three dogs chase each other around the fenced-off dog run, she thought about the concept of celebrity. The truth was it meant very little to Sophia, and the only reason it drummed up any kind of excitement for her was because, depending on who the celebrity was, it provided the occasional reminder that someone with an artistic or creative ambition found success before her, that someone was able to beat the odds and get paid to do what they loved. She envied that part. She wanted to spend her days focused exclusively on developing stories, to be allowed the freedom of self-indulgence to go wherever her emotions and characters took her. Natasha McGavin wasn't exactly her first brush with celebrity since living in New York, just probably her most significant because there was the real potential it could change her life. Writing a book with Natasha could open doors for her. It could change everything.

In second place on Sophia's list of run-ins with the famous—and only second because he hadn't offered her a job—was Kurt Vonnegut. Ben had shared his admiration of

Vonnegut's work with her early on and, as Nonna would have said, it stuck like pasta. This particular expression, one of many in Nonna's arsenal, came from cooking spaghetti when for dramatic effect and to entertain the children, she would toss a server of spaghetti against the wall. If it stuck, it was ready to eat and, as she claimed, meant to be.

The meeting with Vonnegut had happened just a few blocks from where Sophia was now, at the Strand Bookstore, and had nearly been one to remember with regret instead of pride. As Sophia searched through the miles of books the Strand boasted they offered to their customers—a regular and much loved pastime—she practically bowled Vonnegut over while she scurried through the place. She discovered him in an aisle, both in one another's way, each having to hold themselves back from running right into the other. Sophia stuttered, "I'm so sorry." They were the only words she could come up with at the time.

Vonnegut said nothing but gave her a quirky smile and shuffled along his way in the opposite direction.

After the stunned pause subsided, Sophia responded with quick thinking. She knew the store like the back of her hand, so she darted to the back wall and the little cubby hole in the corner where she was sure to find the "V" section. With lightning speed, she found the book she was looking for—*Like Shaking Hands With God: A Conversation About Writing*—that Vonnegut co-wrote with Lee Stringer.

She then searched him out through the aisles, telling herself he *had* to still be there somewhere, and that she would never forgive herself if she missed this opportunity to ask him to sign his book, especially one on writing.

When she found Vonnegut, he was sitting at a wooden table in the middle of a discussion with a manager from the store. She hated herself for doing this, for appearing like a fan, but the truth was that was exactly what she was. This was Kurt Vonnegut, the writer who had inspired her in so many ways with his unique, clever, offbeat writing. His work and the way he told his stories made her believe that her own distinct voice could find an audience, too.

When Vonnegut realized Sophia was standing above him, or perhaps that she was not going away, he looked up. So did the store employee to whom he was talking, and who shot her with a disgusted "can-you-leave-us-alone?" look. But Sophia didn't care what he thought. She was a foot away from Kurt Vonnegut. If only her dad was there! He probably would have passed out that very minute if he had been.

The moment she would share with her idol would be over before she knew it.

"I'm really sorry to interrupt your conversation, Mr. Vonnegut. I love your work and would be honored if you would sign your book for me."

Vonnegut looked at her but again said nothing. He looked at the book, nodded his head, opened the front cover, and scribbled his name on the inside title page. Then he returned to his conversation with the employee. He didn't give Sophia a single word but it was one of the greatest interactions she had ever had.

She departed with an enthusiastic "thank you" and headed for the checkout area at the front of the store to purchase the book she had just pulled off the shelf, which she actually already had a copy of at home. But this one Kurt Vonnegut had signed himself. She was in heaven.

She handed the book to the cashier, a young girl with a mod haircut and practical clothes, who reviewed the book before looking back at Sophia. "You know he's here?"

"I do!" Sophia told her, proud as a kid who just made a painting for her parent in kindergarten. "I had him sign it!"

The girl considered this, and then shrugged. "You're lucky. My friend…she works at a diner. He threw an ashtray at her."

Sophia produced a sour expression. She didn't know if this was true or not and, frankly, she didn't care. Vonnegut had signed his autobiography on writing for her. While he spoke no words of advice or inspiration to her directly, he didn't have to, because his work had already said so much.

When he passed away a couple years later, she lit a candle for him in her apartment, and told Kevin how thankful she was that the world had a chance to know such a creative and unique talent.

When Sophia returned to her apartment later, she had one foot in the future and one foot in the past. The future included a movie star coming back from the dead. The past included a box of her stuff from Kevin's apartment, left by her desk, along with a present and card sitting atop her computer. Filled with dread and expecting a Dear Jane letter, she opened the card first. After all, how bad could it be considering he had already broken up with her? The card read:

> *This meant the world to you and left a lasting impression,*
> *like you've done to me.*
>
> *I will always & forever love you.*
> *Kevin*

Tears splashed the wrapping paper as Sophia opened the gift, a first edition of Kurt Vonnegut's *Breakfast of Champions*. Kevin was right; it had meant the world to her. And so had he.

Sophia cried shamelessly. Even so, she managed to maintain enough self-control to not get tears on, or even near, the first edition. That would have been completely unacceptable, something she'd never allow to happen, regardless of the amount of pain she was experiencing. If Kevin had left her any other gift, it might have found its way spiraling down to the sidewalk outside her window. But with this prized possession, that too was not going to happen.

When she had reached the bottom of her emotional well, she wiped her eyes, changed into a dry shirt and checked her email. She was grateful to find birthday wishes from Kate.

> *Bon jour!*
>
> *Happy Birthday! How's everything? Still going to those crazy focus groups? Witness any eye-gouging over free food lately?*

All's good here. Have spent the last couple of evenings (Yes, evenings! Not nights, thank you very much!) with a man called Philippe. He's very French and very…how you say?…fabulous! He says crazy things like my soul is a butterfly and my eyelids are diamonds. Whatever that means. But he's handsome and very sweet. I know you warned me about the men over here but maybe they're the ones you should be warning. I'm a crazy American woman on the loose! Give me my own video. Call it, "Kate Kinda Gone Wild!"

I'll try to call you later to speak with you live! And I owe you a surprise when I see you next. Happiest of happy birthdays to you! Your luck is about to change. I just know it. I love you!

XOXO Kate

Sophia responded to Kate's email:

Dear French Government,

Please accept this email as confirmation that there is a citizen of the United States of America currently in your country who will crush the butterflies of all of your men. She will, however, increase the intellectual capital of your country as she was born with definite clairvoyant talents. I am pleased to submit into evidence the fact that my luck certainly has turned around. While not all areas are…how you say?…smashing, I believe I am now employed by acting legend Natasha McGavin as her autobiography writer. I will be able to release all the details as soon as I know more on Friday.

Thanks for the wishes. If both of us can't be getting some hot lovin', then at least I know you are. Bom, Chickie, Bom-Bom. (insert stripper music here)
Sophia

PS
Please don't end up on the Internet.

CHAPTER 12
A PEAK FOR EVERY VALLEY

Sophia spent the remainder of her birthday writing, exchanging the final hours for time with her computer, refusing to think about how this year's birthday could not have been more different from last year's. Yet, as hard as she tried, moments slipped through: how Kevin brought her to that nice restaurant on the well-hidden, cobblestone street in The Village; how they jumped on each other when they returned to her apartment; how he presented her with a miniature flourless chocolate cake afterwards, standing naked before her in bed, his brawny body illuminated only by the solitary candle atop the cake and a swipe of streetlight spilling into the apartment. It had been a perfect birthday, and now it was one best not remembered.

Sophia began early the next day, continuing her same plan of attack, trying to tackle as much of her new story as she could before starting her work for Natasha. Dirk would be her focus for the day. She would channel her aggression and heartache through him and, in turn, he would unleash his own, far more complicated version onto his world. She considered how far she would take his pain and how out of control his life would go. The options were endless.

Writing was a roller coaster of a process. When things clicked, the story flowed so smoothly and fast she could barely keep up. The world during those times was complete and she could not be happier. When it didn't, however, the opposite was true in every regard. That was when she felt like hell—worse than hell—and her frustrations did as much damage to Sophia's self-esteem as the good times did to promote it.

Thankfully though, the creative juices continued on her side today. Her greatest challenge, to her surprise, had been a new one. In between the sentences and cornfields of her Midwestern setting, she struggled to block out the thousand questions racing through her mind about how she and Natasha would work together, how much she would be paid, if she would like it, and if Natasha would like her. She tried to relax her mind by telling herself she would know everything soon enough, that she would jump off that bridge when she got to it.

One thing was for certain: that if she needed to, she knew she had her 401k to help make ends meet. It wasn't a great option, and her father would read her the riot act if he knew she was even considering tapping into it, but it was an option nonetheless. Sure, she understood, she would pay for using it, but it was good to know she had it in her back pocket, that it could help subsidize her income. It was a worthy compromise if it meant she could stay focused to hammer out a solid first draft, assuming the rest of the book came as quickly and as fluidly as her outline and the first chapters had so far.

Sophia had been down this road before, starting a new project, becoming completely consumed by it. She found that some things about the process remained exactly the same as before, like when she worked out a chapter, finishing it to her initial satisfaction, but then somehow came upon a wall that halted her from moving forward. It demanded of her, "What do you think you're doing? Do you actually think you have the talent to make this happen?"

Each time, Sophia was left little choice other than psyching herself out, stepping outside her shell of fear—a large one at that—and giving herself pep talks. She rationalized why she had just as much talent, and right, to be a published author as anyone else. She reminded herself that there was a peak for every valley and that she couldn't get to the end of the journey unless she kept her head up and continued the fight. She had discovered early how useful it was to know about these landmines and how to avoid them, remaining mindful to celebrate the little victories along the way and that, despite feeling good about her work at the time of completing smaller tasks, her confidence would temporarily abandon her each time she dropped the period at the end of a chapter. The most recent chapter was no different. This was the adventure she was on to bring her characters to life. After all, Dirk, Anna and their unborn son had destinies to fulfill.

CHAPTER TWO
May 1968

As the unbearable heat held its large, stifling hands around Dirk's throat, he contemplated the purpose of this senseless gathering on the high school's football field and wondered why so much attention was wasted on something so meaningless. Tradition had long since abandoned him and he deemed such celebrations pointless, only serving to remind him that he was trapped, on this day, with these people, in this place. The only reason Dirk had agreed to attend this embarrassing shindig was that it meant something to Anna, although he would never understand why.

From where they sat, he could see the locals, many of whom had left responsibilities far more important on their farms to be there. He watched them as they moved across the grass like cattle, the only difference being that some of this livestock wore their Sunday best. He hardly considered this cause for formality, the women gussied up in summer dresses and many of the men washed and donning monkey suits. This was a graduation, after all, not a wedding or a funeral, although Dirk likened it to the latter.

As he watched, insistent sweat rolled down the gutter of his spine. All of it, every bit of this calamity, reminded him he wasn't the boss in this place or any other, that he was just one of the herd. As he wiped in vain at the perspiration on his forehead and released a heavy sigh back into the thick, suffocating air, he wondered what it was all for. Nothing, he suspected, was the answer for which he searched.

After scanning the crowd, Anna reported that Dirk's father never made it to the graduation. She said it with disappointment, as if George Grant had ever shown up for anything in his pathetic, drunk life. This discovery certainly was no surprise to Dirk, now more focused on the slippery layer of sweat developing between their two bound hands. Seeing no point in wasting energy to confirm Anna's findings, Dirk praised himself for not being the fool to expect anything different from his worthless old man. Anna had insisted she invite him so Dirk did not stand in her way, but George did not show. Dirk was once again proven right.

The last of the audience trickled into the bleachers while Anna waved her hellos to classmates, including Drew Hudson who Dirk tried not to acknowledge. "Condescending prick, always trying to pick up on my girl," Dirk wanted to say, refusing to look directly at him. He pretended to be interested in the town sign just across from the field, now decorated with streamers and paper banners offering the senior class best wishes and congratulations. Through the festive mess, Dirk could still see the hand-carved wood face, the same message that had been there for years.

Welcome to May Valley, Illinois!
Proud Home of the AgriPeople Company

The sign, Dirk thought, might as well say, "Proud Home of Burt Woodward, Bastard Extraordinaire."

Pickups and station wagons drove by, honking their regards to the seniors gathered all around Dirk and Anna. As Dirk stared off in the distance, he recalled the town's saying, a statement he had heard his entire life, a remark that crawled deep under his skin:

"God loves corn—especially corn from May Valley, Illinois."

It was the town motto, and it had haunted Dirk as long as he could remember. So had Burt Woodward and his AgriPeople Company. Woodward had managed to gain influence on everything about this town and the way its people made their livings and it made Dirk sick.

Anyone who spent enough time in May Valley was guaranteed to hear that statement, and to hear it often. Those words attacked Dirk every time he wandered through town, charging him like a thousand angry wasps, reminding him May Valley, a productive farming town on the verge of becoming so much more, was no longer for the likes of the Grant family. This was George's gift to Dirk—one of many—and one he would not be allowed to forget. Gone were the days when a man worked his land his whole life and handed it over to his son to continue the cycle. But even if circumstances had not been what they were, Dirk admitted, he knew George was not exactly that kind of man.

The story was that the saying came from the town's founding forefathers, that they claimed God's love for their corn in 1836 when their first crop of vegetable gold sprang from the newly impregnated ground. The tale and saying had been passed down ever since, from generation to generation, and probably spoken or heard by anyone born and raised in the town. Dirk himself vaguely remembered being forced to say the words in elementary school by one of his teachers, perhaps by Mr. Meinser, in the third grade. The phrase seemed to lose its momentum during the Depression, as so much had during that time, but was refueled for take-off in the 1950's when the town literally found itself the winner of the jackpot—all because of the vision and ruthless leadership of Burt Woodward.

The problem with proclaiming God's love, Dirk felt with certainty, was that God, if he did exist, surely had better things to do with his time than worry over May Valley. It was a farming town like any other in the middle of nowhere and, frankly, the only reason it earned notation on the map was for its financial luck of the draw. If God existed, Dirk claimed, then people were just crops to him, planted in these fields like seed to play their part. When they had produced whatever bounty they were going to produce, they withered and ceased to exist. There was nothing spectacular or special about any of it, and it certainly did not justify making such ridiculous statements.

Dirk was amused by this idea of God's chosen corn and the array of other self-centered and overly generous statements people made about themselves, displaying their inflated and false senses of worth, that it all should somehow make themselves feel better and their lives valuable. He would have pitied them if he hadn't felt such contempt for them. Prayers went unanswered. Didn't these fools know that? It made him wish he knew all of the town's dirty secrets, certain there were plenty of them, because if he did he would turn every secret back on each and every fool. He would expose the town for the shallow, worthless lot that they were. He would show them the truth behind their self-righteousness and give them what they had coming to them. If he could accomplish anything in his life, that would be the best, his ultimate desire.

But how would that happen? First of all, what he was praying for was impossible. Secondly, the town remained sheltered from any kind of reality because Burt Woodward had promised them guidance and riches, and had delivered them from the fire. Yes, he had saved them. Everyone, that is, except George Grant and, as a result, Dirk Grant, because as everyone knew, shit rolled downhill. Chalk him up as one more casualty on the George Grant highway.

"'We have no need for your crops!'" Dirk had overheard George screaming, repeating what Woodward told him.

"The son-of-a-bitch has it out for me," George had thundered through the house in a drunken argument with himself, Dirk hearing too much then, as he had always heard too much.

Anna said something and it brought Dirk back from another place. He mumbled incomprehension to her, indicating he hadn't heard what she said. So she repeated herself, "Here we go. It's beginning!"

She smiled, happy and proud, more beautiful all the time. She was the one good thing remaining in his world.

At no time during the moments of silence, or even after the long-winded speeches had begun and the real boredom had set in, did curiosity ever overcome Dirk. He knew George had not come, that he would not come. It was a surprise to no one, including those few citizens of May Valley who would actually notice such things or cared enough about anything other than themselves to notice. The town had grown significantly in Dirk's lifetime, and money had brought with it blinders like those on a horse. The ones who had prospered wanted not to be reminded of those who had not.

Anna, on the other hand, did an occasional search of the crowd, certain, or at least hopeful, that George would surprise Dirk for this one special occasion. He has to come, she told herself. He's the only family Dirk's got.

She wondered what things would have been like if Dirk's mother were still alive and if his sister, Meg, had not run away and been lost to the world. What became of Meg? Why did she disappear and leave Dirk to fend for himself with George?

Anna was then distracted when her own father came into view, taking his place behind the podium, moving the microphone to better suit his height.

Dirk also watched this man who had been more generous with him in the short time he and Anna had been seeing each other than his own father had been in a lifetime. Clint McCormack cleared his throat and began speaking to the graduating class and its audience. He spoke eloquently and passionately, quoting a name Dirk did not recognize and talking about the future and opportunity. Dirk was certain the person quoted was a writer. English teachers always quoted writers. Anna had told Dirk endlessly about reading stories with her father, sharing his passion for literature, his knowledge of tales old and new. He had submerged Anna's mind deep in the classics years before her friends had ever heard the titles, the same years Dirk had spent in the fields learning to tend the crops, learning to value something that was likely to be taken away from him. Wasn't that how things always turned out, for him anyway?

Mr. McCormack's speech was brief, and when he finished addressing the field of young adults, he closed with a sincerity unique to him. "I have watched you all grow up. I am proud of your accomplishments. And I wish you all the best on your roads."

Dirk and Anna both watched him walk off the stage. He hadn't always been a teacher, Dirk remembered, having heard the stories over dinner at the McCormack house of how he tended crops when he was their age. But, as Mr. McCormack described, Anna's grandfather was blessed with amazing foresight. He had seen the changes in farming coming on like a storm cloud in the distance and had insisted his children have a variety of skills and options. Mr. McCormack was always touting options.

The cost of the choice made by Anna's grandfather was major. He lost one of his best workers by sending his son to college and telling him to pursue a career he was passionate about, one he could practice anywhere he would be happy living. When Clint fell in love with the idea of teaching literature, Anna's grandfather sold the farm to a townie who had graduated several years before his son, a man with big city investors on his side who believed in his ambitious ideas. The man was named Burt Woodward.

Like Burt Woodward, Clint McCormack returned to May Valley after college. Without wasting another moment in Chicago after graduation, he hurried home to marry his high school sweetheart, Anna's mother, bringing his new trade with him. Dirk considered how the stories told it, that there was so much opportunity back then. Anna's family had been smart to call it quits when something more stable, more predictable came along. They had handed in their equipment and picked up books instead because they knew the timing was right.

But Dirk resented the idea that someone made his decisions for him. His grip on their seed and soil was compromised without consideration of his desire or talents. He had learned how to work the field and how to be successful with it, only to be denied the opportunity. When George was useless for periods of time—and there were many of them—it was Dirk who kept things going, making the farm run better than it had in years. But when George took back the reigns, claiming to be in control of himself again, things just returned to their state of decline. It didn't matter that Dirk had better instincts than his father, or that George continued to make rash decisions they would pay for time and time again until there was nothing left, until they had lost the farm altogether.

The heat continued to beat down on them so Dirk leaned forward, resting his elbows on his knees and his head in his hands, as if doing so would provide him with relief. He stared into the grass below his feet, spotting a seedling from a nearby oak that had somehow traveled a hundred feet or so away from the large tree. Looking across the way, Dirk wondered why they hadn't been positioned underneath the tree, in the shade, where there would at least be some relief from the cruelty of the sun. He played with the seedling in his hand, remembering how his older sister had taught him to drop them from a certain height to make them twirl like propellers. To this day, the seedlings reminded him of broken angel wings and of Meg. Where are you, Meg? he wondered. Are you even still alive?

The seedling still in his hand, he thought about the future—always a topic of conversation at these things. Was it really as bright as they made it out to be? People seemed to think celebrations made their lives better, as if noting events with special attention would make life less tedious, less mundane. Stick a candle in it and life will be more joyous, he scoffed. Had these adults looking at them from the bleachers found the future to be all they thought it would be?

Dirk felt Anna's hand on his back and he turned his head to show her he noticed the gesture. In the seven months that Dirk and Anna had been seeing each other, her family had always extended themselves to him, including him in almost everything, circling around him as if he were their own. Dirk knew they felt he was hard to get to know, but that Anna had convinced them of how sweet she found him to be, that he was reserved but also kind. Unlike George.

The McCormacks recognized Dirk's efforts to be polite, to help in miscellaneous ways, like assisting Mr. McCormack around the house whenever he was over visiting Anna. Although he kept a certain emotional distance—a distance they understood, considering the circumstances—they felt he really liked being with them. Mr. McCormack had told his daughter that Dirk seemed to make her happy, and as long as that was the case, there was nothing else to discuss.

Dirk often did not know how to respond to the McCormacks—their direct approach, their sincere questions, their attention—all part of their foreign language he tried his best to comprehend. So he imitated Anna, watching her move about them as if she were doing a ritualistic dance known only to members of the tribe. During their time together, when Dirk was able to break away from the fields, they spent time on her front porch or in town, enjoying being with one another, relaxing, listening to the radio, and getting closer physically, although Dirk sometimes pushed those boundaries.

Anna found Dirk funny, and sharp, and complicated. He didn't feel the need to tiptoe around her like the other boys. If she was to ever have the relationship her parents did, she would have to be friends with the boy, comfortable and relaxed. Most of her girlfriends wanted to be treated like porcelain dolls, and the boys wanted to be idolized. Dirk's lack of finesse attracted her, and she liked the honesty in his crudeness. It made her feel tranquil, without the need to impress, or pretend. He made her feel at home.

Anna also saw a work ethic in Dirk that she admired, and she recognized he was better off when his hands and mind were kept busy. He was more settled, at peace, when he was productive. There was creativity in him she could see when he put his mind to something, which she did not see in his father, but that she saw in her own. Others did not understand why, out of all the boys, she chose him, but she did. She knew the potential he had inside, that he was a diamond in the rough.

Principle Jenkins was the last to speak, welcoming them to their futures, promising them great things. Dirk wondered if he secretly thought most of the graduates would step into the lives their parents had lived, relieving them of their roles, as they too were graduating one rung up the ladder of life. Few would venture far from this place, Dirk knew, infuriated, cursing the impossible hold of this town.

Jenkins spoke with an enthusiasm that both bewildered and sickened Dirk. His intonations, his words, his gestures were all predictable and *disingenuous. Dirk did not understand how a man could be so artificial, wanting a peak inside Jenkins' head to understand him better, to see what drove him, to see what he really thought, to see the truth.*

Dirk imagined Jenkins in high school. He was probably the Molly Swift of his class, an answer for every question, a response in any conversation, always interested, but when it came down to it, not very interesting herself. Dirk had answers, too, but did anyone care to hear them? How many times had he wanted to share his thoughts with George, but steered away, knowing the feedback would only have resulted in confrontations, words interpreted as insults, recommendations decoded in George's mind as betrayal. George was not one for advice, even if it was the best advice, even if it would have saved the farm. Dirk knew he could have salvaged everything, that one day, long ago, there had still been a chance. He could have made a difference.

They reached the conclusion of the graduation, and Anna leaned in to hug Dirk. "Congratulations!" she said, great excitement pouring out of her.

Dirk tried to mimic her enthusiasm, hugging her back, repeating her words.

"Let's go find my parents," she told him.

As they moved their way through the crowd, Dirk considered Jenkins' comments. A "promising future?" His farm was being taken out of his hands because of bad management and poor decisions. And because there was some kind of history between his father and Burt Woodward he knew little about. That was his promising future. What "options" had he been left with? Military service and the Vietnam War? Dirk wanted a glimpse into the future, desperate to know what "promises," if any, it offered for him.

Something in the corner of Dirk's eye caught his attention, making him look for something he didn't know he wanted to find. His eyes settled on a beautiful stranger staring back at him, a woman Dirk had never before seen. She was exotic, her long wavy brown hair flowing past her shoulders, her stunning features shaded by the wide brim of hat, a style Dirk had only seen in pictures. Her lips were sensuous and full, her eyes knowing and inviting. And Dirk felt an intense pressure against his chest as if someone pushed their hands up against his torso and began stretching at the skin to get inside. He froze instantly, eyes wide, mouth open.

The woman seemed to catch herself looking at Dirk, or him at her, and tilted her head to the side, almost embarrassed. She smiled at Dirk, but turned and walked away.

"Who is that?" Dirk asked, risking the chance at sounding like a worked up farm boy.

Anna looked in the direction of Dirk's finger. "That's Tim Johnson's mother, silly."

"No, not her," he replied, but he had lost sight of the woman.

As bodies shifted, he looked for the wide-rimmed hat, the gorgeous hair, the lips, but the moment had passed and Anna pulled him behind her towards her parents. She was saying something but he didn't hear a word of it. He wanted to see the woman again, whoever she was, but couldn't find her. She was gone, like she had vanished into thin air in the middle of the field.

CHAPTER 13
ANOTHER STRAY

Officially back in the rat race, which was both a good thing *and* a bad thing, Sophia rejoined the New York shuffle and made her way across town to Natasha's Upper East Side home. Relieved and anxious, it brought her mixed emotions and she acknowledged that, as the years went by, it seemed that there were fewer and fewer simple emotions, that the only thing she could really be certain of was that she couldn't be certain of anything.

Everywhere around her, people scattered furiously, moving intensely in all directions, like wildebeests on the run from a pack of lions. This frantic time of day had always reminded her of a spectacular IMAX documentary she saw years ago about the Serengeti and the seasonal migration of its animal inhabitants in search of food. The film, with all of its beauty and brutality burned forever in her mind, impressed upon her that there were many basic similarities between life there in the African wild and life here in New York City. There was a constant struggle for the fittest to survive, and people, the same as those herds of animals, moved desperately from location to location because sitting idle meant falling prey to the elements.

Though Sophia couldn't help selfishly hoping for a purpose greater than just making it through another day. The idea that solely managing to exist without being devoured would be her greatest accomplishment felt like setting the bar awfully low. While she felt her dreams and expectations were fairly modest in comparison to many she knew, she did desire something meaningful to come from her life, to leave something to the world like she had discussed with Natasha that people would remember, perhaps be touched by, even if it was in some less-than-remarkable way. She wanted—no, *expected*—better from her life than to just survive. She wanted to leave a message of her own, in her own way, something that touched others. Twain's purpose was his family and the work he did as a geneticist. Austen's was her work as a teacher and, one day, inevitably, as a mother. Sophia wanted to leave something more than disposable, throwaway magazine and newspaper advertisements. Perhaps she would also have a family someday, but for now the difference she envisioned she would make would come from writing, *her* writing. She reminded herself of this regularly as she brainstormed Anna's tragic plight. Her tale needed to be one of emotion and significance. Her journey of love and sacrifice needed to pack a punch that left a mark. Like the fables she loved as a child, Anna's story needed to have teeth.

Pushing her way through the crowds, Sophia had indeed returned to the urban rush hour, where bumper-to-bumper meant wall-to-wall people every which way she went. It reminded her *exactly* of that documentary. Sometimes, she joked with herself, it smelled just like it, too. As she boarded the crosstown bus on 66th Street, she couldn't help but think that even though she had been out of the mix only a short time, the break somehow managed to feel like it had been forever.

Sophia arrived in Natasha's neighborhood twenty minutes ahead of time so she walked around the block for ten minutes to avoid being early, careful to time things as best she could, not knowing what her new employer's expectations or demands would be. Too early might make her look overly eager or nervous, and since it seemed they would be working out of

Natasha's home, it might inadvertently cause an imposition. She also and absolutely did not want to be late. Like everything else in life, there was a fine balance. But, as the day would play out, Sophia would realize later that, despite her best efforts, "balanced" was probably not the best word to use when describing how her first day went.

Natasha's home was not quite what Sophia had imagined. On the grandest end of the imaginary spectrum, she envisioned Natasha living in an attractive walk-up townhouse, perhaps with two, maybe three stories max. She had ruled out an apartment because the address she gave Sophia when they parted ways the other day had not seemed to be one for a condo or apartment. *How much money could she have?* she wondered. After all, including the many years that had gone by, she was a former movie star who hadn't made a movie in twenty or so years, and *that* last movie was a children's film co-starring a band of puppets. Plus, from the research Sophia had conducted on the Internet about Natasha—research that confirmed she and her parents were not the only people who thought she was dead—there was no indication Natasha's success really extended beyond 1990.

What Sophia discovered awaiting her at the end of her trip to East 62nd Street was her most opulent fantasy on steroids. Natasha's home was no humble, little abode. The place was gigantic, as if one greystone building had eaten two others. From the outside, it appeared to be five or six stories tall, with a single door in the front and Natasha's sole street address above it. Natasha's "home" nearly took up a sixth of the city block.

After she picked up her jaw and forced her tongue back in her mouth, Sophia rang the buzzer.

A few seconds passed before someone answered. "Who is it?" asked the voice through the speaker.

"Sophia Connors."

A pause. "Who?" asked the voice, this time with attitude.

"Sophia Connors. I'm starting work for Natasha today."

Sophia heard muffling over the intercom, and then silence. Several seconds passed. She almost hit the buzzer again when the voice returned. "Who sent you here?"

"Natasha McGavin," Sophia replied, a little perplexed.

More awkward muffling came, followed by more silence. Then the voice, still with attitude, commanded, "Please enter."

Sophia wasn't sure what to make of it all, so she did as she was told, pushing through the front door as the buzzer squawked above her. Following the long hallway lined with gorgeous marble, she walked to the end where a door resided. It opened up just as Sophia reached it, and a man dressed in a black suit appeared before her. "Hello. May I help you?"

"Hello," Sophia returned. "My name is Sophia Connors. I was hired by Natasha McGavin. She told me to show up today at 9:00 AM for my first day of work."

The man's face showed confusion and a lack of information; someone clearly had not told him about Sophia. She began having doubts about him as well, but just as she thought she saw him start to roll his eyes, Sophia heard screaming from behind him. With that, the man in the black suit grabbed her by the arm, pulling her inside. "Here! Follow me," he demanded.

The man dragged Sophia through a large oval foyer, also marble, with four major columns holding up a glorious, and presumably, hand-painted dome. As the man hauled Sophia through the room, causing her to fishtail across the floor, they reached an opening that fed into an even wider, more spectacular living room area.

The screams continued like those from a wounded cat. Sophia could locate them this time: they seemed to come from upstairs, up the flight of stairs just off the side of the room they had entered.

"Here," the man said, now no longer pulling at Sophia but pushing her, and with force. "Here! Get in the kitchen! Fast!"

Before she knew it, Sophia *was* in the kitchen just as he had ordered, her back to the swinging kitchen door. She should have predicted what was going to happen next, but wasn't thinking nearly quick or clear enough. The door she entered through swung back again with a violent return, clipping her at the ankles and making her jump forward a few feet.

She looked around for the man in the suit—who had just

shoved her like they were playing touch football—to ask him what was happening but he was nowhere to be found. She realized he must have stayed on the other side. Who was he hiding? Sophia? Or whoever—or whatever—it was that was making that terrible sound?

But Sophia realized she was not alone. Across from her, in the heart of the kitchen, was an older woman staring at her with ridicule. The woman, who Sophia guessed was the chef because of her apron and the bowl of mixed greens her hands were in, said, "Let me guess. Another stray."

Sophia looked around, not sure if the chef was talking to her. When she confirmed that there was no one else in the room, she offered the most unimpressive first introductory statement ever, "What? Who? Me?"

The woman laughed at her. "Yes, I'm talking about you. Take a seat. Jasper will be back in a minute."

Sophia glanced around the room again, this time taking in all of the amazing stainless steel *and* the multiple Viking logos *and* the fact that her whole apartment could fit inside this kitchen. Finding a seat in a bar chair at one of the two islands in the center of the room, she heard more screaming, this time closer. It sounded outside in the room she had just left, or rather, the one from which she had been thrust.

"What's going on out there?" Sophia asked.

"Shhhh," the woman insisted, whispering adamantly, "You don't want her to hear you! Or worse, you don't want her coming in here, do you?"

Sophia didn't know the answer. Did she or didn't she want her coming in there? And who was "she" anyway? Natasha? *That* couldn't be Natasha! She was so nice at the movies. Maybe a little weird, but nice.

"Who are we talking about?" Sophia whispered back.

"Natasha!" the woman said, contempt rolling off her tongue like Sophia was the dumbest person on the planet.

The chaos outside continued, complete disorder in the court, but only the occasional word or phrase could be understood like, "Son of a bitch!"

Sophia also thought she heard crying.

"If you want a *really* good view," the woman told Sophia, suddenly less critical than before, "move your chair to this side over here and twist yourself in the other direction. That door is bound to swing open again…it always does. I think this is gonna be a good one today."

"Good one?" Sophia questioned but did as suggested. "What do you mean—?"

But before she could complete the sentence, the door swung open as the woman had predicted and Jasper entered as if his hair was on fire. He covered his head with his hands like he expected something to follow after him. Over his shoulder Sophia could see Natasha, wailing, something large and shiny in one of her airborne hands, a cigarette ablaze in the other, and she understood why Jasper was rushing.

"Duck! Duck for cover!" he screamed, pushing past her.

Sophia's reaction time had never been too good, even with advanced warning. As a kid, when Twain once threw a Tinker Toy at her because he thought it would be funny, he had warned her he was going to do it, and yet she had still failed to protect herself in time, ending up with a wooden block-shaped knot on her forehead that took two weeks to go away. So when Jasper yelled his warning to her, the best reaction she could come up with under the pressure of such circumstances was to cover her face—an effort she hoped showed that she respected the advice of those who had come before her in this house of unknown chaos and danger. She did, however, peek through her fingers, seeing that just as the door swung back towards the outer room, a horrible crashing occurred, complete with the sound and sight of glass splintering in all directions. Somehow though, the shrapnel, both solid and liquid, never found its way into the kitchen, which provided minimal relief for the group while Natasha's angry banshee screeches in the outer room elevated the terror level an extra notch or two.

The door remained in motion, likely from the force of the object that hit it, and swung inward again. As it did so, Sophia caught a partial view of a man's outline. "There, there," the man said, presumably speaking to Natasha, her high pitch ranting continuing to wail so loudly that Sophia imagined dogs around the neighborhood were able to hear it.

The man's deep voice kept pace with Natasha's and soon completely replaced her emotional cries. Before they knew it, there was no sound at all from behind the door that had ceased to swing.

Sophia slowly removed her hands from her face, unaware of how much time had passed. She looked to find Jasper and the chef, who she didn't see at first, until she realized that they both had taken refuge behind the kitchen island. They too came out from hiding, slowly standing up, almost in unison. The whole incident reminded Sophia of *The Three Stooges.*

"Welcome," Jasper told her, checking out the new girl to see how she was holding up. "Nothing like a trial by fire, huh?"

Sophia gave him an "are-you-out-of-your-mind?" look while asking, "Is this a regular thing?"

"Every once in a while," the chef said. "When she drinks."

"How often does she drink?" asked Sophia.

"Pretty regularly," said Jasper, but with a smile, so Sophia wasn't sure if he was kidding or telling the truth or both.

"Great," Sophia replied, secretly thinking, *That's just perfect. I'm back in the saddle and she's falling off the wagon. What have I gotten myself into?*

"She was expecting Colin Orton for breakfast," the chef said. "By the way, I'm Mary. As you might have guessed, I'm the chef."

"Colin Orton, the director?" Sophia asked.

"Yes," Jasper said. "He cancelled, she cracked, and here we are."

"You're the new assistant?" Mary asked.

"I'm Sophia. I'm here to help her write her autobiography."

Jasper and Mary looked at each other then back at Sophia.

"Really?" Mary asked.

"Yes. Why?"

"Well, I think I can speak for us both when I say we've never heard Natasha even talk about wanting to write an autobiography," Jasper told her. "And I've been around a long time."

"Let me guess," Mary said. "Did she give you the line about no one ever getting discovered anymore?"

Sophia felt ill, wanting to lie to Mary just to prove her wrong. What were the odds they would ever find out? "No," she lied. "What line?"

Mary and Jasper looked at each other again and shrugged. Sophia could see the two of them had their own language, not unlike her and Kate, and that they thought, for some reason, that they knew everything about her, like they had her figured out. Sophia was happy to prove them wrong, at least a little, even if she wasn't being truthful. The combination of this situation and their attitudes was not sitting well with her. While she was trying to give her best first impression, they weren't returning the same thoughtfulness.

The door swung open again, all three of them flinching in response, and a very tall, striking, chisel-faced man appeared.

"You must be the new assistant?" he asked.

Sophia could see a silent, "I told you so" pass between Mary and Jasper.

"I'm the writer," Sophia told him. "I'm Sophia Connors."

He looked at her as if he didn't understand, and Mary and Jasper didn't help matters by shrugging their shoulders. Sophia tried to explain, "Natasha hired me to help her write her autobiography. She told me to come here today—now—to begin working with her."

"I'm Jonathan Kramer. I'm *Ms. McGavin's* attorney," he said, emphasizing the Ms. McGavin part, his not-so-subtle way of telling her that was what she was to be called. He then handed her a business card. "Please go and have an early lunch and meet me at my office. The address is on the card. How about noon?"

Sophia nodded, perplexed, as if she had been knocked in the head with whatever glass object, maybe a decanter, *Ms. McGavin* heaved at the door.

"Now I must ask you to leave. I will see you shortly. Jasper, please see Sophia out."

Jasper did just that, and for the next two-and-a-half hours, as Sophia waited to learn what horror awaited her next, she was grateful she hadn't yet cancelled her unemployment check.

Jonathan Kramer's office hovered like a cloud, high above 59th Street, with a view overlooking Central Park so spectacular that Sophia momentarily forgot she wasn't a tourist. As Sophia approached the receptionist to introduce herself, she said, "That is the most incredible view! That's a nice job perk, huh?"

But the young, snotty receptionist gave no indication she had ever even noticed it before. "May I help you?" she asked, emotionless, and Sophia wondered if the catwalk had noticed its robot had escaped.

"I'm Sophia Connors. I have an appointment with Jonathan Kramer."

Moments later Jonathan's assistant, also chilly, came out to lead Sophia into his office, recommending a chair in front of his desk for her to sit in. It dawned on Sophia that she was in a world she knew very little about with the exception of what she had seen in movies and books.

Jonathan soon joined her. "Sophia," he said, "Would you like an espresso? Or water? Anything?"

"No, thank you. I'm fine."

Jonathan moved around the desk and seated himself. "Thank you for joining me here. As I'm sure you can understand, my first priority is to protect my dear friend, Ms. McGavin.

"Sure," she replied, not sure why he was saying what he was saying, or where he was going with the conversation, or what any of this had to do with her.

"Ms. McGavin did not tell me she hired you. I'm sure you can imagine how surprising I found it when you arrived this morning."

"Sure, I guess," Sophia conceded. "I don't mean to sound rude, but why does Natasha have to tell you when she hires someone?"

"First, I must insist you call her 'Ms. McGavin.'"

"Is that what *she* wants?" Sophia asked, not sure why her instincts told her to present such a question, but they did and she listened. After all, Natasha hadn't told her to call her "Ms. McGavin."

"Secondly," Jonathan said, ignoring her inquiry, "Yes, it is extremely important I know everything that goes on with Ms. McGavin's personal and professional business. It's my job. It's what she pays me for."

A-ha. Sophia was starting to understand but it didn't stop her from getting more annoyed by the moment. Just as quickly as she was getting agitated, she was becoming increasingly certain this opportunity was going down the tubes before her very eyes.

"What is your background, Ms. Connors?"

Sophia didn't care much for this guy. Even though he did just call her "Ms. Connors," which might have normally softened her defenses, he did so with an obvious injection of condescension. Or maybe that was just his snotty way. She opted to overlook it, however, thinking that the least she could do was let him interview her. So she shared all of her vital details with him, including her background and education, her upbringing and work history, her recent departure from RGB, as well as her literary aspirations. It bothered her that he was scrutinizing over details Natasha clearly had not been concerned with, but she guessed she could understand why he was being critical, that his priority was taking care of his client. Before long though, he would explain his focus on such details.

"In order for us to speak any further, I must ask that you sign this," he said, pushing in front of her a legal document. "It's a confidentiality agreement. It's a basic form that commits you to a private arrangement with Ms. McGavin. Signing it means that you may under no circumstances share the..."

Sophia interrupted him. "With all due respect, I understand the contract. At the agency, we signed them regularly to ensure the security of our clients' businesses. I'm not a secret agent, you know. I'm just a writer who wants to help Ms. McGavin tell her story. I hope that makes you feel better about who I am and why I'm here."

Sophia reviewed the document, and after she didn't see anything different from any other confidentiality agreement that she had signed before, she penned her signature at the bottom.

"About that," he said, "the job we're hiring for is assistant. I'm not sure the right thing for Ms. McGavin to do is to write an autobiography. Would you still be interested in the position if it excludes the writing portion you two previously discussed?"

Sophia had a decision to make. She could go back to collecting unemployment and pounding the pavement for some job she could not be certain she would like, or that would allow her the time she needed to write, or she could take the job this apparent control freak was offering that involved working for his nutty client who had an arm like a professional pitcher. At least she would know she had a steady paycheck coming her way, as well as a schedule that supposedly demanded less than the six days a week she used to work.

"I'm interested. Can we discuss the pay?" she asked, broaching a topic that had yet to be discussed.

Jonathan explained those details, which more than satisfied Sophia's needs and concerns, and confirmed her 401k plan would be safe for another rainy day.

"And the schedule?" she asked. "Natasha, er…Ms. McGavin and I discussed it not being a standard, full-time position. I was hoping this was the case so I had more time to work on my own book."

"Ms. McGavin doesn't like people around too much. We think a four-day week average is good for her with her assistant. As you saw today, she does have other staff to help manage her affairs. The schedule may need to be flexible though, meaning that one week you may work Monday through Thursday, and the next week you work Friday through Monday. If she cancels you altogether, I guarantee you will get paid the same."

Sophia liked the sound of that. "That's fine."

"Do you have a driver's license?"

"Of course. I'm from California."

"Ah," he responded indifferently. "Well, Ms. McGavin does have a driver, but from time to time, you may need to do some errands for her that will require driving."

"Ok, that's fine," Sophia said. There was one more question she wanted to ask. "Can I ask you something?"

He must have seen the concern in her face and beat her to the punch. "Is today's behavior a regular occurrence? Is that what you want to know?"

Sophia was relieved she didn't have to verbalize it.

"The short answer is no," he told her, "it does *not* happen regularly. The long answer is that Natasha hasn't worked in quite a while. She's done very well over the years with investments. During the '70s, she made many significant real estate purchases in areas that were once the worst areas of the city but now house large condos and office buildings. Chelsea. SoHo. Hell's Kitchen. The Upper West Side. You name it. The reason I tell you this is that Natasha is not as well-socialized as she likes to think she is. We protect her from certain realities of the world. This means no Internet, gossip papers, etc. We do our part to support and indulge her. She is *still* a star—don't ever forget that. And if *she* is the one to forget, well then, you need to remind her of her status. She is also a very important, successful businesswoman. It is your job to keep her focused on that as well."

"When do I start?" Sophia asked.

"You already did. But come back tomorrow. To the house that is. Once she gets a little rest after today's incident, she'll need you to take her for therapy."

"What do you mean? A doctor?"

"Oh, no," Jonathan laughed, the first real evidence he was human. "Retail therapy, of course."

CHAPTER 14
THE TRUTH SANDWICH

Sophia returned the following day to Natasha's house, or The Estate as she decided to call it, unable to help herself, believing strongly that such a majestic and palatial home deserved the honor of a title. Besides, it was a bad habit she found difficult to break. People, places and things got nicknames, and that was just the way it was.

Initially, as she considered what she would name it, she did wonder if it already had a proper name like all of those great properties seen on *Lifestyles of the Rich And Famous*. But after considering it further, she realized that not only hadn't she heard reference to such a name, but that Jonathan certainly would have insisted she call *it* a specific name, too. Regardless, the wisenheimer in her confessed, it really didn't matter for she probably would have spun the given name into something else anyway.

As she trekked back to the scene of the crime—an event worthy of the record books, at least in Sophia's estimation—she imagined the house surrounded by a gigantic chalk outline and rolls of police tape pulled from one side of the house to the other. Sophia was feeling fairly self-conscious, like maybe she *was* the stray Mary claimed her to be, returning to the place that promised her kibble. With such a questionable introduction, and such a loaded interaction, it was impossible not to wonder how many assistants had come before her. Wasn't that what Mary and Jasper were implying? Didn't they see her as someone who would fail, presumably like the rest?

But what Sophia *really* wanted to know was how often Natasha threw tantrums like the one she saw yesterday. She considered it alarming that Jasper and Mary seemed well-prepared for such dramatics and that Jonathan attempted to pass over it as eccentric behavior, that it wasn't that big of a deal, that it had something to do with Natasha's star status. Sophia had certainly worked with her share of difficult personalities, people who thought they were bigger than life, but could not remember one instance when objects were thrown in her direction or, for that matter, *at* her.

She enlisted reason, telling herself that the best she could do was to just take it as it came, one day at a time. What was the absolute worst thing that could happen? A trip to the emergency room seemed possible but unlikely. Maybe the worst was that this employment wouldn't last as long as she hoped it would. It was still an opportunity for her to make some money, to keep her afloat for a while so she could write. *Remember,* she told herself, *you wanted experiences.*

This time her arrival at East 62nd Street delivered a new surprise, a whole other experience, as if Natasha's world was a big magician's coat and in each and every pocket she could pull out something completely different. *I'd like to see what's up your sleeve now, please...*

Sophia buzzed the front door and was ushered in promptly by Jasper who stated he was expecting her, greeting her with a polite handshake and a warm smile. He went so far as to say, "Welcome to the staff."

The best part was the absolute quiet. There was no pushing or shoving, no screaming or breaking, no trying to explain who she was or why she was there, amidst some cataclysmic fire storm.

She also had the opportunity to actually see the lower level of Natasha's home without the threat of physical harm. The Estate now sounded like it looked—a museum instead of a zoo.

"Come in here and have a cup of coffee," he told her. "Natasha asked me to entertain you while she finishes getting ready."

Still a little overwhelmed by her thoughts, and in the midst of lowering her personal security warning color from red to orange, maybe yellow, Sophia heard Jasper use her name but didn't think enough of it to make a comment. Instead, she took a seat in the kitchen, this time choosing a bar stool with a view of the door, having learned her lesson to not turn her back on that swinging door.

Jasper moved across the room to the coffee pot. "Shall I?" he asked, offering to pour her a cup.

"Yes. Please."

Sophia noticed Jasper was a compact man, short yet strong. What he lacked in height he made up for in stature.

"Do you know if I'll get some kind of job description? Are there specific tasks I'll be assisting Natash, er…Ms. McGavin with?"

Jasper grinned. "Don't worry. We all call her Natasha when Mr. Uppity isn't around. We humor him. Even Natasha does. She refuses to tell him she hates to be called that. I think she likes to keep secrets from him just to throw him off. Would you like milk in your coffee? Sugar?"

"Please," Sophia said, feeling relief from this insight. "He does seem wound rather tight. Has he worked for Natasha for a long time?"

Jasper brought a cup to her, placing it before her then going back to pour himself one. "Yes, forever. I'm sure you weren't even born when they became involved."

"Involved? You mean…"

"No. I just say it that way as a joke because Jonathan might as well be Natasha's significant other, they've been together so long. That's a lot of decades to collect good times and bad times with a person. I think they see each other more as siblings than they do as business partners."

Sophia sipped her coffee, feeling her guard continue to lower gradually. "He seems terribly protective of her. I guess that's a good thing."

"It is," Jasper confirmed. "He just wants to make sure she doesn't get taken advantage of. She's rather fragile, as you saw yesterday."

Fragile? Sophia didn't think that was the word she would have chosen to explain yesterday's meteoric behavior. *Crazed. Destructive. Possessed.* Those were words she would consider using.

"Where's Mary?" she asked, changing the subject.

"She's off today. She usually only works Mondays, Wednesdays, Fridays and Saturdays."

Before Sophia could think through her thoughts, verbal diarrhea got the best of her. "I don't think she likes me very much."

"Who? Mary? Oh, I wouldn't say that. Why do you think that?"

Sophia had seen Mary's kind of resistant behavior before, like there was an invisible shield, or a sign that said, "You don't belong with us."

"She didn't seem very welcoming yesterday," she tried explaining.

"You just caught her at a bad time. Natasha was making us all pretty crazy yesterday. You only caught the end of Hurricane Natasha."

There it was again—another reference to an out-of-control Natasha. "Does that happen often?"

But before Jasper could answer, they both heard the click-clack of heels on the marble in the living room. "Time to go to work," he said without providing any indication of an answer to her inquiry.

Natasha opened the door, this time with a soft elegance Sophia hadn't seen the day before but saw hints of at the movie theater. It was the behavior of a woman in control of herself, who wanted to be thought of as graceful and demure. Sophia saw she was dressed to impress.

"Good morning, Sophia. It is so lovely to see you again."

Sophia wasn't sure if Natasha had seen her the day before, cowering behind her hands, and thought it best not to ask. Seeing Natasha's hand extended, she reached out for it, shaking it warmly. "It's so good to see *you*, too," she replied, really meaning to say she was happy *this* Natasha was present. "Thank you again for this wonderful opportunity. I'm here to help however you need me."

Sophia had also decided not to bring up their discussion about writing Natasha's autobiography, still uncertain what to do, if anything, with the issue. She would leave it alone for now.

"Well, today I need some assistance with shopping. I am feeling a craving to cover some territory," she said with a sheepish grin. "Are you up for that?"

"Of course," Sophia said, trying to sound cheerful and agreeable, perhaps more peppy than her usual self. Hearing it out there though, she decided to tone it down immediately. It had made her flash on her former boss, Russell Griffin, and the way he performed "the dog and pony show"—his form of song and dance whenever clients were around. This thought was enough to remind her to do what she did best: her work. There was a reason she was a writer and not an account person. Account people were about managing the outer world. Creatives were about producing work for the outer world. They were different types of laborers, she thought, one not better than the other, just different, and suited for different personalities.

With that reminder in her head, she returned to the Sophia she was at the theater, before she saw that Hyde-side of Natasha, before she received the ridiculously controlling warnings of Jonathan, even before Natasha was anyone other than a stranger waiting for a theater to be opened. Sophia would be respectful and thoughtful about this world, but she would be true to herself as well. Otherwise this working arrangement would not work for her. Otherwise she would compromise her voice again, like she did at RGB, and that was not acceptable. *Dig me or dump me.* That would be her new motto.

Sophia learned quickly enough what Natasha meant by "cover some territory." Natasha's turf consisted of a significant stretch of Madison and Fifth Avenues. As they ducked in and out of boutiques, most of which Sophia hadn't seen the insides of since they were completely out of her price range, Sophia considered how practical, perhaps boring, she was when it came to shopping. She had an appetite for clothes as much as any of her girlfriends, but she knew she loved other things equally or more, like an apartment of her own, a cell phone with a data plan and the occasional nice dinner out. Dresses and shoes that cost more than her monthly expenses were luxuries left for movie scenes and movie stars. Natasha could afford such extravagances and Sophia would admire them from afar.

Sophia had expected to see some kind of diva moment from Natasha during their shopping expedition, she just hadn't expect for it to happen so quickly...like the moment they walked out of the front door of her home only to step right into a chauffeured car.

"Charles, this is Sophia. Sophia, this is Charles," Natasha said, slipping her sunglasses over her eyes for anonymity, making the introductions as she stepped past the door held open by her driver.

What made it such a diva moment was the fact they only drove around the block and down a couple of streets before Charles stopped and opened the door again—a more than manageable walk for mere mortals.

"The usual place, ma'am?" he asked, helping Natasha out of the backseat.

"Yes, Charles. Thank you."

Charles winked at Sophia as he assisted her—a friendly gesture, she concluded, to tell her she was in good hands.

Before they got to the first store, Natasha stopped to look for something in her bag. A moment later, she pulled out a cell phone and handed it to Sophia.

"I am not very savvy with these things. Honestly, I feel like it has been forced on me. But since I have one, at Jonathan's insistence, please put your number in it for me while I look around."

"Of course," Sophia responded, taking the phone with one hand while the other opened the door for Natasha.

Natasha browsed through the store, touching and appraising the one-of-a-kind items the boutique offered on display. While she looked, Sophia did as she was asked, adding her contact details to the phone. When she finished and pressed save, she checked the address book to make sure it took, which it did. What Sophia also noticed was that for someone who claimed to not like the device much, she certainly had a lot of numbers programmed into it. Sophia looked up to locate her employer, who was standing across the room with two blouses in her left hand, her right hand pointing to a dressing room.

"Okay, I'll wait for you here," Sophia said.

When Natasha had disappeared behind the door, Sophia gave in to temptation, something she knew she shouldn't do, and reviewed the address book. She tried to rationalize with herself that she wasn't being nosy. She told herself she was acquainting herself with Natasha's contacts so she was better prepared to organize her social activities when asked to do so. Bobby, Tom, Liza, Al, Steven…the list went on. For someone out of the limelight for so many years, whom most common folks thought was dead, Natasha knew a lot of A-list entertainment people.

Natasha returned with empty hands. "Nothing you liked?" Sophia asked.

"No, not today."

Sophia followed Natasha out and then up the street to another store, this one larger than the last. "Here's your phone," she said, handing it back along the way.

Natasha hid the phone in her Louis Vuitton bag. It, like almost everything else Natasha was wearing or holding, had a big name label on it. "Thank you."

The process of trying on clothing definitely infused energy back into the subdued Natasha, much like the sun bringing light to the day first thing in the morning. Sophia did her best to respect the quiet between them until they had explored another couple stores. Then she thought it an appropriate time to ask the question, "Would you like to talk about how I can assist you? That is, what you expect of me, and what I can do to make your life easier?"

The phrase came out a little corny, even for Sophia who happened to know what she meant. She wasn't sure if she had spoken clearly enough, if she had communicated to Natasha that she was there to support her in any way she needed, despite the change of direction regarding the autobiography. She attempted to explain, "What I'm trying to say…"

Natasha either understood she wanted to establish some guidelines for her employment or was too focused on looking at jackets because she waved away Sophia's concern. "I know. I know. Tomorrow you and Jasper can discuss everything. He will bring you up to speed on the regular tasks. He is a marvel. He will tell you everything."

"Ok," Sophia said, agreeing to Natasha's underlying request to maintain the silence.

But while Natasha continued scanning the racks, in this store and the next few, Sophia could only think about the autobiography, and how in a perfect world that would be the best way she could assist Natasha because those were the real skills she offered. As Sophia's arms loaded up with the handles of bags from various stores and her shoulders felt the weight of their demands, so did her head fill with a nagging concern. Since Jonathan had been wrong about how to refer to Natasha, maybe he was wrong about the book as well. Sophia knew she wouldn't forgive herself if she didn't ask the question.

"May I ask you something?" she asked as Natasha examined the handbag selection at Barney's.

Natasha stopped looking at the rose bag she had in her grasp, put it down, and lowered her sunglasses. As Sophia stared across the variety of Fendi bags into those exposed eyes, she got the impression that perhaps she had just pushed Natasha too far, and that she herself was about to be added to the list of strays—the ex-assistants—to which Mary had been referring.

But all Natasha said, with composed reservation, was, "Yes. Of course." The way she said it only made Sophia more nervous.

"I met with Jonathan yesterday. While we were filling out paperwork and setting me up to work for you, I mentioned our conversation about helping you write your autobiography."

"Yes, about that," Natasha said, interrupting her. "I do not think I would like to do that."

Sophia didn't know what to say so she did her best to respond with a delicate and respectful tone. "Oh, really? But you seemed so interested the other day."

Natasha returned the glasses to the top of her nose, turning back towards the bags. "Yes, well…I had a change of mind. Who wants to revisit the past anyway?"

Sophia considered this. Maybe Natasha wanted her to present her case. Maybe she even wanted her to make a fuss about it so she could relive some of the glory from the good old days. So she spoke what she felt. "I think a lot of people do. People love Hollywood, and you've had such an amazing career. I'm sure you have a hundred great stories. We'd probably have a hard time selecting which to use and which not to."

Natasha soaked up the compliment as if it were a breath of fresh air. Sophia knew her case had been heard, and valued, but then Natasha returned her answer all too quickly, "You are sweet for saying that, darling. But no, I do not think that is something I would like to do."

Sophia did not want to press any further. She had spoken her mind and, in all fairness, that was all she could expect. She was left with no other choice but to move forward with the terms of employment that Jonathan had established and that she had accepted.

"Like I told you," Sophia reinforced, "I'm here to support you however you need me. If this is how you feel then, of course, I respect your decision."

"Wonderful," Natasha said. "Now let us continue on."

Sophia felt disappointed as she followed Natasha up the escalators into the women's ready to wear area. Her employer perused the aisles and handed a few selections to Sophia. "Would you mind carrying those for me?"

"Not at all," Sophia told her, still contending with her frustration but feeling it begin to dissipate. She still had a job. And she still had her own book, which no one could take away from her. That was hers and no one could change that.

After Natasha had made her selections, she asked Sophia to follow her into the dressing lounge. "Please put them on those hooks and have a seat. I will be right back."

Sophia left the clothes she was carrying in the dressing room and then sat on the bench outside. For a few minutes, she could hear Natasha's "oohs" and "hmms"—the sounds she made as she tried on various outfits. Then she heard the metallic twist of the door jam, and Natasha appeared before her in a strapless number, a vision of lime green and *a lot* of skin. She looked like a glow-in-the-dark Shar-Pei.

Then came the dreaded question anyone would fear—the moment of truth—the inquiry Sophia did not want directed at her. It came towards her like a car crash in slow motion.

"How do I look?" Natasha asked. "Should I buy it?"

Sophia tried to think of something that would get her out of answering the question, like she had left the car unlocked or the building was on fire. But she could think of nothing, her imagination completely betraying her. *Damn you, imagination! I won't forget you did this to me!*

Sophia had always been aware that time played dirty tricks on people, that it took back what it gave out. She had seen this with her elders. Hell, she had even seen certain signs of it with herself, knowing full well that those little pieces of evidence were just the beginning of bigger ones. Things for her, like for everyone else, were in a constant state of shifting. But the problem she faced in that Barney's dressing room was that Natasha refused to obey the most important fashion rule of them all: one size does *not* fit all. She had irrationally crammed her torso into a dress that did not fit her and now Sophia had to deal with the repercussions of an unfair question.

"It's very summery," Natasha said. "Does it fit?"

Sophia continued stumbling on her thoughts. Was this a test? Did Natasha *really* think it looked good or was she messing with Sophia, another part of her initiation? *Day one—throw a drunken tantrum and glass decanter at the new employee you told would be hired to help you write your autobiography. Day two—wear the least attractive item in the store in a size you haven't been able to wear in twenty years and make the new employee lie to you to prove her worth.*

Sophia had a big decision to make in a no-win situation. She could tell Natasha what she wanted to hear: that it looked nice, that it made her look slim and beautiful, like it was still 1979. Or she could take the high road, the one with bumps and curves like Natasha's mature figure, and tell the truth. She did not want to become one of those people who contributed to a celebrity's dysmorphic perception of reality. Natasha was her boss but she was also a woman—a sensitive woman, as everyone insisted on telling her.

"Cat got your tongue? What do you think?" Natasha asked again, twisting around so Sophia could examine her completely, in all of her green glory.

Natasha stopped and stared at Sophia who knew she had to respond. If she was silent for too much longer, she wouldn't have to say anything at all because the silence would be statement enough. But she wanted to be more tactful than that. "It's not my favorite."

Natasha put her hands on her hips, wrinkles everywhere smiling at Sophia. "That does not answer my question. I did not ask you if this was your favorite. I asked you if it fits me."

Ugh. The situation just got worse. Sophia hated herself at that very moment, wishing she had just a little Russell Griffin to get her through this day. With an obvious question mark placed at the end, as she was all too often prone to do, she squeezed out, "Maybe?"

"Well, do you or do you not like it? I asked you a simple yes or no question. As Louis Malle once told me, there is no use for maybe in life."

Gulp. She wanted to change the subject by asking, "You knew Louis Malle?" which would have been a safer, better conversation to have. Instead she blurted out, "No, I don't. I think a couple of the other outfits looked nicer. They seemed to fit you better."

Natasha's face soured like she tasted something bitter, the lime in her dress perhaps climbing into her mouth. Then she stepped backwards, towards the dressing room. "Well, that is very passive-aggressive of you."

Before Sophia could figure out on her own why Natasha had said that, she asked, "What do you mean? Why would you say that?"

"Clearly, you *are* upset with me. It is the only explanation for why you would act this way. I understand you are not happy with my change of mind about the book, but this is not an adult or appropriate way to act. I do not appreciate you taking your frustration out on me, or this lovely dress."

Again, Mary popped into Sophia's mind—Mary the prophet, the knower of all assistants past, present and future for Natasha McGavin.

Sophia could not believe what she was hearing. First, that Natasha completely misconstrued her comments and intentions. Second, that this advice about proper conduct was coming out of the woman who all but threw herself on the ground yesterday and cried like a toddler because someone canceled a meal with her.

"Natasha, please listen to me," she said. "I was sincere when I told you my feelings about the book. And I'm sincere now in what I tell you about the outfit. I think you are a beautiful woman, but that outfit does not look good on you!"

Sophia realized her lips probably took it farther than she intended, the words slipping from her, like soap from a wet hand.

Natasha stepped back, as if she could avoid the conflict by entering the dressing room. "Now you are just being mean," she said, closing the door with a slam.

Mean? thought Sophia. Mean would have been telling Natasha her exact assessment of the outfit: that some clothes are designed with age appropriateness in mind, that if you don't have the body then you shouldn't show it off. *Kind* was trimming the edges from her truth sandwich to make it edible for Natasha's childish sensibilities.

Sophia could hear Natasha moving around the dressing room, talking to herself in a low voice. She just didn't have it in her to be plastic, to lie and tell Natasha things just because it was what she wanted to hear. She was certain that was it for her employment, all two days of it. She was definitely going to get the boot as soon as the dressing room door opened again.

When Natasha did re-appear, all she said was, "Enjoy your figure while you have it, dear. Life will come along and kick you around in due time, too."

Sophia pleaded with Natasha, "I wasn't insulting your body. I was talking about the dress."

"That is not how it sounded."

"The dress…that's what I meant. If you heard otherwise, then I'm sorry. I should have chosen my words better."

Sophia thought of Kevin, and the voice in her head said, *Isn't that what Kevin said to you?*

Shut up, voice! she said back, telling herself the only similarity between the situations was that Kevin and Natasha were both selfishly twisting words to rationalize *their* positions.

"Fine," she replied. "Grab my bags. It is time to go home."

In the car on the way home—all three blocks of the trip—Sophia expected the ax to drop, but it never did. She thought of her character Anna in the prologue dream, her head on the chopping block like she was Sir Gawain. Someone was always taking the fall, making the sacrifice, for someone else.

And as she brought Natasha's bags inside and up the stairs to the bedroom closets—the place was so big that the closets had closets—still nothing happened.

"I'll see you tomorrow?" Natasha asked, escorting Sophia to the door.

"Sure," Sophia told her, hesitated, then added, "Are we good?"

Natasha nodded a confirmation that included a hint she wasn't entirely sure what Sophia meant, leaving Sophia to wonder if they had experienced the same thing. She would, as Jonathan and the others suggested, need to be mindful of Natasha's "sensitivities." She would pay attention to these, not so much for political reasons, but for Natasha's overall well-being. The job issue aside, the last thing she wanted to do was upset her.

"Ok," Sophia said. "See you tomorrow."

CHAPTER 15
YOUR MOUTH TO GOD'S EARS

Sophia's list-making tendencies proved quite useful as Jasper spent the next two days telling her about her many responsibilities as well as all about Natasha's many likes and dislikes, explaining in detail her expectations around The Estate. These specifics ranged from how the largest refrigerator she had ever seen was to be organized *(condiments on specific shelves inside the door; flavored and non-flavored water on the top shelf; Mary's prepared meals went on shelves two, three and four; and the Vueve Clicquot always chilled on the bottom),* to the Montblancs she wanted in the Tiffany crystal on top of her desks in the library *(black ink on the desk to the right where she usually signed professional documents, checks and such; blue and other colored ink on the desk to the left where she sent personal cards and letters).* Sophia learned what dishes were washed by hand *(most of them)* and the rotation schedule of everything that required cleaning or watering. While Alice came to clean the house on Mondays, Wednesdays and Fridays, and David tended to the plants and rooftop garden on Mondays and Thursdays, Sophia would be expected to chip in when extra hands were needed. Sophia methodically scribbled notes and then retraced the details with different colored highlighter pens to add an extra level of classification.

"Impressive organization," Jasper told her. "But the notes are probably not necessary."

"Why? Because she'll get rid of me before I need to worry about anything?" she asked, only half joking.

"No," Jasper said, returning the favor of a laugh, "because the only thing erratic about Natasha is her behavior. There'll always be clues and reminders around the house of what goes where. Natasha lives with a stockpiling mentality. She believes in having enough supplies to rival a nuclear war bunker. If we have another blackout or some other problem in the city, you be sure to come here. The fifth floor is full to the brim with water and canned food—not that Natasha eats that—but she wants to be ready, in case she has no other choice. There are also additional fridges and freezers up there, amidst all of Natasha's archives."

"Archives?"

"You know. Photos, memorabilia."

"I bet that's interesting to look at."

"She's only shown me some of it. Once. But it seemed to upset her. I think it makes her too emotional to look at it."

Sophia admitted to Jasper that she sort of understood Natasha's method to her madness. If she had the space and money, she'd probably keep supplies, too. But space—and money, for that matter—were luxuries she, like many Manhattanites, did not have.

Returning to Jasper's original comment, she said, "I like my notes. I feel if I write things down, I remember them better. I may never look back at them but there's something about jotting things down that helps me retain the information. In order to write a book, you have to be able to keep the details straight."

Jasper laughed. "I have a difficult time keeping anything straight."

Sophia understood his approach and laughed with him. She also appreciated his accessibility, that he was making her feel welcomed.

They bonded further while polishing Natasha's multiple sets of silverware, a task Jasper confessed he had been holding off until Gina's replacement started.

"Am I the new Gina?" Sophia asked.

"Yes."

"What happened to her?"

"Died."

"Really?" Sophia asked, shocked by the answer, hoping he was just joking but knowing that around The Estate anything might be possible.

"No, not really," Jasper told her, pleased with himself for pulling her leg. "She and Natasha bumped heads too much. Turned out she wasn't a very nice girl."

"Have there been a lot of assistants?"

He nodded. "Natasha has had her fair share. I think they think Natasha will introduce them to other celebrities, or that Natasha lives this exciting life. With the exception of the regular mood swing, there's not a lot going on around here. Mostly just maintenance," he said, waving the utensils in the air as evidence. "And these young kids today don't care much about that."

"Speaking of remembering things," he added. *"Are* you going to help Natasha write her autobiography?"

"Nope. Dead in the water."

"That's too bad. That lady has some good stories. Her life has been a real trip. And she's the real deal—a *real* New Yorker. She was here when it was gritty and dangerous. It's like an amusement park now compared to what it was."

"I think New York still has plenty of grit today."

"I don't disagree. I'm just saying the '70s were tough times for this city. I think being a single career woman during those days must have been something else."

"I agree with that. I'm actually thinking of weaving New York during the '70s and '80s into my novel. I'm fascinated by the city, and those times are so potent. There was so much going on."

Jasper scratched the itch on his forehead with his shoulder to avoid getting cleaning solution on his face. "What's your novel about?"

Sophia had yet to talk about her book with anyone, but the

process so far had been a fluid brain dump, like the creative damn had broken.

She thought about what she wanted to tell him, and how to best summarize sixty or so pages of character set-up and story development. "The high-level overview is that it's a thriller, a modern day fable, with a deep human element. It's about the lengths to which people will go to achieve or preserve that which they cherish or desire more than anything. It's about priorities and compromise. It's about good versus evil. Love versus hate."

"That sounds interesting. You know, I read something once that said the opposite of love is not hate, but indifference."

Sophia smiled. "I've had this conversation with myself before. I think that's true, but for this story I felt hate would be more interesting to write about, and read, than the subtle destruction or damage that's done from indifference. Hate is more tangible."

"So you think love is productive and positive and that hate is bad and tears things apart?"

"Actually, I think there's a fine line. I think the two, depending on the viewpoint, can accomplish quite the same things. I also believe someone can love so much that if it's taken away from them they turn into a monster, a broken soul. That's really the heart of my story. A man who was once decent becomes something different when the one thing he loved more than anything in life is taken away. It's about the downward spiral, the ripple effect, that comes afterwards, and who is affected and how. That some people can take tragedy and somehow press on, and some are completely immobilized by it or eaten up."

"That sounds intense."

"I hope it is. I'm pleased with how it's coming out so far," Sophia admitted, then added, "I also want to hint at there being other levels of existence no one knows about. Like on a basic level, how you really cannot know another person, how we each have things about us others don't get to see, that we are mysterious creatures. You can examine the evidence you have before you, but there are always details you will probably never understand. My sister's a teacher. We have this ongoing discussion about nurture versus nature—whether or not people are born with predetermined characteristics and traits or if they are conditioned through experiences."

"What do you think?" Jasper asked. "I think both."

"I think both, too," Sophia said, pointing at Jasper as an example. "Your genes play a huge role in who you are as a person. But what you've seen and experienced has obviously also conditioned you to respond with certain attitudes, and with certain defenses or strategies for success."

"What does your sister think?"

"We pretty much agree, although she believes in something she made up calls 'the mommy gene,'" Sophia shared, adding a roll of her eyes for commentary.

Jasper laughed, grabbing at a pile of forks to polish. "What is that?"

"She believes she was born with this special gene—as if the scientists haven't discovered it but she has—and that maybe she got more than her share. The mommy gene makes women who have it want to make babies more than anything else."

"They do say the instinct is pretty powerful. I have friends who have the mommy gene—both women *and* men. I have some mommy gene in me, too. What about you?"

Sophia shook her head. "If I have it, it's a recessive or dormant one," she said, deflecting the topic with humor.

Jasper remained silent, sensing she had more to say.

"I love kids. I think I want to have a family one day," she added. "I'm just not consumed by it like she is. Does that mean I'll make a bad mother? I hope not. But right now, and in light of my recent breakup, I can't think about stuff like that. If I do, it'll make me crazy."

Sophia realized the live wire in her was close to the surface and she wondered if Jasper could see it, too.

"I *can* tell you though," she said, bringing the conversation back to a lighter level, "I was not one of those little girls who had twenty dolls. I was sort of a tom boy."

"I had dolls," Jasper admitted. "They were all boy dolls, but they were dolls just the same. I always wondered why they called them action figures for boys?"

"It's all marketing. It goes back to gender stereotypes and what is and isn't acceptable in the American household. I think things are changing, little by little, that people are becoming more educated and aware of the complexities of the world, of genetics, to not be so afraid and hateful towards the things they don't understand."

"Your mouth to God's ears," Jasper said. "I do hope you're right, for all of us."

"What about you?" Sophia asked, pointing at his finger. "I see a ring. How long have you two been together?"

"Fourteen years. His name is Clifford," Jasper said. He seemed to stop himself as if he wanted to offer her more details but didn't know if the additional details were appropriate. Sophia wondered if he did so out of sympathy for her.

But then Sophia probed. "How'd you meet?"

"I'd seen him around for years. You know the city can get to be a pretty small place when your 'crowd' haunts the same establishments. Over the years, we'd always smiled at one another but never spoke. We're both pretty reserved, shy. It was probably best we didn't meet the first time we saw each other. I was kind of a mess for a couple years after my ex and I split."

"Years?" Sophia asked, a look of dread filling her face. Was that what she had in front of her?

"Don't worry," he told her, "there's no solid rule about how long it takes to get over it. You just give yourself all the time in the world you need. It'll be out there for you when you're ready again."

"I wish I could be so sure."

"It's funny though. We had seen each other for years, even worked out at the same gym for a while. I remember one time I was out on Fire Island playing volleyball and he and his friends walked by and stopped to watch us, or me, as he told me later."

"That's nice."

Jasper nodded. "Yeah, I think so, too."

"So how did you finally meet?"

"It was a Sunday morning. I was on a firm 'no boys allowed' stretch so I was staying home most nights and getting up early to go to the gym. That's what I did that day, too, and, low and behold, who do I see walking into the Duane Reade on my way?"

"Clifford!" Sophia said, no different than a child being read a story to which she already knew the outcome.

"Yep. And for some odd reason, probably because I was still half asleep, I followed him in. Can you believe that? I'm a stalker!"

Sophia laughed. "Good for you. Then what?"

"I acted like I needed gum. Can you imagine that? I grabbed a pack, any pack I could, and looked up at him in line, totally knowing what I was doing, and was like, 'Oh, hi. How are you?'"

"Slick. Very slick."

"I know. I've got smooth moves."

"I like that story."

"It turned out that his mom was in town visiting. He had left her at the diner to go get her an umbrella. That's why he was at the Duane Reade."

"A sweet man who is good to his mama."

"I know! Ka-ching! After we finished talking, for the first time after who knows how many years, we exchanged numbers. He went back and told his mom that he got *her* an umbrella and *himself* a date!"

"What'd she say?"

"She told him, 'You're not going out with some guy you met on the street!' She called me that for the first month we dated—'the guy from the street.'"

"And now?"

"Aw, she loves me. And I love her. She's wonderful. She raised a great son."

"That's nice."

"Yeah, I think so. Some people hate the rain. Not me. It changed my life."

CHAPTER 16
A NEW TWIST

Sophia's pleasant discovery was that her workdays, or at least the several she had experienced so far, allowed her plenty of time and energy in the evening hours and on her days off to write. Natasha's demands, while different in nature from what was initially discussed, had been accurately described in terms of scheduling and flexibility.

Sophia continued plugging away at her story, celebrating silently, for the most part, every paragraph and every page she accomplished, each rewarded with a not-so-literal pat on the back, as if to tell herself, "See? You *can* do this! Now keep going!"

She built her confidence as she went, brick by brick, despite knowing all too well she still had a long, long way to go, that this structure would take hundreds, maybe thousands, of more bricks. Since starting, she had determined the best way to get through such a massive project was by allowing herself to honor each small victory, reminding herself that a lot of little ones collectively made up the massive ones, and that if it was easy, everyone would do it. This logic wrapped in a challenge—

knowing not everyone would attempt it—for some odd reason inspired her instead of discouraged her. She told herself not to worry about the endeavor as a whole, but instead about the single steps in front of her, that they would eventually bring her to the finish mark. She reminded herself of the long-distance swimming she did as a kid, how no one on the team wanted to swim the 400 freestyle. As co-captain, she felt it was her responsibility to fill those unwanted aquatic shoes when no one else would. While there were times she thought she might drown, she completed the task every time, and sometimes in first place. That, she guessed, was the process of writing a book, and it was the best strategy she could think of to keep herself motivated and productive.

It was her day off and she was in the midst of sending Dirk away from May Valley forever. The driven young man was in pursuit of the older woman he had become intimate with—the one he saw first at the graduation and then later in town. The woman offered, at a great cost unbeknownst to him, a world more promising. He was, however, completely unaware Anna was now pregnant with his child. That was when Sophia received the call from Kate.

Like her characters, Kate and Sophia's lives were changing quicker than either of them could know, and there was little they could do about it, even if that was what they wanted.

"Lady Liberty!" Kate yelled over the phone.

"So nice to hear your voice! How are things on the other end of the pond?"

"Things are good. I miss you so much!" Kate admitted. "How was your first week of work?"

"I survived and lived to tell about it. Like I wrote in my email, those first couple of days were pretty questionable, but the last couple have been really good. I actually think the dust might be settling nicely."

"That's nice. Sounds promising."

"It is. I'm becoming friends with Jasper, the house attendant. He oversees a lot of Natasha's general life—the house, other things. He's lovely and has been so helpful. You'd adore him."

"How's Natasha? Has she been behaving herself?"

"Natasha's complex," Sophia tried to explain, "and hard to follow sometimes, but she seems to trust me more every day. Even Mary, who was rough around the edges, is coming around."

"She's the cook?"

"Yes, that's her. Except when they work for someone in their home they're called chefs. I'm not sure *who* they'd hired before me, but they seem to have some funny stories to tell. There have been some real POWs."

"'Pieces of work!' I love that expression. Any change of mind about the autobiography?" Kate asked.

"It's not going to happen. I'm certain of that. What can I do?"

"You're working. That's a good thing."

"It is, I guess," Sophia admitted. "They have me doing odd jobs, which I actually don't mind. I'd rather be writing, of course, but that's not an option. And the money is much better than I'd expected so I have no complaints there. Plus, the schedule's very fair."

"How's the writing coming?"

"It's coming. I think I'm half way through part one," Sophia told her.

"How many parts will it be?"

"Three. The first is shorter than the other two, I think. But it's all flowing smoothly...so far. Watch, I say that now and then hit a wall."

"Don't talk like that. It just means this was the story you were meant to write. Things happen for a reason."

"What's Paris done to your head?" Sophia teased. *"You,* of all people, don't believe *that."*

"Ha ha. Nor do you, but I do like the sound of it," Kate confessed. "Besides, things are working out for you, for both of us. Change is a good thing, and you're doing some exciting new things."

"Like polishing silverware. I can still smell the polishing

cream," Sophia joked. "But you're right. I don't mean to sound like I'm complaining."

What she really wanted to tell Kate was she was treading water, that while she no longer felt like she was completely under water, she did still occasionally think it was remotely possible to slip back below the surface at any time. The reality was she thought about Kevin all of the time, and the idea that he was no longer one of the exciting things happening in her life to which Kate was referring brought her much sadness. He had been reclassified as a part of her history now, someone standing behind her, waving goodbye as she moved in another direction. How long would it take, going back to Jasper's point, for *her* to get over *her* ex?

"You've got plenty to be excited about, Sophia," Kate demanded. "And don't you dare get lippy. That's *my* job."

"True," Sophia said, and then changed the subject. "How's Paris today? How's *Philippe?*" She said, teasing her with his name with a deliberate schoolgirl tone that should have been followed up with "then comes a baby in a baby carriage."

"He's *good,"* she returned, and Sophia could hear the smile in her voice.

Kate continued. "I have good news, more good news, and a little bad news to report. You may want to sit down for this."

"I don't like the sound of this. Do I?"

Instead of answering, Kate moved forward with her announcement. "The good news is that, like you, I found a job. The other good news is it's an international marketing director job, like I've always said I wanted!"

"In Paris?" Sophia asked, jumping the gun. Where else could it be considering Kate hadn't been in The States for weeks?

"Yes, that the bad news, sort of, if you can call it that."

"That's not bad news at all!" Sophia announced. "I mean, it royally stinks for me, but that's amazing for you!"

"You're happy for me?" Kate asked. "I was so nervous about telling you."

"Kate, please! You're not Kevin. I know what this means to

you. But I swear to God, if you get married and stay there, well…then we have a problem."

"I'm relieved," Kate admitted. "I knew you'd be happy, of course, but I didn't want to add more stress to your life. I didn't want you thinking I was leaving you, too. It's just that this opportunity literally landed in my lap. I just can't believe how lucky I am that things worked out the way they did."

"You know I'm happy for you," Sophia told her. "This isn't about *me*, Kate. This is about *you*. Kevin leaving is very different. You never told me you wanted to marry me one day. I think this is great."

"And guess what?" Kate asked. "Now you'll have plenty of time to visit me. You can get settled with the movie star and then come visit!"

"How long do you think you'll stay?"

"I don't know. They want me to sign a two-year contract. Who knows how this will work out? But it's a really exciting opportunity. The company is growing like gangbusters and they want an American flair. Can you imagine that? The French want an American flair?"

"What about your apartment?"

"I thought about subletting it, but I don't think I want to deal with the hassle. Besides, I'm not sure the building would let me do it for that long. I guess I'm going to give it up and just put most of my stuff into storage."

"That's so hard to imagine," Sophia confessed, realizing how much lonelier New York suddenly became. In her New York migration theory, she never thought that those acquaintances of hers who would flee the city would be her boyfriend *and* her best friend, and certainly not at the same time.

"I know it is," Kate admitted, "but it's also so exciting. I mean, imagine it…*me* living in Paris for a couple of years."

"That's amazing! You'll never regret doing it. You'll never look back at the end of your life and say, 'Geez, moving to Paris was such a big mistake.' When will you come back and pack up your apartment?" Sophia asked, unable to believe she just asked her best friend that question.

"I have to figure that out. I think in a month. They'll put me in a temporary place until I find an apartment. Plus, I have to give a month's notice anyway."

"Well, let me know if you need me to do anything. And I can certainly help you pack."

"Thanks, Sophia. I'm so gonna miss being able to see you all the time."

"Me, too. But, truth be told, I'm getting used to life without you," Sophia joked. "Who knows? Maybe I'll even go out and find a replacement."

They both knew she didn't mean a single word of it but, nevertheless, it felt good acting like she did, every artificial syllable of it. After all, and in the same vein as the chicken and the egg dilemma, she wondered which came first: the statement or the feeling?

The news rattled what remained of Sophia's foundation. One thing she felt for certain was that she would never have another friend like Kate. Life was no longer like school days when there were endless opportunities to be social and meet new people, not in those same easy, open-minded ways. Besides, Kate was one of a kind and the two of them were as similar as they were different. Their chemistry formed a rare, cohesive connection, a sisterhood Sophia knew wasn't found often.

While she was stunned, Sophia acknowledged she had to have different expectations for friends than for significant others, although she admitted it was difficult at times to see the distinctions. How could they not be treated differently? Sophia always figured that at some point, Kate would be whisked away. Maybe it would not happen physically, and maybe not by a Frenchman named Philippe, but one way or another life would evolve and bring about changes. As she had written in her novel for Dirk to say, "Nothing ever stays the same."

Sophia knew she had a choice to make. She could stay in her apartment and feel sorry for herself, or she could go out and be productive, and perhaps put a new twist on the day that had otherwise begun to bring her down. Lacing up for a run, she chose the twist.

She traveled the path following the West Side Highway, along the way racing several freighters down the Hudson and witnessing the many others who dared to be out on this winter day, including boatloads of tourists at 42nd Street boarding the ferries to circle Manhattan as well as other joggers and bikers exploring the outskirts of the island. She cut in at 23rd Street until she arrived at one of her favorite coffee shops in the city in search of her favorite treats.

"That's one way not to feel guilty about eating cookies," said the young man behind the counter as he filled Sophia's order.

"Exactly," she replied, realizing he was referencing the fact she had been exercising.

"As for me," he added, rubbing his belly, "I'm on a guilt-free diet. I don't feel guilty about anything I eat!"

There was a deliberately loud cackle in the open kitchen beside them. It came from another young male employee who stepped out from behind a glass display to provide further commentary. "You *did not* just say that!" Then he looked at Sophia and said in his sassiest manner about his co-worker, "Looks to me like there's nothing free about that diet. How many waist sizes do you think it cost him?"

Sophia laughed and put her hands in the air to indicate she wanted nothing to do with their banter. Secretly, though, she loved every moment of it. It was like dinner theater: there was food *and* entertainment.

She grabbed the cookies, waved her appreciation to the guys and walked several blocks until she got to subway. By the time she arrived home and the reward of her journey had been devoured, it dawned on her that perhaps she shouldn't be the only one enjoying such a treat today.

"Hello, Downtown Cookie Co.," the man said when she placed the call.

"I'd like two dozen of your yummiest cookies," Sophia told him. "It's a gift. Is it possible to have them delivered today?"

"Of course. But you should know that all of our cookies are equally yummy."

Sophia laughed. "Yes, actually I do know that. Perhaps too well."

Before Sophia hung up, she gave instructions for the card that would accompany the surprise.

Natasha, Jasper & Mary,

Thanks for making my first week a good one and for showing me the ropes. I'm looking forward to working with you.

See you Monday!
Sophia

Sophia then continued writing, finding the afternoon's distraction had cleared her head and helped her gain focus. Before she knew it, night overtook day and the glow from her computer screen was the only light filling her room. It wasn't until the phone rang that Sophia noticed how much time had elapsed.

She looked at the phone and saw it was Natasha calling. *Uh-oh,* she thought, expecting the worst possible scenario.

"This is Sophia," she answered in a professional tone that reminded her of the voice she used at RGB.

"Sophia, this is Natasha. What wonderful little morsels you sent over today!" Her tongue sounded thick and heavy, which made Sophia think it was probably from the weight of alcohol.

"I'm so glad you like them," Sophia told her, hoping the conversation wasn't going to get awkward. A college professor had once called her in such a state. Clearly inebriated, he proceeded to describe his attraction for her. While Sophia didn't exactly have the same concerns with Natasha, she hoped her employer was only calling to confess her desire for the sweets, and that nothing would happen they would both regret the next day.

"Yes, they're delicious. They remind me of the ones my mother used to make," she added, confirming Sophia's suspicion that she had been drinking, the slur so strong Sophia could practically smell the booze through the phone. She wondered how often this was the way Natasha put twists of her own into a day.

"You're very welcome. I order them for my family and have them shipped. I just wanted to tell you how happy I am about the opportunity to work with you. I'm really looking forward to everything."

"That's good, dear," Natasha said, and then gave a long pause. If this were a movie, Sophia told herself, the pause would have been replaced with a hiccup. But then Sophia heard Natasha release a breath and she knew Natasha was smoking.

"Yes, very nice indeed," Natasha added. "And I'm glad you don't hate me because I don't want to write the book."

Sophia also realized it was the first time she had heard Natasha speak without affectation, with contractions—signs there was a regular person in there, no matter how deeply covered by daily theatrics and an occasional intoxication.

"I don't hate you at all," Sophia reassured her. "I told you I support and accept your decision."

"Good. Well, anyway…thanks." And then, as if she had lost interest in the conversation, Natasha abruptly hung up.

Sophia stared at her phone a moment before placing it back on the desk. "I couldn't make this stuff up," she said aloud, and then returned to her real work of fiction.

CHAPTER 17
AN IDEA

Life with Natasha McGavin quickly became routine as Sophia got to know everyone involved in her world, from a long list of service providers which included the accountant, the cleaners, the mailbox store, the stationery store and the tailors, to the many other companies maintaining The Estate, such as the window treatment, carpet and flooring companies. Considering the upheaval in Sophia's life over the past couple of months, this shift to the seemingly mundane was both appreciated and embraced.

Sophia was alone at The Estate sorting through Natasha's mail when she received the call about *The Dreyfus Affair*. It was the first time she had ever spoken to Claire Bulliard.

"Who's this?" the woman demanded of Sophia when she answered the phone.

"Sophia Connors," she replied, holding the phone against her shoulder with the side of her face as she pulled fifteen catalogs out of the stack of mail to put them aside, just as Natasha had requested. At least the mail order companies were clearly aware she was still living *and* spending. "May I ask who's calling?"

"Claire Bulliard. I'm Natasha's agent. And you?"

Sophia recognized the name. If she looked in her notebook, she knew Claire's name would be covered with tangerine orange highlighter, the color given to anyone business-related.

"I'm Natasha's assistant. She's not here this afternoon. May I leave her a message for you?"

"Please do. Tell her to reserve the third week of May. I've got an exciting project for her," Claire said, speaking with the speed of a woman who spent her life working the telephone.

"Great. Are there any specifics you want me to communicate?"

"They want her to record a commentary track for the 40th anniversary DVD release of *The Dreyfus Affair*. And if she says she doesn't want to do it, tell her Vanessa Baxter signed on. And that Joseph will be there to negotiate any squabbles that come up."

Sophia knew from the stories that her mother had told her that Natasha and Vanessa *hated* each other and fought like wild dogs during the production.

"Joseph's the director, right?"

"Yes, darling," Claire confirmed. "And let me do you a favor by telling you to be prepared. When you mention Vanessa, she will likely pitch a fit—a *colossal* fit. Have you ever seen one of those from that lady? She may be tiny, but she's got quite a fight in her when she's inspired. And those pipes…New Jersey can hear her roar!"

Sophia knew she was entering delicate territory. Her job was not to gossip with others. Her job was, as Jonathan had described, to protect Natasha. Not wanting to cross the line, she replied with a simple and noncommittal, "I'll plan accordingly."

"Good, Sophia. I'm telling you, just watch yourself. Armor up, put on your battle gear, and get ready to duck and cover."

"Ok," Sophia said, a little humored, but more concerned. She suddenly could no longer help herself. "So all those rumors are true? They hate each other?"

Claire laughed at her question. "Absolutely, dear. Do you mind me asking how old you are?"

Sophia did mind, but before she could answer, Claire continued, "It may be before your time, but did you ever watch *Dynasty?*"

"Sure. My parents watched it sometimes."

"Well, you know how Joan and Linda used to fight?" she asked, saying the names like she knew the actresses personally and Sophia wondered if she did. "Throwing stuff at each other? Wrestling in the coy pond? Crazy behavior like that?"

"Uh, sure," Sophia said nervously, afraid of where she was going with this.

"Natasha and Vanessa inspired those scenes. They *invented* the catfight. I'm not kidding you when I say that there have been scenes in movies and television written based on the fights those two have had."

"They really hate each other that much?"

"Darling," she clarified. "Hate is such a gentle word."

"Wow."

"Yes, wow!" Claire said, validating Sophia's response, which only made her more cautious. "That's why I'm going to let *you* give her the details. Anyway, I must go now. So nice to talk to you."

"Uh, thanks. You, too," Sophia said, officially frightened.

Sophia decided to stay at The Estate until Natasha returned, having spent a decent part of the afternoon brainstorming how to deliver the news to her boss. Her plan in place, she awaited Natasha, practically jumping her upon arrival despite knowledge of the "thirty-minute rule"—advice given to her and her siblings as children by their mother.

"Give your father thirty minutes to unwind before dropping a bomb on him," Diane had told them. "Do not, whatever you do, meet him at the front door and expect him to solve your problems right then and there. A busy day deserves a few minutes of peace and quiet."

"Is anyone here?" Natasha asked, walking through the front door, announcing herself to her home, which to her knowledge may or may not have still had employees roaming about.

"I am," Sophia said, entering the living room with a hot cup of tea, one lemon, one teaspoon of fresh honey, just like Natasha liked it. "And look what I have for you."

Natasha put her bags down and looked at Sophia's offering. "Well, that is a nice way to come home now, is it not?" The affectation was present in her speech like it had never disappeared, back where she must have thought it belonged.

"Guess what?" Sophia said, having decided that if she acted excited then Natasha might just jump on the bandwagon and get enthusiastic, too. Despite the warnings, she figured it was at least worth a try.

Natasha pushed her way into the kitchen, lips blowing to cool the tea, but keeping her eyes on Sophia. "You seem happy about something, Sophia. What is it?"

"Claire Bulliard called."

"Oh, really? That is a bit of a surprise. I cannot remember the last time she called," Natasha said, working her way towards the refrigerator. She took a few sips at the cup before putting it down. "What did she have to say?"

"She called with some fun news," Sophia continued, digging deep to act as excited as she could. Normally, she would have been naturally charged to explain the reason for the call, but Claire's warning had robbed her of that thrill. Instead, she wanted to get the news out as fast as possible, leaping before she looked, come what may. She felt like she was back in school and had just brought home a bad grade, fearful of her parents' disappointment.

"Yes? What was it? Get to the point, please."

"She said they're making a 40th anniversary DVD edition of *The Dreyfus Affair*—a fantastic film, by the way. Did I tell you I think I've seen it three or four times?" Sophia asked, adding the compliment, which was the truth, to buffer what she expected would happen next. "Joseph wants you to do an audio commentary track for the DVD. Doesn't that sound great?"

Natasha thought about this for a moment, and then a smile came over her face. "Forty years? How is that possible?"

"It's such a great movie," Sophia said, feeling relief might be in order. "And I love DVD commentaries. They really give a whole new experience for film buffs."

Sophia wasn't certain if she had begun rambling but thought she might have been since it was a problem she had when she was nervous. "I wonder if they'll restore the picture and sound quality," she added.

"You know I was nominated for that movie," Natasha said proudly.

"I do. And for several awards, too. You were so good!"

Sophia watched Natasha's expression. She actually seemed excited about the invitation, as Sophia thought she really should be, showing evidence she was interested in the prospect of being involved. *Of course, why wouldn't she?* Sophia asked herself. This movie represented a huge moment in her career. And it was a classic, as Sophia would call it, for which Natasha would continue to tease her. Sophia told herself this wasn't nearly as bad as Claire had made it out to be. *What does she know?*

But then, just as Sophia's guard began to lower, and like lightning had just struck right there in the middle of the kitchen, something changed. Natasha's face fell like a soufflé and her eyes darkened. Sophia literally thought she saw them change color.

"Why are *you* telling me this?" Natasha demanded, closing the refrigerator door like she just lost her appetite, as if deciding this question required her complete attention.

"Why am I not hearing this from *Claire?*" she continued. "If you knew Claire, you would know she would have kept this information all to herself so *she* could selfishly have the privilege of telling me!"

Sophia hadn't expected this turn of events. She should have just played dumb, or simply refused Claire's request, or told Natasha to call Claire back. "Um, well…probably because she was going to be busy later and wanted to give you the good news as quickly as possible?"

"That is just the biggest pile of manure," Natasha charged, and Sophia suddenly wished for the protective gear Claire had described. "Did she also tell you to tell me *that?*"

And why do these things always happen in this kitchen? Sophia asked herself.

"Did she? Did Claire tell you to tell me that?" demanded Natasha.

"No, I made it up. I didn't know what else to say. She didn't really go into specifics."

Natasha opened the refrigerator again and pulled out a bottle of wine. She began opening it but then stopped herself, pointing the corkscrew at Sophia, squinting through her suspicion. "What did she say about that bitch, Vanessa?"

"Nothing?" Sophia said, knowing the accidental question mark betrayed her, and that if she had a tail it would now be curling behind her, retreating between her legs.

Natasha kept prying, "She *did* say Vanessa would be involved in the project, didn't she?"

That was when all remaining reason went out the door, the tipping point, the moment Natasha lost her shit to the fan.

"Oh, God! Of course! That explains it! Why am I cursed? What did I ever do to deserve the likes of Vanessa 'Donkey-Breath' Baxter? Was it not enough I had to spend the better part of the '60s and '70s battling with that ox for movie roles *and* men? Do I really have to contend with her ass-face now as well in my golden years? I will not do it, I tell you! It is not worth it!"

"But Natasha, do it for yourself! You deserve this honor. This was one of your best films. Who cares about…'Ass-Face?'" Sophia said, trying to keep a serious face as she repeated the vile term she couldn't believe came out of Natasha's mouth. This woman was a pistol! "This is about *you!* Don't deny yourself because of her!"

Natasha's shaking hands finally got past the cork and poured a glass almost to the rim. Then she pulled out a second glass, filled it and pushed it towards Sophia without asking if she even wanted one. "Do you know that bitch told a critic from *The Los Angeles Times* that I slept with one of the producers to get that role? And the truth was *she* was the one who slept with Jonah Smith, the producer. *She* did it!"

Natasha gulped at her glass and shook her head. It made Sophia's nerves brew.

Natasha continued, "She actually campaigned *against* me from winning. Uh-huh. Yes, she did! When I was nominated, she actually told the press she thought the ballots had been counted wrong. Can you believe that?"

"Well, it just makes her look bad, not you. And she's obviously just jealous. Why else would she do such things?"

Natasha finished her glass and poured herself another. "Because she is evil. Pure evil."

Sophia silently considered that word evil." It was a good word, and it reminded her of her character, Dirk, and she wondered if he was anything like Vanessa Baxter. She wanted to console Natasha, but it was difficult to know what to tell her. How did one go about giving tenderness to a porcupine in the midst of defense mode?

"Oh, God!" Natasha said, starting up again. "And look at me! What am I going to do? I look like a heifer ready for slaughter. Why did you give me those cookies? Are you trying to completely destroy my figure?"

Sophia was about to grab her glass of wine when Natasha took it for herself. Now double-fisted, Natasha brought the day to a close. "You can go home now. I need to be alone."

"Are you going to be ok?"

"Yeah, I'm fine—all five hundred pounds of me. Just splendid."

"I don't believe you."

Natasha spewed a laugh of disgust and questionable sanity. "I can't imagine why you'd ever think *that?*" Her insincerity and self-contempt were obvious, but the presence of contractions gave away that her exposed vulnerabilities were bringing out her wild streak.

Despite multiple rejected offers to stay and keep Natasha company, Sophia headed for home, stopping by the video store on her way to find an old copy of *The Dreyfus Affair* to rent for the night. She also picked up a bottle of wine, craving a glass after having a bottle dangled in front of her by her employer. She was exhausted, not only from a long day that included hand-holding during Natasha's emotional unraveling, but from her demanding work and writing schedule. It seemed there was never a shortage of work, that no matter how much she accomplished, there was still so much to do. But the fight would have to wait another day. She decided she deserved one night off.

After nuking a bag of popcorn and enjoying a few sips—not gulps like Natasha—of her buttery chardonnay, Sophia put in the movie. As she did so, she glanced at the VCR that gathered dust on her entertainment stand. She realized that Natasha was a lot like that once popular technology, that she too had been the desire of everyone once upon a time. But time had moved on, and with it came newer models, different developments, and a lot of wear-and-tear. It had to be difficult on her, to have been placed upon a pedestal at one point, but to no longer command that attention, or, deep down, even feel worthy of it. It could not be easy to go from pinned up to covered up, to look in the mirror and not recognize the face or body staring back. It begged the question, like Sophia's relationship with Kevin, a question that was applicable regardless of topic: was it better to have loved and lost or not to have loved at all?

The Dreyfus Affair was noire melodrama at its best, from the opening scene when Sally Burgess, played by Natasha, walks up the police station steps into the building and confesses, "I did it. I'm guilty…" until the end when the officer tells her, "The only thing you're guilty of, young lady, is loving the wrong man."

Natasha, so young and petite then, was superb as the ingénue at the wrong place at the wrong time, who gets taken advantage of by Burt Packard, played by the now-deceased Kurt Smith. Burt is a complicated man with a questionable past that catches up to him as he starts to have real feelings for Sally. The past, as represented and dredged up by no-good Florence Swift—played, of course, by Vanessa Baxter—crashes down on Burt despite the best efforts of Sally, his only way out, who insists love will save him. What poor Sally doesn't realize, however, is that all the love in the world would not stifle Florence Swift, a desperate woman who would stop at nothing to get her man back, *her* only way out.

Art imitating life? Sophia considered, holding her pillow tight against her chest, wondering what Natasha would say about the men in her past as she watched Sally on screen being escorted out of the police station at the end, just as they dragged in handcuffed Florence, the villain, who wasn't really dead after all. Was *Vanessa* really *that* evil?

One thing for certain was that Natasha's performance was flawless. Her emotional range was generous but precise and controlled, and she portrayed the character's heartbreak in a powerful, gut-wrenching way. She was not the same person she was at the beginning of the story, not when she arrived at the police station, but when the flashback began, when the story *really* began, before she first met Burt. She had gone on a journey, the type of character development and depth of story Sophia sought to unfold in her own work, through Dirk and Anna, over the course of their lives. Natasha was nothing short of brilliant.

Forty years? Sophia remembered Natasha saying, which made her curious.

She shut off the machine and went online to see what she could find out about the film, coming across countless sites dedicated to the film as well as to Natasha. She knew Natasha had a following, which she had discovered before starting her first day, but seeing it impressed her all over again, as if she had never known what influence Natasha had had on so many.

How could she not know about all of this? Wouldn't she be thrilled to know so many fans cherish her, that they consider her a significant contributor to cinematic history? How could Jonathan and the others not want to share this with her? What reason could possibly be great enough to prevent them from doing so?

As Sophia scanned the sites and reviewed many interesting bits of trivia—some about the movie, some about Natasha (including numerous false allegations still out there claiming she was dead)—she learned that Natasha's birthday (if, according to some, she were still alive) was only a few weeks away. It gave her an idea, one that certainly could, and probably would, backfire on her. But as Nonna used to say, "If you're unhappy and you don't try, you only have yourself to blame."

CHAPTER 18
IF THE SHOES FIT

Timing was on Sophia's side the next day. The first part of her good fortune came when Charles took Natasha to see Jonathan about a legal matter and she was asked to stay at The Estate to continue organizing files in the library, or The Bat Cave, as she called it because of its many file cabinets hidden behind facades of bookshelves filled with real and fake books. Sophia felt she had only begun to scratch the surface in terms of learning about Natasha as well as her home, and was confident there was more to the woman on all levels. This place, for instance, started to remind her of The Winchester Mystery House, the famous home in Northern California where the owner—wealthy, widowed Winchester Rifle heiress Sarah Winchester—built endlessly onto her home, adding countless hidden rooms, doors and stairs that went nowhere. The story, as Sophia understood it, was that Winchester was cursed by a Native American woman who said the Winchester Rifle destroyed her tribe, and that the only way to prevent the curse was by continuously building onto her home until she died. Sophia and Twain were obsessed with the story as kids, nagging their parents until they finally gave in and brought them to see it in person.

The second stroke of luck was that Alice was also working at Natasha's today and was in the midst of battling the laundry—a task that surprisingly always gave the impression they worked for a family of six, not just an older single woman. At the risk of setting faulty expectations for the future, Sophia stopped by the laundry room and asked, "Want me to grab a handful and bring them upstairs?"

Alice's face lit up. "Yes, please. You're so sweet for asking. That last girl would never have been so helpful. I tell you, I did not like her at all."

Sophia nodded her head. "I'm starting to hear that a lot," she said, grabbing a basket of freshly folded clothes and towels.

"If you could just drop them in Natasha's room, maybe by the bed, I'll put them away," Alice told her. "Thank you so much!"

Sophia climbed the rounded staircase to the second floor where Natasha's entertaining space began to merge with her personal living quarters. The Estate unfolded as you explored it, much like Natasha. Presented first was what she wanted the outside world to perceive was the real her: formal, pristine and classically tasteful. The first floor was for entertaining people Natasha did not know especially well, at least not in an intimate or familiar kind of way. It was inviting but it kept them at a comfortable distance. In Sophia's limited experience, this included most everyone. The highest floor on the other hand, the 5th floor attic, was Natasha at her most intimate, for that was where she stored her keepsakes—historical and telling evidence of the memories she wanted to hold onto and remember best about the years that had come and gone. Sophia had yet to see this part of Natasha. Based on what Jasper said, she doubted she ever would.

At the landing on the second floor, she crossed over, past the hallway to guest bedrooms, and alongside the private screening room (which she had previously counted could hold twenty comfortably and offered a screen to put some art house movie theatres to shame). Then she passed in front of the second floor "mini" kitchen (a resource still larger than her own kitchen, and one Natasha used for houseguests or entertaining in the screening room, which Sophia had not yet witnessed). She then continued upwards to the third floor, which began the master living quarters.

Natasha's real personal living area, all two floors of it, was nothing less than spectacular. While the main stairwell she had just climbed escalated to the top floor and roof access, the third and fourth floors met on part of the floor in a high ceiling, open air atrium area that reminded Sophia of some of the most beautiful suburban homes she had ever seen. Turning away from the main stairs, she made her way to another staircase inside the great room and followed it as it rose above a large, open lounge-like area with a big U-shaped sectional, a 60-inch flat screen television, and yet another kitchen—this one Natasha's personal, easy-access kitchen (also much larger than Sophia's).

According to the story Jasper told Sophia—as Natasha had told it to him—when she completely renovated her home in the late '80's she refused to install an elevator, saying that if she heard the chime or movement of an elevator in her home in the middle of the night, it would have thrown her into cardiac arrest. She told him she had never been afraid of living alone in a large home, but that an elevator just might make it feel like *The Shining* and that would not do.

Natasha had also told Jasper that all of the stairs would keep her in good shape—a point he wasn't sure was accurate— and if, or when, the time came she was no longer able to climb them, she would hire a "strapping young man."

"He'll just pick me up and carry me around," she had explained with a wink during one drunken, sharing moment, of which apparently she and Jasper had had a few over the years.

Sophia had learned the two were fairly close, or as close perhaps as Natasha let anyone get.

"*And* to look at," Natasha had added as a reason for hiring a "house stud." "Like a statue. Women pay men to do more controversial things, do they not? I'm sure I wouldn't be the first."

That Natasha is a handcrafted, one-of-a-kind, they-broke-the-mold POW, Sophia chuckled, recalling the story as she finished climbing the stairs leading to Natasha's master bedroom. At last, Sophia had made it to her destination, the place she wanted to go for reasons other than helping Alice with the laundry.

She entered the bedroom and moved with the silent quickness of a stealth bomber, dropping the basket of clothes by the foot of the bed, and then heading for Natasha's multiple closets (the master suite was so large that her closets had closets of their own). Not certain where she would find what she needed, Sophia prayed silently, *Please don't let Natasha or Alice walk in on me right now.*

Sophia ventured through two rooms before finding what she needed. Having completed her mission, she retraced her steps back to the library to continue her project in the Bat Cave. She knew she had accomplished the first part of her mission but that she was far from being out of danger.

Lunchtime arrived before Natasha returned, so Sophia decided to take an actual break to run her errand. After informing Jasper and Alice of her brief departure, she ran out, traveling with efficiency to and through the store she needed to visit.

Sophia could feel the nervousness start to get her. Maybe she was doing the wrong thing? She could still afford to just get by. Did she need to risk everything, to go out on a limb and chance destroying Natasha's confidence in her, and perhaps lose her job as well?

It was too late now. She had made up her mind and committed to seeing this through, hell or high water.

Upon returning to The Estate, she learned Natasha was still not back.

"Ok, good," she stuttered, telling Jasper. "I'll be in the library."

"Don't you mean the Bat Cave?" Jasper asked, noticing she missed her cue.

Sophia looked at Jasper, the weight of her recent actions still literally in her hands. She thought she felt the pressure of a suspicious look from Jasper, as if he could read on her face she was up to something.

"Yep, Bat Cave," she said, beginning to exit. "That's what I meant to say."

Jasper had to know something was going on with her. Despite a minor age difference, the two had begun to grow close. She could now recognize when something was nagging at him, so why wouldn't he be able to do the same?

"Ok," was all he said in return, peering at her with the beady eyes of a laboratory rat that knows the scientist has something more than a lump of cheese up his sleeve.

"When you see Natasha, will you ask her to come see me? I need to talk to her about something."

"Sure. Is everything alright?" he pressed.

"We'll see. Ask me after I talk to Natasha," she offered.

"Uh-oh. I don't like the sound of that."

Natasha walked through the double door entrance of the library an hour later, greeting Sophia whose arms were filled with a stack of old files she was preparing to shred. "You wanted to see me?" she asked.

"Oh, hi," Sophia said, thinking, *here we go!* "I do. Thanks for coming and finding me."

Natasha glanced around the room. "It looks like you made some good progress today."

"Yeah, I think we're getting there. I'll fire up the shredder later this afternoon," she added, considering, *that is if you don't fire me in about five minutes.* "That ought to make a good deal more room for you for the next couple of years.

"Great. Is that what you wanted to see me about?"

"No, it's not. There's something else," Sophia said as she put her pile of papers down by the industrial-sized shredder and then walked over to one of the desks.

From a bag hidden underneath the desk, she pulled out a wrapped box, a card taped on top. "This is for you," she told Natasha, crossing the room back to her. *Please don't hate me.*

"What is this?" Natasha asked, looking at it as if it might be ticking inside.

"It's an early birthday present," Sophia said. "Open it."

Natasha face began glowing with curiosity. "You *are* full of surprises, are you not?"

Sophia didn't reply. She just smiled, hoping Natasha would accept the gift with the goodwill she intended.

Natasha sat down in one of the antique desk chairs and began to open the card. "Good Lord, my birthday. Do we need to acknowledge that?"

Sophia wanted to tell Natasha she felt the same way about her recent birthday but stopped herself. For a variety of reasons, it hardly seem appropriate or even equitable, no matter how displeased Sophia had been with the arrival of her own birthday and some of life's recent circumstances. Their two places in life, in all areas personally and professionally—as far as Sophia could tell anyway—were not comparable. What drove the birthday dread for each of them was different, she assumed with confidence, although they likely shared one commonality—that overbearing sense of discontent stemming from the fear that the hands of the clock were moving uncontrollably too fast.

Sophia could try to share her sympathies with Natasha, but for what reason? They were two very different women experiencing very dissimilar lives. Financially, Sophia got by, basically living paycheck to paycheck, while Natasha was fortunate enough, according to Jonathan and everything Sophia had seen so far, to not need to work at all, ever again.

In the love-life category, Sophia's last relationship had come to an abrupt and disappointing end, but was nonetheless a significant, and recent, relationship that had held much promise. There had been no indication of the last time Natasha had had such a relationship, when a man was in her life. It made Sophia sad for her. When was the last time she was told she was loved, or desired, or both?

No matter how much getting older agitated Sophia, Natasha was more than twice her age and was likely feeling twice the pressure from that ticking clock. And the bottom line, Sophia decided, was that Natasha was her employer. Regardless of her best intentions, giving her this gift might be perceived as presumptuous, even offensive. Knowing Natasha's reactions in the past, it perhaps might be seen as an act of aggression, crossing over the line from thoughtful to insolent. It was a bold decision that just might get her fired.

Natasha opened the card and read it aloud. "A gift for a special woman. I wish you all the best on your birthday and throughout the year. Sincerely, Sophia."

"I hope you like them," Sophia said, praying her idea didn't blow up in her face.

Natasha unwrapped the present. As she removed the paper and looked at the world famous logo on the lid of the box, she asked, "The present is inside?" What Sophia knew she really meant was, "This could not be my present. You must have put my present in this box you had lying around."

She removed the lid. "Oh. Look at those. Running shoes?" she asked, evidently more than a little confused. "That is so interesting."

"Here's the thing," Sophia began to explain, making her pitch. "I have an idea, if you would be so kind as to hear me out."

Sophia stopped to take the mental temperature of Natasha, reviewing the evidence before her. Natasha's head hadn't exploded, nor had she grabbed a fistful of black Mont Blanc pens from the desk to stab into Sophia's chest. She seemed visibly stable, ready for Sophia to elaborate. The temperature appeared to be hovering within a healthy range.

So she continued. "The weather's getting nicer now that spring is around the corner, and you said you'd like to get in a little better shape for your voiceover session with 'that awful Donkey-Face,'" Sophia began, hiding behind Natasha's enemy for protection. She knew full well that the best way to make her point was by mentioning Vanessa's name. Natasha's eyes became squinty and focused again.

"I called her '*Ass*-Face,'" she clarified. "She has donkey *breath*."

"Oh, ok," Sophia said, acknowledging the error. "I stand

corrected. In any case, I was thinking we could take advantage of the park and go for some nice walks. It's a lovely park, and if we schedule a short walk every day, we'll both get some good exercise. I know I wouldn't mind walking off some of the damage I've done to myself this winter being locked inside all the time. And it'll make us feel good, too."

Natasha's eyes returned to their normal, non-horrific appearance, as if she regained awareness of some important fact or consideration. Whatever the reason for her reaction, it seemed more important than Sophia's explanation for the gift choice, and Natasha offered a calm expression that hinted she wasn't insulted by the gesture and that she too might have thought it a good idea, or at least one worthy of discussion. Sophia found this to be a huge relief after having replayed this in her head a thousand times these past several hours. The scenario that had stuck with her the most was the worst case, in which Natasha screamed, without contractions, "You think I am fat! I hate you as much as I hate Vanessa 'I-sleep-with-producers-to-get-jobs' Baxter! You are fired! Get out of my house! Get out of my life!"

Natasha stared at the shoes, and Sophia saw firsthand that the anger she had shown for Vanessa had turned into something else. Sophia even thought she witnessed a tear in the corner of her eye. "What's wrong?" she asked.

"No one ever buys me presents," Natasha admitted, confirming she was getting a little emotional.

This stunned Sophia. "No one, really? How's that possible? Someone *has* to give you birthday or holiday gifts. You know so many people!"

"I get them, but they're from work acquaintances. I mean, I don't want to sound ungrateful, but it's not exactly the same. Those feel, for lack of a better description, obligatory," Natasha said.

"This is thoughtful and personal," she added. "And completely unexpected. Thank you so much."

"You're very welcome!" Sophia said, having noticed that Natasha's guard lowered enough to allow both emotion and contractions to come through. "Try them on to see if I got the fit right."

Natasha did just that. "They fit perfectly. How'd you manage that?"

Sophia shrugged, thinking, *I'll never tell.* After all, what would Natasha think if she knew Sophia had checked out her shoe closet to find her size? "I guess I just got lucky."

Then Natasha did the unthinkable, something that in all of Sophia's scenarios she had never done. She stood up, came around the desk and hugged Sophia. In the five long seconds she held on, Sophia really started to understand that this was a woman in an ivory tower, sheltered and protected, easily provided with everything she needed to survive but missing so much that made surviving worth it.

"When do we get started?" Natasha asked.

"How about tomorrow?"

"Terrific," she said, and Sophia knew that, at that moment, she meant it completely.

Sophia went home at the end of the day relieved as well as pleased with herself, knowing it was quite an accomplishment to get an affectionate embrace from the woman who inspired the infamous television hair pull. Excited and motivated, she used the rest of her hours to complete another chapter, thus officially beginning the next part of her novel.

It did not go unnoticed that once again there were parallels between her life and the lives of her characters. One of her strongest connections at the moment was with Dirk, who hungered for new beginnings and whose life had begun to find new possibilities, although discovered and created through very different means. Dirk's life, especially in these later chapters as he worked his way from May Valley to New York City, was driven by greed, his appetite only growing stronger and more insatiable. He was becoming even more dangerous as well, and everywhere he went deliberate and circumstantial destruction followed.

While Dirk made progress though, others touched by his life were forced to make compromises. And as he made a new life for himself, a pregnant Anna was forced to pursue drastic measures in order to keep her child safe from harm—from Dirk and what he was becoming, and from the others Father McKenzie had warned her about. She would heed the warnings and deliver the child where the priest said he would be safe. After months of hiding her pregnancy in a small Arizona town along the interstate, she would bring the newborn into the arms of safety, convinced she would never see him again. It was the greatest sacrifice she could ever make, but it was the right one. She also knew it was what Sir Gawain would have done.

Sophia would soon discover that there were also similarities between Natasha and Anna, that the actress also struggled with something beyond her control, something that threatened her and changed the course of her life.

Part Two
CHAPTER ONE
April 1969

Solitude defined the night as tall wicker walls and a ratted dark green blanket provided the only protection for the sleeping newborn from the brisk scratches of an aggressive April wind. Evening introduced itself to the dawn while the damp Northern California air picked at the infant lying within the reach of its limbs, substituting the tearful whispers of the voice long gone with an angry chill. Although the child sensed the rocking had stopped some time ago, he remained silent and still, the nagging wind blowing its final winter breaths through town and into his abandoned basket. Spring had yet to be seen in Rogerstown, leaving winter on duty like a lioness with her young, protective and dangerous, fearful she would not be able to stand watch forever. The frost of the cement doorstep began to seep through the floor of the woven basket, but the child's bold slumber continued, despite the cold and desperate threats.

St. Teresa's Home for Orphaned Children had long been the residence for such cases, older and newborn alike, abandoned on these steps, or inside the warmer but no less intimidating rooms in which relatives or guardians handed over the lives of their offspring to the care of the nuns. Children from every walk of life found refuge here, each with unique circumstances, but all with a similar dilemma—those who had brought them into the world were unable, for one reason or another, to keep them. The sisters accepted them under their wings and into their order, raising them with religious and intellectual standards, offering a societal and spiritual safety net.

Rogerstown was a place of unfulfilled promise, a village that grew from dust in a matter of years. There had been a time when the block of buildings housing St. Teresa's was the only set of side-by-side structures in the area, lined up, pretending to be like those in a big city. Nestled against one another, holding each other up, it was all there was in the small downtown area. After World War II, the small village grew quickly into a small city until hard times forced the growing to stop almost as quickly as it began, recession corroding much of its hard-earned progress. Despite all of the prosperity and decline, St. Teresa's remained, and because of all of the economic and social challenges, the children continued arriving there.

The darkness of the early morning hours swallowed St. Teresa's like shadow filling the hollow of a mineshaft. Inside, throughout the halls of the enormous three-story building, the youthful inhabitants and their sisterly sponsors slept in unison with the mechanical breathing of the large antique grandfather clock.

It had been another Tuesday night, and just as she had since arriving at the orphanage, Sister Margaret sat in the chair by the stairway on the second floor until eleven-thirty, working the night shift. Close to the children's dormitories, she had monitored the progressive retirements of the boys and girls in the sequence of their respective bedtimes. By eleven-forty, long after the oldest of the children were asleep, she herself had retired to the downstairs bedroom she shared with Sister Alexis. She was in her single bed, her final prayers said, and well on her way into a deep slumber before much of Wednesday had registered on the clock.

Night watch had been Sister Margaret's idea, thinking it best one of the sisters stayed up late to ensure the day ended smoothly with a closely watched send-off to sleep for the children. Out of the dozen-and-a-half adult members of St. Teresa's staff, only three were excluded from the late shift responsibilities—Mother Beverly (who everyone agreed had plenty of other obligations requiring her experience and attention), Sister Rachel (who at sixty-five was under orders from Dr. Wells to get extra sleep and care), and Nicole McMaster (the hired cook, and one of only two non-clergy employees).

Mother Beverly, extremely suspicious of the world outside the tall and very thick, wooden orphanage doors, immediately agreed to the suggestion, saying at the time of putting the procedure into action that she wanted to make sure she and the sisters did everything they could to prevent problems at St. Teresa's. It was typical of the Mother Superior to preach brimstone and fire and the coming of judgment. While she toned it down in front of the younger children, her words often managed to frighten the older children as well as a number of the nuns themselves. "There are terrible evils out in the world," she said regularly. "The Lord is not the only one who works in mysterious ways."

Sister Margaret, although not comfortable with the Mother Superior's particular way, chose to think of Mother Beverly as having a softer, more nurturing side than what she always showed, but that it was one she managed to hide quite well.

The two of them certainly had their share of differences. To start with, Sister Margaret said the children were sent to them as blessings—for both the children and the sisters—that they could provide for them in ways their birth parents could not. Mother Beverly, on the other hand, said the children came to St. Teresa's for reasons that only God could understand, and that they, the nuns, were there to support his will. "Tomato, tomahto," Sister Margaret figured, thinking they were ultimately saying the same thing, just saying it in their own unique ways.

Mother Beverly required the night watchers to maintain a journal detailing any activity while on duty, even though there had not been one late-night wanderer inside St. Teresa's demanding commentary beyond a few words. Sister Margaret therefore wrote in the usual descriptions—a certain boy or girl was up to use the bathroom, there was the occasional need for a glass of water, and she gave a hug or two to a sleepless child. The journals kept Mother Beverly current on all activities so she could keep tabs on the children—who got up in the middle of the night, who was sick, and any other general concerns that might need resolution or monitoring. Mother Beverly had a journal for all orphanage duties, from Sister Katherine's afternoon religion classes to Sam Johnson's miscellaneous handyman duties (she believed Sam might observe misbehaving and signs of acting out, things the sisters might overlook that might need discipline). The Mother Superior ran a tight ship.

Even though Sister Margaret forced herself to stay awake every Tuesday night (occasionally nodding off for which she knew Mother Beverly would be extremely angry, that was if she had written that part in the journal), she enjoyed watching over the children like she was St. Teresa herself. The Saint's spirit of sanctity had always inspired Sister Margaret, and it was her hope that she could provide the children with just an ounce of the same loving and blessing. She had been drawn to the orphanage through a vision she had had years before that forever changed the course of her life. She knew that what she saw that day as a teenager in her dreamlike state was her calling. Purpose had brought her there.

As the minute hand of the old clock beside Sister Margaret's bed reached forward and grabbed onto the next number, the house telephone rang rudely into the darkened room, breaking through the warm envelope of Sister Margaret's sleep. It was now one-sixteen, and the rolling, thunderous rhythm of the ring shook her with a terrible jolt. When the second ring came, Sister Alexis stirred awake, asking drowsily, "Do you want me to get it, Margaret?"

"No, thank you," Sister Margaret responded, moving her body up from under the white cotton sheet. "Go back to bed, Alexis. I'll let you know if I need you."

It was unusual for the orphanage to receive calls at this hour but the phone resided in their room for just such an occurrence. Two years ago, they had received a series of calls from a young man asking to speak with "the penguins." Sister Alexis answered by telling the boy he had called an orphanage, not a zoo. The calls continued over a number of nights, the youngster requesting each time to speak with "the penguins," saying that any of the penguins would do. Days later, after he had stopped calling, it dawned on Sister Alexis how unusual it was the boy would call in the middle of the night to speak to penguins, who really couldn't speak anyway because they were, after all, penguins. The other nuns, enjoying a moment of rest from the children as Alexis shared the story, broke into laughter, explaining to Sister Alexis the young man was doing what kids called "crank calling." Suddenly understanding, she began laughing, too. She announced to Sister Margaret, becoming red in the face, "Isn't that cute? Penguins! I'm a penguin!"

Sister Margaret reached over to the nightstand and turned on the light. Then she picked up the phone and said, "Hello? St. Teresa's," hoping the tone in her voice was more inviting than tired. She heard muffled sounds through the receiver, and then silence.

"Hello?" she repeated. "Are you there?"

There were several more moments of silence before sobs broke through and poured out of the receiver, sounds that made Sister Margaret's heart tremble. Mother Beverly had always accused her of being "overly sensitive" and "too involved."

"We would lose all control of this orphanage if I wasn't here watching you," the Mother Superior once reprimanded her when she had asked to invite a group of unfortunate, out-of-work men to dinner. "The children and God are our priorities here. If you want to do something for the homeless, then organize a food drive within the community. But it had better not get in the way of your commitments to St. Teresa's."

It was also this empathy that made Mother Beverly appreciate her so much, although she would never admit as much to Sister Margaret.

The voice on the phone finally spoke to her. "I'm sorry," she said.

Relieved by the response, Sister Margaret asked softly, "What are you sorry about, sweetheart?"

She listened patiently as more silence and sobs danced together in her ear. She waited for more than a minute before the girl could pull herself together enough to say another word. "I left my baby on your doorstep," the voice continued. "Please believe me, it's for the best! I'm not a terrible person. I don't want to do this, but I have no choice!"

"Are you sure this is what you want to do, dear?" Sister Margaret asked.

The girl answered, "I have no other choice."

Sister Margaret was now wide awake, realizing this was not the time to counsel the girl. Having no idea how long the child had been outside, and suddenly concerned about its well-being, she said to the distressed girl, "I'll tell you what I'm going to do. I need to hang up with you in a moment so I can bring the child inside. Will you please call me later to discuss this?"

The tears escaped, free again, like water from a broken dam. "I'm sure of what I have to do! Just promise me you'll take care of him. Please! He's very special."

"I'm sure he's very special. And yes, we will. But I want you to call me back in the morning so we can talk about this. You have many options. Okay? Please?"

But the voice would not acknowledge the request again. Instead she said, "I need you to do me a favor. Please name my son, Gawain. It's a...family name. It's the only thing I can give him."

"I'll see what I can do," Sister Margaret told her, certain the young girl would not call again and knowing she would not be able to satisfy the

girl's request. She had lost count of how many times she had seen all of this before.

"Please," the girl cried, "It's all I have. And then maybe one day he will know how much I love him."

The sound of her grief was replaced by the cry of an abandoned telephone line, and Sister Margaret returned the telephone to its cradle.

She then rushed to the small wooden cabinet on the other side of the room to grab her robe, and leaned down to speak softly to Sister Alexis, "Dear, I'll be needing your help after all. Please meet me in the infirmary."

"Yes, Margaret," Alexis replied, getting up as Sister Margaret left the room.

Sister Margaret walked down the darkened first floor residence hall toward the light illuminating the building's foyer, the glow from the end of the hallway making her feel like a mouse moving toward the entrance of its mouse hole. On her way, she passed each of the rooms housing the sleeping nuns, certain no one else was awake. When she reached the front room, her hand searched the wall to find the light switch, flipping it to completely brighten the room. She then moved toward the front door and unlatched the variety of locks Mother Beverly had insisted they have installed.

She opened one of the grand doors and, for a moment, briefly exposed St. Teresa's to the outside world. "Keep the doors closed and always locked," Mother Beverly regularly warned. Even half asleep, Sister Margaret could hear Mother Superior's warnings about sin and the modern world.

Sister Margaret looked out onto the front step and saw what she expected to find laying quietly on the stoop. There was the infant just as the caller had stated. She quickly leaned down and picked up the basket, impressed with the lightness of its weight. Morning dew from the wicker wetted her hands, and she held tight to the basket as she brought the baby inside. "There, there," she said. "We'll warm you up in no time."

Back inside, Sister Margaret placed the basket on the floor and closed the door shut, locking away the night again. In the four years Sister Margaret had been at St. Teresa's, she had seen eleven children delivered into the arms of the orphanage, six babies adopted, and four leave because they had reached the age when they were old enough to venture out on their own. "We can't take care of them forever," Mother Beverly would say.

But there was the occasional exception. Sam Johnson, who was now the handyman, had arrived at the orphanage when he was four years old. But unlike most of the children who had been raised by the sisters, he chose not to travel very far, determined to take care of them as they had him. His presence was welcomed, even by Mother Beverly, bringing a sense of security and family to the sisters. He reminded Sister Margaret much of her own brother and had come to view him as such, as one of them, just as the other sisters who had been with St. Teresa's for much longer.

Sister Margaret picked up the basket again and walked the infant quickly into the infirmary, surprised to find Sister Alexis waiting with Mother Beverly by her side. "Mother Beverly, what gets you up at such an hour?" she asked.

"I heard the telephone ring, Sister Margaret," Mother Beverly said, her usual sternness fully awake at this hour, proving once again you couldn't get anything past her. "I wanted to make sure everything was alright."

Sister Margaret gently laid the baby's basket on the examining table. "Well, look at you!" she said, smiling at the infant, only able to see his barely-open eyes through the blanket.

She delicately pulled the layers to the side as if unwrapping a present she knew would break if she weren't careful. Then she gently picked him up and pulled him to her chest to warm him. "A newborn," she said, looking back at Mother Beverly and Sister Alexis, relieved to discover his small body was still warm.

While Sister Margaret held him, Sister Alexis laid out a fresh towel for her, and she slowly placed the child on his back to do a general examination. He was so small and fragile, his tiny fingers and toes reaching out for her the way they did.

"He seems okay," Sister Margaret said, feeling more relieved after checking over his whole body.

"Good," Mother Beverly returned. "Please call Dr. Wells in the morning and have him come here tomorrow. Never can be sure. We need to make sure this child is healthy. Only the Lord knows what he's been through!"

Sister Margaret pulled the new towel up across the bottom half of his body, and then layered the sides across his chest. She picked him back up and held him in her arms again, rocking him lovingly. "Yes, little man. What have you seen in your short, little life?"

CHAPTER 19
WHERE THERE'S A WILL

Kicking off their walking regiment proved to be more of a challenge than Sophia had originally expected and, to her dismay, more than Natasha had led her to believe. So much of life with Natasha was like that—hindsight would provide a much different perspective on matters—a fact that Sophia should have expected by now, all things considered, yet somehow always managed to forget because she continually gave her employer the benefit of the doubt. If there was something Sophia thought would be difficult or would meet with resistance from Natasha, then it ended up being simple and smooth. And those things she considered to be straightforward somehow always managed to be problematic and unnecessarily complicated. Natasha's emotional wiring was exactly like the fuse box in her apartment—not all of the connections and responses made sense.

Natasha had a definite look of disgust on her face when she said to Sophia, "You want to go *now?*" on the morning of their designated start date.

Sophia had indeed expected some resistance, but she thought that it would occur a few days into the new program, when the soreness and fatigue from working muscles long forgotten stood up and cursed obscenities at Natasha. Sophia figured they were at least entitled to the New Year gym honeymoon period: that initial stage every January when people's resolutions to get into shape actually motivated them to show up and get some work done before frustration, boredom or defeat settled in.

"It is barely ten in the morning," Natasha continued, sipping at her fully loaded latte, which Sophia didn't have the heart at the moment to tell her was a wasted use of what should be her daily allotment of calories. That was a whole other topic she had planned on addressing eventually, but today was not that day. All of this was part of the "CD" program Natasha did not know Sophia had started rolling out—cardio and diet—the two key elements to getting in shape.

"Now's the best time for us to get out there and get started," Sophia said, making this up as she went along, trying to sound motivational and knowing she had to tread lightly. She still didn't know Natasha well enough to know what buttons to push or not push, and she wanted this to play out positively. She wanted Natasha to get results that would make her happy, to feel more comfortable with her body, and perhaps even give her a new lease on life. That was what she had discovered from exercise, and what she wanted to share with Natasha. Exercise had been her salvation for many years, during many situations, and it could work its magic on Natasha as well.

But Sophia had her work cut out for her so she deemed it best to take it slowly, enlisting her one-step-at-a-time strategy, which included the decision to not yet dare mention the changes Natasha should make in her diet, like avoiding those favorite yet detrimental objects of her affection such as fatty coffee drinks, alcohol and cigarettes.

"Here's the thing," she continued, "Exercise is best if you do it bright and early. First, you have energy because you just got up. Second, because you did just wake up, you may still be partially asleep. I find it's easier to get yourself to do something if you can't think too much about it or talk yourself out of it."

"I am not so sure about that," Natasha said, getting up

from her chair. "I am quite the powerful motivational speaker."

Sophia could see that was the truth. Natasha seemed to get most everything she wanted, and whatever little convincing she did do in her life came with rewarding results.

"I really mean it," Sophia stated, feeling as if she was presenting a case in a court of law. "I get some of my best work done, writing *and* exercise, when I'm half asleep."

"Hmmm," Natasha said, not buying what Sophia was selling. "And I get some of my best work done after a cocktail or two."

Sophia sidestepped the comment even though she knew plenty of people who tapped into their talents after a little drinking. But this was not an activity requiring creativity other than what was necessary to get Natasha moving. "And, reason number three," she continued her attempt at persuasion, "now is a great time in the city. All the commuters are at work, lunchtime is still a couple hours away, and the park is nice and abandoned."

"Good Lord," Natasha complained, now in motion, placing her empty cup on the counter in the kitchen and moving away. "What have I agreed to?"

Sophia wasn't sure where she was going. She was either walking away or was actually giving in and going to obey Sophia's request. She decided it was best to keep up her offensive play. "I'd like for you to think of me as your trainer for one hour every day."

"One hour? I thought it would take half an hour max! And every day?"

"If we want real results, we need to make it happen. The only way to do that is to tackle it every day. We need to get our bodies moving. It doesn't have to be high impact. It just has to be consistent, quality motion. I'm telling you that we can achieve great things just by walking and by doing it regularly."

Sophia thought she was losing Natasha because she began climbing the stairs to her bedroom, until she said, "'Just walking,' she says. Fine. I will change my clothes."

"Great! Just think…we have more than two whole months until we see Vanessa and make her suffer because you look so good!" Sophia said, deciding last minute to throw in Vanessa's name to show Natasha she was making the right decision, and to help her seal the deal. It was also the move she would make, she had decided—the card she would keep in her back pocket—if Natasha ever gave her too hard a time.

"Bitch," Natasha said loudly. The comment concerned Sophia because she wasn't sure if she was talking about Vanessa, or if she was talking about her for using such a transparent strategy to get her moving.

"You'll love it!" Sophia added. "I promise."

"That is what my ex-husband used to tell me," Natasha said before disappearing around the corner, "and boy was he ever wrong."

It was a good thing Sophia was such a fast learner, because with every day she and Natasha walked, she developed different techniques to combat her employer's impulse to cancel on her which, for the first month, proved both helpful *and* necessary.

She also learned a lot about Natasha during those first few weeks through the topics they discussed, many of which arose from random situations or conversations, as well as through the excuses she came up with to justify not wanting to walk. But, despite all of the reasons Natasha presented and Sophia never accepted (and there were many), the younger woman was always allowed the final say in the matter—a fact that amazed and impressed Sophia every time.

Her time with Natasha gave Sophia insight into the strong and independent woman she was, though very set in her ways and very used to the world bending to accommodate her. The world at large might have thought her deceased, Sophia considered, but the world that knew she was alive also knew she liked to be in control.

"For this to work the way we want, I need you to trust me," Sophia told Natasha on that first walk as they crossed over a bridge on the east side of the park.

"I am not a very trusting person," she confessed. "Not with everyone."

"That's ok. I'm not 'everyone,'" Sophia said as considerately as she could, hoping Natasha would find her sincerity contagious. "Just follow my directions, give me a little time and you'll get results. When I first started working out, a trainer told me the first six months would be the hardest. But you have to show up and you have to keep at it. After that, it becomes habitual, and it's suddenly not as hard to convince yourself to do it because it's become part of your lifestyle. See what you have to look forward to?"

Natasha said nothing, her breathing already a little faster and heavier from the pace and the unusual amount of activity. She darted a "you're nuts" look at Sophia—an expression so out of character for the prim and proper Natasha that if it were spoken it would have been with a contraction.

A few minutes later, she flexed her nerve by asking, "Should I call Charles to pick us up when we tire out?"

Sophia grinned casually in return and then dove deep inside herself for more words of encouragement, a process she had committed herself to until it was no longer necessary. She had faith in Natasha. She knew there was strength inside this woman that, regardless of age or "sensitivity," could be tapped into if only the right approach was used. Sophia remembered the many ways Austen said she got her students to follow directions. After all, how different were adults from children? Not very, she believed.

"If we tire out, we'll find a nice bench and rest. There's no reason we ever have to feel exhausted. This process is all about getting enough movement. And the bonus that comes with working out is it's therapeutic. You'll feel better. You'll sleep better. Your clothes will fit better."

"I like the sound of that," Natasha admitted.

"We can do this, Natasha. Where there's a will, there's a way."

During the first few walks, as they made their way through Central Park, budding signs everywhere provided evidence that winter was slowly conceding to spring. Sophia shared many of her own personal fitness lessons from over the years, including the uncomfortable conversation about how booze and cigarettes would not help their progress. Sophia deliberately used the all-inclusive "we" and "our" in the discussion to sound less accusatory, for which Natasha again shot Sophia a glance, this time a more formal, "you-are-pushing-your-luck-and-are-lucky-I-am-here-right-now" scowl.

But once Sophia felt she had covered most of the important information she thought Natasha needed to know or would benefit from hearing, she decided it was best to give Natasha as much privacy on their walks as she seemed to want. If Natasha didn't indicate she felt like talking, Sophia let her be, allowing her to soak in the experience of their walk. There was nothing quite like Central Park, and the exercise and scenery did wonders for them both.

"Do you ever get tired of it?" Natasha asked once, early on. "Just walking around in circles?"

"Sometimes. We're lucky we have this great park though. That helps."

"I suppose. But do you not ever feel like it is pointless? That no matter what you do today, you will still have work to do tomorrow?"

"That it's never-ending?" Sophia added, helping Natasha finish her thought. "Sure. But then I tell myself how fortunate I am to be able to come out here and move around and physically take care of myself. I can do things to improve my physical state. That's important. I try to remind myself I'm fortunate to have that."

"Jesus, you *are* from California!" Natasha said, laughing at her.

"Why do you say that?" Sophia asked. She had an idea where Natasha was going with the statement, but decided she would make her explain anyway. She had begun to think Natasha liked to be challenged sometimes, so she started to hide behind her so-called trainer status to accommodate her.

"You seem to be so positive all the time, so...what is the California way to describe it? Centered? Or connected? In tune with the universe?" Natasha explained, scoffing at the terminology. "Do you not *ever* have bad days? Do you ever say, 'What is it all for? That one day I am going to be dead so why even bother?' Or are you too young to have those thoughts?"

Sophia had seen this darker side of Natasha before, the overly concerned and critical part of her personality, and wondered what it was that had brought out the clouds when the sun was still shining so bright for everyone else. Sophia wasn't entirely sure they were just talking about exercise.

"Sure, I wonder that sometimes," Sophia admitted. "I actually think it a lot. But then I think, 'What choice do I have?' When I feel like crap, which has been a lot lately, I lay out all the facts for myself. I know I feel and look better when I exercise, and that I'll benefit for it in the long run. I know I want to do everything I can to stay as healthy as possible, for as long as possible."

"Like I said, you are *so* from California."

"You know what they say: 'You can take the girl out of California, but you can't take the California out of the girl.'"

As the days turned into weeks, and as Natasha began to keep better pace with Sophia with less effort, she also began to speak more freely.

It was early April when she made a noteworthy admission Sophia was pleased to hear. "I have not had a drink in two weeks."

"Really?" Sophia said. "That's great! How do you feel?"

"Like crap."

Sophia was confused. "Really? How is that…"

"I am kidding," Natasha barked, showing a little irritability. "I'm just kidding. I feel fine. I feel better except I do not sleep well."

Sophia thought about this. "I thought you'd sleep better. I think booze disturbs your sleep."

"Well, not me. It knocks me out. I have weird dreams sober."

"How weird?" Sophia said, stopping for a moment to stretch.

"Well, last night, I dreamed my friend's deceased

grandfather visited me and told me to tell my friend he can talk to her in her dreams."

Sophia stopped stretching and looked at Natasha, now standing still, the spectacular city skyline peeking over the trees behind her. "Why do you think you dreamed that?"

"I told you, I have crazy dreams."

"Do you think that's crazy?"

Natasha thought about it. "Not really. It was emotional. I remember crying. But not crazy, I guess. Because I do believe that is possible."

"Now who sounds like they're from California?" Sophia teased before going out on a limb and asking, "Have you weighed yourself?"

Natasha shook her head. "I'm afraid to."

"Why? What's there to be afraid of?"

"I'm scared of being disappointed. What if I weigh the same as I did? Or worse, that I gained more?"

"Look at you! You know you've lost weight. Are you cheating on your diet? You know Mary and I have worked very hard to change the food you have available," Sophia said, knowing she probably sounded too harsh.

"I know!" Natasha growled. "You think I haven't noticed? Get off my damn back. Who knew when I hired you to be my assistant I was also getting a trainer, a dietician and a dominatrix?"

Sophia put her hands on her hips, deciding to throw it back into Natasha's court. "Really? Who knew you were hiring me to be your *assistant?* I guess we both had surprises coming our way."

"Oh, just shut your mouth," Natasha said, her porcupine quills raised in jest.

Ten minutes later, as they passed a playground, Natasha said, "I think we should open up the beach house soon. Maybe next week?"

"You have a beach house?"

"Yes, in East Hampton. Has no one told you about it? Not Jonathan?"

"No, nothing. No one said anything about it." Sophia told

her, realizing Jonathan might not have done so because he didn't expect her to last that long.

"I like to stay there a good portion of the summer. Will it be a problem for you to come and stay for a few days at a time? I could have Charles bring you back and forth every day, but that seems like an awful waste of time and gas, especially when the city can be so dreadful with the humidity. You will have your own private room and bathroom. It is a very nice place."

Sophia quickly reviewed her summer plans in her head. Other than writing, there was nothing and she could easily bring her laptop with her to The Hamptons. How nice, she considered, would it be to walk along the beach and enjoy the summer, away from the heat and occasional smells of the city? Hot garbage—she would not miss that odor.

"Sure," Sophia told her, thinking that by the end of summer either she and Natasha would be really close or totally hate each other, though if she saw the latter starting to happen, she would just make an excuse as to why she needed to go back and forth to the city. It was a risk she was willing to take. "Why not?"

"Wonderful," Natasha replied. "Can you go out next week and open up the house?"

"Of course," she said, but then remembered Kate was coming back to move out of her apartment and put her stuff in storage. She would be in town for the entire week but Sophia knew her time was very limited and she had promised to help her out. "The only thing is that my friend Kate is coming back to town to prepare for her move to Paris. If it's alright with you, I'd like to check with her to see when I'll be able to see her while she's in town and then plan accordingly."

"Paris? Lucky girl. You must go visit her. It is a fabulous city. As for next week, go whenever you like. Or better yet, if she has the time, go out to the house with your friend and spend a night or two. Charles can drop you off and pick you up whenever you want. That way, you can take your time opening up the house and have a few days to relax with your friend before she leaves."

Sophia loved the idea and could hardly contain herself.

"Are you sure? You wouldn't mind if she went out with me?"

"Of course not. But no wild parties," Natasha teased. "Not until I get there."

"Parties? Me?" Sophia asked with a feigned look of seriousness. "What a great idea."

CHAPTER 20
DUST

Sophia's brain was spilling over with new information when Charles picked her up to go get Kate for their trip to The Hamptons. She had spent an intense hour talking to Twain, taking notes on an array of specific and general questions for which she needed his insight regarding genetic engineering and its relationship to the food industry. From her own experience at RGB and the three years she worked on the Petsuch Food Company account, as well as from the research she had conducted over the past month, she knew what she needed to know about agriculture for her novel. But she needed her brother's professional guidance to help her fill in some of the story blanks so she could realistically drive Dirk to the dramatic destiny she has been planning for him. It was all coming together, which was a very good thing, but it was also overwhelming at times, too. With her head ready to explode from everything he had told her to consider, she was thrilled to leave her apartment.

"Can you come up and help me with my bags?" Kate asked when Sophia called from the car outside her apartment building.

"Of course."

Sophia was greeted at the door with a big hug, but it was the barren apartment over her shoulder that gripped her the hardest.

"The movers are gone, I take it," Sophia said, surprised by the sights—loose cable wires going wild, floor bunnies roaming where furniture had been for many years, framed dust marks left in place of the pictures that once covered the walls—the last evidence of the life that once resided within these walls. Sophia hadn't properly prepared herself for the shock. It felt so final and left her winded.

"It's so depressing, isn't it?" Kate asked, seeing the empty apartment's affect on her friend, clearly feeling the same loss.

"It is," she admitted. "It's the end of an era."

"Don't be a drama queen," Kate returned. "I'll be back."

"Promise?"

"What else am I going to do? Marry a Frenchie and stay in Paris? Who does that?"

Sophia knew her friend all too well. "You? That's just the kind of thing *you* would do."

Sophia looked around once last time. It *was* the end of an era, regardless of what Kate would admit. Sophia didn't doubt they would always be friends but she knew what time did to people, that it had a way of altering relationships as it marched on, just as it would in Kate's absence. The thought saddened Sophia so she stepped outside as quickly as she could, Kate's remaining possessions in tow, relieved to leave Kate's apartment.

As she turned to see to her friend in her New York apartment one last time, she saw it was Kate who had become emotional, placing her keys on the counter, cupping them over the ceramic tiles with her hands and holding her pose for much too long.

"Let's blow this taco stand," she finally said, trying to mask her own pang of melancholy with humor. But her defenses betrayed her and tears ran down her face—Sophia's, too—all the way through the Queens Midtown tunnel. It was another ten minutes before either of them stopped crying.

"I bet you've never seen anything quite like this, have you,

Charles?" Sophia asked, wiping her eyes.

She saw his eyebrows rise without judgment in the rearview mirror, and she knew she couldn't be sure if he was telling her, "Don't worry about what I think" or "I see this all the time." He was Natasha's driver, after all, so who knew what he'd seen in this car?

It was then that she realized she hadn't been off the island of Manhattan since her trip with Kevin to Cape Cod last August, when they stayed at that quaint bed and breakfast. She had no idea at the time it was to be their last vacation together.

"This is sick," Kate said, scanning Natasha's Mercedes, returning to form. *"Who* has their *own* driver?"

"Jealous? I know I am."

"Hey Charles," Kate said, leaning forward towards the front seat. "Do you only work for Natasha?"

"Yes, ma'am," he replied, remaining face forward but meeting Kate's eyes in the reflection.

"What happens if Natasha doesn't need you for anything?"

"I wait for her until she does," he said.

"And what do you do with all that free time?"

"Kate, leave him be," Sophia said. "Charles, you don't have to answer my nosey friend's questions. She doesn't get out much."

"I don't mind. I do a lot of reading and puzzles, ma'am. I also run errands for Ms. McGavin."

"Man," Kate said with a chuckle, "I have the wrong job."

As the city faded into the distance, and tall cement and brick structures as far as the eyes could see were replaced with towns nestled in the midst of forest and sky, Sophia and Kate caught up for the first time since they parted in January.

"We've been together ever since," Kate said, finishing her story about how she and Philippe met one romantic day she had been sitting at a café, reviewing the book she purchased that morning at the Louvre. "You'll love him. He's wonderful."

"It's been awhile since you dated someone."

"I know, forever. Speaking of forever, are you going to continue hating Kevin for the rest of your days?"

Sophia would have preferred not talking about Kevin, having spent so much time and energy on him the first several months of the year. She had actually grown tired of everything about him but accepted it was an unavoidable topic, and one that surely was going to come up at some point. "I don't hate him."

"Have you spoken to him since his move?"

"He's called but I don't answer. He left a message once wondering how I was doing. He said he saw something with the Jolly Green Giant and that he wanted to tell me he was thinking about me. You know I'll never be able to look at green peas the same way again."

"Prick," Kate said. "What he was thinking about was how guilty he feels. What he wants is for you to forgive him."

"What's there to forgive him for? For having no tact? It's hardly a sin that needs absolving."

"No, but it was the wrong thing to do. There are better ways to break up with someone."

"I suppose, but..."

"Don't make excuses for him, Sophia," Kate commanded. "He did a shitty thing and deserves to be punished for it."

"What good does that do?" Sophia reasoned. "He moved on. Of course, he did it before breaking up with me, but trying to punish him is pointless. I'd only be torturing myself. *I'm* the one who would have to live with all of that misery, while he sits pretty in his new life."

"*Are* you miserable?" Kate asked, taking a softer tone.

"No, not as much now. It comes and goes," Sophia said, looking out the window, pleased to be able to escape into the endless stretch of blue around them, ready to change the subject. "I take it out on my characters."

"That's a good outlet. How's that coming?"

"It's coming. Little by little...the story of my life."

"When do I get to read it?"

"As soon as it's done."

"Am I in it?"

"No. Well, sort of," Sophia told her. "My Mother Superior character is you, turned inside out. She's the complete opposite version of you."

"A nun? Are you kidding me?"

"Like I said, the complete opposite of you. Except she's strong and bossy like you."

"I'm not *strong*," Kate said with a smirk and they both laughed.

When they arrived at the property, Charles gave them a quick tour before heading back to the city. As they walked through the various buildings (the main house, the pool house and the guest quarters, which was connected to the main house through an adjoining hallway, but was just as private as Natasha had stated), Sophia realized she had given the nickname "The Estate" to the wrong property because Natasha's Hampton's house seemed far better suited for the title. On the spot, she decided she had no other choice than call this home "The Sequel" because everything was supposed to be bigger and better in the second part of any story—bigger bells and whistles helped to keep the people coming back for more.

"How many acres is this place?" Kate asked Charles during the tour, continuing her nosey streak. That was her way. She was a fountain of questions, which made her able to talk to anyone, and the reason Sophia had always told her she could hold a conversation with a wall, if she felt so inclined.

"Five," Charles answered. "Ms. McGavin has owned the property since 1980. When she bought the land, there were only a few homes on this stretch of the beach. Billy Joel lives just down the road."

"Ooh, Billy Joel," Kate cooed. "Forget Paris. I'm staying right here!"

Charles hadn't been gone more than a couple minutes when Kate transformed herself from city girl to beach girl, completely casually attired, including flip flops, despite the chill in the air that refused to admit its days were numbered.

"It's forty-five degrees," Sophia told her. "Isn't it a little cold to wear those?"

"Oh, please. I'm wearing them now because I don't know

the next time I'll get to. You don't think I'm bringing these to France with me, do you? I'm leaving them with you."

"What about the French Riviera? Can't you wear them there?"

"I don't think my five buck sandals will go over too well there. Besides, how often do you think I'll make it to The Riviera? I can barely afford to *live* in France. Glamorous vacations are totally out of the question."

"Your sandals aren't good enough for France but they're good enough for me? Thanks."

Sophia pulled out the list of things Natasha gave her to do while out at the house. "Here's what I need to take care of," Sophia said. "I should probably get started."

"Let me help you," Kate offered. "The faster we get things done, the sooner we can crack open the wine."

Their first task was to open several windows to release the stale air trapped in the house for the past seven months. Within no time, cool but fresh ocean air blew life back into the place, while Sophia and Kate went from room to room throughout the house, removing the sheets that covered all of the furniture. Natasha had told Sophia she rarely came out to the house during the winter so it made sense to keep everything protected. After clearing everything off, they pulled out the brooms and rags to do a solid once over, getting a jump start on the cleaning before the professionals came in weeks later.

"Why doesn't she come out here during the winter?" Kate asked. "I bet it'd be nice with a fire and snow on the lawn."

"I think it makes her blue," Sophia replied. "She says she likes the city in the winter and the beach in the summer. She says that's the way it should be."

"Makes sense for her, I guess. But me? I'd be out here all winter, too. Look at this gorgeous view of the ocean! And get a whiff of that salt air. It's amazing!"

As they worked their way through the house, they examined everything in close detail.

"Look at these photos," Sophia said, referring to a wall filled of framed pictures. "There's Jill Clayburgh and Al Pacino.

How old is this photo? Did you know they once were a couple?"

Kate stopped to look at the end of Sophia's pointing finger. "Very cool."

Then she looked closer at the other photos. There had to be at least twenty other frames on the wall. "And look at these. Oh, my God! Is that Andy Warhol? Natasha is the shit, isn't she?"

"Definitely," Sophia replied, unable to keep from noticing how happy Natasha looked in the pictures. There was something different about her now, something that had been added or perhaps taken away.

Then she thought of something else, something deeper, a thought connected to her final visit to Kate's apartment earlier in the day—that no matter how much you covered or tried to protect things, it was impossible to keep the dust from collecting.

Once they had finished putting all of the protective sheets in the laundry room and started a load of wash, they moved into the kitchen, which Natasha surprisingly only had one of at this house.

"Are you hungry?" Sophia asked.

"Sure. And thirsty."

Sophia opened the refrigerator, pleased but not surprised to find the exact same organizational system as at The Estate. She pulled out a bottle of wine and some condiments, then let Kate prepare dinner with the groceries they had brought to the house while she started a fire in the large living room and set the table. Thirty minutes later, both women relaxed comfortably in the house on the hill overlooking the beach, watching the sun fade from view while they ate and enjoyed their second glasses of wine.

"That's quite a view," Sophia said, watching out the window as the moon took its proud position to glisten over the ocean, highlighting the waves as they smiled and frowned, smiled and frowned. The smell of the ocean in the air brought her back to days as a child with her parents, trips to Carmel and Monterey, salt water taffy, random collections of sea shells.

Both women retired to their own rooms soon afterwards,

each exhausted and spent. Sophia knew Kate was fatigued from several days of packing and dealing with movers. She also saw that underneath her driven guard, Kate simmered with nervousness and apprehension about the direction she had chosen for her life. Sophia suspected that if she pressed hard enough, her friend would admit she was right: it was the end of an era.

Sophia was also drained, several months of non-stop life changes, work and writing taking their toll. More than ever, and more than she anticipated, she was grateful Natasha had suggested this little getaway. It was thrilling to think there was a whole summer ahead of her to get away from the city. A change of scenery, with a regular dose of sand and sea, would do her good.

That night she dreamed of Nonna.

"I can talk to you in your dreams," she told Sophia.

Nonna was as real in the dream as she had been just a few years before, standing before Sophia, her arms open and inviting. Everything about her was as it had been during her healthier days, down to last details, from the glasses on a metal leash around her neck, to those chubby feet stuffed into those practical old fashioned, but not fashionable, shoes that no longer were the correct size.

The dream, as dreams went, was fragmented. One minute Nonna was talking to her, the next to Natasha. Andy Warhol and Jill Clayburgh were there, but remained in the corner of the room talking only to themselves. Then Nonna was dancing with Al Pacino who, she said, was very nice.

"I like him," she said. "I'm glad he won."

"I miss you," Sophia told her, crying. "I miss you so much. I'm sorry I wasn't with you at the end."

Nonna continued dancing with Al Pacino, smiling, glancing over him. "You were, dear. You always were. You always are."

In the morning, Sophia remembered the dream when Natasha called to see how they were doing. She wondered what it all meant, amazed that alcohol had such different results for her than for Natasha.

"Are you ladies having a nice time?" Natasha asked.

"Yes, very nice," Sophia told her. "Thanks again. The house is absolutely beautiful. We've taken care of almost everything on your list and the boys are coming over in a half hour."

"Ha! Very funny. I just wanted to make sure you found everything you need and that you two are doing well. Also, I am calling you to tell you I have a surprise for you when you get back. There is something I cannot wait to show you."

Sophia was already surprised just by this announcement. "What is it, Natasha? That you're the one who's had a party and the place is destroyed? Or how about you've been eating and drinking since I left you and gained a bunch of weight?"

"Again, very funny. You will just have to wait and see."

After the two finished their conversation, Sophia told Kate about the call. "She sounded excited but wouldn't tell me exactly what it was."

"What do you think it is?"

"I have no idea," Sophia said, "but it makes me nervous when she tells me that she's been up to something. Left to her own devices usually only means one thing."

Another day filled with minor tasks and major relaxation passed all too quickly and before Sophia knew it, they were back in the car with Charles, almost arriving at the international terminal at JFK.

"I mean it. Just drop me off," Kate insisted.

"But you still have three hours," Sophia said, looking at her watch. "What will you do? I'll just wait with you for a while."

"Forget it. No one ever goes to the airport with someone in New York."

"I would do that. For you. Today."

"I know, but there's no need. I'll shop the duty free and take my time checking in. Don't even think twice about this because I'm not gonna change my mind."

Sophia was silent. This was the moment she had dreaded more than any other moment, a moment she had felt robbed of with Kevin. But then again, she realized, there was no good way to say goodbye.

The tears began again before the car pulled up to the curb.

"I'll get your bags out of the trunk, ma'am," Charles told Kate. "Please take your time if you two would like a moment."

"Yes, please," Kate replied.

"I can't believe this," Sophia said.

"This is for you," Kate said, handing her a sealed envelope. "It's just some things I want to tell you. Read it later. Not now."

"I love you," Sophia said through the tears.

"I love you, too," Kate added, her eyes reddening as the waterworks poured and her voice broke. "You go make me proud, ok? Finish that book so I can walk into Le Barnes & Noble, or whatever bookstore in Paris, and point it out to people and say, 'Look at that! That's my talented best friend! She wrote this amazing book! Aren't I lucky to have such an incredible friend?'"

Loss consumed them both while they embraced in a moment neither wanted to ever release. Kate then quickly exited the car and Sophia could hear her crack a joke before the door closed, "I bet I look like shit."

Sophia's face was still in her hands when the Mercedes reached the interstate to head back into the city. She knew, however, this futile attempt to shield herself from her grief would not change the fact that another chapter of her life had officially come to an end.

CHAPTER 21
IDLE LEGS

When Jasper heard Sophia enter the next morning, he greeted her with a big welcoming hug. "Good to have you back."

As he let her go, he took a closer look, examining the red under her eyes. "You alright?" he asked.

"Fine, but I think I'm having a delayed breakdown."

"Please don't start talking breakdown around here. You know Miss Sensitivity. She's been in the clear for a while and I'd like to keep it that way."

"Ah, the good old days," Sophia joked, remembering the dance of glass all around her like confetti, an event with all the excitement of a party, but none of the fun.

"Must be all that exercise you have her doing. She's a maniac. Have you seen the latest?"

"No. What do you mean?"

"Oh, well, she's very excited to show you. Go on up. She's dressed and having coffee right now. Coffee, no latte, I might add." Jasper laughed as he moved back towards the kitchen. "Who knew you *could* teach an old dog new tricks? I think you might be a witch, Miss Sophia. Seems like voodoo to me."

Sophia put her jacket and bag inside the coat closet, and

then climbed her way up to Natasha's quarters.

"Natasha? Are you decent?" Sophia said, announcing herself as she reached the third floor, pleased to have an excuse to use a favorite phrase that somehow always managed to amuse her.

"Sophia?" Natasha returned, "Yes! Come in here now!"

Sophia immediately saw "the latest"—the purchase to which Jasper was referring. It was difficult *not* to notice it there in the middle of Natasha's great room. Standing not far from the couch was a professional, gym-quality treadmill.

"Where did *that* come from?" Sophia asked.

Natasha's eyes lit up like a child on Christmas morning. "Isn't is fantastic? It arrived yesterday. I've already used it three times."

Sophia studied the equipment, and then Natasha. "Are you feeling ok? What have you done with Natasha, the woman I had to cajole into exercising like a month ago?"

Natasha giggled—she actually giggled! "I know. Funny, huh? I bought it so I can watch the news and just walk. Isn't that a brilliant idea?"

Sophia was tickled by Natasha's insinuation that she was the first person to think of such a plan. But she had probably never stepped foot inside a gym and, regardless, Sophia was thrilled by her boss' graduation to a new level of enthusiasm. And just when she felt like she had officially seen all the cards from Natasha's quirky deck, she was once again proven wrong.

"Wait! There's more," Natasha told her, running into the bathroom and then back, holding a scale in her hands.

"You weighed yourself? I knew there had to be a better reason for your excitement than the prospect of doing more cardio."

"I did and guess what?"

"You gained weight?" Sophia joked, unable to help herself from teasing Natasha.

"Stop it. Of course not," Natasha tossed back. She put the scale down so she could step on it. "I lost fifteen pounds so far! Fifteen pounds! Take that, Ass-Face Baxter!"

"Are you serious?" Sophia asked, forgetting her sadness, feeling better already.

"I am! I thought my clothes were feeling looser but didn't want to say anything just yet. But then two days ago, I put on a pair of pants I know to be tight, and they were so loose! So I went and got on the scale and, sure enough, that was it! It's working! I was so motivated I went out and bought this mammoth thing. Maybe I should take the kitchen out and turn it into a gym?"

Sophia examined the equipment. "This is quite a set-up. And to think I was sure you were going to tell me you've been holed up in here eating cake and ice cream for the past two days!"

Natasha laughed at her and Sophia could see real pride and enjoyment in her eyes. She was illuminated and unguarded. "The one thing you should know about me by now is that I cannot do anything half-assed. I go all or nothing, obsessive compulsive or not at all."

"I can see that."

"Besides, what's the saying, 'Idle hands are the devil's tools?'"

"Or maybe it should be 'idle legs?' Does that mean we're not going outside today?"

"Not at all. Let me change. I'll be down in a minute."

Sophia was unusually quiet during the walk, which Natasha must have noticed because she asked, "How are *you* doing today?"

It was unusual for the topic to turn so directly onto Sophia. While Natasha was generous in her own way, when it came to conversation her favorite topic was still always herself. Besides, Natasha was a real talker. She, like Kate, could talk the paint off a wall.

"Fine," Sophia lied, staring off into the distance, watching a bird chase another into the sky as her feet dragged along the asphalt.

"Bullshit."

It was always a shock when Natasha stepped out of her

Upper East Side mold, into her tough, "take-no-prisoners" alter ego. It was the side she showed when they discussed Vanessa, and a milder version of which came out when she was having one of her moments, but Sophia had yet to see it come to *her* defense. It was the fearless and impulsive side, or at least, the raw, defenseless side, that found foul language and contractions useful. Sophia wasn't sure if Natasha's endorphins had begun taking over. "You're the actor," was how she chose to reply to the claim she wasn't telling the truth. "Not me."

"That's for sure. I've seen better performances on infomercials."

Sophia stayed quiet, watching the trees blow as she continued walking, hoping that if she waited long enough, Natasha might change the topic to something more interesting for both of them, like herself.

But instead Natasha stopped, and Sophia sensed she had no choice but to do the same.

"Are you going to talk to me?" she asked.

"Must I?"

"Yes, you must."

"Fine," Sophia said, rolling her eyes, taking a deep breath before continuing. "This year has been nothing but changes, major ones at that. I try to keep my head up but sometimes it gets the best of me."

"Thank God," Natasha replied. "I was starting to think you were invincible."

"No, you didn't," Sophia returned.

"No, I didn't," Natasha confirmed. "Tell me more." Then she smiled at the younger woman, seeming proud of herself as if she had just had a breakthrough. "Listen to *me*. I sound like *you* now."

Sophia felt her mouth open up and her heart spill out, a release that felt as if she was trying to remove the weight of the world from her shoulders. "In one day, I lost my job and my boyfriend. My best friend just moved to Paris. I spend all of my free time writing. And a moment doesn't go by without my head feeling like it's going to spin right off. There is very little around me that I recognize anymore and it freaks me out."

Natasha gave a knowing nod like she understood. Either she *was* a better actor than Sophia or she was truly engaged.

"You love writing, right?" Natasha asked, a question that seemed a little surprising to Sophia but that she found interesting.

"Sure. More than anything."

"So then you're spending your time doing what you need to be doing right now. Your novel *is* your relationship. And when you're ready for another one, or have more room in your life, then it'll happen."

"That's easy for you to say."

"Oh, dear, you know that's not true. Did I ever tell you about my husband?"

"No," Sophia said, pleased the topic was shifting, more comfortable when the attention wasn't on her. "You don't tell me about stuff like that."

The comment made Natasha laugh, like she knew Sophia spoke the truth. "I loved Mathew very much," she admitted, "but we married young though, and like kids do, we thought love was all we needed to be happy. Eventually reality sunk in."

Natasha paused as if a lump had caught in her throat, which she swallowed before continuing on. "The bottom line is I had to be an actress. It was my top priority and what I wanted before anything else. I forgot that for a while, when we first met."

"So what happened?"

"I left him. Or he left me. After all these years, it's hard to remember exactly which came first. What I am certain of is we pushed each other away in our own ways. I realized by the time it was over that I couldn't be a wife and an actress at the same time. Not at *that* time anyway, when I was a young woman trying to prove as much to myself as the world that I was an actress. It took too much out of me and I didn't have anything left for him."

"But what about once you made it?"

"Oh, I had already been successful by the time we were together, but that didn't matter. Not for me. I honestly don't know if I ever felt confident enough to make myself vulnerable in all areas of my life…at the same time, that is. Besides, the world moves on. I think you'll find you want different things at different times in your life."

All of this struck a nerve with Sophia, more than she felt like acknowledging to Natasha. What if she didn't *want* to want different things later in life? What if she *couldn't* want different things later in life?

"Want my opinion?" Natasha asked.

"Sure."

"Enjoy this time in your life. You're finding out who you are and what you're made of. You have the rest of your life to be who you're going to be—so enjoy this time of figuring it all out, and this time of being creative. You really do have endless options and opportunities."

"It doesn't feel that way. I feel lost, like my life just keeps slipping away from me. Like I'm fighting an uphill battle that never gets easier."

"Sorry, dear, but *that* feeling doesn't go away."

May quickly bumped April off the calendar for another year, and the morning of the voiceover session for the special DVD anniversary edition of *The Dreyfus Affair* arrived before any of them knew it. No one had any idea what was about to hit them.

"Are you Sophia?" a stranger asked her on the stairwell up to Natasha's quarters.

"I am. And you?"

"I'm Nathan. I'm Manny's assistant. Ms. McGavin is looking for you."

"Who's Manny?" Sophia asked, now climbing the stairs with this stranger, Nathan, who had spots of yellow and red dye throughout his hair, looking like a tropical fish.

"Manny is Ms. McGavin's hair and make-up director. He's preparing her now."

"*Director? Preparing?*" *What the hell is she up to now?*

All of this came as a surprise to Sophia, who somehow had been left out of the loop when it came to certain arrangements for the day. Perhaps, she considered, Natasha thought or, rather, knew that Sophia would tease her about hiring someone to make her look beautiful for work that would only highlight her voice.

This was all for Vanessa, the woman who had recently become Natasha's reason for living and who would soon become her reason for other things as well.

"Nathan, you found her! Sophia, dear, this is Manny. He is here to get me ready. He is a star all on his own, you know?" she said, affectations and dramatics present and accounted for.

No, she didn't know this, but she wouldn't let on to this fact. "Hi, Manny. Nice to meet you."

Manny winked at her, his "star" hands doing their thing on Natasha's head, which was when Sophia noticed her hair had been recently colored. When did that happen? Had Natasha organized *that* on her own, too? What would she do next? Drive herself to the sound studio on West 52nd Street? *What's going on around here?*

Sophia watched while Manny continued his work. "Any more pounds I should know about?" she asked. This was their newest hobby—a game in which, every week or so, Sophia randomly tested Natasha, sometimes with the scale, sometimes on the honor system. Natasha had grown to love the competitive nature of the arrangement, and Sophia was pleased it seemed to keep her motivated and inspired.

Natasha smiled, jiggling subtly in her seat, but not moving for fear of making Manny mess up. "Three, baby!"

"What's the grand total to date?"

"Thirty."

"Fan-frigging-tastic, Natasha!" Sophia said with genuine enthusiasm. She threw in a little salty language because Natasha liked it when she used the occasional curse word, a new form of dramatic pronunciation she had borrowed from Natasha to show she was feeling scrappy.

"Are you ready to see *her?*" she continued.

"I've never been more ready."

CHAPTER 22
ON THE RECORD

In the four months they had known each other, Sophia had seen several sides to the "sensitive" Natasha. There was the elegant Manhattanite—the former actress turned businesswoman who spoke properly and deliberately, and sought perfection is everything she did and presented to the world. It was a role of precision and calculation, discipline and construction, intended to appear effortless despite all she put into it. There was also the pugnacious version—a heartier substitute with thick skin and equally threatening bark and bite. This Natasha was just as competitive and self-focused as the other but was much less afraid of what others thoughts or felt because, in this condition, she was consumed by her own temporary state of being, which was reactionary and inspired, coming out like a wave of euphoria or hysteria, depending on the circumstances.

But somewhere in between the two, battling for attention and stage time, was yet another Natasha—non-negotiated and non-negotiable, unable to play well with the others, and comparable to a fault line waiting to trigger an eruption. This was a version Sophia had only witnessed once but had heard much reference to by Jasper and the others inside Natasha's inner sanctum. After a long hibernation, a period when Natasha seemed to have herself pulled together—dare anyone actually thought her more relaxed, content state-of-being brought on by her healthier lifestyle was a permanent, full-proof defense against this other side—*The Dreyfus Affair* reunion would surprise everyone by releasing this other Natasha. Before the day was over, Sophia—a woman who already thought she had seen a lot in her life—would be surprised and realize that she did not know nearly all there was to know about Natasha. It would be a profound day that would not end like it began, a day that could not finish what it had started.

"Charles is downstairs with Jonathan," Sophia informed the descending Natasha as she carefully clicked her way down the stairs to the living room, two palms raised to the sky to complete her Norma Desmond scenario. Her heels, evidence that Natasha had opted for form over function, slowed her down and, as she neared Sophia, she asked, "Ready to go?"

Natasha looked and acted like she was about to walk the red carpet. The only thing missing was the million dollar Cartier necklace (however, Sophia was pretty certain the rocks hanging from her earlobes were worth more money than she had ever seen or made in her life). When Natasha reached the landing, she crossed to the mirror to examine herself one last time, and Sophia imagined the mental checklist she thought she could hear taking place. *Dressed to the nines? Check. Fabulous hair and make-up? Check. Brutally uncomfortable, ridiculously overpriced but très chic dress and shoes? Check.*

Sophia debated for some time whether or not she should say something about Natasha being grossly overdressed, but she eventually talked herself out of it. Who was she, for a variety of reasons, to say what was right for Natasha to do, even in jest? Besides, Natasha had spent the past few months exercising, dieting and denying herself—the denial part alone deserving of special recognition. She had earned this moment in the spotlight, even if the spotlight was only a 100-watt light bulb from a desk lamp in an otherwise darkened studio room.

"Do you have my bag? It has my notes in it," Natasha asked Sophia, attempting to relocate a well-cemented strand of hair.

"I do. Are you sure you don't want to go over these with me before we get there? Like a rehearsal? Just so you're sure to say everything exactly the way you want?"

Natasha turned around and faced Sophia, her hands moving along her hips to flatten the sides of her dress. "No, but I do want you with me in the studio. *You* will be my audience. I will be speaking to you but I want the words to come out fresh. I want *that* to be the first time you hear them."

Okeydoke, Sophia thought, immediately regretting stuffing her laptop in her bag and dragging it with her across town this morning. She had thought that Natasha, not wanting her by her side, would ditch her in a waiting room to go off with her famous friends. "You got it," Sophia told her, flattered in any case by the announcement. "It ought to be interesting."

Natasha nodded. "Oh, it will be. I promise," she said. It was a remark Sophia should have taken as a warning.

The awkwardness of this alternate universe continued unfolding from there as Sophia became more and more exposed to the Hollywood side of Natasha's world which, thus far, had not played much part in her experiences. Natasha had been more of the wealthy businesswoman to her than the former movie star. Once their brief discussion of writing Natasha's autobiography had been completely scrapped, Sophia thought of her employer in the present, not in the past. That was what Natasha had indicated *she* wanted, yet somehow this journey into the past had begun to appeal to her—almost in an increasingly alarming way—and thus the entourage set sail for the old country.

Adding to the mix was Jonathan who on the entire drive over to the recording studio spread a layer of ponderous compliments, remarking on topics that were both valid and believable—like her weight loss and how great she looked, and others less rooted in reality—like how he was sure *The Dreyfus Affair* anniversary DVD would sell better than the latest release of *Star Wars*. There was no doubting that *The Dreyfus Affair* was a great movie, Sophia thought, relieved to be sitting in the front seat with Charles and away from the shenanigans in the backseat, but that it shared the same commercial appeal as *Star Wars?* What was he thinking? If this was what all of Natasha's Hollywood friends were like, she was happy her day job was for the wealthy businesswoman, not the actress. It was still an eccentric role, but one that resided on Planet Earth.

The hair and make-up crew, the driver, the lawyer, the agent, and what she was about to see—it all made Sophia wonder what her boss' life must have really been like back in the day, when *all* people thought she was still alive, when she was working on film after film, at the top of her game. What must her life have been like when there were twenty others like Jonathan sucking up to her and telling her everything she wanted to hear? While Sophia didn't think he was a bad guy, or that he was untrustworthy—at least not until later that day—his relationship with Natasha seemed most definitely about business. He was simply taking care of his client, but the way he went about it sometimes made Sophia question his sincerity. There were some shady people in the world, and if that was what being rich was all about then perhaps it wasn't really worth it.

Sophia began to realize that her relationship with Natasha was unique—a relationship Sophia enjoyed and felt privileged to have—the only other similar connection for Natasha being that between her and Jasper. But, as Sophia considered, how could anyone not love Jasper?

The moment they arrived at the studio, Natasha sounded off with her expectations regarding organization and execution. Again, she was in control, and Sophia felt like she was just tagging along for the ride. "Charles, please open my door first. Jonathan, follow my lead. Sophia, please wait until I am near the front door before getting out."

It was as if Natasha expected Vanessa to be peering out the front window of the studio to watch her arrival. Or better yet, like Natasha expected the paparazzi to be there to take her photo and she didn't want her assistant in the picture. Just to be sure, Sophia looked around, but there was no sign of *Entertainment Tonight* or *E!,* which was too bad for them, Sophia thought. They were sure to miss the wave of saccharine that had been filling up the car from all of Jonathan's schmoozing sweet talk and would pour out once the door opened.

The fact that there were no photographers or press did give Sophia a moment of disappointment because—for selfish, comical reasons—she would have loved it if someone was there shouting, "Who are you wearing?" And it would have been great for Natasha's benefit, too. Sophia had started to understand how much this trip down memory lane, and all of this Hollywood life, still really meant to her.

Jonathan held the door open for Natasha, as requested, and then for Sophia when it was her turn. As they entered the building they were immediately greeted by Natasha's agent, Claire Bulliard, and the studio manager, Jim Kaplan.

"It's such a pleasure to meet you, Miss McGavin," Jim told her. "We're absolutely thrilled to have you here with us today and that we get the chance to be a part of such an exciting and historical project."

"The pleasure is all mine," Natasha told him, playing it up, but meaning her words as well. She looked around the room as if expecting to see others. "And please do not use the word 'historical' with me, at least in front of me. It makes me sound so old."

Claire seemed to read her client and know what she was most concerned with. "Everyone else is in the studio. Shall we join them?"

"Yes, of course. I hope we are not late," Natasha said, stretching the truth. She had said she wanted to be timely for Joseph Stubbings, the director, but insisted on trying to arrive after Vanessa. The alpha female struggle had officially begun.

Jim escorted the group down a hallway, opening a door at their destination, "Here we are. This will be your recording studio for the day."

Inside was a large group of people, all noticeably more modestly dressed than Natasha. Sophia recognized Joseph from his picture on the Internet. He stood in one corner with what appeared to be a few of his people, and looked over their way as the door opened. In another corner resided a circle of bodies, but there was no sign of Vanessa. Then the circle suddenly broke open and Sophia realized the pack was hovering around Vanessa, who she immediately saw was just as overdressed as Natasha. And what was wrong with her face? It was about to get very interesting.

Natasha had to have seen Vanessa but acted like she didn't, moving immediately towards Joseph. "Daaaaaaarling! It is fabulous to see you! It has been much too long," she told him, sounding like Bette Davis herself.

"Beautiful," he returned, "it's been *way* too long. And you look amazing! I don't think you had that figure forty years ago." It was a compliment Sophia relished as much as Natasha did.

"You always were a man who knew how to use his words," Natasha said. "But I think your eyes have started to go south."

"Let them go south," he told her, pulling her into a warm but horny embrace. "South to that waistline, you little vixen. And words are not the only thing I still know how to use."

Natasha giggled at the flirtatious compliments, and Sophia was glad to see her so pleased with herself. "You are still so naughty. What am I going to do with you?"

As he released her, he looked deeply into her eyes and grinned his devilish best, "Anything you'd like. *Anything.*"

Natasha's eyes lowered to the ground, acting bashful. She then pretended to notice Vanessa for the first time. "Oh, Vanessa. You *are* here."

It was then that Sophia got her first real look at Vanessa, or rather her face. It confirmed her initial response, that impulse to want an answer to the question, "What happened?"

Natasha apparently shared the same reaction.

"And *look* at you," she said, making a bold announcement to her nemesis, as well as to the room that had stopped to watch the reunion. Sophia imagined they all knew this interaction was as loaded a situation as they come.

The room was quiet and still, and Sophia wondered if the hushed observers were watching to see who would throw the first punch, as if they had placed bets on their predictions.

"Oh, dear! It's true! You *are* alive!" Vanessa said,

continental kissing Natasha from cheek to cheek. As she said it, her frozen mannequin face refused expression, not moving or bending even a centimeter. Sophia wondered how much, and how many times, she had been altered. Her face was so tight and injected that she was barely recognizable as the young starlet she once was. Natasha showed more than her share of aging, but you could still see the young beauty she once was in this more mature version of the same attractive woman. Vanessa looked altogether like a different person, even a different *species,* Sophia thought.

"Of course I am still alive. Why would you say something so ridiculous?" Natasha said, casually looking at Jonathan for some kind of explanation, not understanding Vanessa's attempt at humor but then shrugging it off like she was talking nonsense.

When Natasha turned back to Vanessa, Sophia saw Jonathan register a look, a slight hint that he *did* know what Vanessa was talking about, and that he was relieved Natasha did not press the matter. If Sophia knew what she was talking about, how could he not? Was *that* part of the Natasha protection program? Was that his idea of keeping her safe? Was she completely unaware of the rumors?

"Perhaps that is just your own wishful thinking," Natasha added, turning Vanessa's comment back on her. "You know I will outlive you all."

"Ah, just like the cockroaches," Vanessa said. She sounded like she was laughing but it was a reaction you couldn't see on her face. "But you're not exactly a spring chicken, now are you?"

"Yes, that is true. But no matter how old I get, I will still be younger than you. And, as I recall, by quite a few years."

"Ladies," Joseph interrupted, and the room released a deep sigh. "Now that we're all here, how about we get started?"

What Joseph didn't know though was that they *had* already begun. It was on.

Jim escorted Natasha, Vanessa and Joseph into an adjoining room with soundproofed glass walls. "We'll be able to hear you in the sound room," Jim explained. "Please let us know if you need anything or want a break."

While they settled into their comfortable chairs, the studio technicians set up the two actresses and the director with microphones in front of a large screen. Joseph took this opportunity to explain how the day was going to work. "Time is a major consideration for this project which is why we really only have one day in the studio to record our commentary. We'll use what we can for the DVD, so let's do our best to share good and interesting tidbits about the production and the movie, maybe share some stories about when it was released, about how the critics responded, etc. Ask yourself the question, 'If I was a fan of the film, what would I want to know?' That's the stuff we're going for here."

As the credits rolled during the opening sequence, Natasha spoke first. "This is Natasha McGavin. I played Sally Burgess. I would just like to say that I do wish Kurt Smith could have joined us for this. He was such a wonderful man and great actor. As people may know, he passed away from cancer in 1997. Also, he was nominated for many awards for his role as Burt Packard in this film."

Not to be outdone, Vanessa stepped up to talk as well, "Yes, Burt was a very special and talented man. I always joked with him that if he weren't married that I would have been all over him like white on rice."

Natasha loved that Vanessa came out of the starting gate with such a ridiculous comment. She took the bait on this one, not that Vanessa expected what was coming to her. "You always were so ladylike in that way. But if I remember correctly, you did not always practice such reservation. What about Kurt's brother, Jonah?"

The sound room was dead quiet except for Vanessa's agent, who began to ask, "Did she just say what I think…" but the crowd unanimously "shhh'd" her so they wouldn't miss a thing. Sophia could practically see money shifting hands across the room as the imaginary betting continued.

The first thing they didn't miss was Jonathan mumbling, "Uh-oh."

Sophia remembered the story Natasha had told, that Vanessa had slept with Jonah to get the part, but that she spread the rumor it was Natasha who had done so. Sophia had a pretty good idea where this was going.

"I will clarify for our viewers," Natasha said, speaking into her microphone but not taking her eyes off Vanessa to show she had been waiting to confront her about this story for some time, "Jonah was one of the film's producers. Vanessa…isn't it true that Jonah cast *you?* As I recall, Jonah was married as well."

Vanessa, as best as anyone could tell with that face, was fuming. "I'm not sure *what* you are implying Natasha, but I'm sure you're not remembering things correctly, dear. That does happen with age. It's nothing to feel ashamed of."

"Oh, honey, I appreciate your concern for my recall faculties but there is absolutely no need for it. My memory is like a steel trap, both solid *and* unforgiving. I am thrilled to be here for this anniversary DVD. I have *so many* great stories to share. It is too bad we only have two hours!"

The women weren't together more than twenty minutes, the movie not thirty seconds into the opening credits, and they were already bickering. Sophia wondered how they would possibly make it through another one hundred and eighteen minutes of screen time without killing one another. And what if they had to spend the whole day together? Surely, if this continued, someone would be dead by the end of the day.

Sophia looked to see if Natasha had her notes. She did, the pile of papers beside her stacked high, confirming she had meant her threat—there were many, many stories. It was no wonder she wouldn't share them with Sophia earlier.

Jonathan glanced over at Sophia and gave her a smile, but she knew it was an artificial one. She could tell he was concerned, and with good cause—the two animals inside the cage had shown their fangs. In one corner was Vanessa Baxter, not a particularly smart woman but whose mean streak had, and would, serve her well. Natasha, on the other hand, was intelligent but more subtle, with a wrath both devious and dangerous. Underestimating either could be a lethal decision.

Sophia reflected upon her belief that some people were probably just not meant to get along, a theory for which her dad was an excellent example. He was perhaps the kindest, most peaceful and grounded man she had ever met, but when it came to his brother, a switch flipped and he became agitated and aggressive. They were oil and water, or better yet, kerosene and flame.

Back in the studio, Natasha was talking about the opening scene in the police station. "The actor who played the officer behind the desk is Darren Mitchell. He went on to play the father on the hit '80s sitcom, *My Family & Me.*"

Vanessa clearly had nothing to say but, refusing to let Natasha be one comment ahead of her, added, "I had salad that day."

Natasha laughed audibly, scoffing at this statement. "Forty years later, after making a movie that is on several top one hundred best American film lists, and all you have to share is that you had salad?"

But the remark didn't seem to bother Vanessa in the least, and she struggled to make a face at Natasha, telling her, "Funny you should say that. I also remember that *you* never ate salad. I suppose that explains how your hair wasn't the only thing that got bigger during the '70s and '80s."

"Oh, but dear, look at us both now. Tables have turned, haven't they?"

The tension was building so Joseph, in true director style, diffused the situation by adding his take on the scene. While describing what inspired his decision to film certain segments with only one camera and long takes, he was meanwhile trying to ignore the snarls passing silently between the two leading actresses.

Natasha shook her head in contempt from her corner, mouthing at Vanessa, "Salad?"

Her nemesis countered with an adolescent, blowfish face made by puffing up her cheeks, extending her arms out wide at her waist to imply an exaggerated body size.

Natasha twisted at her sides to show how small her newly streamlined belly was, and then said loud enough for her microphone to pick up the statement, "I'm surprised your face can still move! Does it hurt when you smile?"

The banter continued like this for another forty minutes as the two passed jabs about everything, from how the other looked in specific scenes (Natasha told Vanessa that back then, the noire lighting was the only lighting that was flattering for her, and that today no lighting would be best), to how they wreaked havoc for one another on the set (including Vanessa's admission that when she baked brownies for the crew, she slipped Ex-Lax into those she gave to Natasha—to which Natasha laughed, saying she had figured something was up, so she gave them to Jonah to punish him for cheating on his wife with her).

"What tipped you off?" Vanessa asked pointedly, her face attempting surprise.

"An intelligent woman always suspects the apple given to her by a serpent."

If Sophia hadn't been so nervous for Natasha, she might have been amused. Jonathan didn't help matters any either, now pacing back and forth like an expectant father in one of those old-fashioned maternity movie scenes, before men were allowed to be a part of the delivery. Sophia would have loved to have sent him on an errand, or asked him to boil water.

It was at the end of the first hour when things got really bad and reached the point of no return, when the ill-will between the two was exposed for what it really was—nothing short of pure hated. The scene they were discussing was one in which Sally and Burt had accepted that they were madly and hopelessly in love, after just being confronted by Vanessa's mischievous character, Florence Swift, who desperately needed both Burt's love and the money he had swindled out of wealthy and powerful men over the years. Sally's father had been his latest prey and Florence was scorned and furious—in shock that he was passing on the payout, and her, in the name of true love.

The sparring up to this point had been comparatively superficial. While both women had shown plenty of teeth, there had been no real wounds and no attempts at blood by bringing up the history that *really* mattered to either of them. Natasha knew, as Sophia would be told later, that Vanessa was proud of her many male conquests, and probably her facelifts as well. Natasha's comments likely brought her a little embarrassment because they were made in such a public forum, but that was as far as the damage went. Vanessa, like her character Florence, operated by different rules and morals. Such controversies were more like trophies to her than reasons for self-consciousness.

But once Sophia and the room learned what was about to be exposed, all would realize the outcome was inevitable. The feud between the two had remained dormant for decades, but the circumstances of this interaction made this confrontation unavoidable. It was Vanessa though who really broke skin first— forty years ago and now—going into territory she should not have gone into. She was responsible for wounds that had never healed and would cause Natasha raw bleeding that would continue for days.

"I love this scene," Natasha shared. "Joseph's direction is so gripping, and Kurt's acting so great, you really feel the conflict that traps this character between two worlds. You experience his struggle yet you truly believe that redemption is possible, that someone so evil could change when someone so good comes into his life. I think the story is beautiful and timeless."

"You just can't give me credit for being a good actress can you?" Vanessa interjected, breaking down on her side of the room, inviting them both back to the late '60s, to an incident they both had been hovering around since arriving at the sound studio. The women hadn't seen each other in forever yet the old feelings came back immediately, like everything had happened only the day before.

"What are you complaining about now, Vanessa?" Natasha reprimanded. "You are not even in this scene."

"Not once have you ever said that *my* acting contributed to the success of this film."

"Is that why you are such a bitch to me? And why you lobbied so hard during award season to get people to *not* vote for me? Because you are jealous that the critics and our peers admired *my* work, and not *yours?*"

Sophia would learn later that Natasha, at this point, still had no intention of bringing up that certain part of the past left unsaid, that she had held *those* stories and feelings away from herself, telling herself, "Don't do it. Don't bring it *all* up. Don't go *there.*"

But Vanessa kept hounding her, angrily pleading, "Would it kill you to acknowledge my talent?"

"If by talent, Vanessa, you mean sleeping with every Tom, Dick and Jonah to advance your career, then sure…I acknowledge your talent."

Vanessa's immobile face began quivering with fury. "You have no idea how many men I've slept with!"

Natasha laughed, throwing her hands in the air. "No, and I bet neither do you."

Joseph stood up, trying to stop this battle from getting worse than it already was. "Ladies, please…"

But both women cut him off at the knees with their words, yelling in stereophonic unison, "Shut up!" It drove him silently back into his seat.

Sophia looked at the studio operator seated in front of her, and then at his monitor—they were still recording. He was smiling and literally sitting on the edge of his seat.

"Natasha McGavin," Vanessa screamed as she got out of her seat to make her point. "I have had *all* I can take of you."

That was it, the moment the third Natasha broke free, when there was no other choice but to confront Vanessa about the one topic that mattered. Vanessa had somehow managed to reach the epicenter of her emotions, breaking through all of Natasha's defenses, sending her to her feet. The fault line had been triggered. The room began to shake.

"Did you say, 'all I can take *of* you' or *'from* you?'" Natasha asked with controlled but powerful fury, speaking clearly and concisely. "Because we both know how much you have already taken *from* me, don't we?"

Natasha had gone from zero to sixty on the rageometer. "You had my friendship but *that* wasn't enough," she continued, laying into Vanessa. "And you had my friends but *they* weren't enough. So you had to have my husband, too."

The room shared a loud, and earned, gasp.

"But he didn't want much of you either, did he, Vanessa?" Natasha pried with deliberate venom. "He didn't stick around long, did he?"

"He left you, Natasha! He left you for *me.*"

"That's where you're wrong. He *did* cheat on me. I have you to thank for that. And then *I* kicked him out. I always knew you were slimy, Vanessa, but I gave you a chance. I thought maybe I misunderstood you, that maybe *everyone* misunderstood you. But I learned what kind of person you are."

"Mathew loved me. It was *you* he had to get away from. Why else did he come to me for love?"

Natasha let out a brutal laugh. "I wouldn't call that trap between your legs 'love.' How many marriages have you ruined? Are you proud of yourself for that? If so—if you have no remorse or guilt about causing so much damage to others—then you really are sick. But now I'm happy to see that your outside is just as awful as your inside. What on heaven's earth *did* you do to your face?"

"I hate you, Natasha McGavin!" Vanessa cried, screeching like a wounded animal, then doing something Sophia did not expect. She picked up her water bottle and threw it at Natasha. She would have made a direct strike if Joseph hadn't jumped in front to take the hit.

"Cut! Cut!" Joseph yelled, holding his head. Sophia ran into the room to intervene. She wasn't sure if he was talking about the recording or the gash on his scalp.

The booth was suddenly flooded with people from the sound room, two wrestling Vanessa to the ground while Natasha waved the wig she yanked from Vanessa's head in the air. "And your hair is fake, too, you deformed monster! Look at this mess!" she bellowed, also sounding like something from the wild.

Joseph, Jonathan and Sophia held their arms around Natasha, pulling her back, hoping to deflate her aggression while also protecting her in case all of Vanessa's flailing freed her to take another swipe.

At this point, Sophia noticed Claire was yelling at the nearly bald Vanessa, "Calm down! Calm down!" while Vanessa's agent, another nip-and-tuck victim, began yelling back at her, "Don't you talk to my client like that!"

Seconds later, without Vanessa's hair, Natasha and her people were led into another studio. They could still hear the other actress hollering like a mad woman in the room they exited. Ten minutes passed before Joseph joined them and asked, "Can we finish this in here? Just us? I'll work with Vanessa separately this afternoon?"

Natasha expressed a deep breath. "Sure," she said, attempting her best game face, but Sophia could tell something in her had shifted.

For the next two hours, Natasha went through the motions, reading her notes with enough mustered energy to get the job done. Someone who didn't know her might not have questioned her enthusiasm, but Sophia did. She knew the actress well enough now to know that behind the soundproof glass window was neither the mature debutante nor the rebellious spitfire. Vanessa had exposed the tip of an iceberg long pushed down by Natasha, ready to break through the surface, uninterested in asking permission to do so.

What had happened reminded Sophia of Twain's favorite expression: "It was a shit show." Depending on the perspective opted for, it was either one of the most tragic or entertaining events ever. Either way, it was Hollywood at its most scandalous and it was on the record.

Natasha was dead silent the entire drive back to The Estate, but when they arrived the crying began and would not stop. It was there she would make significant decisions about her life, giving into confrontations she had managed to avoid for decades. Things for her, and for others, would never be the same again.

CHAPTER 23
THE REST OF THE ICEBERG

Jonathan was the first to see the tears. "Natasha? Are you alright?" But she said nothing, pushing her way past him to get out of the car.

"Natasha!" he called after her. "What is it? What's wrong?"

"Go home," she said, stumbling out of the car door, arms flailing to balance herself.

Jonathan looked in Natasha's direction as he climbed out of the car, then turned back at Sophia, who was trying to catch up. She saw the look of perplexity take over his face. At that moment, she thought she knew what that look meant—that they shared the same confusion about what was happening. She would find out soon enough how wrong she was in that assumption.

Charles had also stepped out of the car, but then reversed his direction and moved back to the driver's door while watching out for traffic. Natasha had gotten out too quickly for him to help her. Perhaps, Sophia thought, he concluded that his assistance was the least of Natasha's concerns at the moment. Before getting back into the car, he demonstrated his polite best, "Will that be all, Ms. McGavin?"

"Yes, Charles," she offered back in a broken voice, pushing through the river of sobs that were gaining momentum.

Sophia straightened up on the sidewalk only to be halted by Jonathan, his arms held out to stop her approach in front of The Estate. "Sophia, that'll be all for today," he said, an impulsive command. "We'll see you tomorrow."

His actions surprised Sophia but brought out a thunder both awesome and terrifying from Natasha. The actress stopped in her tracks, turning to make a stand and weigh in on the matter: "No, Jonathan! *You* go home!"

Jonathan's face shifted gears again, exposing a man scrambling with control—a challenge of which he suddenly became aware he was losing. "Natasha, what are you talking about?"

"GO HOME!" Natasha screamed, showing more ferocity and passion than she had just hours before at the sound studio, or even on that first day when Sophia saw her throw the decanter. "I can't take *this* anymore. I can't take *you* anymore! I want *you* gone. I want *you* out of my life!"

Jonathan's head spun around, looking in multiple directions, as if by doing so he would discover clues to the mystery before him. "But what did *I* do? Why are you saying this?" His rational tone had turned to pleading.

Natasha said nothing in return and Sophia saw she was somewhere else, her eyes proving that whatever she had been holding back had won the struggle. She wiped at her face, perhaps hoping it would stop the pain from taking her, but these efforts appeared in vain. Jonathan responded by putting his hands on his hips—a confused reaction that blended his defenses with perplexity. "I *told* you today was a terrible idea. You can't really mean this."

Natasha bobbed her head, waving her hands in the air at him, like she was swatting something, or him, away. She had been undone by something Sophia did not yet understand, something that had happened, or was happening, between her and Jonathan—something Sophia knew nothing about.

"But I *can* mean this, and I *do* mean this," Natasha told him.

"Your days of telling me how I feel, and what I do, are over. If you don't leave right now, I'll call the police. NOW!"

Jonathan stared at her, silent and confused, growing more upset. He attempted one last plea. "Why is this *my* fault? Why are you blaming *me*? You know how you get. You know I'm the *only* one who understands you!"

This brought out another furious response from Natasha. "You say that like I got what I deserve. Like I don't deserve more out of life!"

"I begged you not to open this can of worms!"

"I SAID, 'GO!' It's over!"

"What do you mean? What's over?"

"You know. YOU KNOW!"

"This will pass, Natasha. Give it time. This will all be behind you again."

Tears threw themselves from Natasha's eyes. "You've told me that before. You've tried to protect me but *look* at me. *Look* at *me!* How many years have gone by and it still just comes back. It never goes away, Jonathan. And your approach has *hurt* me not *helped* me. I can't do this anymore. All of this, you and me, it's over! GO!"

Sophia stepped up, clueless to the depths or reason for the exchange between the two, feeling it was the right time to intervene. She didn't want to hurt or anger Jonathan, but Natasha had made her wishes clear and she felt it was best for everyone to provide some space between the two. "Natasha, please, let's go inside," she said. Unsure of what else to tell her, she repeated herself, simultaneously pushing her hand into her bag to find her keys, "Please, let's go *inside.*"

Jonathan grabbed at Natasha's arm, but she pushed him away. Sophia responded by wrapping herself around Natasha, pulling her back to give her further distance from Jonathan. Then she put herself in front of Natasha to block any additional advances before scrambling to fit her key into the lock.

"Stay away from me, Jonathan! Anything other than *this* has got to be better," Natasha added before following Sophia through the door.

Whatever control Natasha had held onto was lost the moment the front door shut, and she crumbled, immobilized by her pain, by what had been unleashed.

"Here," Sophia told her, taking her arm and leading her into the foyer, "Let's get you inside and changed. Would you like some tea?"

But Natasha did not respond. She followed Sophia's lead up the stairs to her bedroom, unvocal except for the violent crying. Sophia turned to face Natasha to ask her how she could help make her more comfortable when she noticed how completely drenched the older woman's face was, as were her neck and the top of her dress. Sophia had never before seen anything like it.

"Please don't leave me," Natasha begged her.

"I won't," Sophia said, beginning to feel great concern for Natasha. "I won't go anywhere."

Natasha stared at her, shaking her head. "It's over. It's *all* over."

"What is?" Sophia said. "What's over?"

"I can't keep living like this! Things have to change!"

Sophia could not have been more confused. "*What* do you want to change, Natasha? What can I do to make things better?"

Natasha lifted her hand and put it alongside Sophia's face. "Do you know you're one of the kindest people I have ever met? If I had had a child, I would have wanted her to be just like you."

Sophia could see the hurt overwhelming Natasha's body, crippled by something far beyond her comprehension, beyond today's recording session, something deep and lasting.

"What can I do to help, Natasha?" Sophia asked. "Today was a crappy day. Tomorrow will be better. I promise!"

"Help me get out of this goddamned dress," she told Sophia. "Then get me my sleeping pills from the bathroom."

Sophia did as she was told, dressing Natasha in a nightgown and giving her two pills, as noted on the bottle, to knock her out. She also made a mental note to take the rest of the bottle and any other prescriptions to ensure Natasha didn't get crazy ideas later.

Natasha climbed under the covers. "Stay with me? Please don't leave me," she pleaded with the fragility of a child certain she had seen a ghost, and perhaps she had.

"I'm not going anywhere, Natasha," Sophia told her, holding her hand. "I'll stay here as long as you need me."

For twenty afflicted minutes, Sophia was haunted by the heavy sobs of a woman in agony, tortured by something else in the room with them that neither could make go away. She simply could not understand what it was that had brought out such a disturbance in Natasha, or even what had actually occurred. Watching Natasha, who she had come to feel fondly for, feel this way was almost too much for Sophia to take and she prayed it would go away quickly, that slumber would bring her fast relief. She did her best to ignore her own discomfort stirred up by the situation, to choke down her own sadness so she could be there emotionally for Natasha, until sleep was stronger than her sorrow.

After an hour had passed, and Sophia was certain Natasha would not be awakening anytime soon, she went downstairs to hang up her coat, pockets filled with the pill bottles she took from both the upstairs bathroom and Natasha's nightstand. As she grabbed her bag, she heard footsteps behind her. "There you are. What in the world happened today?" Jasper asked.

She turned around, relieved to see her friend who must have heard them storm in. She would have hugged him if it weren't for the fact he greeted her with a drink and a plate of food.

"What an unbelievable day," Sophia told him, sipping the glass. "Please tell me this has vodka in it."

Jasper shook his head apologetically. "We can arrange that, if you'd like."

"I don't know what happened. Something just snapped in Natasha. One minute, she and Vanessa were squabbling. It was ugly but it was manageable. Then, before anyone knew it, they were attacking each other, including Vanessa throwing a bottle across the room and Natasha snatching the wig off Vanessa's head. By the time we got home, she went from crumbling to collapsed. The two hate each other like nothing I've ever seen. I know that there's more to it than what happened at the recording studio today. I mean, it's been forty years! That's four decades! Did you know that Vanessa had an affair with Natasha's husband?"

"Really? Is that why they hate each other so much?"

"I think that has a lot to do with it," Sophia told him, filling Jasper in on the events of the day, a literal blow-by-blow.

"All this came out in front of everyone? Including Jonathan?" he asked, looking dizzy from the story.

"Yes! He looked as uncomfortable as you can only imagine. I was mesmerized and horrified all at once. But I have to say that I feel so sorry for Natasha. She's completely crushed. Somehow, all of that has thrown her into this awful state of despair. You remember how she was the day I started? Well, that was nothing."

"Oh, boy. What's she doing now?"

"She's sleeping. She wanted two sleeping pills, which I was glad to give her, and then she cried herself to sleep. I'm telling you, she was hysterical."

"Why isn't Jonathan here? Should we have him come over? He'll know how to handle this."

"No, we can't! That's the other part of the story I can't believe. I think she just fired him! She told me to stay with her and told him she never wanted to see him again."

"Why? Is that why he keeps calling here?" Jasper asked. "Now *I* need a drink!"

"He's called?" Sophia asked.

"Several times. He says it's urgent they talk. He told me to 'reason with Natasha,' but wouldn't elaborate, not that I would've asked him to. Do you know what that means?"

"I'm not sure," Sophia said, reaching into her bag and pulling out her cell phone. Checking the recent call log, she saw Jonathan's name, and then flashed it at Jasper to show him he had tried her as well. "She just told him that it's all over, whatever that means, and that he knew why she was doing what she was doing. Afterwards, she told me she 'can't keep living like this.'"

"Like what? What does that mean?"

"I don't know. I was hoping you might know. It was awful. She just kept crying, so I let her have two sleeping pills. But I took the rest of her pills and hid them, just in case."

"Good thinking. Better safe than sorry."

"Sleep should do her a lot of good. Hopefully, she'll wake up tomorrow feeling a hundred times better."

Sophia did as she promised, staying in and around Natasha's bedroom for the remainder of the day and evening. She tried to pass the time writing but quickly gave up the idea once she realized it would be impossible to concentrate. Images of a distraught Natasha played over and over again in her head, defeating her concentration and motivation. Instead, she skimmed through uninteresting magazines she found stacked in the great room, dozed off and on, and wondered how it was possible in this day and age that Natasha did not have Internet access she could use.

Natasha seemed to Sophia to be a woman trapped between generations, unwilling to accept she was no longer the ingénue, but even more unready to play the part of the older woman, regardless of the perks and benefits that came with age. There were countless things she had said over the months to imply she was fighting time with everything she had, comments that Sophia—left alone with her thoughts as she watched over Natasha—recalled as she herself battled the hours. All the while, Sophia struggled with the questions the incident raised. What else was there that she didn't know? And why had today triggered such an episode?

It was just before three in the morning when Natasha awoke again. Sophia had been slumbering between unsettling dreams in the armchair next to the bed when she was stirred by Natasha's movement. Natasha was quiet at first so Sophia wasn't entirely sure she was awake. But then she sat up and looked around. It seemed to Sophia that Natasha became aware of her circumstances again and that her troubles sank right back in because her uncontrollable crying started from where it left off. Sophia sat on the side of the bed with her, holding her hand, stroking her head and hair. "I think maybe we should see someone tomorrow. Maybe your doctor? She'll know more about how to help you feel better. Maybe help you with what's going on."

Natasha said nothing, only responding with more sobs, and Sophia realized her hands were now completely wet, as if she had just placed them under a faucet.

"Is that okay?" Sophia asked, already knowing she would do it regardless. "May I call your doctor tomorrow?"

Natasha, defenseless, nodded her permission. Half an hour later, her sobs were replaced with heavy breathing and she was asleep again.

Jasper returned to The Estate at seven in the morning. This time it was Sophia who met him with a drink—a cup of coffee.

"You look like crap," he told her, trading the observation for the offering. "Long night?"

"You could say that," Sophia told him, trying to focus through the blur of exhaustion, unable to remember the last time she slept so little throughout the night. "I think she should see her doctor. This is beyond us."

"What is?"

"Whatever's bothering Natasha. It runs deep. She needs a professional. This isn't something we're equipped to deal with. She's been crying for the better part of the past day."

"That's not good."

"No, it's not. I think something is really wrong. That's a damaged woman up there and we're not going to do her any good by just hoping the problem goes away on its own."

"But can we get Natasha to go?"

"She told me she'd see the doctor. Maybe we can even get her to come here?"

"I think that's possible," Jasper said.

"After yesterday, I believe anything's possible."

Dr. Boni arrived a little after eleven o'clock. Natasha was awake by then, lying in bed, staring at the wall in between emotional bouts. Sophia held her hand and talked to her quietly, but wasn't sure how much of her was present and how much was off somewhere else suffering at the hands of another place and time. "Didn't I tell you? Today's a new day. Don't you feel better?"

But Natasha did not reply. She held onto Sophia's hand with what seemed to be most of her strength, a grip that told her, "If you let go, I will die."

So Sophia didn't let go, not even when Jasper escorted the physician into the room. Her colleague and friend seemed uncomfortable to be in the room, made an "eh gads" face to Sophia, and left as soon as he made the introductions.

"Good morning, Natasha," Dr. Boni said, standing over the bed. She tried to make eye contact with the patient but only Sophia would look her in the eyes.

Sophia glanced down at her own hands, still holding onto Natasha's, and then looked back at Dr. Boni. She repeated this gesture once more. Dr. Boni seemed to understand Sophia was telling her they should change places because she sat on the side of the bed and slid her hands around Natasha's just as Sophia removed hers.

Natasha noticed the switch off and squirmed so Sophia responded immediately to calm her. "I'm still here, Natasha. Don't worry. I'm right here."

Dr. Boni took the lead from there. "You're not feeling so well today, are you, hon?"

Natasha managed to shake her head, forcing tears to rise to the surface. The admission relieved Sophia, giving her hope that help had arrived.

"Do you want to talk about it?" Dr. Boni asked.

Natasha tilted her head until she found Sophia's eyes, filling the room with more unspoken communication.

"Do you want me to share what happened?" Sophia asked her.

Natasha nodded.

"Natasha's feeling pretty blue. We went to an event yesterday that I think opened up some old wounds," she told Dr. Boni, and then looked at Natasha. "Does that sound pretty accurate?"

"Yes," Natasha said.

"Natasha has been sleeping, and upset, the better part of the last day, ever since we got back yesterday afternoon. I think she's depressed."

"I am not depressed," Natasha said feebly, defending herself, an attempt to slip back into the guarded Natasha that Sophia knew so well.

"Don't say it like it's a bad word," Sophia told her. "Everyone gets sad sometimes. Something serious happened yesterday that hurt you. It's nothing to be ashamed of."

Sophia's words struck a chord with Natasha, causing the tears to return with a vengeance. Dr. Boni reacted with a gentle, controlled sensitivity that told them both that she knew what she was doing. "She's right, Natasha. Depression is *not* a bad word. It's actually very common. I'd like to help you if you'll let me."

Natasha gave in again. "Please. I need your help. I can't do this alone anymore."

"Do what, Natasha?" Dr. Boni asked. "Can you tell me what you mean?"

"All the lies. Act like I feel fine when I don't. When I haven't felt ok in forty years."

"Why is that?" Dr. Boni probed. "Why forty years?"

Natasha stared with wild desperation at Sophia, asking for permission to go on but then doubting her choice to say anything at all. After all these years, it seemed like it took less energy to protect the truth than to share it, a theory she was about to discover was so very wrong.

Sophia confronted Natasha's insecurity once again, hoping to provide her with words that would fill her with courage. "You can do this. There is nothing, absolutely nothing, to be afraid of!"

That was when the rest of the iceberg broke free, clearing the surface, exposing the truth. Natasha spoke openly for the first time in decades, recounting the story that changed her life, giving the details of the before and after, and how she had dealt with it for so long. Sophia could not help but cry with her.

"I'm so sorry," Sophia told her, back on the side of the bed, holding Natasha, comforting her as if she was family. "I'm so very sorry."

Natasha's screams at Jonathan echoed in Sophia's head. *"You know. YOU KNOW!"*

Now Sophia did, too. In the short period of their acquaintance, Sophia had easily walked dozens of miles with Natasha, but she'd never walked an inch in her shoes.

CHAPTER 24
WRITTEN ON STONE

For the next week, life around The Estate refused to bounce back to its previous level of activity, a fact the inhabitants accepted almost immediately. As Natasha continued to wrap herself in the escapist comfort of sleep for the better part of each day, Sophia, who Natasha begged to temporarily move into one of the guest bedrooms on the second floor, did just that.

"It's nothing permanent, of course," Natasha assured her. "It'll just be nice to know you're nearby."

Sophia and Dr. Boni both agreed it was best if someone kept an eye on her for the short-term, until Natasha was on the mend and her depression had been managed.

On the afternoon of the physician's visit, while Natasha slept with the assistance of medication Dr. Boni gave her, Sophia returned to her apartment to collect some of her things for this mini non-vacation on the other side of the park. It was then that she came across something she found timely.

Sophia was not a mystical or magical thinker. She did not believe life—or the universe or God—handed out signs for people that told them, "Look this way," or "Do this," or "Do that." Nor did she believe that everything happened for a

241

reason—although she *was* driven by the idea that each person, regardless of their life circumstances, must find their way in the world and discover their own purpose. She felt strongly that everyone must establish priorities in life and, despite what she claimed in her novel, she didn't feel purpose was predetermined. Sophia's belief system contributed to her writing the dark fable she was now calling *Bad Blood*—a title that held multiple levels of meaning for her characters, their relationships and Dirk's evil intentions. She *did* believe that bad things happened to good people, and vice versa, and that they unfortunately happened all the time. Any newspaper or television program would confirm that, and Natasha was evidence of this position as well.

Sophia's sense of empathy caused her to be completely moved by Natasha's confession of the secrets which she had been holding onto. And while she did not believe in hocus pocus kinds of signs—although she found them to be excellent story devices for creative writing—she did believe in the kind of serendipity that was waiting for her at home.

In the past thirty-six hours, since Sophia last left her apartment, the chalk writer had returned to Amsterdam Avenue, marking up cement and stone and sharing new words of wisdom with the world. His efforts had been a regular part of the neighborhood as long as she had lived there, although she had never seen him in person or caught him—chalk-handed, as it were—in the act. She had assumed the chalk writer was a man because of the occasional dedications of his work to the New York Yankees and to the female species, although Sophia knew several women who shared the same interests and conceded that the alternative was always a possibility. The tribute this time, however, was to the past, present and future—and the timing could not have been more appropriate.

A Letter To The Future

Dear Future Me,

I don't know who we will be when one day we meet.
I don't know if you will recognize me or if I will recognize you.

Perhaps there will be a glimmer in your eye that I recall.
Perhaps there will be memories, like flashes of time, that we share from long ago.
Will my head be full of silver and my pockets full of gold?
Will I have figured out my problems?
Or will they have figured out me?
I wonder what I will have discovered by that time.
Have I made peace with what was?
Have I done all that I needed to do?
I'm sending you this letter in hopes all of our good traits make it,
And that you're surprised by some of the new ones I gather along the way.
Please know I also hope I was able to shake some of the bad as well.
In case I've failed, I wanted to tell you I'm sorry.
You deserve better.

Love,
Present Me

PS
I would leave you my email address but who knows if there will be email in the future. Besides, there are crazies in this city. I don't want others emailing me, too.

Sophia's trip to her apartment was a quick one. She was in and out within a few minutes, grabbing her digital camera and clothes for a couple of days, and stuffing them into her J.Crew travel bag. On her way back, she took a picture of the chalk drawing.

Natasha was deep asleep when she returned to The Estate, as she would be for the remainder of the day. As it turned out, Natasha required little from Sophia over the next few days other than the knowledge of her presence nearby. So Sophia spent significant periods of time writing in the great room. Much to her surprise and relief, she managed to get a decent amount of work done. She hoped she would stay as focused and productive this summer in the Hamptons, that was if their plans hadn't changed and if Natasha still wanted to go out there after everything that had happened. Sophia had no idea if and how this might change the choices she would make in the future.

Sophia had just begun Part Three of her novel—the final third of the story. After a lot of debating and problem-solving, she had figured out how to make all of the elements work properly together to get the story where she wanted it to go. Unlike the first two parts, which hovered mostly around a single decade of time as she established the vital backstories and early lives of her characters, this final part would accelerate through the years quickly, jumping across the next four decades, graduating the lives and ages of the characters. But as with the first parts, she would continue alternating between the multiple and seemingly disparate storylines with each chapter until they eventually caught up to one another for an explosive conclusion, an ending that was now amazingly not so far away. Sophia was making tremendous progress and her commitment was paying off with results she could actually now see. It motivated her and made her want to keep pushing forward.

In the first chapter of this final section, Sophia established that years had passed for all of the characters. Dirk, who had long since mastered his evil and powerful ways, was now an adult who had manipulated his way into a successful career in New York City. For solely opportunistic reasons, his eyes were on the daughter of the Chairman and CEO of VCC, the canned goods company where he had aggressively climbed his way up the corporate ladder. Sophia had not yet completely revealed his intentions to the reader—the evil he would unleash once he reached the top—but had hinted throughout that he would stop at nothing to get there, that he was playing people like pawns in order to forever leave his mark. The reader understood by this point, though, that his vengeance would affect not only his home town, May Valley, but the entire world as well.

In the next chapter of this final part, she would continue the story of Anna and Dirk's orphaned son, now a boy, whose well-being the reader finally knew was being closely watched by

Sister Margaret. It had been recently unveiled that the vision the sister had had as a child—her calling to become a nun—involved her heavenly obligation to save the life of this boy. While she knew the orphanage was probably the safest place for him, she suspected that the Bad People might one day find either Anna or Father McKenzie since they were the only two who knew the child's true identity and his whereabouts. When the Bad People did find the boy, the result led to a physical struggle to save him that involved a fire at the orphanage and their narrow escape. Sister Margaret had no knowledge if the Bad People had found Anna, the priest or both, but she knew she would have to continue to protect the boy at all costs. So they fled for their lives, hoping to find a corner of the world they could hide in for safety.

As Sophia wrote the chapter that found Sister Margaret and the boy in their new lives, she thought of Natasha and what she now knew about her life. While not deliberate, she recognized there were similarities between Natasha and this story—the running, the fear of something catching up to her, the sense of loss. Sophia considered that if Natasha were to ever read the story—which, of course, she hoped one day she would want to,—she would have to warn her that some details might strike a nerve and hit close to home.

Part Three
CHAPTER TWO
February 1977

The boy walked home across the freshly fallen blanket of snow, leaving behind boot prints with every step. Long before winter eclipsed autumn, the short path through the quiet neighborhood had become second nature and, as it was with everything he did, he looked over his shoulder regularly to make sure he wasn't being followed. "Beware of strangers," she reminded him regularly, giving him a look from a secret language they both understood. Theirs was a life of precautions. It was how it had to be to ensure their safety, to guarantee they wouldn't be found again.

Even in St. Louis, seemingly a million miles from Rogerstown, he felt it wouldn't be long before they showed up again. They had somehow managed to find him at St. Teresa's, and even though the newspapers reported that they both died in the fire, he was certain they would soon figure out that she tricked them. Not a day went by without him seeing the faces of the Bad People in the shadows, or thinking that they would eventually find them hiding behind different names and lives.

"We're dead to them," she had insisted, showing him the articles she found detailing the tragedy. The world thought they were gone forever, which he could see both relieved and saddened her.

The concept of death, though, and what it meant was still not easy for him to fully grasp. He knew he saw things differently than others and that that was why the Bad People had come for him, but he was unable to understand how one day you could be alive and the next dead. He did not understand what happened to you afterwards, despite her repeated attempts to explain.

"When you die," she told him after their escape, attempting to be convincing as much for her sake as for his, "your soul goes to Heaven. In our case, this time, we've been allowed to start over again—new names, new city, new lives."

Her tone contended with urgency as she said, "No one knows we're still alive. We need to be extremely careful about protecting that knowledge and each other."

He may not have been able to understand mortality but he comprehended the importance of her words. He had seen the Bad People. He knew they had to keep each other safe.

While months had passed since that fateful night, the memory of them being chased through the burning orphanage was present and powerful in their minds, and it still gave them shivers.

But they had managed to escape the fire, fleeing Rogerstown in the darkness, chasing the morning past the California state border and beyond. As they travelled the lonely and consuming miles, they watched their old lives dissolve into the distance. When fear had retreated far enough away and she was finally able to breathe again without looking over her shoulder, Sister Margaret pulled off the barren highway, stopping the car and staring ahead into the abandoned morning. She swallowed a deep breath, held it tight for a long moment, and then exhaled…as if for the first time since she had started to suspect that they might have found the boy. She then turned to face him. Noah?" she asked him. "May I have a hug, please?"

He was still stunned but he happily obliged. As they embraced, he felt her tremble and saw the lights and stars that came from the closeness. He also heard the high pitch of pain as it circulated around her body, sensing that it was now more than her heart that was damaged. It was her soul, too, but he said nothing about it, not sure if she would understand what he meant or how he knew. He had long since realized he saw and understood things others did not.

"You saved me," he told her.

"We saved each other," she answered back.

Sister Margaret hadn't slept in over a day when she finally took them to a motel, the adrenaline pumping through her veins as her mind calculated their next moves. Before retiring for the night, she said there was something she needed to do and left the room, assuring him that she would be right back. He watched for her in the parking lot through the folds of the curtains in the window and saw her return minutes later with the license plates in hand. He knew, even at his age, why she had done that.

By the time they arrived in St. Louis, she had already seen the newspapers. Their story made national news with headlines such as "Tragedy Befalls California Orphanage" and "America Mourns Orphanage Fire Victims." She had chosen St. Louis as the place to stop for good because the local paper hadn't included photos with the article. When they arrived, she shared the assortment she had collected along the way to put his mind at rest.

"You see, Noah? They think we died."

The boy nodded but still did not seem convinced.

It was difficult but there was no other choice than for them to become different people. He saw the struggle in her actions and heard it in her words. But in her eyes, gleaming directly into his the way they always did, he knew for certain that the one thing that remained unchanged was her love for him. And if it had changed at all, it was that she loved him more. They had shared life and death together, their old lives left behind in Northern California in a pile of ashes.

The boy's abilities had always allowed him special insights, but what it did not offer him at that moment was the full comprehension of the loss with which she was grappling. The fine print of the newspaper articles and the declaration of their deaths put a permanent division between this world and the past. What he did not know was that she had already traveled so far in her life, had already fought to move away from bad times and bad people, that she had thought she'd finally found a safe haven. Wasn't that what she had been promised?

But she had been wrong, and at an unimaginable cost that almost included the boy. He was her priority now, she told herself, and she would never make that mistake again. Up close, evil was far more frightening than in her teachings. It was ruthless and relentless and it would stop at nothing to get its way.

When the boy arrived at the house, he walked up the cement path to the front door and pulled at the chain around his neck until he found the keys hidden beneath his shirt. He knew it bothered her to be unable to pick him up from school, that there were times when her own classroom at the middle school demanded she stay late. She had told him that until she could get a teaching job at his school, or until he was old enough to attend hers, they would have to do their best. "Everything is going to work out just fine," she had insisted, and he had agreed with her—not because it felt true but because they both needed it to be so.

As he entered the house, he stepped onto the rubber mat on the kitchen floor, then leaned backward to shut the door behind him, double locking it before twisting out of his snowy boots. He also pulled the chain across and placed the metal head into its slot, just in case.

The house was loud with silence, as he expected. He placed his backpack on the kitchen table and walked across the faded linoleum floor until he reached the small, shag-carpeted living room. On the end table next to the sofa was the book she had brought home for him shortly after they arrived in St. Louis. It always reminded him of the fire and their travels through miles of night, as well as the secret and the love they shared.

"Leave it to me," she had told him, when they first arrived. "I'll find us a home. I'll get a job. I'll take care of everything."

And she did just that.

They had only been in St. Louis a few days when she presented Noah with the book. While he was advanced in reading, he was only able to make out a few words from the cover— "Sir," "and the," "Green." What first grabbed him was the picture—an impressive illustration of a handsome knight standing tall atop a beautiful horse, a sharp and mighty sword in his hand. The knight had a bold and proud look on his face. Noah had looked back at her with wonder, unsure of the present she was giving him.

"I believe your birthmother would have wanted you to have this," she told him.

The boy was surprised and confused because he had never heard her speak about such things. He searched her face for answers. "You knew her?"

"No," she told him, "I did not but I spoke with her once. She asked me to name you Gawain. I believe she got the name from this story."

"Gawain?" he asked, trying to adjust his mouth to the unique sound of it.

"I think she would've liked for you to have known that," she said, a little uneasy as she spoke, not knowing how he would respond to this news.

"Do you know anything else?" he asked.

"There are a few things but, unfortunately, not much."

"Like what?" he asked, attentive and curious. "What else do you know?"

"I spoke to her the night you were delivered to St. Teresa's. She was very upset about not being able to take care of you the way she would've liked," she said, trying to be as honest as possible, deciding that was the best approach. It was just the two of them now—the truth was all they had.

"What else?"

She smiled. "She told me to take very good care of you because you were very special."

"She said that?"

"Yes, she did. 'Very special.' And she asked me to name you Gawain. It's important you understand that no one knows anything about this except for you, me and her. I never said anything at St. Teresa's because I knew Mother Beverly never would've allowed it. But you know we're both going to have to change our names now and I was thinking you might like to change yours to Gawain."

The boy smiled, and she knew he liked the idea.

"I looked it up," she told him. "The name means, 'White Hawk.' I think it's a very nice name. It's unique, like you."

He nodded in agreement. "What's it about?" he asked, pointing at the book in his hand, still wanting more information.

"It's about honor and chivalry. It's also an adventure, with a moral. We'll read it together. I think she would have liked that."

He wanted to start reading the book that very moment, to learn the story he was now named after. "And you?" he asked. "What will your new name be?"

"Well, I don't know," she said. "There are lots of nicknames for Margaret. Maybe I can choose one of those so I don't feel like I completely changed my name. You know, it's a name I've had for a long time. Can you help me decide?"

"Yes," he agreed, still examining the book in his hands.

"One nickname for Margaret is Greta. I always liked that name."

But Gawain made a face, disagreeing with her.

She thought for a few more moments. "Margaret means 'Pearl' in Greek. How about that?" she asked.

He considered the new suggestion. "Pearl is pretty, like you. I like it."

She looked at him with her "I-want-to-hug-you" face which always made him blush.

"Pearl and Gawain. That settles it."

They began reading the book that evening. It was the first of many times they would read it together.

Sophia closed her laptop for the night before heading off for bed, pleased with the surprises she was layering throughout the story. But surprises, she knew, were not limited to her novel. They showed up in real life as well, sometimes making themselves known in the least obvious of circumstances and at the most random of times. She believed life was like that—unpredictable and facetious—sometimes giving her what she asked for or needed, but usually at times other than when she thought she wanted or needed them most.

CHAPTER 25
SWEET

"What do you mean you're staying there?" Sophia's mother demanded.

"Just what I said, Mom. She isn't feeling well so I'm staying here a few days to keep an eye on her."

Diane growled subtly, her standard indicator she wasn't thrilled with something. This time she went so far as to follow it up with the actual words. "I'm not sure I like the idea of that."

Sophia wasn't entirely surprised by the reaction—her mother had a history of being defensive and overly protective. "Mom, don't be like that. Try to be understanding."

"Sophia, she's a grown woman. Doesn't she have friends? Doesn't she have family? You *work* for her. She's paying you to be her employee, nothing more. There are limits she needs to respect."

There were times when her mother's reactions had a way of making Sophia shut down. This was one of them, and she sensed her retreat mechanism kick into full operation. But before Sophia stopped listening completely, or tried steering the conversation into another direction, her own defensive techniques developed over the years gave one final attempt at invoking her mother's sympathy. "Actually, I'm not sure she does, Mom. She may be well off in many ways, but there are plenty where she's not. I'm not going to go into all of the details with you, but just believe me when I tell you she's a good person who deserves a little TLC right now. I feel bad for her."

"Well, I have to speak my mind…"

Yes, Mom…I know!

"…and tell you I think it's a little weird. And while you make an excellent point, I still don't understand. She is a very fortunate person with a lot of money. What does she have to be troubled about?"

"Mom, don't be like that," Sophia replied. "You can't possibly think that because she's been successful that she has no problems. That's ridiculous. Besides, you're being insensitive. *And* suspicious *and* paranoid."

Her mother didn't like the sound of that, not one bit, so she yelled out away from the phone to tattle on her to her father. "BEEEEN! Your daughter called me paranoid. She says I'm sounding suspicious."

Sophia could hear her father in the near distance, first with a loud cackle, then a statement. "Well, Diane, she has a point. Why are you grilling her about that poor woman? They're grown-up, for God's sake."

Diane countered with her own sinister laugh—another reaction Sophia had witnessed as long as she could remember. "She's not *that* old. Besides, need I remind you she's only a few years older that *you?*" his wife told him.

"Than *us,* dear. *Us!*" Ben retaliated.

Diane was quick with the retort and seemed ready for a brawl. "Don't group me together with you two old fogies, dear."

Par for the course, Sophia's parents were getting lost in their own side conversation. She had called them only to give them a quick update while waiting for Natasha, but it had quickly turned into something she hadn't anticipated nor wanted. "Uh, guys. Maybe I should let you go so you two can discuss this amongst yourselves."

"Sure, dear," her mother said, already forgetting she was the reason they were arguing. "That'd be great. But before I do, your father wants to know if you want one or two seats at Austen's wedding."

Sophia knew immediately her mother was lying. She always blamed her father for her inquisitions, particularly in instances where the topic might be controversial or ill-timed. Heaven forbid Diane Connors be discovered stirring the pot when no one else in the family wanted to do it.

"What are you asking me?"

"Will you be bringing a guest with you to Austen's wedding? Your sister is finalizing the dinner arrangements and needs to know if you count for one or two settings."

"Do I have to decide this *now?* Isn't the wedding a *year* away?"

But Sophia knew what her mother really wanted to find out. This was her way of prying, of asking, "Are you seeing anyone?" Why her mother—one of the least diplomatic and most direct people on the planet who had no shame about those qualities— could not just come out and ask the question, she did not know.

"'If you count for one or two?' Your choice of words could not be worse."

"Now who's being paranoid? I don't think I like your tone, Sophia."

"Fine, Mom. Tell Austen to count me for two. I'm bringing Natasha with me. The truth is we've become lesbian lovers. That's why I'm moving into her home."

"Well, now…aren't you just the comedian today? Ha, ha, ha. Do you hear that? That's me laughing. I ask a simple question and you get all snippy and smart with me. I don't appreciate it, I'll tell you."

"Goodbye, Mother. I'm hanging up now. One of us actually has work to do," Sophia said and then did just that, once again amazed at how her parents clearly lived in another world.

Also living an existence quite different from Sophia was her employer and now temporary hostess, Natasha, who emerged two minutes later from her bedroom, finally dressed, running shoes and all. "I'm ready."

Sophia sipped the last of the home-squeezed orange juice Jasper made for them and said, "Me, too!"

"Were you on the phone?" Natasha asked curiously. "I heard talking."

Sophia hoped she hadn't heard what she said, especially the lesbian lovers part. It would have required some explaining she preferred not having to do. "My folks."

"That's very sweet," Natasha said.

Sophia knew why Natasha felt that way. "Most of the time it's sweet. Sometimes, like today, it's just crazy."

Natasha smiled as she zipped up her jacket. "I understand. I had a mother once, too."

As they began their decent to the main floor, Sophia asked, "Is she still alive?"

"My mother? Oh, no. It's been many years now. But you know what's odd? No matter how long it's been, sometimes I forget, like I go to pick up the phone to call her to tell her something, and then I remember she's gone."

The prospect saddened Sophia. Despite the occasional turmoil with her mother, she knew how crushed she would be if she was no longer alive. She also remembered how devastated her mother had been when Nonna had passed away. It was a monumental loss that was always present.

"I've been dreaming about her a lot the last few nights," Natasha continued. "It's like once the emotional dam broke open for me, so did all of these other memories."

Sophia opened the door for Natasha. "Is that hard?"

Natasha considered the question, but wasn't reserved in responding. She was getting used to talking about such things, to trust that they would not destroy her if she did. "Some memories are difficult and some are not. The thing is, when you spend as much time and energy as I have, for so long, trying to cover up bad memories, you inadvertently also hide the good ones, too. They're all interconnected. If one thing has to go, it'll do its damnedest to drag others with it."

As they reached the street and began heading towards Park Avenue, Sophia asked, "What have you been dreaming about? If you want to talk about it. If not, I understand."

"No, I don't mind. I really don't. Dr. Bland says it's good for me and, frankly, I feel like I'm ready to talk about it. I think I've been ready for some time but just didn't know it."

That was where they were headed—to see Dr. Bland, which was part of their new morning walk routine as well as part of the agreement Natasha had made with Dr. Boni the morning she visited The Estate. Dr. Boni had said she would agree to let the patient stay in the comfort of her own home as long as she agreed to a few conditions. The first and easiest of the guidelines was for Natasha to take medication to calm her nerves. Dr. Boni's assessment was that Natasha seemed to be overwhelmed by an emotional awakening that was causing her more pain than she was ready to deal with. "Turning on the light in a closet full of memories can be a challenging thing," she had told Natasha. "Especially if that closet hasn't been opened in a very long time. You might find things you're not prepared for. It'd be ideal if this type of thing happened gradually, but the human mind rarely works that way. It, like people, wants to do things its own way, which sometimes is not the best for anyone involved."

"That rings a bell," Natasha had joked, her first since slipping out of control at the recording session. "It's all or nothing with me."

The second stipulation was that Natasha get started on an anti-depressant to see if that might remedy some of the issues she admitted to having suffered from her whole life. She told Dr. Boni and Sophia that she had never before acknowledged her battle to anyone other than Jonathan.

The third part of the agreement was that Natasha needed to spend time with Dr. Bland to discuss the issues recently dug up. Sophia was a big supporter of this idea and suggested they add the therapy sessions as part of a new walk schedule in hopes the combination of the two activities would help eliminate some of the anxiety from the experience for Natasha.

"I've been remembering all of these things about my mother and what she used to put up with from my father," Natasha said, answering Sophia's question about her dreams.

"It doesn't sound like you were close with your him."

"No, not at all. Honestly, he was a miserable son of a bitch. An alcoholic, a womanizer. Which was probably why I set up shop with Mathew."

"You think you chose Mathew because he was like your father?"

"Yes, exactly. He was what I was looking for because he was all that I knew. I was conditioned to want those same qualities in a man, even though I knew how much my father hurt my mother and how unhappy he made me and my siblings."

The idea rattled Sophia a little and her mind wandered, making her question if the same were true for her, too. There were certainly similarities between Kevin and her father, that was for sure. They shared some good traits in common—humor, work ethic, temperament. But were there other reasons she had chosen him that perhaps had nothing to do with her father and everything to do with her? Had she been attracted to Kevin, or felt it was alright to let down her guard with him, because she sensed on a deeper level that ultimately he would want something else and move on? Had she fallen for the romance of the relationship because she knew there would never be enough time for the pedals of the rose to wither away?

"But like you said," Sophia reminded Natasha, "acknowledging the bad sometimes makes room for the good. Do you have any good ones about your father?"

"He was a hard worker. He provided for us as best he knew how, I guess. Those were different times. Men weren't allowed to show emotion. They weren't supposed to be affectionate. The role of a man and father was not what it is now. I think the only times my parents were intimate were when they made us."

"How many of you were there?"

Natasha laughed, knowing Sophia wanted to do the math. "Three. Can you imagine making love three times in your whole life?"

Sophia laughed right back, not at Natasha but at the term she used. While she had some romance running through her veins, or at least once had, using the term "making love" was dated and out of the question. Natasha saw the look on her face and asked, "What is it?"

"People don't really say 'making love' anymore."

"Really?"

"No, I don't think so," Sophia said. "But you obviously do. Now *that's* 'sweet.'"

Natasha winked at Sophia, communicating to her that it didn't go unnoticed that she had deliberately brought back the same term that Natasha had used earlier. Sophia was clever that way, always managing to connect past and present references, a skill that Natasha had said on different occasions that she respected. She had gone so far as to saying that she appreciated the way Sophia's mind worked, even if it was occasionally at her expense. It had been years since someone had felt bold enough to tease her in such a way.

"You mean old," Natasha said.

Sophia smiled. "No. I mean sweet."

Fifteen blocks north and an hour later, Sophia waited in the coffee shop around the corner from Dr. Bland's office, hovering over her laptop and a troublesome writing snag. She was certain this time she had gone as far as she ever could, that both her talent and luck had run out or run away, abandoning her amongst the cappuccinos and croissants. That was the process—there were good days and bad days, great moment and hellacious ones—and Sophia was considering what she would do if she couldn't find a better way to get an adult Gawain to expose Dirk's villainous plans and bring his world to a crushing halt. Natasha saved the day when she peeked her head through the door. "I'm out here."

"Thank God!" Sophia said, packing up her belongings in record time.

Outside, she joined Natasha and asked, "How was today?"—unable to see the telltale signs hidden behind Natasha's sunglasses until she dipped them in response to the question.

"Does that puffiness mean good or bad?" But Sophia's attempt to charm the sadness out of her fell flat on the cement at their feet.

"It was fine. Let's get out of here please," Natasha said, rushing them to get moving. "I'd rather go hide in the park."

Sophia put her arm through Natasha's. "Let's go then. Dr. Connors' orders: one lap around."

The previous days had followed a similar agenda. After a session with Dr. Bland, Natasha needed time to process and relax, and it took about half a mile before she was able to return to the present world. The break did wonders for Sophia as well, who had been thinking about how she wanted to throw her laptop and herself into on-coming traffic.

"Okay, I'm back," Natasha said as she and Sophia rounded the reservoir.

"Tough stuff, that going back in time, huh?" Sophia asked.

"You could say that," Natasha allowed.

"Does it make you feel any better to know I'm having trouble going *forward?*"

"Writing problems?"

"You could say that," Sophia admitted.

"You'll work it out. Don't worry."

"I hope you're right. But it sure doesn't feel like it at the moment."

"I know the feeling. Believe me," Natasha said.

"Want to talk about it?" Sophia asked.

"Don't think I can't see you trying to change the subject."

Sophia laughed. "Am I trying to change the subject or are you? I lost track!" Their banter brought a smile to both their faces.

"Do you want to talk about it?" Natasha asked.

"Is that a trick question?"

Natasha pulled on Sophia's arm, which was still linked with hers. "It's just a question, dear. You don't have to talk about it if you don't want to."

Sophia pulled back on Natasha's arm, not to get away but to tell her she didn't feel threatened by her inquiry or by her. Natasha had a way of bringing out Sophia's nurturing side, of making her feel like she was with family. They had begun to develop an understanding, an intimacy and kinship that her mother did not see because she was not there with them. Perhaps, Sophia considered, her mother was even a little jealous because she sensed that Natasha was getting some of the day-to-day attention and affection she herself wished she was receiving.

"It can really be awful," Sophia answered, approaching tears of her own because of the frustration that gnawed at her. She realized that what she really wanted to say was that being stuck made her lose confidence in her talent, her value as a person, everything. But sharing those thoughts seemed inappropriate because she wasn't sure they compared to what Natasha was battling with. "Even if I've been on a roll for weeks, I feel wrecked when I run into a wall. I just lose hope."

Natasha comforted her. "Being creative isn't as easy or fun as people think it is. Why do you think so many artists go mad?"

Sophia shook her head. "It can be torture. Sometimes I wonder if I'm kidding myself. What if, when I finish and start shopping it around, people tell me it's terrible? What will I do then?"

"That's the risk we artists take. Give yourself some space. Step away from it and return with fresh eyes later. You'll figure it out."

Sophia let out a big sigh. "God, I hope you're right."

They walked a little further until Sophia's eyes were dry again. Then she broke the silence. "Your turn."

"Today was more of the same," Natasha told her. "But what's nagging at me now is that I'm starting to feel like I wasted so much time. I'm so angry that I listened to Jonathan, that I let him protect me. I should have done things my way from the beginning. I'm upset about all of the opportunities I wasted. And I'm trying to accept all the things that happened, things *I'm* responsible for, too. I feel like I'm starring in my own hellish version of *The Three Faces of Eve*."

Sophia didn't know the best thing to say, but she stopped walking so Natasha would see how serious she was. "You can't go back in time, Natasha. You can't turn back the clock and make different choices. It just doesn't work that way. But what you *can* do is live every day how you want to live. *Now.* You need to *live*—in the present."

"If I *could* turn back time, you know one thing I would do?"

Sophia knew better than to engage Natasha in this conversation, but despite her better judgment, she did anyway. "No. What would you do?"

"I'd have started taking anti-depressants years ago. This stuff really works, too. Who knew I was so depressed all this time? It's like I've been sitting in a room that's gotten darker and darker and I didn't realize it until someone finally turned on the lights. I never knew what it was like to feel ok until now."

"That's a great thing to have figured out."

"It is! Everyone should try anti-depressants."

Sophia laughed. "I'm not sure it works that way."

"Well, it should," she said adamantly. "Maybe the world would be a better fucking place."

Sophia saw that Natasha was serious, but the cussing and the statement itself caused her to giggle. This only made Natasha lose it, too, and the two stood there in the middle of Central Park, laughing so hard it hurt.

On their way back to The Estate, Natasha said words that Sophia was excited to hear. "It's time I rejoin the human race. But I don't know how."

"Now you're talking," Sophia told her. "Let's get busy."

"Well, to start, I want to do some research about this whole depression thing. Dr. Bland suggests I'll feel better about my 'condition,' as she calls it, if I know more about what I'm dealing with and realize how many people struggle with it every day."

"That's easy enough to do."

"But how? Do we go to a library?"

"Yes, that's one way to do it. But I really must introduce you to a nifty invention. It's called a 'computer.'"

"I guess I'll need one of those."

"Or we can use mine. Whatever you want. But it might be nice for you to have your own. And we'll also need to introduce you to the Internet, although I'm sure Jonathan would reprimand me if he knew."

"Please don't mention that name to me. His reign of terror is over."

"Is it that bad, Natasha? Don't you think he just wanted to protect you?"

"I don't want to talk about it, Sophia. I don't want to talk about *him*."

"Maybe we should. Wouldn't Dr. Bland want you to discuss this?"

Natasha stopped in her tracks. "Please," she said in a softer tone. "One day. Not now."

Sophia complied. "Ok."

Natasha moved both her feet and the conversation forward. "How do we get the Internet?"

"We have it installed."

"Can you call the Internet company this afternoon and have them come out?"

"Well, there is no 'Internet company' per say. It's not like the cable company or phone company. Or rather, it may be one or the other."

Natasha was confused. "I don't understand."

Sophia tried to explain where Internet service came from as Natasha seemed to glaze over. She realized then that the Internet was something that Natasha had heard about but had no real idea of what it could do or how it worked. It was a completely new technology to her, a new language, so it was like Sophia was speaking a foreign tongue.

"Are you saying you've never been online before?"

"Oh, I've been on line before. At Saks. At Cartier. At Barney's."

"That's not what I mean."

"I was afraid you'd say that."

Sophia realized the challenge before her was much greater than she originally expected. "Let's start at the beginning. Have you ever worked on a computer before?"

Natasha thought back. "Nope. Never."

"And *I* was afraid you'd say *that*," Sophia said. "But don't worry. We'll have you living in the twenty-first century in no time."

That afternoon, Sophia evaluated Natasha's set-up and developed a game plan to update Natasha's access to technology and the modern world. When she was ready to move forward, she attempted to review her plans with Natasha, who waved the responsibility right back at her.

"I thought you wanted to be more involved in things. I thought you said you wanted more control of your life," Sophia reminded her.

"I do, dear. But must I take on *everything?* If I did, I wouldn't need you. Now, wouldn't that be a problem?"

Sophia wasn't going to argue with her. "Alright. But you're going to learn how to use a computer and how to surf the net."

"Alright," she agreed. "You'll get no disagreement from me. Surf's up."

Sophia pulled out her computer and turned it on. "Let's start with the computer. There's something I want to show you. It's something I saw just after 'Let Ass-Face Baxter Have It Day.'"

"Is that what you're calling it now?" Natasha asked, allowing herself to enjoy Sophia's new nickname for the studio session.

Sophia smiled and nodded but didn't lose sight of her point. "This was something I wanted to share with you when the moment was right, and I think that moment is now."

Navigating through her computer, she opened up her pictures folder. When she found the file she was searching for, she turned the computer to face Natasha. "Please read," she said.

Natasha did just that. When she was done, she looked up from the chalk writer's words. "It's beautiful and profound. You're very talented."

"Oh, I didn't write it," Sophia explained.

"Maybe not, but you could have," Natasha told her. "You certainly know something special when you see it."

Sophia felt herself blush, and then returned the compliment, looking right at Natasha. "Yes, I do."

Natasha, knowing exactly what Sophia was telling her, blushed back.

CHAPTER 26
REST IN PEACE

"What in the hell is this?" Natasha screamed at Sophia over the telephone.

"Oh, crap. I'll be right over," Sophia replied, immediately up on her feet, rushing toward the front door of her apartment.

The Internet experience had started off well enough two days ago. Natasha took to it like a fish to water, curious about her depression and inspired by all of the support and information she found available at her fingertips in the privacy of her own home. The Internet had brought her peace and comfort…until today.

"So you *know* about this?" Natasha hollered. Sophia was certain Natasha's face was fire engine red at that very moment.

"Step away from the computer," Sophia demanded, running out of her apartment, cell crammed into her face. Her motion caused her clothes to blow behind her as her feet scrambled into her shoes. "I mean it, Natasha! Go downstairs now and tell Jasper to fix you a sandwich. I'm on my way."

"This is unbelievable," Natasha continued. "How is this possible? Why didn't you tell me?"

"Natasha, I said I will be there in a few minutes. Go

downstairs *now*. And as soon as I hang up, I'm calling Jasper to tell him to shut off that computer. We'll talk when I get there!"

Timing was everything, and right at that moment it was not on her side. Sophia didn't expect this to be an issue so soon, thinking she had at least a few more days to address and squash the impact of what she knew would be an inevitable discovery. But no, Natasha always did everything to extremes, and learning the computer was no different.

"Pick up, Jasper. Please pick up," she said aloud, earning a few sideways glances from people she rushed past on the sidewalk.

"Hello?" Jasper answered.

"Oh, thank God. Please, *now*, go upstairs and get Natasha away from her computer. She knows! She knows!"

"She knows what?" he asked, before it sunk in. "Oh, my God. You mean, she *knows*. Oh, crap!"

"I'm on my way now. Take that computer away. I'll be there as fast as I can. TAXI!"

Sophia was out of breath by the time she arrived. "Natasha? Jasper?" she yelled, pushing past the front door, running through living room.

"In here!" Jasper yelled from behind the kitchen door before he poked his head out, eyes filled will angst as if to warn Sophia that she was in for a tongue-lashing, too.

Then Sophia heard Natasha from behind him. "Yes! *We* are in here!" She could tell Natasha was livid.

Sophia entered the kitchen to see Natasha sitting at one of the islands, an untouched sandwich and a full glass of water in front of her. The expression on her face told Sophia how she was feeling. The food told her Jasper had unsuccessfully tried to distract her from her anger.

"You knew this? You *both* knew this and you didn't tell me? I thought you had my best intentions in mind! You don't care about me!"

Sophia leaned over, placed her hands on her bent knees and attempted to catch her breath. Traffic had reached a standstill after she passed through the park, so she got out and ran the rest of the way. "That's absolutely not true and you know it."

"Well, what *is* true? You both obviously have known this for some time. Were you *ever* going to tell me?"

"Of course," Sophia told her. "I promise you. I…we...wanted to give you time to get everything back on track. We didn't think this would come up so soon, so we figured what you didn't know couldn't hurt you."

"Just like Jonathan. You two are no better than him," Natasha said, getting up, rushing out of the kitchen like her hair was on fire.

Sophia followed after her—Natasha had to hear what she had to say. "Now just you wait one minute, Natasha. We didn't tell you because you've had more than enough to deal with the past few weeks."

"But what about before that?" Natasha asked in return. "This information obviously has been out there for a long time!"

"We were respecting the rules," Sophia said, trying to explain. "I don't think it's exactly right to blame everything on Jonathan, but we were told to keep you away from certain things. With all of the changes lately, we had every intention of telling you. But we wanted to let the dust settle."

"Don't you know? The dust *never* settles! If it's not one thing, it's another!"

"We thought we had time," Sophia told her. "You've only been online for a couple days now. Who knew you'd pick it up so fast? I didn't think you'd consider Googling yourself."

"Hello? Have we met? *Of course* I'm going to search for myself! I'm an actress!"

Natasha had a good point, and Sophia questioned how they could have missed that one. She gave Jasper a look that said as much.

"Well…I *was* an actress," she continued. "And what do I find out people are saying about me? That I'm dead. Dead, I say! And what's worse, people know *everything!* Now I wish I *was* dead."

"You don't mean that!" Sophia said, her heart aching in empathy, able to see the past catching up with Natasha all over again. "I can't change any of that, Natasha. I would love to and if I knew this was going to be how you found out, I'd have made different decisions. I wanted you to know. I did. But I had no idea how to tell you."

"People have *known* all this time. That's why Jonathan guarded me the way he did. He really thought he could cover it up. And he basically did for so many years. I was stupid enough to think I was protected, that I could look the other way and it just wouldn't be, that it never happened because I wanted it that way. I am such a fool."

"Don't talk like that," Jasper said, standing beside them, coming to Natasha's defense. "There were some decisions that all of us now know were probably not the best, but you have to know we only want you to be happy, to be at peace. We're all in this together. This affects us, too. We love you!"

Sophia agreed, "We do. You *have* to believe that. We would never do anything if we knew it would hurt you."

Natasha stood frozen. "It's all coming back to me. All the depression, the humiliation—the things I've worried most about. I've spent years buying protection, guarding myself from reality. After the accident, Jonathan stepped up to take care of me, but instead of making my life better, he just helped make things worse. He turned his back on the real problems as if they didn't exist. But the only thing that ever changed was that I became less capable of dealing with anything. Life doesn't stop dumping on you, but look how I've handled it all. I've hidden myself in this house, alone. Like money and distractions could make it all go away. I'm so old now, alone and have spent the past four decades—hell, most of my life—running from my problems. After all, I chose a career where I get to pretend to be someone else. How appropriate."

"But you *aren't* alone," Sophia told her. "Not anymore. And you don't have to run any longer."

Sophia saw that Natasha could hear her words but was unable to find comfort in them.

"And you can't hide anymore," Sophia told her, hearing Nonna's thick skin in her own voice. "You tried that. It wasn't the solution. We have to find a new one."

"I've done things I can't take back, made such tremendous mistakes."

The cracks in Natasha were showing again, growing visibly more pronounced, but Sophia refused to back off this time and continued to confront them. "Who hasn't?"

"You haven't," Natasha said. "Jasper hasn't."

Sophia jumped all over this comment. "How do you know? How can you be so sure? Do you think we've told you everything about ourselves? Maybe we have secrets we're ashamed of, too."

Sophia looked at Jasper, as if to say, "Well? Don't you?"

Natasha copied the reaction, giving Jasper a quizzical face, which pressured him to respond, "Oh, God, yes. Ashamed. I'm so ashamed."

"Me, too!" Sophia said, taking back the attention, but just for a moment before throwing it back at Jasper. Only this time, the spotlight she put directly on him was much bigger and brighter. "Tell us something then, Jasper. Give us an example."

His glare back at Sophia said, "Thanks" and "I cannot believe you just did this to me" and "I'll get you for this!" He clearly had not expected the conversation to turn towards him, and once she saw his expression, she realized she might have taken it too far.

"Well, sure," he said, speaking as he was thinking, not wanting Natasha to feel he wasn't willing to bare his soul for her. "Of course there are things I'm not particularly proud of. Thank you, Sophia, for allowing me this opportunity to share them."

But before he could go any farther into the details, Natasha cut him off. "I appreciate you both trying to make me feel better, but it's not the same. I don't mean that to sound bitchy, but the whole world doesn't know your business. It doesn't revel when something bad happens to you. Jasper, you've been with me a long time. You know what I'm talking about firsthand—you were *there*. And you all told me that very few people knew, that I had nothing to worry about. But now I come to find out that the world thought I was dead, that they think I succeeded in trying to kill myself. I've been walking around not aware that everyone on the planet knows. How terrible do you think that makes me feel? And how stupid? It certainly explains the odd glances I get sometimes. It's why that bitch Vanessa Baxter said she was surprised I was still alive. And on one site—celebritiesdeadandalive.com—they say I killed myself with a lethal dose of Coke and Pop Rocks. There is a sign over my picture saying, 'Rest in Peace.' Can you imagine? How am I supposed to feel about that?"

A giggle squeaked out of Jasper, but Sophia gave him the evil eye fast enough to make him stop—another Connors characteristic she tried to accept that she had inherited.

"I'm sorry," he said. "I don't mean to laugh, but are you really worried about Internet gossip? Who believes stuff like that anyway? It's not true. You're standing here with us today. You can't control everything people say or write."

His words did not appease Natasha. "It's a terrible discovery. I've been living a lie."

She began to walk up the stairs defeated but Sophia stopped her, grabbing her hands. "Listen to me, will you? You haven't been living a lie. You've had the opportunity to protect yourself from some decisions you regret. But you can't do that anymore, and I know you don't want to. Sure, it'd be nice if we could all go through life ignoring the bad stuff. Sometimes we can. But this time, *you* can't...*we* can't. That will only bring more bad stuff. So woman-up and face it! And what are you going to do about it? Only *you* have the ability to make this better. I can't do it for you and neither can Jasper. We can help you, but you have to take the steps yourself."

As Natasha absorbed her words, Sophia wondered what her grandmother would think if she had lived to see her become a grown woman—*this* grown woman—and if she would be proud of her for trying to give strength to Natasha. This had been Nonna's way with others. And how would she feel knowing that the Connors tough love that she had taught was living on in her absence?

Sophia's words finally struck a chord with Natasha. Her

manic state seemed to be dissipating as if a lever had been pulled to the off position, decreasing the pressure and returning the operations to normal. Thankfully, the red warning lights were no longer flashing and screaming, "Evacuate! Run for your lives!"

"You're right," Natasha said. "I've spent my whole life running."

"So stand up to your problems now. You have every right to feel depressed and any numbers of emotions, but you need to control them, not the other way around."

"You're right. I care too much about what people think. It haunts me if I think I had spinach in my teeth while talking to someone. So can you imagine what it feels like to realize people know my deepest darkest secret?"

"So what?" Sophia barked at her. "Listen to my words...SO WHAT? WHO CARES?"

This stunned Natasha. It even shocked Sophia a little, but she was getting through to her.

"I mean it," Sophia continued. "Who gives a crap what others think? As far as we know, we get one trip around the block. Knowing what you know now, why let that fear consume you anymore? If it all ends tomorrow, is that how you want to go? Don't you deserve better?"

Natasha began to cry, and Sophia saw the weight of the past few weeks start to lift again.

"So what are you going to do about it?" Sophia asked, repeating her challenge. "If you want to start acting again, then let's get you acting again. If you want to do nothing, then do nothing. But damn it, do what makes you happy!"

That was the final breaking point for Natasha. She fell into Sophia arms, sobbing, but with tears of joy. "I don't know what I did to deserve such good fortune as to find you."

"That makes two of us, Natasha," Sophia told her back.

"Three of us," Jasper said, grabbing both of them and crying as well, which only made Sophia start, too.

A few seconds later, Mary walked through the front door and into the foyer, unnoticed by the hugging group until she said in her most cynical voice, "What happened? Who died?"

Natasha laughed. "I did. Pop Rocks and Coke."

They all laughed except for Mary. "You people are so weird," she said, leaving them for the kitchen.

It was seven o'clock when Natasha called Sophia at her apartment. "What are you doing?" Natasha asked.

"Contemplating throwing my laptop out the window. You?"

"Don't do that."

"Why? Because it might land on someone?"

Natasha laughed. "Seriously. Stop. Everything will start clicking again. I promise."

Sophia liked when Natasha tried to comfort her. For some reason, it was easier to take advice from her than her own mother. It was also helpful to get a pep talk from a fellow artist, even if Natasha didn't quite understand the complexity of trying to link two storylines together, or the challenge of bringing her story to its final climax with the intensity and emotional payoff for which she aspired. "And what are *you* doing?" Sophia asked.

"I know what I'm going to do about it," Natasha told her.

"By 'it,' you mean the gossip?"

"Yes!" Natasha said, a noticeable excitement in her voice.

"What?"

"I'll tell you tomorrow. I want you to wonder for the night. I'll see you in the morning. Come early so we can get started."

"'Started?' What on earth are you up to?" Sophia asked.

"You'll see."

CHAPTER 27
THE BEJESUS

There was no doubting it was a good set-up, that was for sure. The laptop was where it belonged—in her lap. The sun was where it should be—out and overhead. And the sand was perfectly placed—in between her toes. It was one of those flawless moments when Sophia felt amazingly fortunate and without a concern in the world. She relished the feeling, knowing to savor it while it lasted because invulnerable moments such as this were fleeting. The day ahead would once again prove this theory correct.

"And then what?" Sophia asked. Her eyes were on Natasha, but her mind was still in the small Nebraska town Natasha had described, inside a canary yellow kitchen thick with anger and disappointment.

"I told my mother she was wrong. Acting *isn't* the gateway to hell. This *town* is!"

Sophia laughed, having heard plenty of damnation talk in her own life. "You said that? How'd she respond?"

"She washed my mouth out with soap. But while she did it, with bubbles coming out of my mouth, I told her our house was a cemetery and that she was killing my soul."

"I bet that went over well. Nice bit about the 'soul killing,' too." Sophia told her. "Is that what acting is for you? The gateway to your soul?"

"Absolutely. I like that. Put that down like *I* said it," Natasha said. "You're so much better at this than I am."

But Sophia had tripped on one detail so she went back to examine it. "She actually washed your mouth out with soap?"

"Yes," Natasha said, applying more sunscreen even though she was underneath a large umbrella. "Those were 'the good old days,' when parents were allowed to hit their kids in order to scare them into submission. Ah, and such good times they were!"

"Then would you consider yourself abused?"

Natasha thought about her answer. "No, not at all. It was a different time and people managed their children differently. I'm not saying it was right, but it does seem like kids were more in control then. Youth don't respect their elders now. But then again, what do I know about it? Raising children is not exactly a topic in which I'm fluent."

"Are you ready to talk about everything in detail?" Sophia asked, knowing they had arrived at the edge of delicate territory.

"No," Natasha said, clinically and disconnected, staring into the horizon, avoiding Sophia's eyes. "Not yet."

These recent conversations had seemingly come out of left field and served as a collective lesson for Sophia that people sometimes made decisions or acted in certain ways that even they didn't understand until after the fact, until all of the evidence had been presented. It was like that for Natasha and she told Sophia so—as soon as Natasha had figured it out herself. She explained that she had been asking for help without knowing it or even knowing why, like she had subconsciously seen a life preserver floating in front of her that day at the movies. As she described it, Natasha had jumped at the opportunity to let Sophia into her life because something hidden inside of her was asking for help in letting go of the past, and that something about Sophia had indicated that she just might be the person to save Natasha. To this last point, in true Nonna fashion, Sophia told her, "I can't save you. You have to save yourself."

"I know that, dear. But you helped me understand that. You showed me I could make things happen, that I don't have to hide or take things lying down."

Natasha had decided that she wanted to tell her story after all, not necessarily to boast about her many accomplishments—though she would never miss *that* opportunity—but because she could no longer hold onto the past. If she did, it would certainly take her down with it as it almost had before. Her call for help—that spontaneous invitation to Sophia that winter day—had caused a ripple effect in both of their lives, the intersection delivering surprising results.

"Here you go," said Jasper, who was just joining them on the beach in front of The Sequel, a name everyone had adopted and Natasha had embraced by having a sign made for the mailbox.

"Seriously, you two," Jasper continued. "If you need private time, just let me know. I can sit down the beach, in the water, back in the house, in New Jersey."

"Forget it, Jasper. Stop asking us that," Natasha told him. "Besides, if you sit down the beach then I can't look at your body and sexually harass you."

Jasper and Sophia laughed at Natasha's joke—another example of her loosening up in ways she never had before. There had been many such examples of change over the past couple of months. First, there were those affected—the casualties—such as Jonathan and her use of contractions. Sophia asked about this affectation once when the time seemed right but Natasha feigned ignorance. The interaction had reminded Sophia of a friend growing up whose stomach gurgled all the time but who always refused to admit to the sound and attempted to cover the noise by shuffling her papers.

Then came the additions—more signs Natasha was a woman undergoing a transformation, a pupa. This list included Dr. Bland and the autobiography. Sophia was apprehensive when Natasha broke the news that she wanted to move forward with the book, and she remained reserved for several weeks until she felt confident that Natasha or some other factor wasn't going to rip the rug out from under her again. But weeks and dozens of pages worth of notes later, Natasha had only shown a complete and focused commitment to the project. Sophia began to believe the project was there to stay.

"Yes," Jasper remarked, pulling a beer out of his bag, unable to resist Natasha's harassment joke, "this is *such* a hostile work environment."

"Besides," Natasha continued, "with only two days a week in summer, I have to get my Jasper time." Then she extended the joke by awkwardly looking up and down at his torso, which made the whole group laugh.

Summer allowed Jasper a reverse work schedule—five days off, two days on—during the months of July and August, an agreement he and Natasha had negotiated which allowed him to take some of his vacation time. His work time was spent mostly at The Estate to keep the place operational while Natasha was at the beach. But occasionally, he came out to The Sequel and would extend his trip a day or two to relax with Cagney and Lacey—the nickname he himself had so proudly given the women.

Summer had kicked into full stride as had their enjoyment of the Hamptons, where the majority of their time was being spent. Only once a week did Natasha and Sophia return to the city for an appointment with Dr. Bland and miscellaneous errands. But since the psychiatrist also owned a home on the island, he offered to meet with Natasha on Saturday mornings to save her the trouble of traveling back to Manhattan for a second appointment.

Natasha was definitely feeling better, so her visits with Dr. Bland became less frequent. As she regularly told Sophia, the medication and therapy were doing wonders for her. "I haven't felt this good in years."

Dr. Bland supported the idea of the autobiography. "Never be afraid of the truth," he emphasized to Natasha when she told him about the project. "Only be afraid of the lies you tell and of the reasons you tell them."

"Can I steal that line?" she requested. "For the book?"

"Sure," he told her. "It's all yours."

Sophia had found little reason to be in New York City, and since Natasha had extended an open invite to her to spend the whole summer at the beach, it was an easy decision to make. After a few weeks together, she felt confident the temporary living arrangement was going to work out fine.

Spending so much time with Natasha was surprisingly painless. Frankly, she admitted to herself, it was quite joyful. Most days, whether they were official work days or not, were spent brainstorming and talking. Nights were spent writing and relaxing. The lines between work time and personal time became hazy at first and then invisible as the women got into a rhythm with one another that respected subtle boundaries and ensured quality time together and alone.

Most of the writing Sophia was getting done was for Natasha's autobiography—a welcome distraction since Sophia had yet to resolve some significant issues regarding her book's ending. The result was a major case of writer's block that felt like the Great Wall of China was keeping her and her characters from crossing the finish line. Since Natasha's return to mental well-being, Sophia had been surrounded by talk about the importance of truth which compelled her to make certain admissions to herself. Sophia's truth was that she had grown tired of working on her novel. It had consumed all of her free time for the better part of the year thus far and she needed a break. But the decision to take a rest brought on more anxiety, which only compounded her block. Sophia was terrified she would run into the same dilemma as before—burnout led to a break which led to never returning to her novel again. She tried to reason with herself, acknowledging that there were parts of the first story she had salvaged for use in her current one, and that the overall experience had been one large and important writing lesson. But all of that hardly seemed enough to justify the sweat and tears she had put into a project she never completed. The prospect of not finishing *Bad Blood* scared the bejesus out of her, and she decided to share this with Natasha. They had been at the beach two weeks when Sophia broke her silent self-torture. "I need to fly a red flag."

"You do? Why?"

"I'm burned out and freaked out," Sophia shared, taking a deep breath and a large swig of wine, preparing to give her confession over dinner. "I've spent the better part of the last six months thinking, breathing and living my book. Now I'm in the final stretch, tired as hell of it, and faced with issues I still have to work out. I'm not sure what I'm going to do with a couple of the characters, I don't know exactly how I want to end it, and I'm facing a brain block I cannot seem to get out of. I mean, when I look at the words, they just dance across the screen without making any sense anymore."

"Oh, geez," said Natasha, "I bet my autobiography is going to come out great then."

Sophia was not in the mood to joke. "I'm being serious."

"And I'm *not,*" Natasha clarified. "Lighten up. It sounds like you just need a break. We've discussed this before. Take some time away from it. It'll do you good."

"Do I sound like a broken record? Oh, God, listen to me. I know you've told me that before, but I'm afraid if I do it then I'll never finish. I'm feast or famine. You know how that works. If I'm doing something, I'm compulsive about it. If I get out of the habit, it's murder to get back into that groove."

"I won't let that happen. I promised you that before and I'll promise it again. And I'll keep saying it until I'm blue in the face and you get it into that thick skull of yours. You and me. We take care of each other. I'll kick you in that ass when the time is right, so take a break. Put it away and have faith that the moment will come when you think, 'A-ha, that's what I'm going to do!' Besides, no one's telling you that you have to finish it right now. The only deadline you have is the imaginary one that you've given yourself."

Sophia pointed at herself with her index finger, waving it in a crazed way. "Obsessive!"

"There's nothing to be worried about. You have my word," Natasha told Sophia. "And just think of what you've already accomplished. Most people would never be able to do that."

"But most people don't want to be writers. It's what I aspire to. It's my career goal—my *only* career goal. It's all I want to do." Then Sophia remembered Natasha was still her boss. They had become friends, but Sophia would never want Natasha to think that she took her employment for granted.

"I'm sorry. What I meant to say is—" she began, trying to rephrase her words better, but Natasha cut her off.

"You have nothing to apologize for, Sophia. I know I won't always be able to keep you. You're meant for bigger things. But you have a place with me as long as you need or want it."

"Thanks, Natasha. I appreciate that."

"Listen to me when I say that I have every confidence you'll succeed with whatever you set your mind to. You seem to be a person who gets what she wants."

"Not always. Want to hear the long list of examples? It might take awhile."

"That's ok. Just try not to be so hard on yourself. Remember, it's good to have goals but don't let them make you miserable. Would it be so bad to go through life working towards something, doing something you love, even if that something doesn't comes to full fruition? Isn't most of the excitement in the anticipation of something?"

"I'm not so sure. I think the thrill is in the destination, not the journey."

"Don't be smart," Natasha scolded. "You don't seem to be the type to spend time on things or people that you don't enjoy. That's a trait we share which I take as a compliment."

"You should. I do enjoy my time with you," Sophia told her.

"Me, too, dear. I just want you to enjoy your life. It goes by awfully fast. Don't let one little tangle get you bent out of shape. If you're doing what love and focusing on what's most important to you—which even under the best of circumstances will give us the occasional hard time—it'll be fine. You'll never regret following your dream."

"I dream about chocolate cake," Sophia joked. "I love that more than anything."

"Don't get crazy on me. That's my thing, not yours."

"You're not crazy."

"No, but for a while I sure thought that I might be," Natasha admitted. She got up from the table to bring her plate to the sink. "Enjoy the creation process. You'll look back one day and realize how important these times are. Some of my best memories are from when I was in my twenties and thirties being creative. They were also some of the hardest times but my work made me feel alive."

"What about now?" Sophia asked.

"Oh, I feel alive, but in a different way. There's something about the hunger you have at that age," Natasha explained. "You want to absorb everything. You want to get your hands dirty and are starving for success. For better *and* worse, that changes with time."

"What do you miss from those days? We can use all of this in the book."

"Lots of things," Natasha shared. "I miss having a career. I want to work again. The DVD project reminded me of that, seeing the film on the screen again, reflecting on what we did and how we did it. The therapy and our conversations remind me of that as well. I stopped trying because the work wasn't what I thought it should be and, truthfully, I didn't need the money. Jonathan has a brilliant business mind. He made really smart decisions with my money. I never would have known how to turn a little into a lot like he did."

"You sound conflicted. About *all* of that."

"The one thing you can be sure of is that nothing is ever simple or straight-forward," Natasha advised. "With acting, I thought that getting a few great roles would keep me working forever, that they'd keep coming. I knew people fell in and out of love, but lost sight of the fact that fans, *my* fans, could, too. Aging and time mess with you. Then the bad things happened and my depression got worse, as did everything else. It was a roller coaster."

"You should start acting again," Sophia declared.

"I don't know if I still have it in me."

"Of course you do. You wouldn't be craving it the way you are if you didn't. You got into amazing shape because you set your mind to it. You can do the same with your career. Give yourself some credit for being the get-it-done gal you are."

"Right back at you," Natasha returned.

Sophia remembered the discussion with her father and said, "You should explore cable. There are lots of great shows with really meaty roles for fine actors."

Natasha seemed skeptical, so Sophia added. "It's like riding a bike. It'll all come back."

Natasha smiled and said, "I'll think about it." That was her standard phrase for changing the subject.

"It's a lot easier to give advice than to take it, isn't it?" Sophia asked.

"Absolutely."

Days later, as they were packing up their belongings and returning to the house after finishing another afternoon discussion at the beach, Sophia presented an idea to Natasha. "Maybe one of these days, when we're back in the city, we can spend some time going through some of your belongings in the attic. You can share with me whatever stories you think of."

"Probably a good idea," Natasha replied. "However, there are a lot of cobwebs up there so we'll need to make sure Dr. Bland is on call that day." Sophia was glad Natasha was open to the suggestion but wasn't sure if she was joking about possibly needing her doctor to do so.

When they returned to the house, they went to their rooms to clean up before dinner. Just as Sophia stepped toward the bathroom to grab a shower, her cell rang. Because her mind was busy wondering what secrets Natasha's top floor might uncover, she answered it without checking caller ID—a regrettable mistake.

"Hey there," the voice said, at first unrecognizable, only because it was so unexpected he should be calling.

"…Kevin?" she asked, knowing it was him before he said another word.

"It's me. How are you?"

Unprepared for any conversation with him, Sophia choked on a long pause. She had moved past the desire to yell at him—to tell him what a huge mistake he had made, how angry and confused she had been—but she had not yet reached a place where polite conversation seemed possible. Could they ever become friends? It wasn't the logical next step, and she wasn't convinced it could be, ever.

He sensed her response was slow in coming so he picked up the slack, filling the empty space. "Long time, no talk. Did I catch you at a bad time?"

Is there ever a good time to talk to you?

She didn't really know what to say, not wanting to sound mad or give him the impression that she walked around devastated all day. She'd lost track of how long she'd been coaching Natasha to move forward. Now was her chance, on one topic at least, to take her own advice. No matter how much she hated the idea.

"How are you?" she finally got out, certain it came out forced, knowing he would notice. But it was something, which had to be better than continuing nothing.

"I'm good!" he said, his tone overly enthusiastic, compensatory. Sophia was pleased the conversation wasn't awkward for her alone.

"That's good. What's going on with you?" she returned. What she really wanted to ask him, of course, was why he was calling but feared it would come out hostile. *Know your limitations,* she tried to remind herself.

"I've been thinking about you. I wanted to see how you are. Are you in the Hamptons?"

"I am. How do you know about that?" Sophia asked, regretting her words the moment they left her mouth.

"From Kate," Kevin explained. "We spoke. She told me you're working for Natasha McGavin. I didn't think she was still alive."

"Yeah, she gets that a lot." *Why are you in touch with my best friend?*

"Kate says you're working on *two* books. That's really impressive. How's all that going?" Kevin asked. Sophia acknowledged that he was certainly making an effort, although she couldn't be sure if it was out of guilt or for some other reason she didn't see clearly yet.

"It's going. One page at a time." *And why are you keeping tabs on me?*

"It's nice you get to spend some time at the beach. It's always good to get away from the city, especially during the summer."

"Well, you know I actually like the summer in the city, how quiet it can be on the weekends," she reminded him. "But it's good to break away. The beach is beautiful and Natasha's home is gorgeous."

"Sounds nice," he said, still working for the conversation, probably also afraid of saying something wrong.

After the surface-level discussion seemed to run its course, Sophia finally drummed up the nerve to ask, "Is everything ok? I don't want to sound rude but do you need something?"

It was Kevin who choked on the next pause. "I just wanted to touch base—see how you're doing. I think about you. I wanted to make sure you're doing well."

"I'm good," she told him. "Busy. Really busy all the time, but things are good." *So busy I never think about you, Kevin.*

"I bet you miss Kate," he told her, seeming to change the subject.

It struck her as unfair that Kevin would use her love for her best friend—a friend who remained in good standing—as a bridge to connect with her. "I do," she replied. "But she's happy, enjoying her new adventures, as *you* must know."

"She told me all about it. Sounds like she loves Paris. And this Philippe guy."

"Yes, that's true." *How often are you talking to Kate? And who are you to talk about love? Who are* you *loving, Kevin?*

"Do you think she'll go back to New York when she's done?" Kevin asked, the word "go" standing out as so distant and removed, reminding her Kevin no longer lived there either.

"I don't know," Sophia admitted. "I hope so. But she gave up her apartment and all of her stuff is in storage."

The small talk continued for another couple of minutes. They exchanged details about the friends they had shared for the three years they were together, and discussed current events regarding their families. She found herself battling the urge to ask if he was seeing anyone but denied herself that question. She knew how she would feel if he said "yes."

But she discovered a surprise right in the middle of the conversation: part of her feared that he would tell her he'd made a mistake, that he wanted her back. While this was an unlikely reason for his call, she didn't know what she would say if that actually happened. So much had changed in the past six months and something in her had shifted. She had been forced to become a different person than who she was when they were together—a survival instinct—and the results were not all bad. As much as she'd missed him, she now wasn't sure she wanted him back. Backpedaling had never been appealing to Sophia and this was no exception.

After another long pause, Kevin blurted out, "I miss you, you know?"

The comment stunned her. Kevin always did have a way of stopping her in her tracks. *No, I don't know. How would I know that?*

She wasn't sure how to take his remark or how to respond. So for lack of anything better to say, she punted with an ambiguous, "I should go. We have dinner plans." The statement was partially a lie since the only plans they really had were to meet in the kitchen and attempt to throw something together— the two of them barely made one complete cook.

He released a sigh from deep within his chest—which she used to sleep against—and, for a moment, she remembered the warmth of his skin on hers, the stubble of his chin on her neck, his breath in her ear.

"It was good talking to you," he said.

"You take care, Kevin." Before she knew it, she had hung up, alone again in her room but not feeling totally alone because he was there in her head, in her chest. She felt his presence like they had just had drinks at Le Bon, and he had just dropped his bomb on her all over again.

She took a long shower before joining Natasha in the kitchen, hoping the spray of hot water from the rain showerhead would wash him from her mind. But it didn't, and while preparing dinner with Natasha, she said little.

"What is wrong with you?" Natasha finally asked as they ate. "The book?"

"Kevin called."

Natasha gave her a serious look. "Really?" she asked. "Why?"

"I'm not exactly sure," Sophia remarked, pushing food across her plate.

"He didn't say?"

"No. Something about how he wanted to see how I was doing. He sounded nervous though."

"He's afraid of you. He knows he did you wrong."

"I don't know," Sophia said. "It doesn't matter."

"Why do you say that?" Natasha asked.

"It'd only be relevant if I still wanted him back."

"You don't?"

"I don't know. I don't think so," Sophia told her. "I think it's too late for Kevin and me. I can't get my head around the possibility that, after all I've been through, he'd want to get back together, or that I would even allow that."

"Then why are you in such a crappy mood?" Natasha asked, pushing Sophia the same way she pushed her. Nonna's tough love was alive and well, summering in the Hamptons.

"Because I feel it all over again. How I invested three years of my life in that relationship. How I thought we were thinking and wanting the same things. And how incredibly wrong I was."

"You don't know that he never felt those things," Natasha reasoned. "You just know the end results. You wouldn't want Kevin back if he apologized and said he'd screwed up?"

"No. I really don't think so. Once upon a time I would have changed my life for him. But now...how could I forget about this whole year and act like nothing even happened?"

"But isn't it a good thing to know that you wouldn't want him now?" Natasha asked.

Sophia's head was somewhere else. "I'm not so sure."

They ate a quiet dinner outside around the fire pit, the crackle of the embers covering the silence from the absent conversation. Natasha allowed Sophia to spend time with her thoughts during the meal but occasionally tried to focus Sophia's attention on the stars in the sky or on other evidence that beauty was all around them. But Sophia couldn't get away from the feeling that the universe seemed such a lonely place.

"You'll get through this," Natasha told her when they parted ways before bed. "If you need to talk, just knock. Any time. Okay?"

Natasha hugged Sophia goodnight. It wasn't something they did regularly.

"Thank you. I will."

Minutes later, Sophia laid in bed staring at the ceiling, the reflection of the pool lights flickering across the ceiling as the night at Le Bon replayed in front of her. As she watched it unfold, she experienced the loss and anger she'd felt that night. And while both had faded since winter, they were present enough to remind her that there were things she'd like to say to Kevin—but did not dare.

I would have done anything for you. I would have moved to Chicago and given up my life here, if you had asked me to. But you thought you wanted to go on without me. You drew a line in the sand and now we both *have to live with that decision. It's been really hard for me, but you know what? It was for the best, even if it doesn't always feel like it.*

Sophia heard shuffling at the door so she turned on the light and leaned out of bed to see what it was. At the foot of the door was an envelope she picked up and opened—a note from Natasha written on the personal stationery Sophia recognized well.

Sophia,
I want to let you know that I'm thinking of you and that I'm here to talk any time you want or need. I promise this will get easier. I also want to encourage you to be grateful for the

moments of love you get in life. They are precious. It is a wonderful thing that you had a period of time when <u>you</u> loved someone so much. It may not have been meant to last forever, but you should cherish what it was. And don't worry...you will have that and so much more, again. I promise that, too.

Love you,
Natasha

PS
Sorry I don't have a more appropriate card to give you.

Sophia closed the card and placed it on her nightstand. While the weight of her problems had not disappeared, she was warmed by Natasha's concern and efforts. But Natasha was wrong about one thing: the card could not have been more appropriate.

CHAPTER 28
A CROWN WITHOUT THE SPARKLE

Sophia and Natasha returned to the city to begin the dreaded (for Natasha) and anticipated (for Sophia) journey to the attic. One woman's keepsakes were another woman's research. *"This Is Your Life–Cardboard Box Edition,"* Natasha called it. "God help us both. Are you certain you want to go through all of that old crap? I'm warning you—that place is a total mess."

"Absolutely," Sophia assured her. "And I'm sure it's not crap. Why else would you keep it?"

"Because I'm too lazy to get rid of it?" Natasha said unconvincingly.

Sophia was certain that Natasha was minimizing the personal worth of her possessions. "I think what you've kept will tell me a lot about you. But don't worry. We'll only stay as long as you feel comfortable. I think this will be beneficial for both of us."

Sophia warned herself to tread lightly and abort the mission if she felt they were going into dangerous emotional territory. Natasha had made amazing progress, but it was important to act with caution. There were new boundaries, but neither of them could be entirely sure where the borders lie. Those lines stretched and retracted depending on the day, the hour, the moment.

But, to Natasha's relief, the trip to the fifth floor would not happen that day after all. One bite into a breakfast burrito—a purchase Sophia knew she was going to regret for much different reasons—and a spear of unimaginable pain hit her tooth. Feeling like she'd been shot in the mouth, she vowed to never trust huevos rancheros again.

"Go to the dentist," Natasha insisted—a convenient decision on her part. Sophia could see a weight lifted from Natasha as she added, "The attic's not going anywhere."

Minutes later, Sophia did her best to talk through the pain into the telephone, "This is Sophia Connors. My tooth just broke and I need to see Dr. Soriano as soon as I can. May I come in today?"

"He's booked," said the receptionist without hesitation or concern. Sophia thought she could hear the smack of chewing gum which only made the moment that much more exasperating.

"Please…this is an emergency. I'm in terrible pain."

"Like I said, *Miss*…he's busy." the woman replied rudely, stretching out the sentence as if that would get her point across better. Adding insult to injury, she said "Miss" with an unusual tone that told Sophia that she had something *much* better she could be doing than talking on the phone with a mere patient.

"Can you tell me when his next opening is?" Sophia asked, trying to find other options to get this matter resolved. The exploration of the attic might wait but her tooth wouldn't. Unable to think clearly through the pain, she gave Natasha a look as if to say, "I don't know what to do."

Natasha yanked the phone from her hand—a movement that, despite being minor, sent a thousand jagged pins through Sophia's jaw. "Sorry," Natasha whispered, seeing that she'd contributed to the pain. Then she spoke into the telephone with precision and determination. "Hello? Who is this?"

There was a pause, then Natasha spoke again, "Well, Brittany. You sound like a reasonable woman. I'm sure you can appreciate the urgency of the situation."

Another pause.

"Oh, I see," Natasha continued. "That does sound like a scheduling challenge, now doesn't it?"

One more pause.

Sophia had no idea what would come next, but she knew that Natasha was adept at getting what she wanted when she wanted it. Brittany was being prepped for a clobbering.

Natasha smiled at Sophia, whispering away from the mouthpiece, "Don't worry. We'll straighten up this little twit in no time."

Then she dropped her chin and went in for the kill. "Listen, dear. I do understand that you are challenged with the incredible demands of your position. It must be both stimulating and satisfying, so I need to enlist your resourcefulness. You see, my friend needs to see someone *today*. Huh? Dear, I'm not finished yet. Please let me finish. Thank you. I think it's important you know that my lawyer, Jonathan Moore—you probably know his name—well, he plays golf once a week with the editor of *New York Magazine*. Surely you're familiar with their annual write-up about the top medical practices in the city. I'm certain Dr. Soriano is, too. It's quite influential. Now I'm sure if you can help us out then we can help you out. Wouldn't it be something if *you* got your boss in this year's publication? That's got to mean a raise and job security, and wouldn't that be comforting in these troubling times?"

There was a final pause.

"Yes, dear," Natasha said after a few seconds. "That'll be lovely. And the flowers that arrive later today…they'll be for you. A token of my appreciation, Brittany. Please be sure to tell your boss *that*, too."

Natasha hung up the phone. "They'll see you at noon. She looked a little harder and found an opening."

"Thanks," Sophia said, holding her chin like it would fall off if she didn't, trying not to laugh because it would hurt too much. "I'm not exactly in the right shape to negotiate with anyone."

"My pleasure. There's no reason we can't all play nice in the sandbox. I was tempted to tell her, 'You scratch my back and I won't scratch your face!' But I thought better of it. Now let's get you a good, old-fashioned painkiller to help take away some of that nasty pain."

Natasha climbed the stairs toward her bedroom. When she was near the top step, Sophia managed to ask, "Is that true about Jonathan?"

Natasha smiled mischievously. "No, he doesn't play golf. I must have mixed him up with someone else."

"I meant about him being your lawyer. You said it in the present tense," Sophia explained, pressing despite some concern that Natasha might press back.

Natasha turned around on the landing and looked back. "Are you asking me if I fired Jonathan?"

"Yes, I guess so."

"Yes and no. Not officially. I can only take on so much at one time. Do you think that make me weak?"

Sophia shook her head. "Not at all. I guess I just assumed, based on the things you said…" she said, her voice trailing off. She then threw out a line for Natasha. "Maybe it's good that you're taking a little time to think about it first."

"Why do you say that?" Natasha questioned, sounding less than confident in her tone.

Sophia gulped, awakening the pain all over again. "I don't know. Maybe once the dust settles, you'll see you don't really want to fire him after all. Didn't Dr. Brand suggest you repair relationships that need mending? Wouldn't that be a healthy step?"

"Why are you sticking up for him? He was always critical of you. You told me that yourself."

"That's true," Sophia admitted. "But he only did what he thought was best for you. He made mistakes. So did you. And there were a lot of good things he did, too. Right?"

"I'm not ready to talk about this," Natasha responded. "I'm going to get your painkiller."

Sophia threw out one more consideration, "And he's been a part of your life for so long…"

"So has depression. But that didn't stop me from trying to get rid of *it*.

Two pills and three loopy hours later, Sophia sat slightly stoned on a leather waiting room sofa, trying to be interested in Dr. Soriano's copy of *Time Out New York*—a useless attempt to distract herself because she couldn't focus to read. Instead, she looked at the pictures, buzzing in a nice way from the very strong pills that Natasha had sworn off but kept in case of just such an emergency.

The receptionist (presumably Brittany) leaned around a large floral arrangement (presumably from Natasha) wearing a consoling face and dramatically altered disposition to announce that room three was ready for Sophia.

"Thanks," Sophia said, zig-zagging her way to the back recesses of the medical office. Gifts and threats might have bought her an appointment but not a formal escort to her room.

Sophia sat in the reclining chair, folded her hands in her lap, and waited. The pain, while still present, had been managed well enough that she was no longer immobilized. She was lost in thought considering this when footsteps announced someone arriving through the door behind her. Her head, which was fuzzy and bubbly when she arrived, was about to feel another intense rush.

"Hello," said an unfamiliar voice, one that transitioned right before Sophia's eyes into an extremely handsome man. Sophia was taken aback. This was *not* the much older, follicle-challenged Dr. Soriano she'd expected to see. This doctor was attractive—*very* attractive. It gave her a cartoon moment—her chest went "Ka-pow!" and her eyes "Vroom! Vroom!"—complete with three dimensional spiral effects.

"Good afternoon. I'm Dr. Hale, but please call me Neil."

I certainly will, she said to herself, then prayed she hadn't said it aloud.

Sophia quickly assessed her situation and came to the conclusion that if she had no choice but to go through this unfortunate and uncomfortable ordeal, the least that life could do was throw her a bone. The bone, in this instance, was this hunka-hunka burning love dentist who gave her a little pitter-patter sensation she hadn't felt in the longest time. Out of nowhere, Sophia found herself wondering how she looked and trying to remember if she had brushed her teeth that morning.

He must have seen a look on Sophia's face. "What's wrong?"

Busted, she told herself, feeling a rush of embarrassment as if he could read her mind.

"Sorry, I thought I was seeing Dr. Soriano today," she said, scrambling, pushing through mental clouds to recover. Simultaneously, her mind did its best to review the grooming issue. If only she could remember how much, or how little, she had done to herself that morning. She and Natasha had planned to spend the entire day amongst boxes. *Damn it!* she told herself, suddenly aware that she had taken multiple short cuts.

But that didn't stop her from trying to recover, so she returned his question with a question of her own, adding on a smile this time in hopes it might help move the scales of physical appeal that perhaps were not tipped to her side at the moment. "Was it not my most inviting look?" she asked. She prayed it didn't come off as flirtatious and obvious.

"Not so much," he said, playfully. "But it's okay. Going to the dentist isn't exactly people's favorite pastime."

"Sorry, Dr. Hale. It must be the pain," she returned. She wondered what her expression had been, hoping the face she made was not a "damn, you're adorable" face. Or did she actually make a cartoon face instead?

"Please, call me Neil. Dr. Hale makes me sound too old and too much like my father. As for Dr. Soriano, he's actually out this week. His daughter is getting married tomorrow."

"That's nice," she said, thinking, *That's nice his daughter's getting married and nice that I get to call you Neil.*

"It is, isn't it? Should be great weather for it, too."

Sophia started to agree, but all of the smiling reminded her of the pain, grabbing onto her like someone had just smacked her across the face. Her agony was audible and expressive.

"Got some pain going on?" Dr. Handsome asked.

"Yes. A lot. I think I cracked my tooth."

"Uh-oh. We can't have that now, can we?"

She shook her head. She didn't know if it was the medication or the blues of his eyes, but she felt helplessly hypnotized. When he smiled, her belly felt warm. "We'll have you feeling better in no time."

We?

That was when Sophia realized another person was in the room. Dr. Handsome's assistant had entered, but Sophia had no idea how long she'd been there. The only thing she could sure of was that Natasha's pills did little to remedy humiliation.

"Dolores, could you prep Sophia?"

He swiveled his chair to look at Sophia's chart. As he turned away, he gave her an unsolicited smile—a comforting glance.

Dolores did as requested, moving around Sophia. She took a seat opposite Neil, making Sophia the center of a patient sandwich.

"You doing alright?" he asked, returning his attention to her. She nodded.

"This might hurt a little," Neil said as he and Dolores began stretching and pulling at Sophia's mouth. It caused her obvious pain so they stopped.

"Here's what I want to do, Sophia," he told her. She liked the way he said her name with kindness and sexiness all wrapped together. She wondered if that was bedside manner he had learned in dentistry school, but hoped he did it especially for her. "I'd like to give you a little shot to numb your mouth and minimize the pain. Then I can examine your tooth a little closer and see what's going on. It probably hurts worse than it actually is, which is good news, right?"

She nodded again, and then smiled, doing her best not to give him an unattractive, "I'm-dying-here-from-the-pain" look.

Moments later, after the injection, Neil sat on the rolling stool next to Sophia's chair. He smiled at her, looked at her charts, and then smiled more. Something unusual seemed to be happening between them. Without a doubt, she found him attractive and, she reasoned, it wasn't completely impossible to think he just might find her attractive as well, despite her questionable grooming habits for the day.

"Are you feeling anything?" he asked. For a moment, she forgot he was referring to the shot.

She nodded, her mouth thankfully growing more numb, tingling from the combination of influences. "Are you going to the wedding?" she asked, her lips beginning to reject their responsibilities.

"No. It's a small wedding. Besides, Dr. Soriano and I are friends, but..." he interrupted himself to look around in a deliberate and overly dramatic fashion. "Between you and me, we're not *that* good of friends." Then he laughed to show Sophia he was trying to be funny. She wanted to tell him he was succeeding.

Dolores also found him amusing, adding laughter from her side of Sophia. This served as a reminder to Sophia that she and Neil weren't the only ones there. Dolores turned back to her, dropped into a more serious mode, then motioned with her fingers to indicate that she wanted to pry Sophia's mouth open to prep it for further investigation.

Over Dolores' fingers, Sophia attempted to see if Neil was wearing a ring. As best as she could make out, his fingers were bare. Perhaps life *had* thrown her a bone—a guy *and* a spark of interest. Of course, the only spark she could be certain of was hers, which was pretty remarkable considering it had been ages since she'd felt even a sliver of interest in a man.

"To tell you the truth," he told Sophia, "I'm kinda happy about not being invited. I enjoy weddings and all, and his daughter is a doll, but I'm happy to spend my Saturday with Zoe in Union Square Park. It's our ritual."

Sophia's stomach dropped, this time in a bad way. *Zoe?* He *was* married, or at least committed. And worse, he must have sensed she was throwing herself at him so he was letting her down nicely. *How could I be so incredibly stupid?*

That was when Dolores threw her the next bone. As Neil

turned around to reach for something on the counter behind him, she gave Sophia a dead serious look, shook her head a couple of times, then flicked her chin in Neil's direction like it was a fishing rod and she was casting a line.

Sophia didn't understand. Was she telling her to back off? Perhaps she saying, "He's married, you idiot! Back off or I'll give you more pain than you already have!"

Sophia shrugged, not having a clue what Dolores was trying to communicate. She mouthed, "What?" This, of course, only brought more pain.

Dolores looked in Neil's direction. He was preoccupied with the instruments so she turned back to Sophia and gave her the same serious look along with a series of moves. She started by flipping her head back at Neil again, and then brought both hands up towards her face, bent her fingers forward toward Sophia at ninety degree angles, and stuck out her tongue.

Sophia still didn't get it, finding herself in a weird game of charades—one she was most definitely losing. "I'm sorry. I don't understand," she mouthed.

Dolores rolled her eyes, letting out an annoyed but almost silent sigh. Then she gave Sophia a pretend smile, and asked, "How old is Zoe now?" It was a question she directed casually at Neil.

Neil turned around again. "Three, almost four," he told them both.

Dolores then shot Sophia a look the patient thought meant "go" not "stop." So Sophia stumbled ahead. "Is your daughter in preschool?"

Neil smiled and laughed. Dolores, more subtle this time because Neil was facing them, laughed with him, but rolled her eyes one last time.

"Zoe's my dog," he explained. "I mean, she *is* my daughter, but the only school she'll ever attend was a dog training course I took her to once. Which she failed miserably at. She can be rather strong-willed—a French Bulldog from head to toe."

Ah! Now Sophia got it—Dolores' fly fishing head movements meant "get back in there" and her hand gestures were paws. Sophia squinted an apology and rolled her own eyes in ridicule of herself.

Still amused, Neil told her, "Open up," and she obliged.

"Zoe's your dog," Sophia repeated, but it came out as "O-ez er og."

Neil smiled. "Hard to talk, eh? This isn't exactly the best job for socializing."

Socializing? Is that what we're doing?

He continued examining her tooth. "Does that hurt?"

"Uh-uh," Sophia told him, confirming she now felt nothing—other than interest in him, of course. And she loved that Dolores was on her side—*that* had to be a good thing.

"Good," he said. She enjoyed hearing him talk, and his story distracted her from the activity in her mouth. "We go to the dog run in Union Square on Saturday mornings. I spend time with the paper and a large cup of coffee, and she hangs out with all of her boyfriends. She's a bit of a flirt."

"Ah," she mumbled to show she was listening and interested, giving Dolores a wink to communicate her gratitude.

He alternated between talking to Sophia and his assistant, shifting from giving personal information to professional requests, and then removed his hands from her mouth altogether.

"What does she look like?" Sophia asked.

Neil glowed. He obviously liked talking about his dog. "She's brindle. Black mostly, with flecks of orange scattered around and a big white patch on her belly. I always say it's white because I've rubbed the color off."

Sophia understood. "We had a dog growing up that loved her belly rubbed—Taffy. She'd literally throw herself on the ground in front of you to tell you it was time."

In the corner, Dolores returned Sophia's wink before saying to Neil, "Hmmm…sounds like some girls in my neighborhood." They all laughed.

Neil indicated that he needed to look into her mouth again and asked, "Have you ever been down to that farmer's market? I love it. Tons of great stuff."

She confirmed with "uh-huh" as did her new best friend, Dolores.

"Ok," he told his assistant, and they both removed their hands from her mouth at the same time. "I have good news and bad news. The good news is that I can stop the pain and get you fixed up. The bad news is you're going to need a crown and, unfortunately, they're not cheap. Dolores, could you please get the molding kit?"

Dolores left the room, and Sophia hoped she would take her time coming back.

"I'll give you a temporary one today," Neil explained. "We'll fit you with a mold and order the permanent one. It'll take a couple of weeks."

"So much money and all I get is a crown without the sparkle?"

"Yep," he replied with a laugh. "Sorry, there'll be no bling. But, like I said, at least we'll get rid of your pain."

"That's good to hear. Thanks."

"It's my job. And what do you do for a living?"

"I'm a writer," she told him, hoping she didn't sound incoherent. It was difficult to sound alluring when her face was half frozen.

"A writer? That's impressive. I could never survive doing that. No one would ever pay me for the way I write."

Neil was handsome, charming *and* gracious, providing her with the type of compliment she appreciated. While writing came naturally to her, it wasn't easy, and it was always validating when people respected that. Her life as a writer had been one of multiplicity—her mind residing in various locations, focused on countless topics, at all times doing her best to juggle the life she lived and the lives she created. But at that moment, the life she was most interested in was the one sitting on the stool right next to her.

"The same goes for you. It's a long road to become a dentist," she told him, matching his praise with her own. "That's impressive."

"Sure, I guess. It's a good career."

Then something happened to Sophia. She wasn't sure if the pills were turning on her or if she was getting scared, but she suddenly felt overwhelmed by the situation. Something inside her told her to slow down—a sensation that took her over almost as fast as her intrigue for Neil.

This was the first outing of this kind for her in a long time, and certainly an unexpected twist to what normally would have been a not-so-routine trip to the dentist. Sophia realized she would see Neil in another couple of weeks when she had to come back for the permanent crown. That would give him time to think about her. Then, she told herself, if she felt this connection again she would be better prepared—physically and mentally—to do something about it. So without showing him any less interest—because she certainly didn't feel that way—she shifted into neutral and coasted through the remainder of the appointment. This new gear allowed her to enjoy the natural interaction as it pleasantly unfolded without her inner dialogue stressing her out.

The rest of their time together was just as congenial. Sophia might have, oddly enough, even used the word "fun" to describe her time in Neil's chair. She considered how everyone should be so lucky to have a little crush on their dentist...until she realized that when it came to Dr. Neil Hale, there was a pretty good chance that most probably did.

For the next two weeks, while she waited for her permanent crown to arrive from some distant crown-making factory—made by crown elves or cap fairies, she imagined—Sophia thought about Neil, his beautiful blue eyes, and his warm, inviting smile. As her mind drifted between the sentences she wrote for her novel and the ideas she drafted for Natasha's autobiography, she was confronted with the significant realization that she was lonely. The warmth and comfort evoked by the potential love from a special man, for the first time in quite a while and after so many months of heartache and frustration, began to invite her into its fold.

There was a part of her that knew her little crush, as she had begun to regard it, may have easily been due to the fact she was not exactly sober at the time of her appointment. There was also the whole hero scenario—that he'd saved her from her pain. Wasn't it normal to feel an instant connection with someone under those circumstances? Dr. Bland surely would have a field day if she ever sat down with him to discuss this.

But then she reasoned with herself. No, that was actually not a natural reaction for her, under the influence or not. She never would have felt that way about Dr. Soriano if he'd been on duty that day. Neil's charm had made her feel something. It had given her the extra heartbeat that came with romantic attraction.

Two weeks later, when Sophia return to the dental offices, she received another surprise: Dr. Soriano was in attendance while Neil was nowhere to be seen. She didn't even see Dolores, who she could have asked to pass on a "hello." She experienced something else she had not expected: disappointment. She'd had no idea that a broken tooth would remind her that there were other things still broken. It was then that she realized that it was time to allow herself to finish healing. It was time to move on.

CHAPTER 29
THE WHOLE STORY

"Are you sure we have to do this?" Natasha asked, still trying to avoid the attic at all costs. It had taken Sophia weeks to get her back to this point, and even though her hand was already on the door handle leading them into her private shrine, Natasha threw out bait one last time. "Your mouth is feeling fine? How are your eyes? Can I bribe you with a day of shopping? My treat?"

"That's tempting, Natasha. It really is. But the sooner we do this, the sooner it's over. And if you want to include *everything* in your book the way we discussed, it's important we do this."

"Fine," she said, accepting that resistance was pointless. "But I'm not promising you anything. I don't even remember half the stuff I have in there."

With that Natasha turned the handle and pushed the door inward, presenting a set of stairs. They began their ascent.

Awaiting them in the attic was a very large room that looked nothing like the cluttered mess that Natasha had led Sophia to believe it was. All of the walls were lined with orderly, well-labeled boxes, leaving the center of the room clear and easy to walk. Natasha must have sensed that Sophia was considering making a comment because she spoke first—a cheap attempt to redirect Sophia's attention. "Speaking of teeth…any word from Dr. Handsome?"

"No. How could he call me? I never gave him my number."

"Surely your number is on file."

"I'm sure it is," Sophia said, "but what doctor would do that?"

Natasha glanced around the room trying to decide where to begin. "You know, you could call him."

"It'd be too weird. What would I say? 'Hi! Remember me? I'm the woman whose mouth you had your fingers in. I was high on pain pills. We talked about your dog. I threw myself at you. Does any of that ring a bell? Well, I sensed we had a moment. Want to go out sometime?' He'd probably tell me he wasn't the kind of doctor I should be seeing and suggest I be committed."

"Oh, please. I'm sure it wouldn't be the first time that happened to him."

"No, Natasha," Sophia returned, "probably not, which only makes it worse. And I don't want it to happen like that. It makes me sound…I don't know…pathetic. It has to happen organically or not at all."

Natasha picked at a few boxes and contemplated her next comment. "It's interesting how you've gone from one end of the spectrum to the other. First you don't even notice men or want anything to do with them. Then you meet one and it's all about rules, how something should or should not happen."

"Ouch."

"Don't take it like that," Natasha told her. "I just mean that you seem a little conflicted."

"I'm sure I am. I'm also pretty sure that I'm not totally over Kevin. Things like this take time."

Natasha extended her arms and waved them at the boxes like a game show host. "Don't I know it? Why do you think I never like coming up here?"

The last part made Sophia feel like she was never going to heal so she redirected the conversation. There were more important issues at hand. "Where do you want to start?"

"I don't know. What works best for you? You're the one

writing this thing."

Sophia thought about her plan of attack for a moment. "Let's start at the beginning. I may not end up telling your story chronologically, but it's the simplest way to do the research. And while we're at it, let's pull a selection of pictures and such to include in the book. Readers love pictures."

"You mean they love embarrassing fashions and bad hair choices."

"Those, too."

So they began in one corner with boxes labeled "home," which were filled with smaller boxes of loose black and white photos never put into albums, and a few childhood toys. Natasha picked up a teddy bear and gave it a long squeeze and smell. "This takes me back," she said before describing the soft vanilla and lilac scent it still held after more than half a century. She pulled the bear's fluffy forehead from her nose. "I can't believe how powerful the sense of smell is. It's like I'm there. I actually recall the day my parents gave him to me."

Over the course of two full days, they would work their way around the room, opening box after box. Natasha shared countless stories as the memories flooded her mind. Sophia took notes, made recordings, and took hundreds of pictures. She knew she would only use a small percentage of these details, but she was pleased to have too much, rather than too little, information. All of this helped her form a picture of Natasha's life and prepared Sophia for what she knew was still to come.

"It's weird how your whole life can fit into a few boxes," Natasha shared.

"It's not exactly your whole life. Unfortunately—or fortunately, depending on how you wish to look at it—you can't hold onto everything."

The first day brought an occasional tear and several "I-forgot-all-about-this" comments, but it was the second day that proved much more emotional. That morning, as they picked up where they had left off, Natasha admitted to having had a significant breakthrough. "I had the most vivid dreams last night."

"Really? What'd you dream?"

"They were memories about Mommy and Daddy. I felt like I was really with them. To tell you the truth, I don't remember the last time I called my father 'Daddy.' But in my dreams, I remembered what it was like to still trust him, to feel like he was perfect, the way only a young child can."

"What a treat," Sophia shared, touched by the confession, "to be reminded of how you once felt about him, even if things played out differently."

Natasha nodded, tears in her eyes. "I've missed that. Being an adult and 'mature,' I forgot what it was like to feel unedited love for someone, free of cynicism and doubt."

Sophia knew what Natasha meant. "Life has a way of forcing you to build walls around yourself in order to survive."

"I never felt good enough for him. Or that he ever approved of me. That's what replaced love," Natasha said, now crying.

"I'm sure he loved you. You said before that he wasn't a great communicator, that there were generation issues."

"The sad thing is he never understood me. Or Bruce."

Sophia knew that Natasha mentioning her brother Bruce was the beginning of the conversation they both needed to have, but for very different reasons. "Do you think it would have made a difference between you and your father if Bruce had lived longer?"

"I don't know," Natasha said. "I'll never know. I'm not sure he could have ever accepted Bruce and that would have always been a problem for me. How can a parent not be proud when their child accomplishes something? You have to be pretty horrible not to feel joy when your own son or daughter makes something of their lives."

"True," Sophia added, without saying anything else. She knew it was probably best to let Natasha talk as freely as possible, only asking occasional questions to fill in missing information.

"I also dreamt I saw my brother, that Bruce came and visited me. We were in a café in the village, laughing and gossiping. When I woke up, I found that I'd been crying." Natasha's tears really let loose, and Sophia put her arms around her.

After a few moments, Sophia made a suggestion, "Maybe now's the time you want to tell the *whole* story. Are you ready for that?"

"I am," Natasha said, pulling herself together in preparation of looking her past directly in the eyes. "You're gonna want to record this."

Natasha moved into a small area that they'd skipped over the day before. At the time Sophia had thought to ask about it, but decided against it. It was a section of boxes without any labeling. As Natasha began opening containers and removing their lids, Sophia started to record.

The first box contained children's clothes and toys from another time. To Sophia they looked unworn and unused, older than the clothes she herself had as a child. She flashed back to the day at the recording studio and knew where Natasha would start.

"The beginning," Natasha said, picking up the clothes like there was life in them. "I realize now that I've always suffered from depression. I just never knew it. It's a terrible thing to think something might be wrong with you that no one would understand, that it would ruin your life if people knew. So you try to keep it from everyone you know, no matter what."

Natasha took a breath before continuing. "There were always signs—symptoms, the professionals call them. I never had the energy my siblings or friends had. I never had the same self-protection system they had either. Sure, I knew how to fight for things I wanted and needed. But where some people can let things roll off of them, I can't. Or at least I *couldn't,* until recently, that is."

Sophia listened and typed some of her thoughts into her computer, describing her own initial reactions to inspire her writing later.

"People didn't talk about depression back then, not the way they do now. And even today, there's still a stigma, a lot of misunderstanding and, I think, shame. I want to help change that."

Natasha stopped talking for a moment, holding a baby sweater to her cheek, smelling it like she had the teddy bear. "I've had many emotional breaks throughout my life. We—and by 'we,' I mean myself and the people around me, and there have been lots of people around me over the years—we never knew what to do about it. There were times when I didn't believe I needed help, and I would fire anyone who made the suggestion of getting help. And then there were times when I was crying out for assistance yet was unequipped to take the steps necessary. And the people around me…well, they were probably still afraid I would fire them. These episodes, my depression—on more than one occasion—they almost killed me."

Natasha smelled the sweater again, unaware of the tears rolling down her face, seeming to have gone somewhere far away. "Vanessa Baxter and I were once friends. We were studio girls together, in the final days when such things still existed— two young and very green newbies who arrived in Hollywood at the same time. We were both under contract and were often up for the same roles. But we were friends. Once upon a very long time ago, we were actually friends."

"What happened?" Sophia asked.

"Success. Success happened. Not just to me, but to her. We both started getting roles. We both began working a lot. We should have been happy, right? I was, for the most part. And while my depression was an issue, I masked it by working all the time, or through parties and alcohol. My life was better than I had ever known it could be, so I was able to look the other way for a while. But success brought out bad things in Vanessa. She became competitive and it made her mean. She became insatiable."

Natasha put the sweater down and grabbed a tiny yellow dress with pink baby ducks on it. "After *The Dreyfus Affair*, I went to film *The People on the Bay* in San Francisco. Production broke for a long weekend."

Sophia realized she didn't know Natasha was in *The People*

on the Bay. How could she have forgotten or missed that?

Natasha's eyes turned black and distant, and Sophia knew the actress was far away—reliving a night so many years ago. "So I went home to surprise Mathew. It was a rainy, stormy night—how cliché is that? When I got home, I found Vanessa's car in the driveway. And when I got into the house, I found Mathew in Vanessa."

"Did they see you?" Sophia asked.

"Not at first. So I went down to the kitchen, filled up a large pot with ice cold water and threw it on them. I wanted to use hot water, scalding even, but I knew better."

"And?"

"Well, they saw me alright. Mathew was angry, asking why I was home, why I hadn't told him I was coming. Can you believe that? I inconvenienced *him* by coming home to *my* house—which was bought with *my* money—to the man who was supposed to be *my* husband. He realized pretty quickly that he had no right being angry so he started apologizing profusely, begging for my forgiveness."

"What did Vanessa do?"

"She started yelling at me. How's that for another surprise? She was naked—crooked boobs and all—and screaming at me in my own bedroom. She told me I didn't deserve Mathew. That she treated him better than I did and that she'd been doing so for some time. She wanted me to know that it had been going on behind my back for a while."

Natasha stopped for a moment to catch her breath. "How does someone do that to someone they love? We were in love. We hadn't been married so long that there was no passion left. There *was* still passion between us."

Sophia didn't know how to answer that question. It was one of the hardest to explain, and one with which she herself battled. "So what'd you do?"

"I started hyperventilating. Two, wet naked people in my bedroom, a house full of yelling—I had a panic attack. I felt like I'd been stabbed in the chest. So I left. I just had to get away. It was one of the worst decisions of my life."

"Why?"

"I got into my car, drove half a mile…" Natasha said, hesitating, now crying uncontrollably.

Sophia remained silent. It was important Natasha be able to speak about this.

"…I lost control of the car," Natasha concluded.

Sophia felt her own tears climb out of her eyes.

"Do you know why I had gone home to surprise Mathew?" Natasha asked.

Sophia nodded. She knew what had happened next.

"To tell him I was pregnant. I had found out while I was on the set and wanted to tell him in person," she said, leaning her forehead into the dress, the pink ducks turning red from her tears. "I woke up two days later in the hospital. The only thing I remembered about the car crash was a loud slamming of metal and the crisp shatter of glass."

"The baby?" Sophia asked.

Natasha shook her head. "I told you I'm not the motherly type."

Sophia hugged Natasha. "I'm so sorry."

After a long moment, Natasha broke from her and said, "Me, too."

She took a minute to collect herself before continuing. "They replaced me in *The People on the Bay* because I couldn't work. I didn't work for a year after that."

"Did Mathew know about the baby?"

"I told him. I told him because I knew he'd leave Vanessa if he knew."

"And did he?"

"Yes. He did."

Natasha took a deep breath. "But that was a breaking point for me. I went spinning out of control."

"What'd you do?"

"I left Los Angeles. I wanted out of the city and I never wanted to drive again. So Jonathan packed me up and shipped me off to New York. It was the early '70s and a lot of films were being made in Manhattan. And the economy was a mess so

Jonathan found investment opportunities. We put a lot of money into real estate, turned some money into more money. I'll admit, I've had as much fortune as I've had tragedy. Maybe what Newton said was correct—that for every action there is an equal and opposite reaction."

"And then?"

"My depression got worse. I drank a lot. Took pills. Spent late nights out partying, doing my best to lose myself. I made some movies, but only a couple of them were worth the cost of their celluloid. So I drank even more and took more pills. I thought I managed it, but really it managed me."

Sophia knew this was hard for Natasha, but she pressed on, knowing where they were headed. "When did Bruce come to New York City?"

Natasha smiled at the mention of her brother's name. "'74, I think. Bruce was much younger than me. He was the baby—a surprise for my folks who had thought their childbearing days had passed. He was a dancer, which our father had a terrible time accepting. Men weren't dancers. Men, in his old-fashioned mind, worked with their hands, not with their legs. Dancers were either women or sissies. In school, he lied about taking classes but our father found out. He told Bruce to stop, that people would talk. Bruce said he would, but he didn't. He couldn't. It was who he was, what he was born to do. It was his way of expressing himself, of communicating. Who has the right to tell another person that what they have to say, or how they need to say it, is wrong? When Father found out, he beat him. Can you imagine? A father beats his son because he was doing the one thing that brings him happiness. It meant nothing to anyone else and it certainly didn't hurt my father. What is wrong with this world?"

Sophia shook her head. She would never be able to explain that behavior to Natasha or anyone else.

"When I found out, that my father had given him a black eye and a bloody mouth, I sent Bruce money and told him to move to New York."

"And?"

"He did."

"He was lucky to have you," Sophia said, but Natasha wouldn't look her in the eyes.

"It was nice being together as adults, out from under the thumb of our small town parents and small town lives. New York, despite all of its challenges and temptations, was a city of hope and promise. It was the Land of Oz. And there were days when things were perfect. Bruce had *everything* to do with that. I was so many years older yet we had so much in common."

"That's wonderful," Sophia told her as Natasha took a moment to collect her thoughts.

"Yes, it was. But as they say, 'What goes up, must come down.' You didn't know I knew so much science, did you?" Natasha added.

"No, I didn't," Sophia said, wanting to enjoy the light-hearted moment but knowing it wouldn't last. "Did Bruce find work in New York?"

"He did. He was quite successful. And, I might add, without any help from me. He was in several Broadway shows and a member of the Martha Graham Dance Company."

"Those are some great accomplishments. I'm sure you were proud."

"I was. I am. *Very* proud."

"Did his success change things with your father?" Sophia asked.

"He came around a little. Until the '80s. Until the ground opened up and ate generations of special, lovely men." All at once, anger and sadness climbed from Natasha's chest into her face. "No one knew what was happening, but suddenly everyone we knew started to get sick. First was our friend John David. Then Rick. And Craig. And Scott. And then Bruce—my poor, sweet, innocent baby brother. Did you know it took the government five years to launch an AIDS education program? Five years *after* scientists had figured out that the disease was infectious! And do you know why? Because people don't care what happens to homosexuals. Five years! Do you know how many lives could have been saved?" Natasha stood up and paced in front of Sophia. "It makes me sick. It absolutely makes me sick."

"Do you want to take a break?" Sophia asked.

"No, thanks. I don't need a break," Natasha responded. "I've been on a break long enough. I need to keep going."

"Ok. When did Bruce get sick?"

"The first time was in '85. Then again in '86. By '87, he was blind and emaciated. By that point, my father retracted what little support he had given. He wanted nothing to do with a son who had the 'gay cancer.'"

Natasha's fury made way for her sadness. "My beautiful brother didn't even know me at the end. It should have been *me* that was wasting away, not him. I wanted it to be *me.*"

The tears poured out of Natasha like a faucet. "I would have given anything to change places with Bruce."

Sophia felt her loss—it ached in her chest.

"I've battled with a lot of guilt over his death. I deserved that death, not him."

"Why do you say that? Why do you feel guilty?"

"Because I was already damaged. At the time, and for many years, I felt worthless. I would have, without even a second thought, given my life if it meant saving his. And a huge part of me feels responsible because I moved him to New York. I always thought that maybe he wouldn't have gotten sick, he wouldn't have died, if he hadn't moved here."

"You gave him a life, Natasha!" Sophia told her, deciding it was important Natasha hear what she had to say. "Who knows what would have happened to him if you hadn't helped him get away? You helped him follow and find his dream. How many people get to say that they did that in their lives? Surely you know how many gay people try to kill themselves because they don't know there is any other option. You gave him options!"

"I hope you never have to know what it's like to be left alone after most everyone you ever loved has been taken from you. We lost so many of our friends—wonderful men whose only real crime was being creative and expressive. I should have been grateful to be alive, right? But that's easier said than done. Life becomes subjective when your reason for living is taken from you, especially when it happens time after time. I went spiraling downward after that."

"When did you try to commit suicide?"

"In 1995. I'd felt so alone for such a long time and I didn't know how to ask for help. Jonathan didn't help matters because he refused to believe things could be that bad. He'd sheltered me for so many years, thinking it was working, so that's what he continued to do. But it was slowly killing me, all of it. So one day I decided to take matters into my own hands."

Natasha paused and considered it all. "I had no idea the world knew about it," she added. "How's that for isolated and deluded? Jonathan lied to me. Everyone around me did. And while I know they thought they were protecting me, it was actually hurting me. How could I possibly get better if my life was made up of lies?"

"Jonathan kept you away from anything that might have exposed the truth?" Sophia asked. "Like the Internet?"

She nodded. "He must have figured it was a technology I'd have no interest in. After all, I'd shown little interest in doing things for myself so why would I want to begin now?"

Natasha's hardships swam around Sophia. "You've had a lot of struggles."

"It's time to put them to good use. I want them to make a difference for someone."

"Then that's what we'll do."

The weight Natasha had carried for so many years continued lifting off of her shoulders, and it would still take time for it to be properly dealt with, to be put in a place where it no longer controlled Natasha. But for five minutes, she and her friend, Sophia, cried together for lost loved ones and newly found possibilities. Together, neither of them felt alone in the world that day.

That night, before leaving The Estate, Sophia left an envelope of her own for Natasha, placing it on her bed, propped in front of her pillow so she was sure to see it before going to sleep. Inside was a card with the prewritten message, "Now & Always You Are In My Thoughts." Sophia wrote a message of her own:

> *Natasha,*
>
> *I'm incredibly sorry for your losses. Thank you for trusting me with your past and future. Your strength, courage and compassion are going to make a difference in a lot of lives. You're a very special woman and we're lucky you're in the world.*
>
> *XOXO*
> *Sophia*

CHAPTER 30
ALIVE & KICKING

Sophia finally felt ready to begin connecting all of the dots of Natasha's life. After months of conversations, interviews and research, which she had drafted and organized in her usual meticulous fashion, she was confident that she had collected enough snapshots of Natasha's history to start painting an honest and complex portrait. They both wanted it to go beyond her career and show the life of a woman who had accomplished tremendous things, but at a significant cost; and to share the hard-earned lessons, some discovered late in life, from which she knew others could benefit, too. Sophia was clear that Natasha saw this as an opportunity to turn the mistakes she had made into something good. There were many decisions she would have made differently if only she had known then what she knew now. She had paid a hefty price and she hoped her tale just might give others the courage and strength they needed to avoid the same pitfalls.

All you have to do is ask for help. You are not alone.

It had been a long process for Sophia to get to where she was now, but that was how writing went—a series of steps forward and backward until she got it right. Since their time in the attic, Sophia had finished mapping out the themes that drove and consumed Natasha's life. Then she started to link these concepts to her history and began fleshing out the story they would tell. Creating this project was both similar and different than her novel, and each was uniquely easier and more challenging than the other.

The day my brother arrived in New York City was one of the greatest days of my life. It would also haunt me for decades.

As Sophia began to put all of the disparate pieces together, she reminded herself each and every day that she did not want to write a boring autobiography weighed down by mundane facts that started from the day Natasha was born and ended with a summary of what she was doing now. What value was there in telling a story like that for either the reader or Natasha? Sophia wanted to write the story of a complex woman: fiercely independent, hungry for the approval of others, conflicted from being stuck between generations. She wanted to show all sides of Natasha—good and bad, strong and weak, healthy and ill. She was a woman who came from nothing who, like many people, struggled with enormous challenges. Sophia now felt that she understood the intricacies that made Natasha who she was.

There were times I didn't think I would make it another day. How could I? How would I?

Natasha loved to say how she was not the same person she once was, or had once tried to be, and Sophia agreed. If they had begun to write the autobiography back in the winter as originally discussed, it never would've had the depth that it was going to have now. She was grateful things had worked out the way they had, if for no other reason than for Natasha's well-being.

Without knowing it, I had asked for help. I threw out an invitation that was actually my own life preserver. A random intersection would put me on the right track.

Out again at The Sequel, alone in her room, a hot August

breeze from the ocean blew through the open window and kept Sophia company as she began writing the first chapter. She had taken her time to find the right words to establish the tone and intention of Natasha's memoirs. It was a hurdle she had struggled with for some time. *How to start it? First person or third person? What to tell and what not? What kind of tone? What to imply and what to withhold?* The questions seemed endless. Once she had decided what to say, she worked on finding the right way to say it—a negotiation with which every writer wrestles, a dance that requires patience and perseverance. Once she got past this initial chapter, she thought that the rest of the book would fall into place.

Chapter 1
A Little Something You Should Know

I've spent much of my time on this earth in motion but, as I'll say now and I'll say time and again, I'm really no different than anyone else. Under the layers of what makes me seem different from the next person, I'm just a human being trying to find my way in the world. But because of luck and circumstance, I just happen to have a voice bigger than most—which is one of the reasons I've decided to tell my story.

First, I must confess that I was not one of those women who fought on the frontlines for women's rights. I tell you this because I wish I had been. Perspective, of which you collect a lot over the years, provides you with a laundry list of such wishes. For one, I wish I had been bold and strong like those who stood up against discrimination, risking so much to challenge the status quo because they knew they deserved better. But I wasn't. I wasn't strong back then. It took me years to build my armor and defenses, and then more years to rip it off again and bare my soul for you today. I suppose one could argue it takes strength and courage to tell a story like mine, but I don't look at it that way. It seems more like something I have to do because it's the right thing to do. I see now that those who fought for my rights must have felt that same way.

Back then, I was too busy worrying about what others thought of me, and too afraid to risk standing out or being thought of as too loud or too angry or too aggressive. I have certainly done little things along the way to help drive equality, but I was not out there doing the real heavy-lifting like so many of our brave and dedicated sisters and brothers (yes, we must give credit to the men who took a stand for us as well). And I should have been. But I'm here now to show you it's never too late to make a stand. These days, I'm championing a number of causes because our world needs more love and attention, because we need as many people as possible to stand up for what's right. But I don't consider myself bold or strong today—just less afraid.

Perspective is an interesting concept and a powerful ally. There's much I can tell you that may help you on your own journey—lessons I would have much preferred to learn from someone else rather than from firsthand, in-the-trenches experience that cost me blood, sweat and a lot of tears. (And that is no exaggeration by any means, as you will soon find out.) I can tell you that I'm not the same person now that I was back then. Who is? And I can tell you that I know different things now—things that would lead to different choices. There are many great lessons I've learned over the years that I'd like to share with you. The most important piece of advice has become the motto for my life and is the main reason I'm writing this book: you cannot outrun the past—it has strong legs and a determined spirit.

My current perspective tells me that my story could make a difference for someone else. Wouldn't that be something—if each of us woke up every day and said, "I'm going to make a positive difference in someone else's life today?" Just think how much we could accomplish.

I have indeed spent much of my life in motion, always on the move, never in one place for long, because I've been running. I fought to get out of Nebraska to find a life more fitting for me. I struggled and climbed my way to find success in my career. I jumped into decisions, roles and relationships that were both healthy and unhealthy. And I spent a good portion of my life running from both facts and fictions. Now time and good fortune have allowed me the opportunity to right some of my wrongs. I hope you find my stories entertaining and, more than that, inspiring. If this book touches just one life out there in the world we share, then I'll feel the effort put into this was worth it. After all, we really are in this together.

I've come to believe that truth is one of the most powerful forces around. It's more important that fame and wealth. It's as important as love and trust. Deep inside your heart and your head, you know certain things to be your own truths. I've had my share, too, many from which I ran for years. Maybe you know that about me already, or think you know that. (But I'll venture a guess that you don't know nearly as much about me as you think you do.) Perhaps you were lucky to have learned this lesson early on and I'm just a slow learner who took her time getting to that realization. The truth is, without a doubt, something powerful. If you embrace it, you might be surprised by what it'll do for you. And if you don't, you may be shocked by what it does to you.

This is my story. It's been a journey full of many loves and losses, many lies and truths. I have been inspired and touched by some very talented and special people over the years, and I hope that my stories might help you follow your dreams and find your way, wherever you may wish to go.

There's one more thing I'd like to share before we begin our journey— a little something you should know: I'm not running anymore. Maybe you're running—from whatever it may be—and you'd like to stop, too. Know that I'll be standing there with you. My story is for you.

By the middle of the afternoon, Sophia pushed herself away from the desk, seeking refuge and a clear head by the pool. It wasn't until she was sitting on the edge with her calves lowered into the cool water, her heavy head resting backwards so she could soak up the sun, that the sentences and ideas twisting up her mind began to melt away. Natasha poked her head through the French doors in the living room to ask, "You feel up to going to the market?"

Sophia drank in a few more moments of the rays before answering. "Sure. Are you driving?"

"Don't push your luck," Natasha returned.

"One of these days. *I am* going to get you behind the wheel again."

"I usually am *behind* the wheel. There just happens to be a driver between me and it, that's all."

"What'll you do when you get to Los Angeles for your meetings?" Sophia asked, referring to the trip Jonathan had set up for Natasha.

After some serious thinking and soul-searching, as well as at the repeated suggestions of Sophia, Natasha decided to have a heart-to-heart sit-down with her old friend and business partner. At the meeting, Natasha told Jonathan that she loved him more than she hated him, and concluded that as long as he never lied to her again, even if it meant telling her things she didn't want to hear (within reason, of course), she needed him in her life.

"I'll hire a car, of course. Dear, these days, having a driver is less about fear and more about ability. I don't drive because I don't have to."

"I think you're making excuses."

"And I think you're acting like my mother again. I had one of those. I don't need another."

Sophia grabbed the car keys and her sandals—the pair Kate left for her—and met Natasha in the driveway. Her mind was elsewhere as they drove away from The Sequel towards town, but she was present enough to enjoy the beautiful drive, which was like touring a watercolor painting with a bouquet of oceanic aromas. Deep down, she was still a California girl, always able to enjoy two things—the beach and driving—and, by her standards, the combination couldn't be beat.

"When do I get to read it?" Natasha asked.

Eyes on the road, Sophia could see in the corner of her vision Natasha was fiddling with her hair in the mirror. "When I'm done."

"When will *that* be?" she prodded, which Sophia assumed she did more so for her own entertainment than for any other reason.

"Soon enough. But if you keep pressuring me, I'm not promising anything. And you'd better not sneak a peak."

Natasha gave her a mocking look, like she just might try that, and Sophia barked, "I mean it. I'll be upset."

Sophia heard herself talk and, unhappy with her tone, she said, "I'm sorry. There's too much going on right now."

"You have been awfully cranky lately. Are you always this irritable while you write?"

"Sometimes. I'm just distracted and my head is on seven different things at once."

"Maybe it *is* a good idea for you to hold off from dating until you're done with your books. Cranky is not a good look on you."

Sophia gave Natasha a dead serious look. "Are you done

harassing me now?"

"No," Natasha said, with a look of her own—hers showing she thought she was being cute and amusing. "One more question. Will you at least tell me the name?"

Sophia thought about it. "It's a working title, but I'm thinking, *Alive & Kicking.*"

Natasha smiled. "I love it! Is that a reference to the death rumors? You're including all of the Internet rumors, right? Like I'm dead, and I died in a pool of my own vomit, and the Pop Rocks and everything else?"

"Yes, I'm including it all. I think it adds to your mythology."

"'Mythology?' You really think I have a mythology?"

Sophia kept her eyes on the road. "Of course. You're a movie star. That'll get people's attention. But, as I see it, it'll be your wisdom that'll make you a *legend.*"

She didn't have to look to know how Natasha would respond to that comment—she knew it would have her jumping up and down in her seat.

"You are so good!" Natasha gushed. "So good! Oh, my God, let's go home. You have to finish by dinner."

"Yeah, right. And that's all you get for now," Sophia told her, knowing Natasha would likely ask for more information.

Natasha settled down before inquiring, "And how's the novel coming?"

"Very good. I'm at the end, but I don't know how to end it," Sophia shared.

"That sounds like a problem."

"Well, sort of. My climax has already taken place, so that's not the issue. I have some loose ends to wrap up and I haven't decided what should happen with a couple of the players. I think part of the reason I can't decide is that I don't want it to be over. Is that strange? I mean, I've fallen in love with these characters. I feel like I know their lives so well, and the minute I finish that last sentence they'll cease to be living people. It's like they'll be part of my past. I'm going to mourn them."

This quieted Natasha. Sophia figured she wasn't sure what

to say, until she added, "I always felt sad at the end of making a film. It was like camp. You spend intense periods of time with people only to go back home. And even if you live in the same city, it's not like you'll have breakfast with them every morning, or spend ten hours together on a set ever again. I always found that really sad. Then there's also the character you're playing. One day you're a waitress with a winning lottery ticket. The next, that character is finished and wrapped. You'll never say another word, or take another breath, for them. So I know what you mean."

"I'm also afraid of sending my work out," Sophia admitted. "What if no one likes it? It's the whole living-in-a-bubble issue. I *think* I've worked out all the problems and developed this well-thought-out story. But at the end of the day, how can I really be sure of anything other than that I've denied myself any personal time for the past eight months?"

"That's the risk you take, baby."

Sophia pulled up to the parking lot and into a spot. As she turned the ignition off and turned *on* a sigh, Natasha leaned over and whispered. "I'm sure people will love it. How could they not? Listen to how much *you* love it."

"I don't *feel* like I love it."

"You may not right now, but you do. Who spends that much time doing something they don't love? And I'm sure it's great because *you're* great. People will love it."

"Your mouth to God's ears," she said, repeating Jasper's words.

Natasha and Sophia grabbed a grocery cart as they entered the market, hitting the delicatessen first. As they finished there and rounded the corner, it became obvious that the cart Sophia had chosen was disabled by one very lazy wheel that dragged and screeched as she struggled to steer it. While in the midst of cursing it under her breath, her cart collided with another.

"I'm so sorry," she said, looking up to see who she nearly mowed down.

"Sophia Connors?"

Sophia instantly recognized the accident victim and then

silently cursed more than just the wheel. If she'd seen him first, she would have run the other way. It was one of those days she would have been better off staying home, in hiding.

"Hello, Trevor," she said, fuming about her bad luck. Here, in the middle of a market in East Hampton, surrounded by canned goods, she had managed to literally run into her former employer, Trevor Duncan—the owner of RGB and the person who at the beginning of the year had *canned* her. The sick coincidence of the situation was not lost on her.

"How are you doing?" he asked, seeming sincerely interested, which Sophia found surprisingly disarming. "It's so good to see you."

She picked up her chin from off the floor and managed a response. "I'm doing well, thanks. You?"

He smiled. "That's great to hear. You look well. We sure do miss you at RGB."

And as quickly as she had let her guard down, her artillery was back out again.

"Oh, really? Is that why you fired me?" she asked with venom.

"I'm so sorry about that. I really am. But you know how the business goes. If we lose accounts, we can't keep the overhead."

Trevor was only making matters worse. "'Overhead?' Is that what I was? That's so personal of you. And it was really nice how your minions ushered us out the front door seconds after you canned us. Did you think we were going to run off with copiers and paperclips?"

"Those were security measures, Sophia. Our lawyers tell us to do that to make sure that private information doesn't get stolen by disgruntled employees."

"The only reason I *became* disgruntled was because you managed the whole process so poorly," Sophia clarified. "If you had been respectful and considerate of what we were going through, then maybe I wouldn't be so pissed at you right now."

Natasha came around the corner just in time to hear the last of Sophia's comment. "Pissed? What are you pissed about?"

"This guy," Sophia said, throwing mental darts at Trevor,

"and the damage he's caused."

Natasha looked at the carts, still face-to-face, and then at Trevor. A large smile grew over her face and she said, "Hello." There was a slight hint of flirtatiousness.

Trevor smiled back. "Well, hello. I'm Trevor Duncan," he told her, extending his arm.

She took his hand and shook it, then removed her sunglasses. "I'm Natasha McGavin."

From where Sophia stood, something was very wrong here—a feeling that only worsened as Trevor and Natasha remained facing each other, locked in an awkward, smile-filled stare that only Sophia seemed bothered by.

It was Trevor who interrupted the moment. "Wait! You're not *the* Natasha McGavin, are you?"

"The one and only," Natasha said, cooing just enough to make Sophia sick to her stomach.

"Goodness gracious," Trevor said. "Wow! Am I a huge fan or what?"

Natasha pretended to be bashful, making it official—she was an actor again. "Well, I don't know. Are you?"

Sophia couldn't help but be dumbfounded. *Yes, I should have stayed home, under the covers!*

"I am!" Trevor proclaimed. "I think I've seen all of your films. You are phenomenal. How come you haven't done anything lately?"

Natasha actually turned red, as she flipped her hair to the side—a very Farrah move. "They don't write a lot of parts for women my age."

"Oh, I don't believe that," he said, flirting back. "You can't limit talent."

Trevor was an attractive older man—Sophia would give him that—but he was an advertising guy and that gave Sophia more than enough cause to be apprehensive.

"You're sweet, but I'm no spring chicken. Who wants to see this old bird in anything?"

"Nonsense! Just look at you! You're gorgeous."

Sophia was getting more and more uncomfortable with the

weird body language being spoken by these two people from very different chapters of her life. If Natasha wasn't yet swept off her feet, she was getting there. As for Sophia, she was getting annoyed. Having had all she could take and no interest in being in the middle of this—whatever it was—she excused herself.

"Watch where you're going, Trevor," she warned him and then looked at Natasha, "You can find me when you two have finished...*visiting.*" Natasha wouldn't have known it, but Sophia used the word "visiting" because it sounded like something her grandmother would have said—her subtle message to Natasha that her behavior was not easy to watch.

It wasn't until Sophia was at the checkout that Natasha appeared again, giggly, like a school girl.

"Your friend, Trevor, is quite the attractive gentleman."

Sophia rolled her eyes, finished paying the young woman at the register, and pushed the broken cart as best she could through the front door. "He's *not* my friend. And I'd hardly regard him as a gentleman."

Natasha followed close behind. "He told me you didn't like him very much. That you're still probably sore about him letting you go."

"Uh, yeah! I think that would be a logical conclusion on his part. You can tell by his keen sense of observation that he's intelligent, too."

"Don't be like that, Sophia. If he hadn't fired you," she said, suddenly taking on the voice of reason, "you wouldn't have been unemployed, and we wouldn't have met at the movies, and I'd never have been able to hire you."

"I'm thrilled we met," Sophia told her as she opened the trunk to Natasha's Mercedes and put the packages inside. "You know that. I just happen to also harbor some serious resentment for the corporate power structure that Trevor runs. Bad behavior deserves punishment."

"He's attractive. And witty. And he has excellent taste," Natasha told her. "I like him."

"How do you know he has good taste?"

"Because he says I'm beautiful," Natasha gushed.

"You can't date him. He's hippy-dippy!"

"Hippy-dippy? You're from San Francisco, for God's sake."

The truth was that Sophia didn't really hate Trevor. The only reason she disliked him was because of *how* they terminated her employment, not *that* they terminated it—not anymore at least.

"I think I've lived in New York too long," Sophia said as they exited the parking lot and headed home.

"Yes, my dear. You've become a bit jaded."

"Did you ever read the college graduation address that was incorrectly credited to Kurt Vonnegut?" Sophia asked.

"No, I didn't."

"As you know, I love Vonnegut. I met him. Did I tell you that story yet?"

"Yes, dear. I think you might have mentioned it. A couple of times, at least."

"Well, there was a column written by a *Chicago Tribune* writer—Mary Schmich. What she wrote was brilliant and it was used as a speech for a commencement address at MIT. For some reason, Vonnegut was credited for writing the speech. Which makes sense because of how clever it was. Anyway, in it she wrote that everyone should live in Northern California but leave before getting too soft, and everyone should live in New York but leave before getting too hard. Maybe that's me. Maybe I've become too hard. Maybe it's time to leave New York."

Natasha became serious again. "Quit that talk. First, you're not *that* jaded. And I won't hear another word about you leaving New York. If you need a break from the city, you stay out here all you want. And you can go to Los Angeles with me whenever you like. I haven't offered it before because I know you want to focus on your writing and I didn't want to tempt you with distractions."

Sophia inhaled the sea air and tasted salt—she loved that sensation. A few moments later, she asked Natasha, "Are you actually going to go out with him?"

"I'd go out with him if he calls. He asked for my number."

"That's very adventurous of you," Sophia told her. "But

wait a second. Only if he calls you?"

"Maybe I'll call him, smarty pants. I do know where he works."

Sophia laughed, imagining Natasha dialing RGB. Or better yet, Sophia calling RGB on her behalf. "I think that's a great idea since you keep telling me to call Dr. Handsome. Take your own medicine."

"I think I just might."

Sophia shook her head at the turn of events. "The world is definitely coming to an end."

Later that night, staring into the glow of her computer screen, Sophia thought about their conversation. If Natasha could get out there and start dating then so could Sophia. Maybe Natasha had the right idea—maybe it was time to make something happen.

She reflected upon Natasha's concept of motion. It struck a chord with her. *I'm tired of running,* Sophia admitted to herself. *Just sick and tired of it.*

CHAPTER 31
A MIRAGE

Sophia greeted Jasper at the door of his and Cliff's apartment on West 12th Street, a loud announcement making her presence known to anyone within earshot, "Operation CPA is in effect."

But Jasper didn't quite follow. "CPA?"

"Yes, CPA. Canine…Pick-up…Assistance."

Cliff emerged from the kitchen, joining them in the entryway with a snarky, meaningful grin. "Are you really going through with this?"

"I won't be judged," Sophia told him with a laugh, "by someone who picks up strangers in Duane Reade."

"What's wrong with that?" Cliff returned. "It was like a scene in a French film, and pretty damn romantic. Besides, doesn't this guy know you don't have a dog? He's gonna see you at the dog run with a full-grown dog—that, by the way, is not *your* dog—and he'll be the one running…the other way."

Jasper intervened. "Don't say that to her," he told Cliff. "He's not going to run. Look at her. Would *you* run from her?"

"She's not exactly my type, baby," Cliff told Jasper before further interrogating Sophia. "Do you even know anything about dogs?"

Sophia laughed with excitement, fueled by both the teasing and the anticipation of what might happen later that morning. "Sure. What's to know? Besides, that's why Jasper's going with me. I just happen to be on a walk with my friend and his dog."

"That's your story?" Cliff asked Sophia. He then turned to his partner. "And she's dragging you into this, too?"

Jasper nodded. "I gotta stand by my woman."

"Well, have fun, kids," Cliff told them. "Good luck, play nice with the other boys and girls, and don't let Libby get into trouble."

"Trouble?" Sophia inquired. "I thought she was fixed."

"She is, but sometimes a girl's got needs, you know?"

"Oh, I know," Sophia told him, and then repeated for effect, *"I know!* That's why I'm here!"

"Baby girl, let's go for a walk!" Jasper called out, and the cocker spaniel came tearing out from the bedroom.

Sophia, Jasper and Libby headed north up University to Union Square. "So you've taken her there before?" Sophia asked.

"Yes, a bunch of times. Stop worrying."

"Does she like it?" Sophia asked, but lost interest in her own question when she felt her pocket come alive. "Hold on."

She pulled out her cell phone, and answered, "Natasha? Hello. How'd it go?"

"It was so great!" Natasha said, beside herself. "It was for that legal series. The producers took me to dinner last night and told me they want me for the part of a Supreme Court justice. And it's a recurring role. Can you believe that?"

"Of course I can!" Sophia said, stopping at the intersection because the light had turned red.

"Listen, there's another reason I'm calling. Have you seen *Entertainment Weekly?"* Natasha asked.

"No, why?"

"You have to check it out! I would've called you last night but it was so late when we were done. Page 35. All I'm going to say is that the timing couldn't be better. At the meeting last night, they pulled out this article and asked if I'd seen it. They absolutely loved it. We're back in business!"

"What's in the article?" Sophia asked.

"I want you to see for yourself. Get a copy as soon as you can!"

"I'm with Jasper and we're headed over to Union Square. I'm sure we can find one on the way."

"Oh, my God!" Natasha said. "How could I have forgotten that today's the day? Well, I know he'll be excited to see you and I want a full report later. And I can't wait to hear what you think about the article. Yes, indeed—we are back in business!"

When Sophia hung up, she told Jasper about Natasha's news and then dove into the first bodega they saw to grab the magazine. She had reached page 35 by the time she was back outside with Jasper and Libby.

"What is it? What does it say?" Jasper demanded, also curious about what could've gotten Natasha so worked up.

"This is too much!" Sophia told him, scanning the piece before handing it to him. "It just goes to show you: you just never know."

Still Wicked After All These Years
- A Can't-Be-Missed DVD

Out this week is the 40th Anniversary DVD release of the film noire classic, The Dreyfus Affair, *a flawless production with star turns led by Natasha McGavin and Kurt Smith, and inspired direction by Joseph Stubbings. This DVD is evidence of two important rules to remember in Hollywood. One: good filmmaking always stands the test of time. There are few audiences today that wouldn't find this flick a nail-biter. Two: a good commentary track, when done right, can be just as entertaining as the best of movies. This special anniversary edition is like two films in one. The audio commentary with Natasha McGavin and Vanessa Baxter is entirely captivating and is alone worth the price of the DVD. It's like experiencing a two-hour verbal mixed martial arts contest between the two notoriously feuding divas. If you've never seen this film, this*

DVD is a perfect introduction, especially to McGavin whose talent is skillfully precise and honest—both onscreen and off as we discovered so memorably on the commentary. If you're ever in a fight, pray she's on your side. We hope the recent rumbling that McGavin is making a comeback is not just a rumor.

Jasper looked up, a grin stretched from side to side. "This is unbelievable."

Sophia nodded in agreement. "I'll call Jonathan and Claire later to see when we can our hands on that DVD."

"I can't wait! And since Natasha's in such a good space with it, she has to watch the commentary with us!"

"We'll make it a party! We can play games like pin the tail on the Donkey-Breath," Sophia suggested. They laughed, both glad that Donkey-Breath Baxter's power over Natasha was gone.

When they arrived at the park, Sophia's nerves took over. "Should we be doing this? Is this too bizarre? I feel like I'm back in junior high and I'm trying to get Robert Schaeffer to notice me."

"You're fine," Jasper assured her. "Don't worry. Remember our story—we're here for *me,* not for you. Besides, he's lucky you're interested in him. Any guy would be."

"You sure you don't like girls?" she asked, knowing what a treasure Jasper was and how blessed she was to have him in her life. "I'd marry you in a heartbeat."

"Sorry, babe."

They climbed the stairs into the park, following the paved walk until they reached the dog run. Sophia tried to act casual as she scanned the crowd, telling herself she was looking for a free bench while knowing that she was searching for Zoe, the black French bulldog, and her dad, Dr. Handsome.

Jasper led Libby through the gates to the run arena before turning to Sophia. "Do you see him?"

"Not so loud!" she told him, the words coming out harsher than she had planned.

"Crazy, please!" he returned with a snap, pretending to be offended.

"Sorry," she told him. "I'm losing it."

Jasper shook it off. "No need to apologize. Love and lust always lead to crazy. Should I get a prescription for you from Dr. Bland? Or better yet, from Dr. Handsome?"

Sophia finished her review of the dogs and their owners but didn't see Neil or Zoe anywhere, so they parked themselves on an outer bench looking inward towards the dog run and the park. They knew this would be a good spot to see them when they arrived.

While Libby, in her own crazed state, moved around the fenced-in area, Sophia and Jasper chatted casually about miscellaneous topics, including Cliff's desire to purchase a weekend home and Natasha's busy fall schedule.

"Will you go to California with her when she's working?" Jasper asked.

"We have to figure that out. For now I think we've agreed that I'm more useful finishing her book."

"Maybe she should hire an assistant in California? Sophia, Part Two?"

Sophia smiled at Jasper. "I don't know. We'll see. It's not like I can't travel or bring my laptop anywhere she goes. I think Natasha knows I get more accomplished when I can just focus on writing. It won't take me that much longer though, so if she needs to be in L.A., I can go out there with her. Unless, of course," she hoped, "my new lover objects."

"Libby!" Jasper screamed, jumping off the bench to run towards his dog as she jumped on the backside of a large golden retriever. "Libby, get down!"

Sophia took the opportunity to scan the crowd again, but there were still no sign of Neil. Jasper returned, saying, "It's a dominance thing when she does that. She humps to show who's in control."

Sophia laughed. "That's one way of looking at it."

Jasper took his seat again. "So where's your man? He said he comes here *every* Saturday?"

"Yes, every Saturday," she said, starting to question herself. *Did he say Saturday? Or was it Sunday?* It had been weeks since they met and she was suddenly nervous she had gotten her facts wrong.

"Why don't you just call him instead of this stalking business?"

"Stalking worked for you, didn't it?"

"Touché."

The first hour passed quickly, as did the second, but by hour three they had long since run out of things to discuss. Sophia was lost in thought, finessing the final details for *Bad Blood* when Libby gave up, showing she was done by dropping dramatically at Jasper's feet.

Jasper threw in the towel, too. "While this has been nice, I think it's time to leave. Libby's exhausted and it'll be a challenge just getting her home. Besides, this bench is murdering my ass."

Sophia was disappointed but understood.

"Just call him," Jasper pleaded. "Will it really be *that* terrible if he tells you he's not interested? You'll never know if you don't ask."

They had discussed this before but Sophia shook her head to confirm she hadn't changed her mind.

"But you went through this much trouble to see him again. Why not just pick up the phone and call him at work?" Jasper asked, standing up to stretch his legs. "I bet your gal pal, Dolores, would agree that's the best idea. It's what you should have done in the first place."

But Sophia wouldn't hear of it. "I just can't do that. I know it's hypocritical. I know all the advice I've given Natasha. But it's not how I want it to happen."

"Is *how* it happens more important than *if* it happens?" he asked. "Who knew you had this little old lady living inside you?"

She laughed, which brought her a sense of relief and the realization that she was reacting ridiculously. "Look—it's not a big deal. It really isn't. It just wasn't meant to be. Two strikes and I'm out. That's how I'll look at it."

Jasper moved around to get the blood flowing to his feet. "You just said, 'I'll look,' meaning that you don't look at it that way now, but you *will* sometime in the future. I don't know. I'm not buying this 'I'm centered' attitude. You have Natasha convinced you're all Zen, but not me." Jasper leaned down to encourage Libby to start moving, then spoke to Sophia again, "You sure you're not upset?"

"I'm a little disappointed," she admitted, "but I just have to believe the universe is telling me it wasn't meant to be."

"But you don't believe in stuff like that."

"Geez, aren't you fluent in Sophia-isms today? I know I've said that before—*many* times—but when push comes to shove, a little faith comes in handy."

Jasper took a seat again as if he needed the stability of the bench before he made his next point. "Maybe all of this is just a mirage."

"What do you mean?" Sophia asked, curious about his meaning. She could tell he was being serious.

"You know, an illusion, like in the movies when the guy is crossing the desert and thinks he sees a palm tree hovering over a pool of water, only it ends up being a pile of sand. It's something you see off in the distance because that's what you want to see, or need to see—something that inspires you and reminds you that you're looking for something, or someone. It keeps you believing that there's good on the horizon, that good things do happen—and if you continue pressing on, you'll reach your happy ending. Maybe this Neil guy was that for you. And maybe you should take all of this as a sign you're ready to get out there, that you're looking for that love again."

Sophia let it all soak in. She knew he was probably right.

"Besides," Jasper added for levity, "What are the odds he's even the right guy for you? I mean, how can you even be sure he's not gay? You did say he was yummy and sweet, and you know my peeps got dibs on all the yummy, sweet ones."

She smiled. "You're right."

"I usually am," he said, standing up again, lassoing Libby with her leash.

"It's good to know one of us is going through this world with such unquestionable confidence," Sophia replied.

"Yep," he told her, "you should try it on some time. I believe it comes in your size. You're alright?"

"Seriously, I'm fine," she said, standing to leave. "This wasn't wasted time. I got to spend quality time with you and Libby in a beautiful park in the center of this amazing city. Plus, I got a little work done while we were waiting. I now know how to end my book."

"Your character will swear off men altogether?"

Sophia laughed at him. "Yes, that's *exactly* how it'll end."

Sophia had been holding herself back from finishing her novel—from declaring it complete and putting the last period at the end of the final sentence—until that day in the park. She had been learning to accept that she needed to let go of her characters and that it would soon be their turns to make their ways in the world.

With the last chapter of *Bad Blood* before her, Sophia faced her final paragraphs. It represented the end of her own journey as well as that of her characters. Several weeks before, she had said goodbye to Dirk, whose devious plans for biogenetic terrorism had been exposed and thwarted at the hands of his biological son, Gawain—now grown and the catalyst for several final and unexpected twists. While neither Dirk nor Gawain knew they were related until the very end, Gawain's survival and success had been helped by an anonymous source who sent him information describing Dirk's plans of destruction and explanations of why the younger man was the only person who could stop him. Regardless of the explosive climax and the demise of Dirk and his secret society, the story hadn't felt entirely finished to Sophia. After much consideration, she decided it needed something more, something beyond the page-turning climax—a reminder to the reader that love was the driving force behind the story.

Influenced by everything she had experienced throughout the year, including her friendships with Natasha and Jasper, Sophia realized how important it was to include an ending more similar to that of *Sir Gawain and the Green Knight.* Like *Gawain,* love had driven her characters to make unimaginable sacrifices. And like *Gawain,* she wanted good deeds to not go unnoticed. Sophia wanted to make a statement that, regardless of how long it might take to get there, good things do happen to people, and that travels across life's sometimes brutal terrain could, and should, conclude with a happy ending.

When Pearl answered the door, she had no idea how her world would again shift. The woman standing in front of her was unrecognizable, but there was something more than the tears in her eyes that should have told Pearl that nothing would ever be the same again.

"Are you alright? May I help you?" Pearl asked.

The woman looked as if she had seen a ghost, holding her hands cupped together against her chest like something might fly away if she didn't grip firmly enough. She remained silent but her body communicated for her.

"Ma'am, are you okay?" Pearl asked again, growing concerned, beginning to understand that the emotion on display went beyond what she saw in front of her.

The woman quivered a few seconds more before managing to force out the words, "I've waited almost my whole life for this moment."

Pearl stepped back involuntarily from the rush of emotion that flooded through the door. Was this really happening? Could it be?

The stranger continued speaking, "Did you once call yourself, 'Meg?'"

Pearl felt as if she had been punched in the stomach. While she would never forget that name, it was barely familiar after all of these years—a part of a life she had stopped wondering about long ago, mostly for reasons of survival. She had stopped asking herself how life would have turned out had things been different, had she not had the calling. She'd stopped asking herself about the people she once knew and cared for, and what life would have been like had she always been called Meg, or even Sister Margaret. And what about now? Would she always be called Pearl?

"How do you know that?" she asked the stranger, her mind still unable to wrap itself around the idea that the past was at her door.

The response was confirmation enough for the woman, who crumbled. "I have waited forty years for this moment."

That was when clarity came to Pearl and she knew for certain what was happening, that God did work in mysterious ways. She reached for the woman, grabbing her, embracing her as hard as she could—as if it would transport them back to another time. "It was you, wasn't it? You were the one who warned us."

The woman folded into her, removing any space that remained between them, unable to get close enough to the woman who had once been Dirk's older sister. "My name is Anna McCormack," she said. "I gave birth to Gawain."

Pearl pulled away to get another look at Anna, feeling something travel through her chest as if God had just shared a breath. She then collapsed back into her. "It was you, wasn't it?"

Anna's nod was absorbed by the embrace, and tears of joy poured down both of their faces. "You named him Gawain like I asked you to," Anna announced. "I never would've found you if you hadn't."

"And you've been sending the letters all these years," Pearl said. "We had no idea it was you. I prayed one day you would come to us. The first time we heard from you, I thought it was them—the Bad People. We considered fleeing, changing our names again and starting over. But I decided there had to be good in the world, that someone was looking out for us."

"There was, you know," Anna told her, stepping back to have another look at the past standing in front of her. "Someone other than me."

"Father McKenzie?" Pearl asked.

"Yes."

"Is he still alive?"

"No," Anna said, her face growing sad. "They found out about him. He saved my life, you know. And he saved Gawain's, before it even began."

Pearl pulled Anna into the house without taking her eyes or arms off of her. "Is he here?" Anna finally asked.

"No, but he can be in no time. Would you like that?" Pearl asked, adding, "I know he would."

"Oh, yes. Please," Anna confirmed.

Pearl made the call but told Gawain nothing of the reunion, only that she needed to see him as soon as possible and that she had something very important to share with him. While the two waited for his arrival, they began sharing the stories of the separate lives they had led over the past four decades.

"I'm sorry about your brother," Anna told Pearl. "I wish things had been different for Dirk."

"Me, too."

"Does anyone know how he managed it?"

"Not exactly," Pearl shared. "Much of it is still a mystery. But his *accomplices, the people he got to help him—those they know about anyway—are being dealt with. The list seems to get longer and longer, though, as they continue to uncover everything. From what we've learned, the investigation seems like it's never going to end."* But then she changed the focus to Anna. *"And I'm sorry for you—the sacrifices you must have made, the things you've endured."*

"God has a plan. Isn't that what we're to believe?"

Pearl nodded. "We didn't know if you were alive. We prayed you were, that you were safe."

"We're all safe now," Anna told her.

"He's a good man," Pearl said, referring to Gawain. "You'll be proud."

"I already am."

Twenty minutes later, when he walked through the front door and saw the two women crying, Gawain knew he wasn't the only one who had come home.

CHAPTER 32
TURNING ANOTHER PAGE

Summer quickly gave way to autumn and before Sophia knew it, hints of winter arrived as well, wiping the leaves from the trees and once again testing the thickness of her blood. Every year was the same: it took time for her California coat, regardless of her years in New York, to prepare itself for the winter challenges that were just around the corner. Not helping matters was the fact that she and Natasha had spent most of the past few months going back and forth to The Coast, as Natasha liked to call it because she thought it sounded very blue blood and was appropriate for the recurring acting role she had landed. Natasha also admitted to enjoying the affectation in her off-camera life because it made Sophia cringe—a new favorite pastime. Working again had lifted Natasha's spirits, giving her room to explore lighter, more creative sides of her personality.

They had only been back in New York a week when Natasha was summonsed again for a fitting, this time for a Showtime movie an old director friend, Lorenzo Cabrini, had insisted she be in.

"'Don't make me beg, Natasha,'" she said he had told her, imitating his thick accent. "And so then I told him, 'Lorenzo, I know you're flirting with me. I explained thirty years ago I wouldn't sleep with you…*ever*. Today still counts as part of that timeframe.'"

According to her recount, Lorenzo reacted with monkey-like hysterics which she found surprisingly sexy. "Is it weird that I was a little excited because he acted like a gorilla?" she asked Sophia. "I expected him to start pounding his chest."

"Are you sure you'll feel safe with such a brut without me?" Sophia asked in return, mostly because it was a chance to tease Natasha about one of her male admirers.

"Absolutely. He's harmless. Besides, I've dragged you back and forth plenty already—much more than I thought I would. When we got this ball rolling again, I never thought it would roll so quickly. Now I'm just hoping I get some work here soon so I can go home after a long day of shooting instead of to a hotel room."

"That'd be nice, but it's not like they're sending you to a Motel 6. Last week, we were in a suite at the Four Seasons."

"I know," Natasha said. "But you know me. I'm spoiled. I like my own bed. I like being home. I miss you, when you're not around, and Jasper and Mary. I miss my space. I miss my treadmill."

There was that treadmill comment again, which Natasha had already made several times. "Who knew I was creating such a cardio monster?" Sophia asked, proud of Natasha (and of herself as well).

Sophia had spent the morning helping Natasha pack her luggage and get ready for the short jaunt. "It's not too late," she told Natasha. "I can still go with you."

"Don't spend another second thinking about it. I'll be back before you know it. Charles Two," she said, referring to her California driver, "will pick me up and take care of whatever I need. Stay here. Work on your birthday trip!"

As Sophia made sure Natasha's laptop was in her carry on bag, she thought about how excited she was to finally be visiting Kate in her new home. Natasha was sending Sophia to Paris for a week in February to celebrate both their first year together and Sophia's birthday.

"I can't stand surprises," Natasha confessed when she broke the news. "Besides, how do you surprise someone with a trip to a foreign country? There are some things with which you just can't surprise a person."

Sophia was beyond thrilled, as was Kate, and they were enjoying planning all they would do and see together.

"Will you help me bring my things out to Charles?" Natasha asked.

"Of course," Sophia answered.

As she grabbed the bags and carried them down the stairs, Sophia struggled with the question that had been anxiously waiting on her lips. *Have you read the manuscripts yet?*

But she realized the question was pointless. Natasha surely would have said something if she had read either of the books by now.

Unless, Sophia thought, her mind going to a dark place, *she has read them and is trying to find a gentle way to tell me she hates them.*

Tortured conversations such as these were taking place in Sophia's head all the time and they were making her crazy.

Sophia had spent the past several months editing, rewriting, editing, rewriting, editing then rewriting some more, alternating between the two book projects. When she got tired of one she jumped to the other, the distraction a welcome relief. As things turned out, she finished them at approximately the same time, so she presented them both to Natasha in a formal and dramatic ceremony that included a homemade dinner—a feat that was remarkable in and of itself since Sophia hadn't had the time to cook for months.

"Here's the deal," Sophia had said when she handed them over. "I'm completely terrified you'll be disappointed and not like them, but I really want your honest opinion. You're very important to me so I want you to be the first to read them."

Natasha cooed over the manuscripts that night but seemed to have lost focus since then. With her newly busy schedule, she hadn't said much of anything since the latest trip to Los Angeles, other than throwing out, "I know you're wondering how much I love the books. I'm reading them now but I'm such a slow reader. Please be patient with me."

Sophia tried hard to abide by Natasha's request, which was more than reasonable but still not easy. After all, she had waited her whole life for this moment: to get honest feedback on a finished novel that she had written. But patience was not a strength of hers.

She did her best to talk herself off the ledge, trying to remember that she had just handed Natasha nine hundred pages to read. It had taken years to develop some of the ideas and then many months to write them into two complete books, so why would she expect Natasha could read all of that in only a few days? Her internal, neurotic dialogue continued. *Give her time. Calm down. Be patient.*

On the way to the car, however, Natasha finally brought up the books on her own, calming Sophia significantly. "I have your manuscripts with me and nothing else to do for the next couple of days but try on clothing and read. You'll get my undivided attention, I promise. I've read a little so far, and I think they're wonderful. I can't wait to finish and tell you how much I love them!"

So Sophia waited some more, doing her best to distract herself. She planned her holiday trip to California to visit her family, then her anniversary and birthday trip to Paris. She took advantage of the dry weather while it lasted and ran in the park, observing that there were more leaves on the ground than there were in the trees. She considered starting another round of edits through one or both of her books but decided against it when Natasha called to say that she had finished her business on The Coast and was coming home early. She mentioned nothing of the books and Sophia felt frustrated and discouraged all over again. But she rationalized with herself that she could wait a little while longer.

"Charles will pick me up at the airport," Natasha told her. "We'll swing by your place and run some errands. Ok?"

"You sound tired," Sophia replied, feeling guilty for her impatience with Natasha.

"I am. All this travel wipes me out," Natasha admitted. "I don't know how people do it all the time."

"What time does your flight land tomorrow?"

"7 AM."

"You're taking the red eye?" Sophia asked, surprised.

"I am. I'm so tired of L.A. and hotel rooms. I can't sleep on a hotel bed another night. I just want to get home and stay home for a while."

Natasha's tone concerned Sophia. Dr. Bland had told them that Natasha had to be careful not to take on too much, that fatigue and stress could trigger an episode if she didn't watch out. It was also alarming that Natasha was taking an overnight flight. She had to be exhausted in order to have made that decision, and Sophia feared she would only be more wiped out by the time she landed, even if she was traveling in first class.

In the morning, Natasha called from the car when she was two blocks away, giving her best Bob Barker: "Come on down."

As Sophia joined them, she said, "Welcome back. Where are we going first?"

"First, let's get coffee. I desperately need the caffeine. Then let's see Jonathan. He should be in about now. He has a couple contracts I need to sign."

"Contracts? Did you get another part?" Sophia asked, pleased Natasha was in better spirits than she'd expected.

"I did! Actually, it's another project from Lorenzo. I can't wait to tell you all about it. I'm on a roll!"

"You sure are! When you set your mind on something, there's no stopping you! Good for you," Sophia told Natasha, happy to see her making up for lost time.

Two coffees to go later, the women were in Jonathan's office. His assistant, still frosty and devoid of personality, led them in while Jonathan finished his telephone conversation.

"Have you seen the paper today?" Natasha whispered so as not to disturb Jonathan.

"No. Why?" Sophia inquired.

"Oh, I'll have to show it to you. There's a little story in there that's pretty amazing."

"Really?" Sophia asked. She was about to ask Natasha another question when she heard her cell phone ring. Without looking to see who was calling, she slipped her hand into her bag and switched it to vibrate just as Jonathan ended his conversation.

"Good morning, ladies," he asked. "How are we doing today?"

"Fine," Natasha said.

"Fine," Sophia repeated. She liked that she and Jonathan were now on good terms. Ever since Natasha had let him back into the fold, he had been genuinely warm to her. Natasha said he trusted her now.

"How was your trip?" he asked Natasha.

"Really good. Really, really good."

"It sounds like it," he said, grabbing his coffee cup off his desk. "I heard from Lorenzo's people. Maybe I should also draft a pre-nup. He sounds quite smitten with you."

"Just stop it," Natasha said with a girlish giggle. "Speaking of papers. I was just asking Sophia if she'd seen *The Post*. Have you?"

Then Sophia's phone began sounding off again. Silenced, she could still hear it as it rumbled against the keys in her bag, producing a metallic chorus. It was unusually early for the phone to be ringing, let alone twice in a row, so she started to wonder if something was wrong.

Natasha must have known what she was thinking because she assured her, "We'll be done in a minute."

Sophia understood Natasha was asking her not to answer it so she obliged.

"No, I haven't," Jonathan said, answering Natasha's question about the newspaper. "Why?"

Natasha grabbed for her purse. "Well, you both have to see this. This is something!"

She pulled the folded paper out and handed it to Jonathan. Then she leaned over his desk and pointed at the article she was interested in, tapping twice to emphasize what she wanted him to see.

He took a moment to read it before saying, "Natasha! This is fantastic!"

"Isn't it?" she responded, a huge grin on her face.

Sophia had been thinking about her phone but now began to feel out of the loop. "What is it?"

Jonathan pushed the paper in her direction. *"Page Six,"* he told her. "Second item."

Sophia quickly found the article that had made them both so excited. Scanning it quickly, she couldn't believe her eyes so she looked up at them for an explanation.

"Read it," Natasha told her. "The *whole* thing."

> *Too Hot To Handle. Who says it's a man's world? Two Manhattan women are sure to make us question that idea this year. One is back from the dead (as rumor had it) and the other is writing her way to the top. What's amazing is they are linked together like a female dynamic duo. Natasha McGavin, actress turned New York businesswoman turned depression/suicide prevention spokeswoman, finds new life in multiple, high-profile projects, including a tell-all book, new acting roles and the not-to-be-missed DVD anniversary release of* The Dreyfus Affair *(in which she rips off Vanessa Baxter's head during the audio commentary track). McGavin has been laying low for too long and is ready to show the world she's still got it. By her side is wonder writer Sophia Connors who has not one but two incredible books being shopped around: her debut novel,* Bad Blood, *an intense and emotional psychological thriller, and* Alive & Kicking, *McGavin's autobiography the two penned together (although the actress insists it should be called a biography because, as she puts it, she couldn't construct a proper sentence to save her life). Both books are said to be immensely entertaining and thought-provoking, and are the focus of bidding wars taking place as this article goes to print. It goes to show you that you can't keep a good woman down.*

Sophia lowered the paper, stunned. "I don't understand."

Natasha and Jonathan glanced at each other, smiled, and then looked back at Sophia. They both began laughing, and Natasha clapped her hands.

"What is this?" Sophia asked, still confused. "Is this a joke paper? Is this supposed to be funny?"

Natasha's claps got louder, as did her laughter. "A joke paper! That's so funny!" she yelled.

This response made Jonathan howl, too. "I wasn't expecting that. Were you, Natasha?"

Natasha laughed even harder. "Not at all! I'm gonna pee my pants. Stop laughing, Jonathan! Just stop it!"

Sophia wasn't following a thing that was happening, but her confusion was quickly leading to annoyance. Her books were nothing to laugh about. "What's so funny, guys? Is this a *real* paper?"

Natasha settled down, wiping the tears from her eyes. "Yes, dear. Of course it's a real paper, silly! It's today's *Post!* And it's one hundred percent real!"

But Sophia still grasped at comprehension. She did not—could not—understand what was happening, and why they, including *The Post,* seemed to know something she did not. Jonathan pushed forward a folder, just as he had the paper, in a cool and self-assured manner across his desk.

"Please open this," he told her. "I think it will explain everything."

Natasha sat watching, eyes glued to Sophia, hands on her mouth.

Sophia leaned forward and grabbed the folder, her head throbbing with bewilderment. Placing it on her lap, she pulled the cover to the side and saw several unfamiliar documents with her name on each of them. So were the titles of her books and dollar amounts. She looked up to see Jonathan, smiling and nodding at her, and Natasha, who was now crying.

"Are these what I think they are?" Sophia asked, feeling her guts turn inside out, her own tears beginning to climb out.

"They are," Jonathan said. "We have two offers for both *Bad Blood* and *Alive & Kicking*. With today's *Page Six* article, we're expecting more. In fact, I just got off the phone with a contact at Random House who wants to throw their hat into the ring. Congratulations. You're quite the rising star."

That was when Sophia broke and crying took over. "I can't believe this," she said, staring at the folder like it was an object from another world.

Natasha got down on her knees and leaned into Sophia for a hug. "Believe it! You deserve every bit of this success. Both books are *so* good!"

"But you never said anything about them," Sophia said, trying to understand the logistics of everything. "Did you actually read them? *All* of them?"

Natasha looked at Jonathan and then back at Sophia, before starting to laugh again. "Of course I read them! I just wanted to surprise you. I've been acting this whole time! But when we found out they were running this article…well, that's when I booked my return trip so I could make sure you heard about this the right way."

Sophia thought about her phone again and wondered if this was why it had been ringing. Had others seen the article?

"I thought you hated surprises," Sophia told her.

"I just said that to throw you off!"

"How did you get this to publishers so fast?" Sophia asked, then thought of something else. "Oh, God. Is it even ready to be seen by others?"

This triggered more laughter. "Apparently so," Jonathan said, "Look at the responses we've had."

It was all too much to process at one time. "I still don't understand. *How* did all this happen?" she asked, trying to put the pieces and the timeline together.

Jonathan took the question. "I know some people in publishing."

Sophia considered this and a look of concern came over her face. "I don't mean to sound ungrateful, but I hope they're interested because of the quality of my work and not because you're friends."

Jonathan found this comment amusing. "That's a good one, Sophia. Listen to me when I tell you what I'm about to say. Contacts will get your foot in the door, but talent gets you inside and keeps you there. You did this all on your own."

"Congratulations, Sophia," Natasha repeated. "And by the way, they want to option *Bad Blood* for a movie."

Sophia cupped her head with her hands to keep herself from passing out and falling over. She was concentrating on her breathing when she heard Natasha say, "There's one more thing."

One more thing? How is that possible?

Sophia looked up to find Natasha holding a wrapped gift in her hand. "What's that?" she asked, perplexed all over again, unable to stop herself from crying.

"I'm going to give this to you but you have to promise me that you will follow my instructions. No 'ifs, ands or buts' about it. I have followed your guidance and suggestions for almost a year now, so you must promise me you will do what it says—word for word! And you cannot cheat or jump ahead. No compromises or excuses. Okay?"

Instructions? Jump ahead? Sophia agreed, thrilled and curious, accepting she had little choice in the matter. "What do I do with this?" she asked, now holding the present.

"Open it and follow the instructions. *Word for word.*"

"I get it," Sophia told her, giving a sinister smile to Natasha and removing the ribbon and wrapping paper. "What are you up to?"

Sophia uncovered a small Tiffany sterling silver stationery box. "It's beautiful," Sophia told her, thrilled at the thoughtful gift. "It reminds me of the notes we write to each other."

"Yes, exactly," Natasha said. "But that's not all. Open it up."

Sophia did as she was told, finding inside a stack of envelopes and cards, neatly organized and already sealed. On top of the pile was an envelope that had a bright red number one on it.

"These are your instructions. *Word for word,* dear. You may open up number one now. The rest is self-explanatory."

So Sophia opened envelope number one and pulled out the card.

Enjoy your day! Go home and call your family and friends to tell them the good news! But know this: you have plans tonight. Cocktail attire required. Open envelope #2 at 7 PM—not a minute sooner.

Sophia looked up as Natasha told her, "I'm so proud of you, dear. And I love you very much. Now go take the day off and celebrate. Charles can take you home while I stay here with Jonathan to go over some things. Congratulations!"

"And I'll be in touch later for us to discuss the book deals," Jonathan added.

Sophia hugged them both as hard as she had ever hugged anyone before and then left the office, having said the words "thank you" a minimum of fifty times before taking the elevator down from the phenomenal offices in the sky. Even on street level she felt on top of the world.

When she reached the corner, she remembered the phone calls and checked her messages. The first was from Kate.

"Have you seen *Page Six?* What in the world is going on? Call me! I got an email from my friend, Tara. You know, the one I brought to your apartment that time you had a party and she passed out on your bed? *That* friend. She said, 'They wrote about your friend Sophia, the author.' I looked it up online. What's going on? Wow! You're holding back from me. I need to know *everything* right now! Call me!"

The second message was from Kevin and, surprisingly, she didn't feel sad to hear his voice. "Hey, it's me. Your ears must be burning because it seems everyone's talking about you. I heard about *The Post* article. I'm looking at it right now. This is amazing! I'm so impressed and happy for you! Call me when you can. And congrats!"

There were messages from other friends as well that she must have missed while talking to Natasha and Jonathan. She couldn't believe what was happening.

Sophia immediately called her parents, and while she knew there was a possibility she would awaken them, she decided this news warranted the interruption of sleep. Within minutes of sharing the details, the rest of the Connors clan was calling, abusing her call waiting like only they knew how.

Sophia's head spun the entire day as she walked Manhattan to process the pivotal twist her life had just taken. The idea of being published and having a book on a shelf in a bookstore—much less two books at the same time—was too much for her to absorb while sitting idle at home. She had to get out of her apartment and feel a part of the city. She needed to jump into its arteries and join its frenzied flow, going wherever it would take her. New York was her city, her home, and she felt proud she could rightfully claim that she accomplished what she had come here to do.

She was thankful Natasha had made plans for them that night. Even after hours of aimlessly perusing neighborhoods and shops that she hadn't had time to visit in months, she found sitting still difficult and was looking forward to seeing her friend. Throughout the day she had thought of so many things she wanted to discuss with her, like knowing how all of this came together, and what Natasha's thoughts had been about certain parts of the books. There was just so much she had battled with to piece everything together, both on paper and in her life, that she needed Natasha, as it turned out, to pinch her and tell her that this was not going away.

Sophia wondered what Natasha had planned. Were they having dinner? Seeing a show? She hadn't a clue. But, like all topics and considerations that day, she was unable to focus on it for more than a few moments at a time.

By five minutes before seven, she was showered, made up and wearing a cocktail dress she rarely had the occasion to wear. It, like Sophia's new life, fit surprisingly well, albeit strangely, too. She sat on the edge of her favorite chair, her precious Tiffany gift placed on her lap, watching the clock until it reached the promised time. She lifted the lid, pulled out the second envelope and removed the card just as the clock struck seven.

This is a warning card. You better not be cheating. I will be so mad *at you if you do! Don't ruin the fun. You may now open envelope #3 (as long as it's 7 PM)…*

That Natasha, Sophia thought. Following the directions, she read the third message, which was accompanied by a twenty-dollar bill.

Take a cab with the money included to the corner of 58th and Madison. When you arrive, you may open envelope #4.

Sophia did as she was instructed, carrying the box and envelope number four against the waist of her coat with both hands. Grabbing a cab on the corner, she soaked in the electric twinkle of the city night as they slowly made their way through evening traffic. She was in no rush, not anymore, not tonight anyway.

Arriving at the designated corner, Sophia thought she must have looked like a debutante in search of a coronation. With only two unread envelopes remaining, she also figured she was close to her destination. As the cab drove away, she opened the next envelope.

Go to the south side of the street and proceed east. At building number 57, stop and open envelope #5. FOLLOW THESE INSTRUCTIONS TO THE WORD OR ELSE!!!

Again, Sophia did as instructed by the cards, touched by the amount of thought Natasha had put into this, happily clicking her heels down the street. She began to feel as if she had walked these steps before which was likely in New York. When she arrived at the given address and looked up, she realized why Natasha had warned her so heavily to follow the directions. The awning had two words she was surprised to see: Le Bon! She was back at the restaurant where Kevin had broken up with her almost a year ago.

Has Natasha lost her mind?

Shaking her head in disbelief, Sophia followed through with her promise and opened the fifth envelope.

Dearest Sophia,

You changed my life and I love you like my own child. I don't know what would have happened to me if I hadn't met you. Now it's my turn to return the favor. It's time for you to face the past so it no longer has power over you. Life is too short, and far too precious to not embrace only the loveliest of things and people. Come to the bar and look for envelope #6.

Natasha

Sophia dabbed her eyes with her index finger, sucked in a deep breath from the chilly night, then pulled at the front door to show the past that it didn't want to mess with Sophia Connors.

Oh, Natasha, Sophia thought. *You're not the only lucky one. What would have happened to me?*

When Sophia walked through the door—much to her surprise—nothing terrible happened. There she was, standing in the entryway, and all around her was life. People everywhere shifted as if on a dance floor, moving about with vibrant and kinetic activity. This was a place for the living, not the dead and not haunted memories. People were laughing and talking, and eating delicious food and drinking fabulous wine. It was the first time Sophia really knew she could do this. She was ready to enter the world again.

She did as the card instructed, moving through the crowd, making her way to the bar. Natasha's attention to detail had been proven many times before, so Sophia expected to find her sitting at the bar, in the center. It was where she had told Natasha she had found—and left—Kevin once upon a time ago.

Sophia pressed forward through the crowd. *I feel nothing,* she told herself, relieved the lift in her step returned.

She looked for Natasha as she searched the shifting bodies in front of her. When she finally found a familiar face, she understood why she really was there. It *all* made sense now.

Natasha, she thought, *you have really done it now.*

The sea of bodies parted and she received a clear view of the center of the bar. There was the envelope with a large red #6, but the hand holding it wasn't Natasha's. This hand belonged to a person she'd never expected to see there—Dr. Handsome Neil Hale—sitting at the bar, waiting there for her and only her.

This is no mirage, she told herself, as she finished her trek across the room, almost in a daze.

When she reached him, he stood up smiling and greeted her warmly. "Hello, Sophia," he said.

She smiled back. "Hello, Neil."

There was a silent pause between them, but it somehow wasn't awkward. "You must be really special to have friends who'd go out of their way to make this happen."

She shook her head. "They're the ones who are special. I'm just lucky."

They stood close, eyes staring into each other's. Sophia felt fuzzy and lightheaded, just as she had remembered feeling in his office, only this time she hadn't taken any painkillers.

"How's that tooth?" he asked.

"Better now."

"Me, too," he told her.

"You've been having problems?"

"Lots of 'em," he said. "Before *now.*"

She blushed, unable to remember the last time a man made her do that until she realized the time had been with him.

"I hear you've had quite a day," Neil told her.

"Yes, quite."

"I'm happy I can help you celebrate. You know I've been hoping to see you again."

"I didn't know that," Sophia admitted.

Neil smiled again. "Now you do."

"Me, too," she told him. "I've been hoping to see you again, too."

"I didn't know that either."

"Now *you* do."

Sophia wanted to give Neil a hug but she held herself back. He handed her the sixth envelope. "This is for you," he said.

Sophia smiled, doing her best to open it.

Surprise! Your final instructions:
Have fun tonight!
Don't be shy.
Don't talk with your mouth full.
Remember that good things do happen to good people.
Have a lovely dinner on me!

XOXO
Natasha

Sophia shook her head but remained silent, unable to believe that her friend—no, Natasha was her family—had done all of this for her. It was amazing and so was Natasha. Sophia felt like the most fortunate person alive.

"Shall we?" Neil asked, suggesting they relocate to their table.

"Sure," she told him, looking into his eyes and feeling the warm tingle in her chest.

He extended his arm and she took it. Then she surprised herself and put her head on his shoulder, nestling into him. It seemed like the thing to do. Everything about him felt comfortable.

"Sorry," Sophia said. "I don't mean to be forward. I'm just very happy. It's been an unbelievable day. And then seeing you here…"

"You have nothing to apologize for. I'm thrilled I can be a part of it. Of course, I'm not sure what I can possibly do for our second date to beat this."

Neil guided them through the bar, past the host's station and through the restaurant. It felt good to trust a man's lead for the first time in a while.

"We have a private table," he told her, steering her past the main room.

"That Natasha," Sophia said. "She thinks of everything."

They walked through a dim, elegant hallway until Neil stretched out his free hand to open a door to another room. Before them, candlelight flickered as if inviting them in.

As Sophia's eyes adjusted to the darkness and she settled into the seat Neil offered her, she felt suddenly, almost strangely, at home. In that moment, Sophia Connors knew she was turning yet another page. A new chapter had begun.

ABOUT THE AUTHOR

Jay Jacuzzi lives in Austin
with his husband, their son
and two hysterical French Bulldogs.
He is currently at work writing his second novel.

www.ingramcontent.com/pod-product-compliance
Lightning Source LLC
Chambersburg PA
CBHW070151260626
47160CB00002B/314